The Viking Princess

College Romance in 1970

The Viking Princess

College Romance in 1970

A Novel

by

Sandlin

Second Edition

This is a work of fiction. Names, characters, places, and incidents either are the product of the authors' imaginations or are used fictitiously. Any resemblance to actual events or locales or persons, living or dead, is entirely coincidental.

Cover design by Simona Molina through Fiverr.com

DEDICATION

This book is dedicated to my son, Gregory Sandlin Buck, and my daughter, Laura Jean Buck Smith. (This is not exactly the way Jean and I met and lived in 1970!)

Contents

Preface

AS AN AVID READER, I always wanted to write novels, and I made various unsuccessful attempts over the years. Oh, I wrote books—engineering technical books, operating manuals, computer books, technical papers, and countless memos. I blamed that style of writing for preventing my writing novels.

My maternal grandfather, James Warren Hale (1886—1966), was primarily a laborer for the railroads; however, he was also an aspiring and prolific writer. From 1942, and likely earlier, he wrote 28 short stories, novels, and plays—about 4400 pages—in 35 journals. Although I knew he was writing "stories" during his retirement, I had no idea he had written so many. We recently found his stories, and I've been sorting, grouping, skimming, and reading them to learn more about my grandfather. Frankly, his stories are not the best—but he still wrote them.

J. W. Hale's wife, my grandmother, Annie Lena Bennett (1890—1940), died on December 25, 1940. He finished his first story in 1942 when his children were in military service. Did he write to occupy his time after his wife's death? Was this a hobby, or did he hope to publish his work? No one knows.

I created this story as an experiment and vehicle to learn how to write, but I must admit writing it was fun. Perhaps that is what my grandfather discovered years ago.

Acknowledgments

MY PERSONAL THANKS and appreciation to those who helped me by reading early drafts or listening to me ramble on about my "Hallmark" novel, especially Marlo Hymel, Terri Valentine, Paula Munier, Laura Buck Smith, Wesleigh Smith, Lindsay Redhead. Susan Shackelford proof read the first edition and offered suggestions which I've incorporated into this second edition.

The cover was designed by Simona Molina through Fiverr.com.

Part 1

Fall Semester

1970

Sandlin

Chapter 1: Introductions

O wad gift the giftie gie us;
to see oursels as ithers see us!
-- Robert Burns

"NO WONDER THEY CALL YOU 'THE VIKING PRINCESS.'"

Fiona was leaning over the desk and reaching for a book on the top shelf, her long, wavy auburn hair falling off her shoulder and hanging to the desk when Mary came in.

Mary smiled, wondering what Gaelic words or phrases Fiona would use in her reply.

Fiona's welcoming smile disappeared. "I'm a Scot, no a Viking. Vikings dinna exist anymore."

The 1970 fall semester was into its third week at Mississippi University, and student routines were taking shape. Students re-acquainted themselves and made new friends in the process. Fiona was Mary's newest friend; they roomed on the same floor of the dormitory and had met on the first day of the semester. A six feet one-inch tall beauty, Fiona towered over Mary, a short, plain brunette.

"I love your accent. You know you're a Scot, but to most people, you're a Viking."

Fiona made no bones about it. She was exceedingly proud of her Scottish ancestry. Scottish landscapes, castles, and the poetry of Robert Burns adorned her dormitory room walls. She was raised in Aberdeen, where her late father had been an extremely successful business owner.

"Anyway, I think 'Viking Princess' is an excellent description. You certainly look the part, and I mean that in the most positive way."

Fiona regained her smile. "Weel, if others see me the way of it, I canna deny being a Viking Princess."

"I wish I could get books off the top shelf."

Fiona smiled and sat down, her book in her long, slim fingers. Mary sat beside her in a frilly, lace-covered guest chair.

As Mary expected, Fiona had been alone and deep in study at her desk. As far as Fiona was concerned, Sunday nights were for studying—as were all nights.

"What's on your mind?" asked Fiona.

Mary sensed Fiona wanted to return to her studies, but Mary had a discussion in mind. "I want to introduce a friend of mine to you," Mary began. "In fact, he's my best friend. We were neighbors and grew up together."

"He?" Fiona peeped up from her desk. "Is this the same boy ye wanted to introduce to me the day we met?"

"Well, yes, but then I wanted to show you off and watch his reaction."

"Mary, I must concentrate on my studies and no on my social life. This is my first semester. That's how I'm no getting out much. It may be next semester or even next year until I feel like circulating—much less dating. I dinna ken."

Mary argued, "Now that I know you better, you definitely should meet Alexander. Believe me, you will like him. Besides, you need to overcome your shyness and do something other than study. He can help you." She smiled.

"Aye, very well, I need a break. Tell me of your friend." Fiona turned down the volume for the Beethoven and Burns collaboration playing on her stereo.

Mary adjusted her glasses. "He is tall, even taller than you, six feet - seven but not skinny. In fact, muscular. Extremely good-looking, with longish brown hair. Very smart—probably the smartest guy you'll ever know. He is majoring in mechanical engineering with minors in math and music."

"Music? What instrument?"

"Mostly guitar but also violin—except he calls it 'fiddle.' He also plays mandolin and keyboard. In high school, he played trumpet in the band."

"Acoustic or electric guitar?"

"He prefers acoustic, but I can tell you, he plays a rocking electric guitar."

"Weel, I have to admit your friend sounds interesting. Tell me more."

"Alexander is an outstanding athlete. He played all the sports in high school, made all the all-star teams, and holds several state records. Even though he doesn't have a scholarship––in fact, he did not want one—he is a major player, frankly the star, on our football team."

On hearing that, Fiona stated firmly, "I'm no interested in athletes and certainly no American football players."

"What's wrong with football players?" Mary had learned Fiona was not particularly interested in sports but was unaware of her aversion to football players.

"Football players made fun of me when I first moved in with my aunt and uncle. They are ignorant bullies. I will have nothing to do with American football players."

"Alexander is not that way. He would have prevented them from bullying you," Mary assured her. "I've seen him do it. In fact, he protected me from the bullies."

"A boy protected me from bullies once," Fiona spoke wistfully, "but then he disappeared. I didna even thank him."

"What happened?"

"Auntie convinced me to play piano at a talent show as a way of making friends. I chose Beethoven's Adelaide. Afterward, a group of senior football players confronted me in the hallway. They made fun of Adelaide as rock-and-roll. They called me 'Skinny Red' and would not let me pass. They made fun of my braces and wanted to rub them with their tongue. No one touched me, but I was that scared."

"Who saved you?"

"A boy I didna ken hurried to the group and commanded 'Leave her alone.' They turned from me to him. He telt me to go, and I did. I didna thank him; I just ran away."

"Was there a fight?

"I dinna ken. No one witnessed the confrontation, and I have stayed away from football players ever since."

"Did you learn the boy's name?"

"Nay. He didna attend oor school. He was older than me but seemed younger than the seniors, although he was bigger. I hope he didna get hurt on my account. I still think about him when I feel vulnerable." Fiona's voice resumed its wistful softness.

"Did you report them?"

"Nay, I was too embarrassed. Ye're the only one I've ever telt the way of it."

"That's the kind of thing Alexander would do."

"Ye make him seem so nice."

"Alexander is more than nice; he is a true gentleman, a Christian and active in the Baptist church. He was so involved in school and church activities, it's a wonder he even graduated. Still, he was Class President and Valedictorian."

"Are ye making this up? It sounds too good to be true."

Jane, Fiona's roommate, came into the room and asked, "Are you talking about your friend, Alexander Gordon?"

"Yes, I want to introduce him to Fiona, but she is not interested."

Jane exclaimed, "Well, introduce him to me!" She eyed Fiona. "Alexander is <u>the</u> Big Man on Campus!"

"Fiona," appealed Mary, "Alexander is unlike any football player you've ever met. He is unlike any guy you've ever met. Don't make a serious mistake; allow me to introduce him. You don't have to marry him; have a cup of coffee, and then you can resume your studies—that is, if you still want to."

"Noo ye have me nervous about meeting Mr. Perfect. What will ye tell him about me?"

"I will tell Alexander you have a good personality."

Jane giggled, and Fiona hesitantly agreed to meet Alexander.

"I'll call him right now. May I use your phone?" Fiona nodded, and Mary picked up Fiona's pink Princess telephone and began dialing.

*****

OUT OF HABIT, ALEXANDER ducked his head slightly and entered his small, plain dorm room carrying a sack of beef sliders. His roommate, Donnie, was studying at his built-in desk as expected and glanced up when Alexander entered.

"In already? Donnie asked. "Must have been a short interview. I don't listen to the Sunday broadcast."

"Well, you missed a good one. Don't ask me to repeat it." He handed Donnie the sack of sliders, and Donnie took three.

"Thanks. They may be small, but they taste great!"

They lived in one of the older, less expensive dormitories. Built in the late 1950s, rooms were distributed alongside a hallway with a bathroom near each end. Recent remodeling added air conditioning and a telephone in each room.

Alexander nodded towards a poster of Farrah Fawcett. "New girlfriend?"

"I wish. Ed gave it to me. Patsy won't allow it on their wall."

Ed was a mutual friend who had recently married his longtime girlfriend. "Now that they're married, Patsy rules the roost. Ed's entire life is changing. I bet he doesn't go hunting this season."

"Patsy always called the shots even before they were married. But I knew you hadn't bought the poster." Donnie was notoriously frugal.

Alexander picked up his guitar, flopped on his cot, and strummed a few chords before moving to his desk.

"Don't tell me you're going to study!"

"Of course, I'm going to study. Mechanical engineers study too—you chemical engineers aren't the only ones. Besides, tonight, I'm studying calculus, just like you."

"So, how did you do on the calculus test?" asked Donnie. "I made a 70."

"95."

"Not 100? What happened?"

"Well, you know how old Prof Williams insists we do everything his way. On one problem, I followed the book and used a 't' transform instead of the 'v' transform Williams taught. I got the correct answer, but Williams still deducted five points."

"You are foolish to argue with Williams. Why do you do things like that?"

"I just want to be right, I guess. Why couldn't I use the book Williams forced us to buy?"

"You sure can be stubborn! And now, you don't have a perfect grade anymore. You might not be perfect after all!"

"I realize I'm not perfect." This was a typical topic of debate between him and Donnie.

"You sure aren't perfect, but everything goes your way so easily that you take good fortune for granted. I don't understand what all those girls see in you. I should make a list of your faults and put it in the school paper."

The telephone rang and interrupted their good-natured ribbing. Alexander wished the telephone was wall-mounted so it would not take up space on his desk. The calls were almost always for Alexander, so Donnie had insisted on putting their phone on Alexander's desk. Alexander hoped this call was not another request for an interview. It was not; instead, it was his best friend—more like a sister—Mary.

Mary was majoring in psychology and would one day be an outstanding psychologist; she already behaved as a psychologist through her understanding of people, their needs, and their problems. Everyone asked Mary for advice.

"Hey, Mary. What's up?"

Like always, Mary got right to business. "I want to introduce you to my newest friend. She lives down the hall from me."

Mary's request was unexpected. By unspoken agreement, they did not arrange dates or introductions—nothing dealing with romance.

After hesitating, Alexander replied, "OK, tell me about your friend." *Something was up, and he was curious.*

"As soon as I met her, I knew you'd like her. She is a fine art and music major. Very talented. Very smart. Tall and slim with an outstanding personality."

Now Alexander understood. Mary was doing someone a favor—perhaps returning a favor. Alexander was a Big Man on Campus—a near-celebrity who constantly downplayed his status. He didn't care to be introduced as a Big Man on Campus, and Mary was well aware of his feelings. *Why did she want to introduce him to this girl?* Still, Mary usually got her way, so he might as well go along.

"OK, I guess so. When and where?" he asked reluctantly.

"How about tomorrow at three o'clock in the Student Union snack room?"

Monday football practice would be short and light after winning the Saturday game. Mary knew Alexander's schedule and habits and had matched her request to them. He had no excuse to avoid meeting Mary's new friend.

Alexander said, "OK, see you tomorrow." But he wondered, *What is she up to?*. He was the favorite target of Mary's mischievous streak. He heard a giggle in the background as Mary hung up.

Donnie asked, "What's going on?"

"Mary wants me to meet a new friend of hers."

"What's she look like?"

Just like Donnie—straight to the point.

"I didn't ask about looks. I did not want the lecture about guys only wanting to meet hot babes. Based on Mary's description, I expect her to be a tall, skinny nerd with a good personality."

"Serves you right. You should spread yourself around among all the girls and not just the pretty ones. What's her name?"

"I don't know. Mary didn't say, and I forgot to ask. I'll have a quick cup of coffee, make polite conversation and be on my way. Shouldn't take long; besides, I need to revise my latest patent application."

"Well, good luck. At the very least, Mary will owe you one."

*****

IN FIONA'S ROOM, Mary hung up the Princess phone. "Easier than I thought," she laughed.

"I'm impressed," said Jane. "You must really be good friends."

"Oh, we are," replied Mary. "Like brother and sister. Now, I'm the one who must study. See you tomorrow." She left the room.

"I shouldna have agreed to this," said Fiona to Jane. "But I didna ken what else to do. Mary was determined."

Jane and Fiona had been randomly assigned as roommates but discovered they were well matched and fast becoming good friends. Jane was a curly haired business major of average height from central Mississippi. She was a serious student, but not to the same degree as Fiona. Attractive, Jane did not have a boyfriend but was fun, outgoing, and very popular.

"I'm so glad you are finally getting out and about. I know lots of boys who want to meet you. You'll have fun. Maybe we can even double date sometime."

"I'm meeting Alexander as a favor to Mary and to satisfy my curiosity. I dinna ken about getting out more."

"Relax, Fiona. Just enjoy the thrill of meeting this Big Man on Campus. He's supposed to be quite nice. Most likely, nothing will come of it except that you'll be out of this room for a few minutes. That, in itself, is a good thing."

"I dinna ken how to act."

"Alexander is probably accustomed to girls going gaga over him, so just be kind of reserved. You probably won't even have to talk much. Just open those big green eyes wide and gaze at him as he brags." Jane laughed. "Now, how should we dress you?"

"Nothing risqué, please."

"Do you have a miniskirt? Mine would be too short on you. Maybe one of my regular skirts would serve as a miniskirt for you."

"Nay to a miniskirt or one of your lowcut blouses. I'll wear one of my church outfits."

Jane laughed. "Well, at lease find out if he has a good looking roommate."

*****

THE NEXT AFTERNOON, Thomas Bennoitt got out of his new metallic blue GTO and strutted across the parade grounds while daydreaming about becoming governor of Mississippi. Ahead, a small group of excited students gathered at the steps of the Student Union. Thomas recognized the subject of their excitement: "*Alexander Gordon! The Big Man on Campus and signing autographs, of course. If he were not a star football player, he might not be so popular, but he wouldn't care. Everything comes so easy to him; it isn't fair."*

Thomas was also a big man on campus, although not nearly as prominent as he wanted. Not quite handsome, he stood a slim six feet three inches tall with black hair already thinning.

Thomas sauntered alone for a short distance, but two fraternity brothers soon joined him. Thomas was a member, in fact, president of the Iota Theta Phi fraternity or, as he called it, "I Felta Thigh." He enjoyed fraternity social life, and his grades greatly benefited from its database of previous coursework and tests.

"Hey, Prez! Think you can win the election for Student Body President?"

"Why not? Besides, the campaign experience will come in handy for my political career. After all, I'm majoring in political science."

"You have an ambitious plan for your life, and it seems on schedule!"

They moved on, checking out girls. Thomas fancied himself a playboy and continually searched for the ideal playmate— preferably one with money.

His train of thought shifted to the tall redhead he had seen at a distance the previous week. *Big Red is fine and looks sophisticated. With luck, she might even have money.* He wondered where she was and resolved to introduce himself as soon as possible.

Thomas watched jealously as Alexander climbed the steps to the Union.

*****

DESPITE HER DIMINUTIVE SIZE, Mary was assertive and had commandeered an excellent table in the snack room with a good view of the general area. She watched as Alexander entered the Union, followed by a small group of students.

Good, Mary thought, *his curiosity brought him here—and on time too.*

The snack room was a natural meeting place, though noisy with chatter. It adjoined a small cafeteria, and the aroma of pizza and coffee overpowered even the men's cologne.

"I'll be back in a few minutes," Mary assured Fiona.

Fiona's shy behavior precluded visits to the snack room— especially alone. "No too long, please. I'm a wee bit nervous." She had dressed conservatively in a dark maroon skirt and white blouse. Betraying her nervousness, she ran her fingers through wavy hair falling over one shoulder.

Mary could sense Fiona's curiosity and gaze as she stepped outside the snack room to get Alexander. The students around him wanted a football conversation, but Mary pulled him away. Instead of looking forward towards Fiona, Alexander peeked back at his fans and laughed at his plight as little Mary dragged him along. He tried to acknowledge and answer his fans, but Mary pulled him on.

Abruptly, Mary stopped, and Alexander almost ran over her. "Fiona, I'd like to introduce my friend Alexander."

Alexander turned politely towards Fiona.

Nothing. Alexander could say nothing. He just stood there with a blank face.

Mary glanced at Fiona. She had a startled but pleased expression and a shy smile.

Still, Alexander remained silent.

I know he was expecting a nerd instead of an incredibly beautiful girl, but this is ridiculous, Mary thought. *Come on, Alexander, say something—even if it sounds stupid.*

Seeing Alexander still could not speak, Mary desperately issued instructions. "Alexander, go get us some coffee and think of something to say." In a daze, Alexander obediently plodded to the service area.

Mary turned back to Fiona and was astonished at her transformation. She was positively glowing—her green eyes bright with excitement and wide with determination. *She is impressed and has resolved to make a good impression on Alexander.*

"Well?" asked Mary.

"He's big and good-looking," Fiona conceded, "but can he talk?" They giggled.

Alexander returned with three cups of coffee plus tea, water, soda, and lemonade. He carefully placed the serving tray on the table and stammered, "W-W-Would you ladies like something to drink?"

Mary replied, "You have an excellent selection to choose from!" and began sniggering.

Fiona held out her hand and, in a dulcet voice with no attempt to disguise her Scottish accent, invited, "*Madainn mhath.* I'm Fiona. Ye must be Alexander. Please join us."

Instead of shaking Fiona's hand, Alexander bowed low and kissed it. Mary had tears in her eyes from laughing so hard at yet another faux pas by "Mr. Perfect." She had never seen Alexander react this way.

Seeing Alexander's beet-red face, Mary wondered if he had lost his speech again. She tried to will words his way.

"Fiona, I realize first impressions are the most important," Alexander finally regained his voice, "and there's never a second chance to make a first impression, but please let me explain. Although Mary is my best friend, she has a mischievous streak that sometimes causes me problems. This time, Fiona, Mary conveniently neglected to advise me that you are incredibly beautiful. Good personality indeed! Obviously, I was stunned speechless. In fact, I'm still stunned."

Alexander turned to Mary. "You've outdone yourself this time." He returned his gaze to Fiona. Fiona blushed through her smile; her eyes bright.

"Fiona, I hope you will give me a second chance. I'm not just a big dumb football player. Please allow me to sit and get acquainted."

"Aye, let us do that."

Mary smiled. "My job here is done. Anyway, I must go to class." She rose and sashayed away, still laughing. She would enjoy retelling this story.

*****

ALEXANDER FORGOT about working on his patent application, but he desperately needed something to say.

"D'ye ken we met three years ago?" Fiona flashed a beautiful smile, and her eyes twinkled.

"Surely I would remember meeting you." Alexander frantically searched his memory without success.

"Ye kept bullies away from me after a talent show at my high school."

"Are you sure? I..." Alexander abruptly recalled the incident. "No, wait! I remember! Was that you? You, uh, look so different now."

"Aye, well, it was three years ago. Ye've changed a bit as weel, but I recognize ye. Ye telt me to get away, and I ran as fast as I could. I hope ye didna get hurt."

"Just as those thugs were about to attack, the security guard came around and stopped them. I tried to find you, but you had disappeared."

"I was that scared. I didna thank ye. I'm glad to have the chance to thank ye now. *Moran taing! Tapadh leibh!* Thank ye!"

"It's a small world sometimes—imagine that! We've met but don't know each other."

"My full name is Fiona Flora MacKenzie MacDonald." She focused on Alexander expectantly.

"Are you related to the Jacobite, Flora MacDonald?"

Fiona's beautiful smile showed his answer pleased her. "How d'ye ask? D'ye ken her?"

"Only of her."

"I am a direct descendant. There has been a Flora MacDonald in every generation of my family."

Alexander thought, *Thank you, Uncle Herbert, for telling me about Flora MacDonald!* His uncle was the family genealogist.

Fiona continued. "My mother was born MacKenzie; they are Scottish Highlanders, as are the MacDonalds. Clan MacKenzie supported Robert the Bruce during the Wars of Scottish Independence. Long ago, Clan MacKenzie feuded with Clan MacDonald, and Mum would sometimes tease Da about the feud. D'ye ken, 'Gordon' is a Scottish Highlander clan?"

Transfixed, Alexander marveled, "You have the greenest eyes I've ever seen. Like back lit emeralds."

"*Moran taing*," Fiona smiled and repeated, "D'ye ken, 'Gordon' is a Scottish Highlander clan?"

"Oh. My great-grandmother named my dad Alexander Malcolm Gordon after her Scottish ancestors. He is trying to learn more about them. I'm named after my dad."

"Tell me about your family."

"I grew up in Mississippi—in fact, I lived next door to Mary. I have two younger sisters. My parents work regular nine to five jobs. Most of my relatives did not attend college. I'll be the first of my cousins to get a college degree."

"How did ye choose mechanical engineering?"

"Mechanical things—especially automobiles—intrigue me. Math and science seem natural, so mechanical engineering was my obvious choice. What about you?"

"Music is my passion. Classical music and voice are my majors. I'm minoring in philosophy."

"I play guitar a little."

"Mary tells me ye are quite good. I play piano, guitar, and cello, so perhaps we can make music together." Fiona smiled at her double entendre. Alexander, still recovering, missed it.

"I'd like that, but I'm better at sports than music." Fiona did not comment, and Alexander could tell sports did not interest her.

After a more general conversation in which they searched for common friends and common interests, Fiona glanced at her watch. It looked expensive.

Alexander thought, *Please don't leave.*

"I dinna want to leave ye after finally finding ye again, but I must get my English assignment now."

"May I walk with you?" Alexander wanted more time with Fiona, and he had no more classes that day.

"*Moran taing*, I'd like that."

Leaving the Student Union, Fiona stopped expectantly at the door. Alexander opened the door for her, and they continued.

Although accustomed to people looking his way, Alexander was conscious of increased glances, looks and even stares as he walked with Fiona. *It must not be easy being a Viking Princess.*

After retrieving Fiona's assignment, Alexander said, "Since we are near, let me get my computer program results."

"Ye do the computer?"

"Yes, I'll show you." They walked to the Engineering Building where Alexander pointed to a room on the first floor. Much tapping and noise emanated from the room. "This is where we punch cards for the computer programs. The actual computer is on the fourth floor. You can wait here, if you want, while I get my program results."

"I'll go with ye. I want to see the computer."

"You'll only get a glimpse, but I'll be glad to show you."

Three stories higher, Alexander retrieved his computer printout--wide sheets of paper wrapped around a stack of punch cards and secured by a rubber band. He showed Fiona an example of a punched card.

Fascinated, Fiona watched cards fed rapidly into the card reader while the printer printed an entire line at a time of letters and numbers. Paper seemed to fly from the printer.

Alexander took a quick glance at his printout. "An error. I'll have to make corrections tomorrow and run it again. But I'll leave it here for now."

"Ye made an error?" Fiona laughed.

"Fortunately, only a small one and it is easily corrected."

"So, MU requires engineers to take computer courses?"

"Not really, but knowing how to use the computer simplifies some assignments. One of my professors noted computers were the coming thing and recommended I take computer programming. Frankly, I enjoy using the computer. It's like learning another language. We use the 'Fortran' computer language—a blend of 'Formula' and 'Translation.'"

They strolled around campus and continued to get acquainted. Fiona asked, "Ye made a perfect 36 on the ACT test, didna ye?"

"Yes, but how did you learn? Mary?" Alexander's perfect ACT score was another private matter that Mary was not supposed to discuss.

"No from Mary. In registration, the student assistant said my ACT score was the highest she had ever seen, except for a guy on the football team. Then she asked me not to tell anyone."

"Well, since you told me, what was your ACT score?"

"35. I'm weak in math and science."

"Not exactly a weak score!"

"How many times did ye take the test?" asked Fiona.

"Just once."

"Ye must have had a braw study guide."

Alexander laughed. "I did not use a study guide. I did not even know about such things until after I got to MU. My high school was small with limited resources, but its size was an advantage. I did many things there that I could not have done at a large school."

"Such as?"

"Play football and be in the band. I just couldn't be in the marching band during football season."

"I used an ACT study guide," Fiona admitted. "I had an ACT class and took the test three times for those last few points. It was hard work."

"You were determined to do well, weren't you?"

"Aye. I was, and I did."

"You have a lot of resolve."

"I resolved to study and practice and stay away from the teasers and bullies." Fiona smiled at him. "Ye weren't always around to protect me."

"Guys that age are ignorant. They have no social skills or sense of behavior."

"Mary says everything comes to ye easily and naturally."

"I don't know about all that. I study and practice also."

"Och, tell me something ye canna do."

"Well, a couple of hours ago, I could not talk," he laughed.

Fiona joined in his laughter. "That was sweet—funny too!"

As suppertime approached, Alexander's stomach growled. He chuckled. "I've really enjoyed meeting you and being with you this afternoon. As you can tell, I'm starving. At the risk of monopolizing your day, would you have supper with me?"

"Is it that time already?"

"According to my stomach, it is."

"I'd enjoy supping with ye and continuing oor conversation. But after supper, I really must return to my room and read. Where should we sup?"

"I eat a lot, and the best place for me is the main cafeteria. Is that OK with you?" They took a shortcut to the cafeteria.

Fiona stepped to the cafeteria door and stopped. Alexander opened the door for her. In the buffet line, Alexander habitually overloaded his plate with beef and potatoes. He glanced at Fiona's tray ahead of him; she selected a small salad and a glass of water. Alexander reluctantly put back a second plate and added a small salad instead. *"Conversation! She did not come to watch you eat. If you want to see her again, you'd better make pleasant conversation. You can get sliders later."*

They found a table, and Fiona stood expectantly beside her chair. Alexander pulled her chair out, and she sat. He sat beside her. She regarded his plate and smiled.

"Weel, ye did say ye ate much!"

"I need the calories for football." Alexander scolded himself, *"No, no, not football, she doesn't like football."*

"I played soccer in Scotland, so I ken well the need for calories. In America, I don't play soccer, but I dance a lot. Do you dance?"

Alexander had taken dancing lessons to help his footwork for football, but he did not mention his reason. "I can dance a little, but nothing like what you must do."

"What kind of dance?"

"Mostly a sort of athletic jitterbug, I'm afraid."

"I like jitterbug too. Perhaps we can try it someday."

"You might be disappointed, but I'm game." *No, no, not game.*

After a few minutes, Alexander chuckled. "You hold the fork upside down! Is that a Scottish custom?"

Fiona laughed. "It is ye who holds the fork upside down! In Scotland, in fact, all of Europe, the fork always remains in the left hand with the tines down. One of the first differences I noticed in America was that the fork is held with the tines up. Americans constantly change the fork from the left to the right hand and back again."

"I'll try it." Alexander put his fork in his left hand with the tines down and picked up his knife with his right hand. Although awkward, he could manage it, especially with meat. He inspected the peas on his plate with dismay and changed the subject. "I've not traveled much; tell me about your travels." He changed the fork to his right hand and flipped it to tines up.

Fiona smiled and spoke matter-of-factly about visiting museums and art galleries in Scotland, England, France, and Italy. She especially enjoyed the Louvre in Paris and had been there more than once.

"So you've seen the Mona Lisa?"

"Ye know of the Mona Lisa? In Paris, she is called 'La Joconde.' Aye, I've seen her several times. What a beautiful painting! I'm trying to learn to paint."

"Do you speak French?"

"Aye. Or perhaps I should say oui."

"I'm American and speak only Southern English, but I want to learn other languages. What do you suggest for a second language?"

"French or Spanish would be good choices. Perhaps German for your interest in science. I speak Scottish Gaelic, French, and Italian."

After supper, Fiona again noted she must return to her dorm.

"May I walk you to your dorm?" He wanted still more time with Fiona.

"Are ye going that way? I'd enjoy the company." As they strolled past the library, Fiona stopped and surprisingly said, "I can study in the library. Would ye join me?"

Alexander wanted to shout, "Yes!" but simply replied, "I'd like that very much." He had no books, paper or even a pencil, but no matter. After all, the library was full of books, and surely he could find something to study.

"Let me return to my room and freshen up a wee bit." They continued walking towards her dorm.

At her dorm, Alexander waited in the lobby while Fiona went upstairs to her room.

*****

ON REACHING HER ROOM, FIONA exclaimed, "I canna believe it! I canna believe it, and I canna believe what I've done!"

"What? What have you done?" asked Jane.

"I met Mary's friend Alexander today, and already I've asked him to study with me in the library. I canna believe I've been so forward. Is Mary in her room?"

"She is. I'll go with you—sounds like a good story is developing and I want to hear it.

They rushed to Mary's room with Fiona shaking her head and fussing at herself. "I canna believe it! I canna believe what I've done! I canna believe it!"

Mary's room was Spartan, especially compared to Fiona's. Mary lay in bed reading her psychology textbook. Her poster of Bob Dylan peeked over her shoulder as if to comment. Mary's roommate, Anne, reviewed class notes with their neighbor, Sara.

Mary raised her head inquisitively as Fiona and Jane entered through her always open door. "What can't you believe, Fiona?"

*****

"*MO CHARAID*, D'YE KEN I telt ye about a boy who once protected me from bullies? Ye said Alexander would have done that."

"Yes, he would have."

"Och, Mary. That boy <u>was</u> Alexander!" Fiona was glowing in excitement. "I canna believe it. I've found him! Weel, ye found him. *Moran taing*"

"Are you sure?"

22

"Aye. Alexander remembered it as well," Fiona assured her. "He did say that I looked different now," she said through her blush.

Uh oh, thought Mary. *What have I started?* Fiona bubbled excitement and was upset at the same time.

"Now that you've met him again, how did you like Alexander?" Mary asked. "But first, what's wrong?"

"*Mo Charaid*, I liked Alexander fine. In fact, he's remarkable, just as ye said. He can even talk!" Fiona giggled. "Thank ye for the introduction. *Moran taing*! We spent all afternoon together and even supped. I've found him!"

"But you seem upset; what's wrong?" Mary had not anticipated this connection and especially Fiona becoming upset. She had been looking forward to retelling her introduction story and hearing Fiona recount a pleasant afternoon.

"I said I must return to my room and study, and Alexander walked with me. Then in front of the library, I heard myself saying I could study in the library and asked if he would join me. He said yes and is waiting in the lobby."

Jane laughed. "You asked Alexander Gordon for a date?"

Mary sighed in relief; this was manageable. "So, you met my friend, liked him, and found a way of spending extra time with him." Mary teased. This was more involved and better than expected. "Congratulations."

"I canna believe I've been this forward. I've never done anything like this in my life. What must he think of me? What can I do? I dinna ken."

"Here's an idea," Mary smiled. "I can go to the lobby and tell Alexander you've changed your mind, and he should leave."

"Here's a better idea," jested Anne. "I will go to the lobby and tell Alexander you've changed your mind, but I will go to the library with him."

"Nay, nay!" Fiona shook her head. "I just want some advice. I dinna ken what to do."

Mary gave Fiona and the other girls a knowing look. "Here's what you should do," she advised. "First, change into something green to match your eyes and a little low cut to catch <u>his</u> eyes."

Jane interrupted, "I have just the blouse she needs."

Mary continued, "Anne, lend her your necklace with the circular pendant, the one that hangs low. Jane, help me brush out her hair and touch up her makeup. Sara, you're the perfume expert; find something alluring but not overwhelming."

"My Mum's Penholigon's Helfeti perfume from Scotland is on my dresser," Fiona suggested. "Da liked it."

Mary noted Fiona's change in attitude and smiled. "Now you're talking!"

A girl entered Mary's room and excitedly exclaimed, "You'll never guess who is in the lobby!"

"Guess who he's waiting for?" Jane bragged.

The girl assessed Fiona and conceded, "I should have known!"

"Anne," instructed Mary, "Go to the lobby and tell the receptionist that Fiona will be down in a few minutes. You might stay there in case Fiona needs help." Mary winked.

Fiona listened intently as Mary gave further instructions. "Step out the door onto the stairway landing, hesitate for a few seconds and look around for Alexander as though you don't know where he is. Once he sees you—well, you're on your own then. Oh, and I'm especially pleased you liked him for more than one cup of coffee."

Jane added, "Remember, eyes wide open."

Fully primped, Fiona stepped out the door and onto the landing with a book, a pad of paper, and a small purse. Following Mary's instructions, she hesitated and assessed the lobby. Alexander, waiting eagerly, noticed Fiona right away and broke into an enormous smile. He stood and hastened to the stairway with his eyes locked on Fiona. Bounding up the stairs, Alexander missed a step and stumbled to his hands and knees. Undeterred but red-faced, he recovered his balance and laughed.

Instead of laughing at his clumsiness, Fiona glowed at the sight of Alexander. Alexander took her book, paper, and purse. He took her hand in his own, and Fiona closed her long slim fingers around it. He smiled and croaked, "Y-You are so beautiful!"

Fiona, luminous green eyes wide and smiling, replied, "Flatterer."

Holding hands, they stepped down the stairs together and turned toward the main entrance doors.

Martha, a dorm resident, came in as Fiona and Alexander were leaving. Martha gave them a puzzled smile and stepped to the stairs. Fiona and Alexander exited hand-in-hand and turned toward the library.

*****

IN THE HALLWAY, Martha found Mary and nearly a dozen girls excitedly discussing Fiona and Alexander. Martha said, "I didn't know Fiona had a boyfriend. He certainly is handsome. How long has this been going on?"

Mary glanced at her watch and answered, "About four hours." Everyone burst into laughter.

"Did you see the look on his face when Fiona came out?" Jane marveled.

"Yes, but did you see the look on her face when he came up the stairs?"

A newcomer added, "I don't even know him, but you can take him off the available list!"

"Yes, but we can take _her_ off the competition list as well!"

Jane smirked at Mary and surmised, "He doesn't stand a chance, does he?"

"Of resisting her, none. Of winning her, every. Let's go to my room, and I'll tell you about introducing them. It will probably be the best story you've ever heard."

*****

ON LEAVING THE DORM, after internal thoughts and arguments, Fiona reluctantly but gently released Alexander's hand. He kept her books and smiled.

"In Scotland," Fiona began, "it wouldna be warm enough for us to walk to the library dressed so casually. We'd be bundled up."

Alexander's eyes drifted over Fiona. She definitely was not bundled up. "A good reason to be in Mississippi."

"My friends were that impressed ye would accompany me to the dorm, wait and are now walking me to the library."

"What are your friends doing now?"

"Och, they're talking about us, of course." *What are they saying about us?* Everyone seemed to have a positive attitude and was even excited—as she was.

"I'll bet Mary is telling them about my stunned reaction to you. She probably added a few embellishments. I'll have to live with that story for a long time."

"But ye must admit, it makes a great story. I canna wait to hear Mary tell it. Also, everything worked out. I'm glad to have met ye and been with ye this day."

"And I'm glad I accepted Mary's invitation to meet you. I almost did not. What a mistake that would have been."

"Mary did a good job of selling ye. I was reluctant at first, but I'm glad she convinced me to meet ye." Fiona smiled. *I canna believe I almost missed this opportunity. I really must get out more often.* It was fun to be out and about with Alexander.

They ambled on towards the library. Birds chirped around them as though listening to their story and commenting on it.

"Tell me more about yerself," Fiona asked. "What are your goals?"

"Most people assume I'll be a professional athlete, but I won't."

"Are ye saying that because ye ken I dislike football?"

"No, it's the truth. Everyone does not like football. I'm enjoying your company even though you do not like football."

"There is more to ye than football, Alexander Gordon." *Much, much more.*

"Thank you. Still, most people assume I'll play professional football, and I leave them to their own conclusions. Sure, the money is good, and the fame and competition tempting, but professional sports are not for me."

"What will ye do instead of sports?" Fiona was not just making conversation; she was genuinely curious about Alexander's ambitions. She, too, had assumed he would play professional football.

"My goal is to invent things and develop my own business and company. I need multiple advanced degrees in engineering. I also want to be well-educated, so I'm taking extra history, art, and languages courses. I want to be creative in music and writing, and photography. I guess I want everything—at least, that's what Mary says."

"Mary is extremely proud of you."

"She has been my friend and advisor all my life. However, she does enjoy playing tricks on me." He laughed.

"Your goals are high but obtainable. I wish ye every success and expect ye will achieve your goals."

"And what are your goals?"

"Goals?" sniffed Fiona, suddenly emotional. "Unlike yours, my goal is unattainable. I would return to the wonderful life and love of my parents if it were at all possible. Can ye invent a time machine?"

"If I could, I would invent a time machine for you even though it would take you away, but I'm afraid you must develop your own life instead."

Fiona regained her composure. "But I do have plans. I love learning and, like ye, intend to get multiple degrees. Mine will be in fine arts, especially music. I'd love to sing opera or dance ballet, but I'm afraid I'm too tall--especially for ballet. I'm learning to draw and paint. I want to tour the world. I'm not sure about finances and may be forced to compromise, but I have faith everything will work out."

"I was taught to set goals and then make plans to achieve them. Your plans reflect your interests and a goal you don't recognize now. It will all come together for you someday, and your life will be wonderful."

"I canna believe I've telt ye these things. Ye are a good listener and that easy to talk to." Fiona had never stated her dreams so concisely to anyone—even her Aunt Ellen.

They reached the library and found an empty table. As Fiona arranged her things, Alexander searched for a book to read for his literature class.

*****

ON RETURNING TO THEIR TABLE, Alexander was about to sit across from Fiona when he realized he would stare at her. He moved around the table, wanting to be closer.

"I like your perfume."

Fiona smiled. "*Moran taing*! It is my Mum's Penholigon's Helfeti perfume from Scotland."

Alexander opened the literature book and began turning pages.

After a few minutes, Fiona whispered, "Are ye reading or skimming?"

"Reading. Why?"

"Ye turn the pages that fast."

"I've always been a fast reader and recently took a speed-reading course to increase my speed. It's been tremendously helpful."

"How is your comprehension reading that fast?"

"Usually, my comprehension is good, but tonight I'm having a little trouble concentrating," he admitted.

Fiona smiled. "A speed-reading course sounds like a good idea. I'll try it."

After several more minutes, Fiona sighed. "Hmmm, you're supposed to be good at math. Are you good at trigonometry? I'm a wee bit confused about this problem."

"Well, I've taken the trig course. Let me see the problem." Alexander stood, moved closer to Fiona, and leaned towards her book with his hand on her back. "Ah, the substitution you are using makes the equation more complex. The tangent of an angle can be expressed as the sine of the angle divided by the cosine of the angle. Use that substitution and simplify the equation."

"Aye, *taing.*"

"I didn't know fine art majors had to take trigonometry."

"They don't. I'm taking trig as an elective. It will probably be my last math course."

After a couple of hours, Fiona announced she really, really must return to the dormitory. She and Alexander left the library with him holding her books, but not her hand. They began in silence, then spoke simultaneously, "I've enjoyed being with you," and laughed at the coincidence.

"In Scotland, we might say '*oidhche mhath,*' which means this was a good and interesting night."

Alexander attempted to repeat it, "*oidhche mhath,*" but botched the pronunciation, and Fiona laughed. He added, "A good and interesting night, indeed."

At the dorm, Alexander took Fiona's hand, gave it a light squeeze, and held on. She gazed up at him and smiled. He asked, "Would you have coffee with me tomorrow morning?"

"I'd love to. *Taing.*"

Fiona entered her dorm. Alexander trekked away, lost in thought. *What a girl!* He was already looking forward to the morning and coffee with Fiona.

*****

MARY'S ROOM WAS A POPULAR gathering place; her door was always open. Girls were seated on chairs and beds in Mary's room as they waited for Fiona's return and the story of her day. Fiona arrived with a blush and a smile.

Sonya, an attractive blonde from down the hall, spoke up immediately. "I saw you with Alexander Gordon and want to warn you about him. As you probably know, we dated."

Mary slipped behind Sonya, held up one finger and mouthed, "Once."

"Alexander is notorious for impressing a girl and then dropping her like a hot potato. I wanted to make sure you knew this. You may never see him again."

Fiona countered with, "We are having coffee together tomorrow morning." She gave Sonya a sweet smile.

Sonya muttered, "Humph," and left the room.

Mary grinned at Fiona and answered her unspoken question. "Sonya is not his type."

"What is his type?" asked Fiona, now curious.

Everyone started giggling and spoke in unison, "You are, Fiona. You are."

Everyone then joined in. "You are tall and beautiful. Exotic even, with that thick auburn hair and those bright green eyes. Your Scottish accent and European culture add to your appeal.

30

Not to mention you are extremely intelligent, talented, and fun. Oh, you are Alexander's type, all right."

"But what if Alexander is not <u>my</u> type?"

At that, all the girls howled in a fit of laughter.

Mary interjected, "You and Alexander appear to be a perfect match—that's why I introduced you. All the same, a loving and meaningful relationship must have a certain '*je ne sais quoi*,' that cannot be easily described. I think you two have it, but only time will tell."

Many girls were nodding their heads in agreement.

Mary continued, "Now, Fiona, tell us about your day with Alexander."

Jane interrupted, "But first, everyone wants to know: Did he kiss you after coming back from the library?"

Fiona blushed bright red. "He did not kiss me; that would not have been appropriate. However, as we neared the dorm, it occurred to me he might try, and I realized I would not turn away."

Much giggling ensued.

*****

ALEXANDER RETURNED to his dorm carrying a sack of chicken sliders but still dazed. He had never met anyone like Fiona.

As usual, his next-door dorm mates had their stereo turned loud, and Donnie was studying at his desk. Donnie pointed to his watch. "Long day?"

Alexander offered him a slider, but he shook his head.

"Your little record player cannot compete with the monster stereo next door," Alexander observed.

"I know. They just turned theirs on." Donnie turned his record player off, removed the Johnny Cash record, and put it carefully in its cover.

"So, how was the nerd—or should I say nerdette?" Donnie asked. "Did you ever learn her name?"

"Her name is Fiona. She is really something. It turns out we briefly met three years ago when I stopped some bullies from harassing her. I didn't recognize her today, but she recognized me. She was skinny with braces back then, but she certainly has changed. She is absolutely beautiful now."

"Of course, she is beautiful, smart and talented. Probably likes you already. Of course, you are her hero. You have all the luck in the world. There's none left for me."

"Fiona has the greenest eyes I've ever seen. She's from Scotland—yes, her hair is red, actually auburn, and wavy. She is majoring in music and voice. Fiona still has a slight Scottish accent, but some Southern drawl occasionally slips in. She also speaks Scottish Gaelic, French, and Italian fluently."

"Sounds like you were impressed. Does she have a good personality, like Mary said?"

"Indeed, she does. She is, by far, the most beautiful and fascinating girl I have ever met."

"So not just a one cup introduction then?"

"No, in fact, I spent the rest of the day with her."

"Uh oh."

"... and we're having coffee in the morning."

"Double uh oh."

*****

FIONA'S ALARM CLOCK rang loudly at six a.m. She slapped it off and sat on the side of her bed for a moment. Jane slept soundly, her curly hair ruffled on the pillow. Fiona stepped to Jane's bedside and urged, "Jane, wake up. Time for exercise." Jane moaned.

Fiona began putting on her exercise outfit. "Come on noo. Ye ken we must exercise to avoid the freshman fifteen."

"We walk so much during the day, doesn't walk count as exercise?"

"I dinna ken, but I'm exercising." Naturally slim, Fiona resolved to gain muscle tone, but not the rippled muscles of Alexander. Her face flushed slightly at the thought of him. She wondered what exercises he did. Probably weight lifting.

Their dormitory included an exercise room that could be located by its perfumed sweat and machine noise. The room was not large but outfitted with treadmills, stationary bicycles, a snow ski simulator, elliptical trainers, resistance machines and even light free weights. Usually, the exercise room was sparsely populated, especially at this hour in the morning. This morning only Fiona, Jane and two others were exercising.

After her stretching routines, Fiona began exercising on the elliptical trainer. At six forty-five, a dance instructor came in and led the small group in 'Jazzercise.' At the end of the Jazzercise routine, the instructor approached Fiona and complimented, "You're great at this. You should become an instructor."

"*Taing*. I've considered that. I'm studying dance and really enjoy Jazzercise. It seems right for me."

"I'll get you more information and train and certify you."

*****

ALEXANDER ARRIVED at the coffee shop early in case Fiona was early as well. He mused about the previous day, meeting Fiona and discovering how different she was. He glanced at his watch; Fiona would be here soon. Mary came to him, smiling.

"Well?" Mary teased.

"Thank you very much for introducing me to Fiona, but why did you do it that way?"

"Alexander," Mary said thoughtfully, "I did not know you and Fiona had met previously. I should have introduced you some other way. Listen to me carefully now. You are her hero. Don't you hurt that poor girl."

"I have no intention of hurting Fiona, believe me. In fact, I want to get to know her. More than beautiful, she is fantastic."

"I didn't anticipate the effect she would have on you," Mary laughed, "but you recovered quite well, and now I have a great story to tell."

"Oh, no!. Please don't have me fainting or drooling."

"A drool would be a good embellishment! Thanks for the tip!"

Mary continued, "To save your having to ask, Fiona was extremely impressed with you—even discounting that you are her hero. In fact, one of the girls who only saw you meet her on the stairs said Fiona could be removed from the list of competitors."

"I don't know about that, but you girls can be scary. Sports are competitive, but sports are nothing compared to female social competition."

"We have to be competitive; it's innate. This is not about games, sex, or love; it is about survival."

Mary teased, "Oh, and another girl noted you could be removed from the list of available men."

Alexander reddened. "Well, I'm certainly impressed with Fiona. I'll be glad to see her again. She should be here in a few minutes."

Just then, Fiona waltzed in wearing a big smile. "*Madainn mhath.Ciamar a tha thu?*"

Alexander briefly took her hand. A refreshing morning scent wafted about her. He opened his mouth to speak the line he'd made up, but nothing came out. He tried again. "G-G-Good morning! I'm so glad to see you were not just a b-beautiful dream."

"Flatterer!" Fiona flashed a huge smile.

Mary laughed and shook her head.

"Mary is writing a short story she calls 'The Introduction,'" said Alexander. "It is somewhat familiar but unbelievably exaggerated and embellished."

"That tale was telt more than once last night. It's a good one!" laughed Fiona.

"Time for my class," Mary said. "Enjoy your coffee." She left them, and they entered the coffee shop.

Fiona selected an empty booth and sat down on its bench. Alexander was about to get coffee but then turned around, embarrassed. "I can't believe this, but I've forgotten how you fixed your coffee yesterday. I guess I was distracted after all; anyway, I don't remember."

Fiona giggled. "I dinna drink coffee. I take tea with a slice of lemon. I have a bag of Scottish tea and need only hot water and lemon."

Alexander left but returned quickly, pleased no one had joined Fiona at their table. He sat beside Fiona. *Had she chosen a booth so he could sit near her?* He scooted over until his leg brushed against hers. She did not move.

"Here we are. Hot water for your tea and coffee for me. I also got some scones." Alexander was very pleased with himself for thinking of the scones.

Fiona made a face. "The scones here are no good. My aunt has a fabulous family recipe. I'll make scones for ye one day." She retrieved a tea bag from her purse.

That offer sounded great to Alexander. "So, you can cook too?"

"I was learning in Scotland, but I'm adapting to Southern-style now and learning to cook that way."

"What's your favorite Scottish food?"

"My favorite is Scottish salmon."

"Do you eat haggis?"

"Aye. Non-Scots make fun of haggis, but it is delicious. Ye should try it sometime."

Changing the subject, Fiona asked, "Do ye ken a blonde named Sonya? Her room is on my floor, down the hall."

Alexander had a quick, *"Uh oh,"* thought, but admitted, "Yes, I know her. We <u>once</u> had a date." He emphasized 'once.' "I quickly learned Sonya is not my type."

"Och? She's a bonnie lass."

"Let me just say Sonya is not academically minded."

Fiona smiled. Changing the subject again, she pointed to Alexander's books and slide rule. "Is that a slide rule? Some guys and occasionally a lassie or two carry them around."

"Yes, a slide rule. Mine is a fancy log log duplex decitrig version. Engineers and scientists use them for difficult mathematical calculations. Slide rules are indispensable for now, but electronic calculators will probably replace them in a few years. Calculators are very expensive and not as versatile as slide rules."

"Someday ye can show me how to use one."

"Slide rule classes are available."

"I'm more interested in private lessons," Fiona smiled.

One of Alexander's teammates approached their table. Alexander whispered to Fiona, "Here comes a guy from the football team. Get ready for anything."

With a big grin on his face, John sat without asking permission. After a long admiring gaze at Fiona, John remarked to Alexander, "So, this is the girl you wanted me to meet? You're right. She is far too pretty for you."

"Fiona, I'd like to introduce my friend and teammate, John."

"Hello, John. Nice to meet ye."

Without hesitating, John began, "Alexander said you liked guys to cut to the chase. Will you go out to dinner with me tonight? We can become better acquainted then."

Fiona calmly declined. *"Taing,* but I have other plans."

John stood, stepped past Alexander, and whispered, "You lucky dog!"

Fiona and Alexander burst out laughing. Alexander said, "Like I said: be ready for anything! Can you believe him? He's really a nice guy, but what a character!"

"Well, aren't ye going to ask?"

"Ask what?"

"About my plans for tonight." Fiona's eyes invited him to ask.

"I must admit being curious, but my asking would be more than a bit presumptuous."

"My dormitory is sponsoring a social event tonight called the 'Meet and Greet,'" said Fiona. "It is a chance to meet and get acquainted with new people. Would ye come as my guest?"

Alexander was familiar with Meet and Greet socials; he was a prized guest. He usually declined such invitations to avoid being shown off, as in "See who I invited." Fiona's invitation appeared more personal, and he wanted more time with her. Her Meet and Greet social provided an excellent opportunity. Besides, she would otherwise be unavailable tonight.

"Of course, I'll come. Thank you for inviting me."

"I want ye to ken my friends and have them ken ye."

Hmm, Alexander wondered, *Maybe I'm making a mistake.*

*****

PREPARED FOR THE "MEET AND GREET," Alexander entered Fiona's dorm amid the sweet mixed smells of perfume and hors d'oeuvres in the lobby. Recorded popular music played softly in the background. He stepped to the receptionist.

"I'm Alexander Gordon."

The receptionist smiled and replied, "I know." She flipped a switch and spoke into the microphone, "Fiona, your guest is here." She handed Alexander a name tag reading "Alexander Gordon / Fiona MacDonald."

As Fiona came down the stairs, Alexander went up to meet her. He took her soft hand in his, conscious of its warmth. She was breathtakingly beautiful and wearing the same perfume as the night before. Alexander stuttered his line, "A-A-A thing of b-b-beauty is a joy forever."

"Flatterer," Fiona replied with a smile. They stepped down the stairs together. "I like your cologne; what is it?"

"English Leather aftershave."

"I can detect the leather scent."

In the lobby, Fiona explained she was part of the program and would play piano and sing but only one song. Until the talent portion of the program officially began, they could have hors d'oeuvres and circulate among the hosts and guests.

"Remember this is a 'Meet and Greet.'" Fiona teased. "If ye see someone ye might be interested in, just ask, and I'll introduce ye."

Fiona's teasing tone was unnoticed by Alexander. This was precisely the situation he wanted to avoid. "I came to be with you—not to be passed around. Perhaps I should leave instead."

Fiona stepped closer to Alexander and put her hand on his arm. "Please dinna leave. I'm that sorry. Let me try again."

Fiona's eyes were tearing up, and Alexander realized he had misunderstood.

Fiona took a deep breath. "Alexander, I selfishly invited ye to be with me, not to meet other lassies. I want to come to know ye. But surely ye ken ye are a big man on campus, and everyone wants to meet ye. I want my friends to ken ye and ye to ken my friends. Please dinna leave. Noo, please excuse me for a minute or two." Fiona turned and stepped up the stairs quickly.

Alexander, now standing alone, thought, *You idiot! What is wrong with you?*

*****

FIONA RUSHED TO MARY'S room. Mary took one look and asked, "What's wrong?"

"I was explaining oor 'Meet and Greet' to Alexander and teased him, saying I would introduce him to anyone he found appealing. I'm afraid he believed I was trying to get rid of him. Alexander said he came to be with me and not to be passed around. He wanted to leave, but I asked him not to. I hope he's still in the lobby."

Mary sighed. She explained that Alexander was accustomed to being the center of attention, but often he did not like it. People sometimes invited Alexander to events so they could show they knew him. He avoided those situations by simply not attending.

"Fiona, I'm sure Alexander came to this Meet and Greet just to be with you," Mary explained. "He was not thinking about meeting and impressing your friends, the big ox. Alexander is a guy. Guys are not particularly smart in social situations. He has probably realized his mistake by now. Now, dry your eyes, and go down there and find him before someone else does. I'll be there as soon as I can blow dry my hair and get it brushed out." Mary's hair was short, so Fiona knew she would be downstairs soon.

Fiona retouched her makeup and was about to return to the lobby. However, first, she peered through the door pane to see if Alexander was still there, and, sure enough, two girls were talking to him. She took a deep breath, opened the door, and stepped down the stairs.

*****

FIONA EASED TO THE GROUP, put her hand on Alexander's arm, and smiled sweetly as she said, "*Moran taing* for waiting." The girls glanced at Fiona, then Alexander, then at each other, and walked away, leaving Fiona and Alexander standing alone.

Alexander studied Fiona's eyes before speaking. "I'm an idiot. I'm sorry for what I said. Please forgive me."

"Mary explained your reluctance to go to Meet and Greet and such socials. Now I dinna ken the way of introducing ye to my friends. I want ye to ken my friends, and them to ken ye, but I might be guilty of showing ye off as well. I dinna ken. D'ye ken that showing ye off isna the same as showing off that I ken ye?"

"I think I understand, but, honestly, I'm a bit confused right now."

Fortunately, Mary came up to them. "Hello, Mister B.M.O.C.," she laughed. "Finding it difficult talking with your foot in your mouth?"

Alexander could only shake his head.

"Oh," Mary noted. "Here comes Jane. Jane is Fiona's roommate. Fiona, I'll let you handle the introductions." Mary gave Alexander a glance that he correctly interpreted as, *"You'd better make a good impression on these girls if you know what's good for you."*

"Jane," Fiona said rather formally. "I'd like to introduce my guest, Alexander Gordon."

Jane held out her hand. "Pleased to meet you, Alexander. What is your major?"

Alexander understood. Not a word about size, looks, football, or last night's library date with Fiona. He was a guest, not even a friend—much less a date. He took Jane's hand gently. "Mechanical engineering; I'm a sophomore from Oceanport."

Anne joined the group. "Anne," Fiona said, still formally. "I'd like to introduce my guest, Alexander Gordon."

Anne held out her hand. "I'm Mary's roommate. You must be the one that Mary considers her brother. Nice meeting you."

"Are you enjoying our Meet and Greet?" asked Jane, a smirk on her face.

"I really arrived only a few minutes ago." Alexander took stock of Fiona. "Frankly, I'm intimidated and not handling this well at all. I don't know what to do or say."

The girls giggled.

"Just relax, you big galoot," cajoled Mary. "Let Fiona introduce you to her friends."

The girls strayed away, still giggling.

"Fiona, after you left, it occurred to me that every guy in this room wants to meet you. I'll try to be polite, but I may not get far away from you. I'm not in my element here. I hope I won't cramp your style."

"I could say the same to ye. Let's relax, stay together and meet people."

They headed for the hors d'oeuvres. Alexander wished he had eaten more supper.

*****

AWARE OF THE MEET AND GREET SOCIAL but uninvited, Thomas Bennoitt sauntered confidently into the girls' dorm and up to the receptionist. He announced, "I'm Thomas Bennoitt."

The receptionist reached for a name badge and retorted, "I know who you are. Who is your host?"

Thomas answered, "Just write 'Student Council Representative' as my host. Like everyone else, I want to meet people."

The receptionist did as Thomas requested and handed him his badge. He strutted away and into a group of co-eds.

After a half-hour of hors d'oeuvres and circulation, the Dorm Mother called for everyone's attention. "It is now time for our program."

The Head Hostess thanked everyone for coming, introduced the organizers and introduced the performers. "Our first talent has traveled the farthest distance to be here—that is, if you consider she is from Scotland instead of East Mississippi. Ladies and Gentlemen, Miss Fiona MacDonald!"

Thomas smiled. *Big Red!* This was beyond his wildest dreams: A sophisticated European pianist who sang and really was fine. He could imagine the positive effect she would have on his political campaign. *I've got to meet Big Red, and what better situation than a Meet and Greet? This is perfect.*

Fiona waltzed to the piano, adjusted the microphone and advised, "Your program says I will sing 'Loch Lomond.' If understood correctly, Loch Lomond is a sad song. Instead, I will sing an anglicized variation of 'My Love is Like a Red, Red Rose' by the Scottish poet and songwriter Robert Burns." She played and sang:

> O, my love is like a red, red rose,
> That's newly sprung in June.
> O, my love is like the melodie,
> That's sweetly play'd in tune.

After the applause died down, Fiona floated over to Alexander, sat beside him, and placed her hand in his.

Thomas Bennoitt could not believe his eyes. Had Fiona sung to Alexander? Thomas was infuriated, given yet another reason to be jealous of Alexander Gordon. He was more determined than ever to meet Fiona and steal her from Alexander.

After the program, Thomas sauntered purposefully towards Fiona. She instinctively edged toward Alexander and put her hand on his arm. Unswayed, Thomas reached them in a few steps and ignored Alexander as he spoke to Fiona. "Allow me to introduce myself; I'm Thomas Bennoitt. I've seen you on campus and hoped you'd be here. Could we talk a moment?"

Fiona tersely answered, "What about?" and kept her hand on Alexander's arm.

Since Fiona would not walk away for a private conversation, Thomas boldly asked, "Would you go with me to my fraternity's party this weekend? We'll have food, drinks and even a band for dancing. It will be a lot of fun."

"*Taing* but nay."

Thomas tried again, "I'm sorry. I was a bit abrupt. Perhaps we should first become acquainted over dinner tomorrow night?"

"Nay." Fiona shook her head.

Thomas suggested, "Perhaps some other time?"

"Nay. I'm no interested."

Thomas cursed, louder than he intended, "Bitch!" and grabbed Fiona's forearm. He immediately felt Alexander's large hand clap on top of his own.

*****

"TAKE YOUR HAND OFF HER!" Alexander's command was calm, but his eyes turned to ice.

"Or what?" Thomas dared.

"I will crush your hand like an egg. You will never use it again."

Alexander's tightened his hand around Thomas's fingers but protected Fiona's arm. Thomas made a kind of "Ouch" sound, relaxed his grip on Fiona's arm and pulled his hand away from her.

Alexander maintained his hold on Thomas's hand, glared at him, and demanded, "Now apologize to Fiona and get the hell out of this dorm."

Thomas mumbled to Fiona, "I'm sorry. I don't know what came over me." However, he challenged Alexander, "But I don't think you can force me out of the dorm."

"I'm sure I can toss you out the door and probably through it—which will cut you up badly. If I can't, the security guard will, and that will not be good on your campaign literature." He released Thomas's hand but added, "One more thing. If any—I mean any—harm ever comes to Fiona, then I personally will come looking for you. Do you understand what I'm saying?"

With no other choice, Thomas conceded, "I understand."

The security guard reached them and asked if there were problems. Fiona answered, "Nay. We're fine."

The security guard watched intently as Thomas exited the dorm, leaving Alexander and Fiona standing together.

Alexander took a deep breath and, shaking his head, apologized. "Fiona, I'm so sorry this happened. Thomas does not like me, and I usually avoid him. That's two social screwups in an hour for me. Perhaps I'd better leave."

Fiona again placed her hand on Alexander's arm and spoke softly, "*Dinna fash yersel. Taing.* I'm glad ye are here. Please stay and meet my friends."

About nine o'clock, the Dorm Mother announced the social was over and asked all guests to leave. As Alexander was leaving, he asked, "Fiona, would you have coffee with me tomorrow morning?"

"I'd like that much. *Moran taing!*"

*****

JANE WAS WAITING EXPECTANTLY in their room for Fiona. She had not expected Fiona and Alexander to be so attracted to each other so quickly. This was a side of Fiona that she had never seen.

"Weel? What d'ye think?" asked Fiona.

"I knew he was big and good-looking from seeing him on your library date," smiled Jane.

Fiona blushed. Everyone was calling last night's library visit her "library date." She had to admit that she also considered it a date.

"But he seemed even bigger and more handsome in person. I was surprised, though, that he was so reserved. He actually was uncomfortable in that lobby full of girls—not at all what I expected from a big man on campus."

"Aye. Alexander was uncomfortable, especially at first. Mary explained that he usually does not participate in Meet and Greet socials. He doesna like being shown off."

A slight smirk grew on Jane's face. "How would you feel at a Meet and Greet if it were held at the boys' dorm?"

"Och, I wouldna go. Well, that is, unless Alexander invited me. Aye, I get your point."

"I did learn one thing about Alexander, though," Jane smiled. "He really does like you. He may have been introduced to other girls, but he had eyes only for you. He literally lit up whenever you looked at him."

"I ken, and I like him as well."

"Is Alexander the jealous type?"

"I dinna ken, but I dinna think so. How d'ye ask?"

"He certainly did not like Thomas Bennoitt talking to you. What was that all about?"

"That was more than talk." Fiona related the encounter with Thomas. "I hoped no one noticed. Please don't tell anyone."

"Thomas Bennoitt is a troublemaker. His goal is to be a big man on campus, and he is jealous of Alexander, who actually is a big man on campus but doesn't care."

"Let's go to Mary's room. I have a question for her."

*****

IN MARY'S ROOM, FIONA ASKED "Does Alexander get into many fights?".

"Not anymore. Alexander used to fight often when he was younger. He's always been big for his age, and the older kids would pick on him. He studied martial arts, and those skills and philosophies were a big help. Now he's so much bigger and stronger than everyone else that he rarely has a problem. Usually,

45

if he just stands up, the antagonists back down. But sometimes, someone simply wants to challenge him."

Fiona told Mary about Thomas Bennoitt hitting on her and grabbing her, as well as Alexander's response. "It happened so quickly and calmly that no one noticed."

"Thomas is ambitious to the point of being ruthless and cruel, but he is a coward," said Mary. "He is lucky that Alexander did not hurt him. Thomas will attempt to get even for tonight's confrontation, but I doubt it will be physical. Thomas is many things, but stupid is not one of them. Alexander tries to avoid him."

Fiona added, "I hope Thomas Bennoitt stays away from me. I dinna like him and want nothing to do with him. He gives me the creeps. I'm glad Alexander was here tonight."

A few more girls entered the room, and the conversation shifted to the Meet and Greet social.

One girl observed, "Well, Fiona, you would get the prize for having the most handsome and interesting guest except you did not share him." The other girls laughed.

"That is one fine-looking man," agreed Anne. "I tried luring him away from Fiona, but he wouldn't leave her."

Fiona's face warmed. "We had a wee misunderston about that. I teased Alexander by saying I would introduce him to anyone he wanted, but he took it wrong. He said he only came to the Meet and Greet to be with me. Ye ken we met yesterday. So, I stayed near him."

"Is that why you put your hand on his arm when Marilyn came up to him?"

"Och, did I?"

Jane added, "She also put her hand on Alexander's arm when guys approached her!" Everyone giggled.

*****

WHEN ALEXANDER ENTERED THEIR ROOM, Donnie said, "*Hola Pepe! Como estas usted?*" complete with his southern drawl.

"I hope Spanish does not cause you to flunk out," Alexander laughed. Donnie recited Spanish lessons repeatedly but could not get rid of his drawl.

"Just wait! Your time is coming."

"Now that I've learned Spanish from you, I may not need to take it. Fiona suggested I take German."

"Tell me about the Meet and Greet. How'd it go?"

Alexander recognized that Donnie wanted a break from his studies. "It was great. You should have come. I could have easily got you an invitation. Mary would have invited you. She did not have a guest."

"Unlike you, I must study. Besides, you just wanted to be with your new girlfriend. You didn't need a wingman."

Alexander ignored the jab. "Fiona was part of the program. On top of being beautiful, she is a wonderful pianist and singer."

"Did she introduce you to a bunch of good-looking girls?"

"We had a misunderstanding about the purpose of the 'Meet and Greet.' I didn't want introductions to other girls—I just wanted to get to know Fiona. Anyway, Fiona is always the most beautiful girl in the room. The most interesting, too."

"Insurance, Alexander, insurance. Besides, what about me? You could have met some girls for me."

Donnie was tall and slim, nice looking, but without a girlfriend, and he did not date often. He had little extra money and was frugal with what he had.

"What would you do with them? Study?"

"Weren't you studying with Fiona last night?" Donnie laughed, but Alexander missed the irony.

Alexander spoke quietly, "I had a run-in with Thomas Bennoitt."

"What happened?"

"He asked Fiona for a date, but she said no—several times. Then he called her a bitch and grabbed her arm. I couldn't believe it! I was standing right there."

"What did you do?"

"I grabbed his hand and forced him to let her go. Then I made him apologize and leave the dorm."

"What did you ever do to Thomas Bennoitt that he hates you so much?"

"I don't know, but someday he and I will have a major run-in."

"Be careful. His father is a rich doctor, and his mother is a well-connected socialite. He gets and does anything he wants."

"Well, he's not getting Fiona, and he's not free to do whatever he wants if I'm around.

*****

THE NEXT MORNING, Alexander invited Donnie, "Why don't you join me for coffee, and I'll introduce you to Fiona? Mary will also be there." Donnie and Mary were well acquainted and had become good friends.

"You sure talk a lot about this Fiona girl. What's going on? You're even wearing your best bell bottoms to an everyday class."

"For one thing, she's easy on the eyes. She's also interesting. Different. Sophisticated. You'll like her."

"I've seen her from a distance, and I must admit she is a beauty. She's called the 'Viking Princess,' isn't she? She looks the part."

"Fiona doesn't like the 'Viking Princess' label, so better not bring it up. Also, she doesn't particularly like football, so let's not get into that either."

"How does she feel about engineers?"

"She is more into fine art, music and philosophy, but she has lived on a farm with her aunt and uncle for the past three years. You can talk to her about farming."

Although Donnie was raised on a farm, he was serious about chemical engineering and getting away from farming even though he wanted to live in a rural area.

"So, this Fiona is not into football or engineers. Why would she hang out with you? Does she know about your money?"

"Please say nothing about my having money. Maybe Fiona heard I play guitar. I don't know, but I'm glad to have met her."

Alexander knew Donnie was teasing, but he too wondered why Fiona was interested in him. She could have any boy on campus, and she did not care about his sports or engineering. He had already made several social errors in her presence. He wasn't even from Scotland.

"I doubt I'll be able to add much about fine art, music and philosophy, but maybe she can give me advice about shoveling manure."

"I doubt it. You have a lot of BS."

"Well, I haven't seen Mary in a while. OK, see you in the coffee shop."

*****

DONNIE FOUND MARY, Fiona, and Alexander at a table in the coffee shop. Alexander said, "Fiona, I'd like to introduce my friend and roommate, Donnie."

"*Madainn mhath*, Donnie. I'm glad to meet ye."

Alexander left them for coffee and hot water. When he returned, Mary teased, "Can you talk?". Everyone howled.

Red-faced, Alexander retorted, "I knew you couldn't resist telling your 'Introduction' story. At least wait until I've left to finish."

"So, Alexander tells me you're a farmer," said Donnie to Fiona. Alexander groaned.

Fiona smiled, "Nay, but I've lived on my aunt and uncle's farm near Easton for the past three years."

Jane came to their table, dropped her books and complained, "That was a hard test. I'll be right back." She left to get a soda.

"That's a good-looking girl," said Donnie. "Please introduce me."

"Jane is my roommate. We were randomly assigned, but I'm certainly pleased to ken her. We are fine friends now. She is majoring in business. Alexander met her last night at the Meet and Greet."

"And you could have too," grinned Alexander.

Jane returned, and Fiona said, "Jane, I'd like to introduce Donnie. He is Alexander's roommate."

Donnie stood, and Jane briefly shook his hand. "Pleased to meet you, Donnie. I'm sorry I neglected you at first. I'm flustered by my business law test." They both sat down.

Mary entered the conversation. "Donnie is a Chemical Engineer. Am I right, Donnie?"

"Well, a chemical engineering student. If I can pass all my courses, then I'll be a Chemical Engineer someday." Turning to Alexander, Donnie added, "Some people must study more than others."

"Well, I certainly have to study," said Jane. "I'm afraid I didn't study enough or perhaps the right information for that business law test."

"What do you do when you're not studying?" Donnie asked.

"I used to play tennis in high school, but have neglected it recently."

"Me too. Would you like to try to shed a little tennis rust with me?"

"Thanks. I'd like that."

*****

FIONA GLANCED AT HER WATCH and fretted, "Speaking of courses, I must go to class."

"I'll go with you," said Alexander.

As they walked out of the coffee shop, Mary laughed and said, "… so there I was, little Mary, pulling this huge football player into the snack shop. Everyone was laughing and pointing at us. Alexander was not looking forward, and he had not seen Fiona…."

"I'm still surprised you didn't just excuse yourself and leave after I blew that introduction," Alexander mused to Fiona.

"That was my most memorable introduction ever," Fiona smiled.

"Speaking of introductions, what did you think of Donnie?"

"He seems quite nice and has much respect for ye but likes harassing ye. Perhaps more serious than ye. More frugal as well. Nice looking, too. He liked Jane."

"You got all that in just those few minutes?"

"Aye. It was obvious."

"Would you have lunch with me today?"

"*Taing*, but I canna. On Wednesdays, I often join a group of lassies visiting the nursing home at lunchtime. We help serve lunch and visit with the auld folks. Sometimes we bring them wee gifts. Today I'll entertain by playing the piano. The men especially like us." Fiona blushed.

"I'll bet!"

"Perhaps another day? Or supper tonight?"

"I'll take you up on supper tonight."

They walked to class with smiles on their faces, oblivious to admiring glances tossed their way.

*****

IN THE COFFEE SHOP, Donnie questioned Mary. "He's a goner, isn't he?"

"Oh, yes. I've never seen anything like this. I'd never seen Alexander flustered until he met Fiona. Usually, it is the girl who gets flustered. As shy as Fiona is, I'm surprised at how quickly she became comfortable around him. My theory is that Alexander revealed his imperfections to Fiona by being flustered and stunned, and she relaxed. Not to mention that he is her hero." I feel sorry for anyone who tries to get between them or even in their way.

"I heard about him stopping bullies some years ago," Donnie said. "Amazing that they've met again. What a story."

"Fiona just raves about Alexander," said Jane. "She is becoming a different person right in front of my eyes."

"Alexander is still stunned every time he first sees her," said Mary, "but, fortunately, he recovers after a few minutes. He could not have written a better script for getting to know Fiona. I'm embarrassed for him, but it is actually funny. Don't worry, he'll get over it."

"You mean he'll get over Fiona?"

"Oh, no. As you said, he's a goner. But he will get over being flustered and stunned."

"After they spent that first day together," Donnie said, "Alexander told me Fiona was the most beautiful and fascinating girl he ever met."

"That's pretty much the same thing she said about him," Jane added. "She also said that although she ran away and left him three years ago, she would never leave him again."

"And she won't," Mary acknowledged.

Jane smiled at Donnie. "I took a chemistry class once. It was very difficult. You must be smart. Tell me about yourself."

*****

52

WEDNESDAY NIGHT IN THEIR DORM ROOM, Alexander wanted Donnie's opinion of Fiona. He opened the conversation, "I'm glad you met Fiona. Now you can understand why I'm impressed. I'm learning more about her every day. Today I learned that she donates time and visits to the nursing home. She played piano and sang for them today. We could not have lunch together, but we had supper. Did I tell you that she uses her fork upside down? She said that's the proper style everywhere except America. I tried, but it's awkward. She played soccer in Scotland but now concentrates on dance. She's Presbyterian."

Donnie smiled but remained silent. He opened his record player and thoughtfully placed a record on the turntable. The voice of Johnny Cash boomed, "Ring of Fire."

Unable to resist any longer, Alexander asked directly, "Well, what did you think about Fiona?"

"She is certainly beautiful—just as you said—and she has a good personality—just as Mary said. She's no farmer or farm girl, though; in fact, I'd say she's accustomed to having money. She's smart, all right, except that, for some reason, she likes you."

"Ring of Fire" ended, and Donnie carefully returned the record to its album touching only the edges with his fingers.

"Alexander, you may be a rough, tough football player," Donnie grinned, "but you're no match for a Viking Princess. It's only taken her a couple of days to wrap you around her little finger."

"I wouldn't go so far as to say that."

"I would. I've never seen this side of you—neither has Mary. Your entire life is changing. Mark my words."

Alexander changed the subject. "How'd you like her roommate?"

"Jane is a good-looking girl and easy to talk to. I'm glad to have met her. We're going to play tennis tomorrow. I might ask her for a date.

"Good. Maybe we can double."

"I'd like that."

*****

THURSDAY MORNING as Sonya left the coffee shop for class, she noticed Fiona enter and sit at an empty table. *Probably waiting for Alexander*, she thought. Sonya knew Fiona rarely went to the coffee shop or sat by herself, but Fiona's routine had changed since meeting Alexander. She gained confidence each time she was with him. Sonya ambled on.

Just outside the coffee shop, Thomas Bennoitt passed by and ogled Sonya in her miniskirt. She smiled at Thomas and then smiled again at her sudden idea. "Oh, Thomas," tempted Sonya. "If you are looking for Fiona, she is waiting in the coffee shop."

Thomas stopped and smiled in return. "Thank you." He turned, "I found her." Thomas entered the coffee shop, sauntered to Fiona's table, and immediately sat down beside her.

Sonya remained outside the coffee shop. One more cut class would not make any difference in her grade. She intercepted Alexander on his way to the coffee shop and invited herself to walk in with him. Once inside, Sonya said, "Oh, there's Fiona, but she has company."

At the sight of Fiona sitting with Thomas Bennoitt and in conversation, Alexander's face took on a shocked and confused appearance.

"Why don't you and I find a table and talk?" suggested Sonya. She smiled at Alexander, but he turned toward Fiona's table instead.

*****

"Hello. I'm pleased to find you again," Thomas said to Fiona as soon as he sat. "I feel I owe you a deeper apology for my actions at your 'Meet and Greet.' Please forgive me."

"I can forgive, but canna forget."

"As I said that night, my fraternity is having a party on Saturday. I hope you will come. We will have a grand time with music and drinks. Please come." He was more than willing to give Fiona another chance.

"*Taing*, but such parties are not for me."

"I hope you'll change your mind. If you do, just come to the party and say you are my guest. My fraternity brothers will be watching for you."

"I willna be there."

"If you don't have transportation, I'll be happy to give you a ride in my new GTO. You'll like it—it is quite sporty and fast."

Alexander stepped with purpose towards Fiona and Thomas.

"So there you are," Thomas grinned. "Care to join us?"

Alexander glanced from Sonya to Thomas to Fiona. Fiona looked troubled and shook her head slightly. "No," Alexander responded. "I think not," and turned away.

*****

"ALEXANDER!" FIONA NEARLY SHOUTED. She rose and took his hand. "We need to talk." She led him to an empty table.

"I don't understand," Alexander admitted. "What is happening here?"

"I could ask ye the same question. How are ye with Sonya?" Fiona's voice quivered. She wondered, *"Not his type, eh? Am I jealous?"*

"I'm not with Sonya. She told me you were with Thomas, and then she walked in with me. Why are you with Thomas? He is nothing but trouble. You said you did not like him."

"I'm not with Thomas. He sat at my table uninvited. I was trying to get rid of him when ye came in with Sonya." Fiona suddenly understood. *Sonya.*

"I'll go have a little talk with Thomas."

"Nay. Stay with me. Talk to me." She put her hand over his.

"You're right. That's certainly more pleasant."

"Alexander," said Fiona. "If Thomas Bennoitt is ever near me, ken I didna invite him. I dislike him."

"I understand."

"And, Alexander," Fiona teased with a twinkle in her eye, "D'ye ken that ye were outsmarted by a blonde?" Fiona used her head to point towards Sonya and Thomas, who were still sitting together, talking, and laughing.

Thomas said to Sonya, "Good. I'll see you at the party."

*****

That night in their room, Alexander asked Donnie, "How was the tennis game?"

Donnie laughed. "When Jane said that she played tennis in high school, she meant that she was on the tennis team. I just played casually. She had me running all over the court trying to get to her shots. She's fun to be with but I doubt we'll play tennis again. How was your day? Full of Fiona, I suspect."

Alexander related how he was outsmarted by a blonde.

Donnie shook his head. "These girls plan and discuss their social lives in great detail. We are simply accessories."

"I don't think Fiona does that."

"Ha! Besides being guys, we're engineers—a double whammy."

"Tomorrow I've got to tell Fiona about being out of town for the football game. I doubt she's aware of the football schedule. I'm a little worried about how she will take it."

"Surely she knows there's an away game and that you'll be travelling to it. Besides, she may not even care. Gives her a chance to study and get away from you for a while. Who knows? Maybe someone will ask her out on a real date."

* * * * *

Jane looked up from her book as Fiona entered their room. "Supper with Alexander again?"

"Aye. He likes to tease me about how I use my fork. I'm trying to teach him the European way."

Fiona reached into a drawer and removed a bag of oatmeal. She put a handful of oatmeal into a bowl, added cold water and raisins, covered the bowl, and set it aside to soak overnight.

"I don't see how you can eat that stuff," said Jane. "But at least, it is tasteless."

"I canna get proper Scottish oatmeal, so must use American rolled oatmeal. Cold oatmeal and warm tea make a good start to a new morning. I'm glad oor tap water is hot but wish we could have an electric kettle in the room."

"You could have a kettle as long as the Housemother does not know about it."

"I dinna want to get in trouble."

"I know," Jane laughed. "You'll have me saying 'I ken' soon."

"How was your tennis game with Donnie?"

Jane laughed again. "He's not a tennis player but we had a good time and I enjoyed being with him."

"D'ye let him win?"

"Oh, no. Of course not. I'm not letting a guy beat me at tennis even if he is good looking."

Chapter 2: The Football Game

Offensive or defensive,
amid the struggle of this turbulent existence.
--Robert Burns

FRIDAY MORNING in the coffee shop with Fiona, Alexander ventured, "I really enjoy beginning my day by having coffee with you. Thank you for accepting my invitation."

"Is this truly the beginning of your day?"

"Well, I usually get up about five o'clock. I don't even set the alarm. I don't seem to need as much sleep as most people. But I'm coming to think of coffee with you as the beginning of my day."

Fiona giggled. "I need my beauty rest."

"Well, it is working."

"*Cuideigin a nì flatter.*" She laughed.

"Och, by the way. Jane liked your roomie," Fiona continued. "They are having lunch together today."

"I know. Donnie told me about their lunch date. Good for him. He needs to get out more. He studies too much."

"Donnie thinks ye do not study that much."

"Now, now. You've seen me studying."

"Just once in the library reading a book."

"Donnie said that Jane is a terrific tennis player. She beat him soundly."

"Was he upset at being beat by a girl?"

"No, not at all. He enjoyed just being with Jane."

Knowing Fiona did not care for football, Alexander usually avoided the subject. However, he must leave soon and travel for tomorrow's game. Alexander suspected Fiona was unaware of preparations for game-day, and he wanted her to understand what was about to happen. He took a deep breath. Fiona smiled expectantly.

"We have a big football game tomorrow in Alabama," Alexander explained, "and the team will leave early this afternoon. I'll be away until late tomorrow night."

Fiona's smile disappeared. This was not at all what she expected, and she did not like the news.

"Och. Fine. I hope ye have a braw journey and play a good game. I'd better go to class noo." Fiona stomped out of the coffee shop on her own.

Fiona's response was unexpected. *"What in the world was going on? Surely she did not expect him to remain behind?"*

*****

FIONA ARRIVED AT HER CLASS and sat next to Mary. This was the only class they had in common. "You seem upset," observed Mary. "What's going on?"

"I thought Alexander was about to ask me for a date. I was wondering what he planned for oor first official date. I thought probably dinner and dancing. But instead, he telt me he would be out of town the rest of today and all of tomorrow for a stupid football game. I dinna ken. I was looking forward to spending this weekend with him."

Mary gave Fiona a big smile. Fiona scolded, "Dinna keek at me like that. Ye ken what I meant."

"Just because Alexander is away doesn't mean you must stay cooped up in your room," teased Mary. "Now that you are coming out of your shell, many boys want to meet and date you.

They are asking me for introductions. I can easily get you a date for tonight. Plus, there are several fraternity parties tomorrow, and you could have your pick. You need not be alone this weekend. Let me help you."

"Alexander would no like if I dated someone else or partied at a fraternity house. Besides, I dinna want to. If I canna be with Alexander, I'd rather be alone and study in my room."

"Has Alexander asked or even suggested you go steady with him? You two have not even had an actual date—at least not in the way most people think of a date. He might get a little jealous, but he'd get over it. Might even be good for him."

"We've had at least one date every day since we met, and ye ken it well. I'm not risking whatever relationship we have— even this early. Mary, I canna believe ye are suggesting this. Ye claim to be his friend." Fiona collected her books and papers, stood, and took a step away.

Mary put her hand on Fiona, smiled and elaborated, "Take it easy, Fiona. You passed."

"What? Och."

"With flying colors."

Fiona sat down again by Mary.

The professor came in, and class began.

*****

THAT NIGHT, SEEING FIONA'S DOOR OPEN, Hannah came in. Alone in her room, Fiona was reading "Introduction to Football for Women."

"Learning about football?" asked Hannah.

"Aye. I checked out this book from the library today."

Hannah was a big football fan. She attended all the games and watched or listened on the radio to those she could not attend in person. "If you have questions, I'll be happy to answer them."

61

"*Taing*, Hannah. I'm sure I'll have questions, but let me first read this book. Then I can at least ask intelligent questions. Noo, I'm that ignorant of football."

"If I tell you a few things now, you can better relate to the details in the book."

"Seems a good approach. Aye, go ahead."

"I'll randomly pick a player, say, Alexander Gordon, and tell you what he does."

"Is it that obvious?" Fiona laughed.

"Oh, yes."

"Please go ahead."

"These days, a football team is divided into several groups, but the most obvious groups are the offensive and defensive teams. It's not always been that way, but that's the way it is now. Substitutions were limited when my dad played football, and the same players remained on the field no matter who had the ball."

Fiona interrupted, "Soccer has limited substitutions and opportunities for substitution. I played soccer in Scotland."

"Alexander plays, mostly, on our defensive team. That is, he comes on the field to stop our opponent from scoring. He plays a position called Cornerback. If we were watching the game, you'd see that Alexander is usually on the second row of defensive players. Come to think about it, would you like to watch the game with me tomorrow? I can tell and show you more."

"That sounds super. *Taing*."

*****

FIONA'S TELEPHONE INTERRUPTED her conversation with Hannah. She answered, "Hello?" It was Alexander. On realizing this, Hannah excused herself and left the room.

Fiona was glad to have a private telephone in her room and not be forced to use the payphone in the hallway. She kept a dime in her pocketbook for emergency calls when she was not in her room.

"I'm happy ye called, "Fiona confessed. "I'm sorry for being a wee bit brusque today. I should have kent ye would be away from campus, but I didna, and so was that surprised. I wanted to see ye this weekend, so I was that disappointed." *I thought ye were about to ask me for a date.*

"That's OK; I should have told you sooner, but I did not want to upset you by talking about football. Your reaction today troubled me and I've been thinking about it all day. I'm glad I called. I'm sorry to have upset you. I'll be more considerate next time."

Fiona smiled. "Alexander, ye can talk to me about football. I may not underston, but ye can explain and teach me." *He said, "next time."*

What are you doing now?"

"I'm in my room studying. What are ye doing?"

"We're in a hotel and have a little time for ourselves, so I was able to call you. We'll go to a movie soon—probably something to psych us up for tomorrow. How was your day?"

Fiona smiled. *Alexander had been curious whether she was in her room or out and about.* After all, it was a Friday night; he was probably wondering if he should be jealous. She could not tell him about Mary tempting her or about checking out a book about football or about Hannah offering to explain tomorrow's game. "Just a routine day, ye ken, classes, piano, and voice lessons. How was yers?"

"The best part of my day was having coffee with you this morning. Then I had a long, boring bus ride with lots of time to meditate. That's when I realized I had upset you. Well, they're calling me to go to the movie. Wish I was going with you instead of with the guys. I miss you."

"Me too. Bye."

Smiling and nearly bursting with the need to talk to someone about Alexander, Fiona picked up her telephone and dialed.

*****

AT THEIR FARM, Ellen Johnston answered the phone, "Hello?"

"Auntie? It's Fiona."

"Of course it is. Is everything OK? I know your voice, Honey."

"You don't seem surprised that I called."

Ellen sometimes had the gift of second sight and was difficult to surprise.

"I had a feeling you might call." *She sounds excited.*

"Aye. I'm fine. College is fine. I'm learning the routines and my way around campus. My studies are going well, and my grades are good. I miss ye and Uncle Robert, but I'm finding new friends. People call me the 'Viking Princess.'"

"Viking Princess?" Ellen smiled. "How do you feel about that?" Like her mother, Fiona had a regal presence.

"At first, I kept reminding them I was a Scot, not a Viking, but noo I just accept it."

"I'm sure you appear to be a Viking to most people."

"Auntie, I've met an interesting boy—well, a young man. When d'ye stop calling them boys and change to calling them men?"

"That change will come naturally, Honey, although some are always boys. An interesting young man? How did you meet? Do you have classes together?" *So, this is why she called.*

"A lassie from down the hall, Mary, introduced us. Mary grew up with him and has kent him all her life. She says he is like a brother to her. She was eager for us to meet, and I finally agreed to meet him."

"Tell me about him." Ellen was more than curious. She had never had such a conversation with Fiona.

"He is that tall and handsome—the best-looking man on campus, in fact. He is a sophomore and majoring in mechanical engineering. Also, he is minoring in music. And get this: He is a football player!"

"A football player! You could not have surprised me more! I thought you did not like football or football players."

"Alexander is different. Ye'd like him, Auntie. Noo, I'm trying to learn about football so I can discuss it intelligently with him. Today, I checked out a beginner's book on football from the library. Perhaps Uncle Robert can answer a few questions for me after I've read it."

"I'm sure your uncle would be happy to explain football to you. You know how he loves that silly game. When did you meet Alexander?"

"Mary introduced us on Monday."

"So, you've just met him. You haven't known him for very long?" Concern showed in Ellen's voice. Until now, Fiona had shown little interest in boys and seldom dated.

"Aye, but we've spent a lot of time together since we met. I'd be with Alexander tonight, except tomorrow's game is in Alabama, so he is not on campus. He called me, though, and we talked for a long time."

"Be careful, Honey. This seems extremely fast. In fact, it sounds like you have not even had a date with Alexander."

"Every day has been like a date."

"Obviously, you like him. How does he feel about you?"

"He always tells me I am beautiful."

"You are beautiful, in fact gorgeous. No one is more beautiful than you. You are always the most beautiful girl in the room, just as your mother was."

"Tonight, Alexander said he was missing me."

"Be careful, Honey. I'd hate to see you get hurt. Don't rush into anything serious." Ellen smiled to herself. *Like I did.*

They changed to a more general conversation for a few more minutes, then hung up.

Smiling, Ellen walked into the living room, where Robert watched TV. She said, "Fiona called." Ellen knew Robert would never believe this.

"How is she doing? Does she need anything?"

"I think she called just to tell me about a young man she met."

"A boy? Well, that is unexpected. I hope she is studying and keeping up her grades and music."

"She is. But guess what? This young man is a football player!"

"Now you're messing with me. What position does he play? What is his number?"

"You know Fiona doesn't understand football. She did not tell me what position he played or give me his number. She just said his name was Alexander, and he played football, and he was in Alabama tonight."

"Surely not Alexander Gordon?"

"Who is he?" Ellen did not follow football—even MU football, her alma mater.

"Only the best player on the team. Some say the best player we've ever had. Most likely, he will be an All-American. Let me find my program, and I'll show you his picture. He's team captain, so there will be an individual photo of him."

Robert searched for a few minutes and returned with his football program. "This is Alexander Gordon."

"Oh, my. As Fiona said, he is very handsome."

"He is six feet seven inches tall and weighs two hundred and seventy pounds. A big man on campus and extraordinarily popular. But this is probably not the guy Fiona was talking about. Why would Alexander Gordon be interested in our Fiona?"

Ellen found Robert's statement hilarious. Sometimes he could be utterly oblivious to his surroundings.

"Have you seen Fiona recently?" Ellen laughed. "She is no longer the skinny, freckled-faced kid you met three years ago."

"Let me see if there is another Alexander on the team." Robert turned the pages of the program. "No, no other Alexander."

"This guy, whatever his name and football ability, greatly impressed Fiona. She has never shown any interest in a guy before. Let me have that program for a few minutes." Ellen found the write-up about Alexander Gordon. "Alexander Gordon has to be the guy. Like Fiona said, he is a sophomore majoring in mechanical engineering, and his hobby is music."

"Probably someone introduced her, and now she has an early crush and infatuation. She will get over it."

"Somehow, I seriously doubt that." Ellen's gift of second sight often gave her insights that others were unaware of.

*****

ON SATURDAY AFTERNOON, Fiona went to the lobby to join Hannah and a few other girls already there to watch the televised football game. Even Jane was there.

"I didn't know you were a football fan, Jane," said Hannah.

"I'm not," answered Jane. "I just want to watch Fiona watch her boyfriend." Several girls giggled and admitted that was their reason as well.

Someone said, "Wouldn't it be great if we had television in our rooms?"

Many agreed but Fiona said, "I dinna watch the telly that often. A telly in my room would interfere with my studies. I'm glad to socialize in the lobby."

"Has the football book helped your understanding of the game?" asked Hannah.

"Aye, m*oran taing*, Hannah," Fiona replied. "Noo that I've read parts of the football book, I ken the game a wee bit better, but much I dinna ken."

"Before we were interrupted," Hannah smiled, "I said Alexander played a position called cornerback. He is in the second row of defensive players and somewhat on the outside. Sometimes he will try to block or intercept a pass. Sometimes he will rush into the opponent's backfield to make a tackle; this is called a blitz."

"Alexander is a tremendous football player. Sometimes he plays on the offensive team instead of only on the defensive team. He's already made four touchdowns this season. He also kicks the ball using soccer-style."

Fiona interrupted, "I played soccer. That style might seem natural to me. Alexander didna tell me he was a kicker."

"I suspect, knowing you did not care for football, he was reluctant to bring it up."

"Ye are correct. After the day we met, Alexander did not mention football again until yesterday morning when he telt me he must leave for Alabama. I was so surprised. I was even scunnered, but Mary used a wee bit of reverse psychology to help me discover my feelings. Then, last night, Alexander telephoned me, and we discussed the situation. He understood, and we are OK now."

"I assumed that was Alexander who called last night."

"I was so glad he called. I even called my aunt and telt her I met an interesting football player. It is difficult to surprise Auntie, but she was that surprised at my news." Fiona laughed.

*****

"WELL, HERE WE GO." Robert Johnston leaned toward his television to see the kickoff better. "I still can't believe Fiona is dating Alexander Gordon. Let's see if she has affected his football game."

"Fiona just said she had met Alexander and liked him. She said they spent time together every day, but I don't think they've had an official date yet."

The television announcer noted that Alexander was the kickoff returner for the first time since high school. Alexander caught the ball on the five-yard line, dodged one tackle, powered through another, moved behind two blockers, and took off down the field. Touchdown!

"I guess he can still play ball," Robert said. "Too bad Fiona doesn't like football, but maybe she will adapt. Wonder if she is watching anyway?" He settled back in his chair to watch the point-after-touchdown and ensuing kickoff.

$$*****$$

IN THE LOBBY OF HER DORM, Fiona jumped up and down with excitement, even though she didn't understand what had happened. Jane watched her in amazement.

Hannah exclaimed, "That happened so quickly I didn't have time to explain it. Let's hope there is a replay." Hannah was quiet during the replay in favor of the announcer's description.

"He is that fast a runner," observed Fiona. "Especially for such a big man."

"Alexander is one of the fastest on the team," added Hannah. "Now, let's see who kicks the extra point."

Alexander remained on the field and easily kicked the extra point. Hannah said, "I wonder if he will also do the kickoff." He did but then came off the field for a few plays.

"Och, he is tired. Let him rest."

"You can bet he is tired, but he never comes out for long."

Alexander was soon back in the game. Within a few more minutes, he made several tackles and intercepted a pass.

"This is an incredible start," Hannah explained to Fiona, "even for Alexander."

Fiona, her eyes now locked on the television screen, learned where Alexander played and how to find him. She jerked involuntarily every time Alexander contacted someone. After one such brutal hit, Alexander was slow to get up.

Fiona exclaimed, "Och, he is hurt!" She stared anxiously at the screen.

Alexander limped a few steps, stretched, and jogged in place but did not leave the field.

Fiona sighed a sigh of relief. "This is exciting," she said. "But I'll be glad when it is over."

*****

"FIONA'S BOYFRIEND is well on his way to an outstanding game!"

"Be careful with your choice of words, Robert. Fiona did not call Alexander her boyfriend—only that she had met him and liked him. Besides, I thought you did not believe Fiona had even met Alexander Gordon."

"I'm pulling for Alexander Gordon whether or not he is Fiona's boyfriend, but I must admit her dating him could be interesting. I've not met him, but he comes across as a good person in interviews and in the press. People who have met Alexander say he is very impressive."

"Well, he certainly impressed Fiona. She must have impressed him as well because he called her from the team hotel last night. I'm sure we'll learn more as time goes on. Don't rush this."

The game ended, and Robert said, "That has to be the best game anyone has ever had. Three touchdowns from a defensive player! Two intercepted passes, three sacks and no telling how many tackles and hurries Alexander caused. Five extra points and two field goals. I'll bet he's in the post-game interview; let's see what he says."

They settled back in their chairs as the television announcers scrambled to organize the post-game interviews.

*****

AT THE POST-GAME INTERVIEW, ALEXANDER STEPPED UP to the microphones. Ellen said admiringly, "Oh my word! So tall, and those muscles! So handsome! Just as Fiona described him. I wonder if she watched the game? I hope she is watching this interview."

The announcer gave a quick review of the game and Alexander's performance and statistics. He then asked Alexander for his view and comments.

Speaking into the microphones, Alexander testified, "First, I thank God for blessing me and giving me the opportunities that he has. I've been blessed all my life—especially with my parents. Football is not a one-man sport, and I thank my teammates for their support and protection. I thank Coach Guffy for allowing me freedom in how I play the game. And I'd like to acknowledge and thank a new and special person in my life."

The interviewer asked, "Anyone you'd like to name?" Alexander smiled but did not respond.

Ellen added, "Ahem, that question has been answered."

*****

IN THE LOBBY, the girls listened to the post-game interviews. When Alexander said, "I'd like to acknowledge and thank a new and special person in my life," everyone turned to Fiona, who was misty-eyed.

Jane said to Fiona, "I'm so glad I was here for your special moment. Congratulations!"

"Fiona, did you know we can meet the football team's bus and welcome them home?" Hannah asked. "It will be late, but there will be a special bus for us, and we can return to the dorm late as long as we are on that special bus and welcome the team."

Fiona was eager to see Alexander. Would he be as keen to see her? She would take the chance. "I didna kent. Aye, let's do it."

"I'll find the schedule and reserve a seat. Hmm, Fiona, sometimes the girls hug the players. Somehow, in this case, it is not a Public Display of Affection or else is conveniently ignored." Hannah smiled. "Good thing too, otherwise quite a few girls would be Campused."

Hannah glanced at Fiona. Yes, she was blushing.

Jane said to Hannah, "I'm going as well. I'm not missing out on this. Something is about to happen."

"In the meantime, I'm calling Auntie," said Fiona. She left the lobby for her room, a change of clothes, and her telephone.

*****

Fiona dialed her aunt's telephone number. Ellen was waiting eagerly for her call and answered immediately.

"Auntie, did you watch the MU football game on TV?" *I bet she did.*

"You know I usually never watch football games," Ellen teased. "But I certainly watched this one. I told Robert about you meeting a football player named Alexander. He quickly figured out the player must be Alexander Gordon, even though he couldn't believe it. We watched the game together. Did you watch it?"

"Aye. The first American football game I've ever watched on the telly. One of the lassies explained the game and showed me where Alexander was playing. It was that exciting. I worried about Alexander getting hurt, but he didna."

"Did you watch the post-game interview?" teased Ellen.

Fiona's voice cracked. "Och, I did. Och, Auntie, I'm so happy. I want ye to meet Alexander. He is much more than a handsome football player. Ye will like him."

"I want to meet Alexander as well. So does your uncle. But, Fiona, don't rush this relationship. Give it time and get to know each other."

"I ken." But Fiona also thought, *I'm still going to see him tonight.*

*****

THE FOOTBALL TEAM BUSES arrived late at night to a crowd of fans, including several "Welcome Home" buses from the girls' dorms. Fiona, Hannah, and Jane sat together in a "Welcome Home" bus. Fiona sensed the excitement of the win and anticipation of welcoming the team. Many guys were in the crowd as well—laughing and cheering. Some were even sober.

The fans gathered around the buses, and the players exited. Hannah observed, "The news media is headed toward the first bus; that must be where Alexander is." Hannah and Fiona moved closer to the first bus. Alexander sat near a window towards the middle of the bus. Fiona moved closer and waited impatiently, but Alexander did not see her and did not appear to be searching for anyone.

Television and newspaper reporters had set up a speaking area with microphones and lighting. Alexander finally exited, and the news media pushed him ahead of the crowd towards the speaking area. No longer in their playing uniforms, Alexander and his teammates dressed in maroon short sleeve shirts with cream-colored ties.

Fiona wanted to get to the speaking area. Jane ran interference for Fiona. Some people recognized Fiona and helped them through the crowd. Fiona knew Alexander would not be expecting her. What would he say and do? Would he be glad to see her? Fiona chewed on her bottom lip nervously.

*****

ALEXANDER SPOTTED FIONA AND RUSHED TOWARD HER as she rushed towards him. They met in an embrace, saying, "I missed you" and laughing at themselves. Holding hands, they moved together to the speaking area. A television reporter attempted to clear a path for his camera by moving Fiona away from Alexander, but Alexander insisted she stay, and she did.

Coach Guffy was the first to the microphones. He thanked everyone for their support and for welcoming the team, but he gave Fiona a hard stare.

Alexander was the first player to speak. He answered reporters' questions while Fiona beamed in admiration. The reporters ignored Fiona. Photographers' flashes lit the scene.

A megaphone blared out: "Girls, it is time to leave. Please go back to your bus." Hannah and Jane prepared to leave, but Fiona lagged behind, hanging on to Alexander's hand.

Alexander asked, "Would you go with me to church tomorrow and then to dinner?"

"I must play piano for my Sunday School class," Fiona answered, "will ye go with me instead?"

"Of course. What time?"

"The bus leaves my dorm at 9:30."

"I have a car, well, an old truck. If you don't mind riding in an old truck, I'll pick you up at 9:30. We'll go to your Sunday School meeting, then Worship Service, then dinner. Is that OK?

"Aye, *Moran taing.*"

"See you tomorrow."

I'm so glad I came tonight, Fiona thought.

Back on the bus, Jane teased, "So, you've asked Alexander for another date?"

"Ye ken, he asked me first." *And now I'll see him tomorrow.*

74

*****

ROBERT'S SUNDAY NEWSPAPER HAD BOUNCED and stopped against his brick mailbox. He brought it into the house and laid it on the table without unfolding it. He made coffee, curious about what the sportswriters had to say about yesterday's game—and especially about Fiona's boyfriend. He could hardly believe Fiona was dating Alexander Gordon. Life might become very interesting. This was exciting.

"Robert, have you seen the paper?"

"Yes, I put it on the table."

"I found it, but have you seen the front page?"

Ellen opened the newspaper and spread it on the table. The front page featured a large color photograph of Alexander Gordon during the post-game interview on campus. By his side, looking up in admiration, stood Fiona MacDonald—stunningly beautiful. The caption beneath the photograph read: "Alexander Gordon, star of yesterday's football game, answers questions as a beautiful unknown admirer looks on."

"I shouldn't be surprised," Ellen said, "but how in the world did she manage to do this? I hope she didn't sneak out of the dorm."

"That's a great photograph, and Fiona certainly is beautiful, but that doesn't mean they are dating." Robert wanted to believe but was skeptical.

"Let's buy extra copies on our way to church," Ellen suggested. "We'll get Fiona and Alexander to autograph them. I believe we'll be meeting him soon."

"You'll make a believer out of me yet!"

*****

MR. GORDON PICKED UP HIS NEWSPAPER at the end of the driveway, unfolded it, and glanced at it while walking back to his house. "Rachel, I think I've found the special person Alexander mentioned in his interview last night. This must be her picture in the paper. They don't give her name, but she is beautiful."

Mrs. Gordon studied the picture of Alexander and his admirer. "She certainly is beautiful. Notice the look she is giving him?"

"Wonder what her name is and when we will get to meet her? Let's get extra copies of the newspaper today."

Malcolm observed, "Whoever she is, Coach Guffy does not approve of her being there. See him glaring at her? Alexander said Coach Guffy runs a tight ship and does not like surprises. He obviously was not expecting this girl to be present at the interview. Wonder what Coach Guffy will say to Alexander? I hope this girl does not cause problems."

Caroline and Liz came out of their rooms, ready for church. They noticed the picture of Fiona and Alexander in the newspaper. "Alexander's got a girlfriend," giggled Liz. "What's her name?"

"Now, Liz," cautioned Mrs. Gordon. "We don't know that this girl is his girlfriend. She might just be a football fan. We don't know her name either."

"Maybe you can't tell," replied Caroline. "But I can tell from the look she is giving him he is more than a football player to her. If she's not his girlfriend now, she soon will be. She is beautiful— see how tall—and that hair!

*****

ALEXANDER PUT ON HIS MAROON MU SPORTS JACKET and adjusted his tie again. Although a little sore and stiff from yesterday's game, he was too excited about seeing Fiona to pay much attention to his aches and pains.

Alexander's "old" truck, loosely based on a 1931 Ford Model A pickup truck, roared to life when he turned the key. Compared to the Model A, the stretched engine compartment contained a modified Ford 4.7 liter V8 engine. The extended passenger compartment accommodated Alexander's six feet seven-inch muscular body. Painted metallic maroon with cream pinstripes and chrome trim, it was his pride and joy. He drove to Fiona's dorm, left his truck at the entrance, and entered. The receptionist called for Fiona.

Alexander climbed the stairs to meet Fiona. He was pleased with himself for not stumbling. On the other hand, his heart pounded in anticipation of greeting Fiona. She appeared in her conservative Sunday best, and he took her hand. He praised, "You are so beautiful," without stammering and was again pleased with himself.

Fiona replied, "*Cuideigin a nì flatter,*" and laughed. They stepped down the stairs and out the door, still holding hands.

Alexander guided Fiona to his truck, bowed and said, "*Maighdeann,* your chariot awaits."

Fiona gasped. "This is your auld truck? It's beautiful."

"A beauty for a beauty. Let's walk around it."

"I ken a story here. How did ye get this?"

"I made it—or more correctly, assembled it from a kit. I needed lots of help, including professional help, and I learned a lot. Don't worry, it actually is not old; it is modern and safe. It is even air-conditioned."

Alexander opened the passenger door, and Fiona stepped in. "If you'd like, I can remove the top, and you can feel the wind in your hair as we ride around after dinner."

"That would be bonnie. Ye do nothing halfway, do ye?"

Alexander took the long route to church to show off his truck. Fiona appreciated not being cramped. She marveled at the truck and Alexander's attention to detail. The interior had the new car smell and wood, chrome, and Naugahyde furnishings. Church organ music played on the cassette player.

Parked at the church, Alexander assumed that the admiring glances from incoming church members were directed at his customized truck. However, inside the Sunday School building, a young girl approached them with a newspaper in her hand. She asked, "Will you autograph my newspaper?"

Alexander, showing off for Fiona and accustomed to signing autographs, responded, "I'll be happy to."

The girl handed the paper to Alexander but turned to Fiona, saying, "You too, please." About that time, Alexander guffawed.

"Would you look at this!"

"I canna believe it!"

The front page of the newspaper featured a large color photograph of Fiona and Alexander. Fiona's long auburn hair would have dominated the picture, except the look she was giving Alexander entirely overrode her hair. This was a prize-winning photograph. Fiona took the girl's pen and signed her name beneath her picture. The girl thanked them and left.

Alexander teased, "You may have a busy day, 'beautiful unknown admirer!' We should get extra copies after church." They signed several more newspapers on their way to Sunday School.

*****

IN HER SUNDAY SCHOOL ROOM, Fiona sat at the piano and played as students gathered. Alexander sat nearby and assured an empty chair was next to him. The group leader called the session to order, and they sang several songs. Fiona then left the piano and sat by Alexander. She whispered, "Ye have a bonnie voice!"

After prayer and a brief message, the group leader asked everyone to go to their discussion classes. This meant separating the girls and boys, which Alexander did not favor, but he had no choice.

The chief topics in the girls' classroom were Alexander, Fiona, and the photograph they called 'The Look.' One girl exclaimed, "Just last week, you were a quiet piano player and said you didn't have a boyfriend! Today your picture is on the front page of the newspaper, and you've brought the captain of the football team with you. How has all this happened in a week?"

"We didna meet until the next day." Fiona smiled.

"So you've only known each other for six days?"

"Aye. It was a good and busy week." Was Alexander her boyfriend? *Mo leannan?* She was anxious for the Bible lesson and a change of subject but wanted to get back to Alexander. *What are the guys talking about?*

*****

THE GUYS TALKED ABOUT THE FOOTBALL TEAM and the previous day's game. They praised and congratulated Alexander for his fantastic performance. Someone asked about his customized truck, and Alexander explained how he made it.

Alexander suspected some of the guys were not particularly welcoming and were probably jealous that he was with Fiona, but no one mentioned her. Then one of the guys said, "So, will you be coming to our church regularly now?"

"I'm not sure. I'm Baptist and usually attend the Baptist church and Sunday School." He grinned, "Fiona kindly invited me today, and I could hardly refuse. We're having dinner after church." He thought, *Shame on me for bragging and teasing, but they were dying to ask. Now they are wondering if Fiona will be here next week. That will give them something to talk about.*

"What about next week's game?"

Eventually, the discussion shifted to the Sunday School lesson.

*****

SUNDAY SCHOOL ENDED, and Fiona and Alexander signed autographs before attending Worship Service and even more afterward.

As they were leaving the church for the restaurant, Alexander suggested buying a few more newspapers while they were still available. He pulled the truck into the parking lot of a small store and asked about buying a newspaper. The sales clerk asked, "How many?"

"All you have."

"Today's paper has been selling like hotcakes, but you can buy them all if you'll autograph one for me and get your girlfriend to autograph it as well."

"OK, it's a deal." Twenty-three newspapers remained. Alexander took the stack of papers to the truck and explained the deal to Fiona. She laughed and autographed the photo. Alexander placed the stack of newspapers in the shortened truck bed and covered them with a tarp.

"Now on to the restaurant. Oops, wait a minute." Alexander returned to the store with an autographed paper for the sales clerk. He bought two good ballpoint pens, gave one to Fiona, and put the other in his shirt pocket. "Well, here we go!"

As they approached the restaurant, Alexander attempted to put on a serious face but grinned as he said, "You know, in America, by law, Protestant church services must begin and end on the hour. Catholic services must begin and end on the half-hour. This assures restaurants are not overcrowded after church services."

"There is no such law!" But Fiona laughed anyway.

Once inside the restaurant, Fiona and Alexander attracted much attention and autographed several photographs. Their waitress also asked for their autographs.

Fiona commented, "I've never been to this restaurant. What do ye recommend?"

Alexander grinned. "Their haggis is excellent."

Fiona caught the joke and retorted, "They do not have haggis. Ye canna get proper haggis in the United States, but I ken a restaurant in Scotland that serves the best haggis, neeps and tatties you'll ever have. Maybe I'll take ye there one day."

"What's a neep?"

"A neep is a kind of Scottish turnip. A tattie is a potato. Restaurants often serve neeps and tatties with haggis."

"Do you miss Scotland?"

"Sometimes, but not as much recently." Fiona smiled.

"Think you'll go back to Scotland?"

"Maybe." Fiona had a strange expression in her eyes, and a tear was forming.

"Well, if you return to Scotland, be sure to let me know where you are so I can cash in my raincheck for some haggis, neeps and tatties."

Fiona patted her eyes with her napkin.

"Are you OK?"

"Perhaps more homesick than I realized."

Now you've done it, thought Alexander.

Their waitress returned and asked for their order. Alexander ordered a large steak, baked potato, and cold sweet tea. Fiona ordered a small grilled salmon with asparagus, salad, and hot tea with lemon. They each ordered cheesecake with strawberries for dessert.

"Weel, at least we agree on the dessert," laughed Fiona. "Scottish strawberries are the best in the world."

There were more autograph requests while waiting for their meals, and they smilingly obliged their new fans.

After dinner, Alexander suggested, "If you can spare more time this afternoon, I'd like to take you for a ride. I can remove the top."

"I'd love to ride around with ye. First, let's go to the dorm, so I can change clothes and freshen up."

On arriving at the dorm, autograph seekers immediately surrounded them and, again, they obliged. With the autograph seekers satisfied, Fiona excused herself, "Let me return to my room for a few minutes."

"Take some of these newspapers. Do you want the entire paper or just the first page?"

"I'll take one complete newspaper and several front pages." Alexander separated the pages and threw away the unwanted sections. He entered with Fiona, helped her up the stairs, and handed her the papers. Instead of staying in the lobby, Alexander returned to his truck to remove the top. Several guys and girls came up to the truck to admire it, and Alexander explained how he made it.

*****

INSTEAD OF HER OWN ROOM, Fiona rushed straight to Mary's room. Mary laughed, "Welcome, beautiful unknown admirer!" Fiona bloomed and handed her the stack of front-page photographs.

"Are you OK?" Mary detected a problem in Fiona's eyes.

"Well, aye and nay, I dinna ken. I was having a wonderful day with Alexander until he asked if I would return to Scotland. I answered, 'Maybe,' and he said to let him know where I was so he could take me to my favorite restaurant for haggis."

"Fiona, I hope you know Alexander is falling in love with you." Mary knew Alexander like the back of her hand and had been expecting this.

"I ken I am falling in love with Alexander."

"Of course, you are. Everyone, well, that is, all the girls, can see. Guys are not as sensitive or socially aware as we girls."

"But Alexander is extremely intelligent!"

"Alexander is a guy, Fiona," explained Mary. "His intellect is telling him that something is changing, but he hasn't figured it out yet. He's just enjoying being with you. Believe me, when Alexander realizes he is falling in love with you, it will hit him like a ton of bricks. He has always been independent and goal-oriented. There's no telling how he will react to discovering he loves you. You'll have to be patient and understanding with him when he does."

"Do ye really think Alexander is falling in love with me?"

"Fiona, if you returned to Scotland today, Alexander would be on the next flight to find you. Now, go dry your eyes and change clothes for your joy ride. I'll meet you at the truck. I want Alexander to autograph this picture. But first, you sign it." Fiona signed.

*****

MARY FOUND ALEXANDER alone at his truck and teased, "I have the autograph of your beautiful, unknown admirer. Now I want yours."

Alexander chuckled and signed, "To Mary, Love Alexander." He then asked, "Is Fiona OK?" *Mary would know.*

"Why do you ask?"

"I think I upset her by talking about Scotland. I must have made her homesick. She says she might return to Scotland. I sure don't want her to leave MU."

"Alexander Gordon, you are the most intelligent person I know. But you're still a guy. You'd better tell Fiona you don't want her to leave." Alexander did not take hints well and often had to be told directly.

While they were talking, Fiona came out of the dorm, smiling and gorgeous. She strolled to Mary and Alexander standing by the truck and said, "Of course, ye kent Alexander's auld truck. Ye wanted him to surprise me."

Mary snickered, "Turnabout is fair play!"

Alexander asked, "Fiona, do you want to drive my old truck? Can you drive a stick shift?"

"I ken. In Scotland, most cars have manual transmission."

Alexander thought, *Oh no. I've done it again. Please don't start crying,* but he replied, "OK, let's go," and handed Fiona the keys.

Fiona gave the engine a little too much gas and let the clutch out too quickly. The tires gave a sharp chirp as the truck lurched forward. Alexander chuckled.

Fiona drove the truck around campus for a while, then turned into a parking lot. "Taing. That was fun, but I'm more comfortable with ye driving." Alexander got out, walked around to the driver's side door, opened the door for Fiona, helped her out and accompanied her to the passenger side door.

Recalling Mary's advice, Alexander blurted, "Fiona, I know how much you love Scotland, but I hope you will stay here. The hours I'm with you are the best part of my day."

"I'm not leaving MU." Fiona hastened to say.

"Good. I'm glad." Alexander silently thanked Mary. *Why hadn't he thought of this?*

Alexander got in the driver's seat, and they rode around the town and countryside with Fiona's long hair flying.

After riding a while, Alexander asked, "Would you like a soda?"

"Aye, and I need to brush my hair before returning to the dorm."

*****

AFTER THE BIG PARTY FOR SATURDAY'S GAME, Thomas welcomed Sonya back to the Iota Theta Phi fraternity house's lobby and guided her to the couch. Sonya was careful with her steps. The place was a mess. Although now Sunday afternoon, the pretend cleaning done after last night's party left the aroma of beer and a hint of vomit. Thomas was a mess as well; he still wore last night's party clothes.

Thomas sat beside Sonya familiarly on the couch. "Welcome back for more. How did you get here?"

Sonya removed a set of car keys from her purse. "In your car. Here are your keys. You'll have to take me back to my dorm. You weren't in good enough shape to drive last night. In fact, you passed out after you gave me the keys."

"Sorry about that, but I don't remember it at all. I don't remember much of anything about last night. You'll have to tell me all about it." Thomas grinned.

"Nothing to tell, but I have something for you."

Thomas put his arm on the back of the couch and leaned to Sonya expectantly, but she reached into her purse and removed a copy of 'The Look' front-page picture.

"Here's a souvenir for you. By the way, you need to brush your teeth."

Thomas said indignantly, "Damnit! How does he do that?" He studied the picture, becoming angrier and angrier all the while. "He doesn't even try and still gets all the attention. Front page too. Not to mention Big Red."

"Notice how Fiona is admiring Alexander? teased Sonya. "Everyone calls their photo 'The Look.'"

"I've got to do something about this, but what?"

"There's nothing you can do. You'd best be glad that Alexander is not running for Student Body President—he'd win in a landslide. I can see him speaking with Fiona by his side."

Thomas was thoughtful for a few moments. "One of the football players owes me a favor. I'll get him to put a bug in Coach Guffy's ear about Big Red and Alexander. He could ask, 'Why can Alexander date and not me?' Guffy will put pressure on Alexander to drop Big Red, and I can pick her up. Sure, I'd get her on the rebound, but it will be worth it. I'll be the one making campaign speeches with Big Red at my side."

Sonya laughed sharply. "You think you have a good plan, but I can tell you it will not work. For starters, there is no way Alexander will drop Fiona—even I've had to admit it. On top of that, you are not Fiona's type; in fact, she dislikes you." *Someone has to tell him.*

"I still think my plan will work. At the very least, it will make life uncomfortable for Alexander."

"You're more interested in hurting Alexander than in attracting Fiona."

"Oh, I want Big Red, all right. And I will have her."

"Face it, Thomas, you have no chance with Fiona. As a matter of fact, you have no chance with me either after last night and today. Now, take me back to my dorm."

"In that case, you can walk, bitch."

Sonya spun quickly to the door and slammed it on her way out.

*****

ON THEIR WAY BACK TO FIONA'S DORM, Alexander pulled into a small soda shop. Fiona entered the ladies' room while Alexander bought two bottles of soda. Fiona emerged with her hair neatly brushed over one shoulder. Alexander stood politely as Fiona approached her chair and waited expectantly. Smiling, he pulled out her chair. Seated, Fiona glanced at the bottles of soda and asked, "Are there no glasses?" Alexander returned to the counter and came back with two glasses full of ice.

"I dinna ken how Americans use so much ice."

Alexander laughed as he took Fiona's glass to the counter and emptied the ice. He returned to Fiona's smile. She took his glass and, using a spoon, placed two of his ice cubes in her glass. She smiled expectantly at Alexander, and he drizzled soda into her glass. Her smile broadened.

Lessons, Alexander thought. *She's determined to civilize me. Well, at least she is not giving up on me.*

"I'll put the top up and save your hair."

"*Moran taing.*"

Alexander drove back to Fiona's dorm, where he expected her friends waited to learn about her day. It had been a wonderful day. He wished he could listen to Fiona relive it with her friends.

* * * * *

ALEXANDER OPENED THE DOOR to his room and offered, "Here, you can add this photo of me to your collection."

Donnie recited Spanish while listening to Ernest Tubb sing "Waltz Across Texas" on his record player. He interrupted his recitation to say, "Ahh, pick it out, Billy Byrd."

"Trying to change your Mississippi accent to a Texas accent for Spanish?"

Donnie laughed. "I've already seen your picture. Besides everything else, now you're turning into a publicity hound."

"Fiona and I autographed this one for you."

"I'm familiar with your scrawl. As expected, Fiona has beautiful handwriting—almost calligraphy. Why didn't she sign it 'Viking Princess?'"

"Because her name is Fiona."

"Let me tell you something. The picture you have is from the local paper. I got the Jackson paper which apparently has a different photo. Coach Guffy is in the Jackson picture. He is staring at Fiona and seems angry."

The picture in the Jackson paper must have been taken from a different angle. Coach Guffy was visible in the background, his ever-present whistle around his neck and partially covering his tie. He glared past Alexander and scowled at Fiona.

"You're right. Coach Guffy is not happy."

"Could be he does not like Fiona being taller than he is, but I've heard he despises women," advised Donnie.

"Coach Guffy discourages players from dating during football season," explained Alexander. "But he's not said anything to me about Fiona, and, frankly, it doesn't matter if he does."

"You and Fiona are too new and unexpected. You surprised him. He believed you were as dedicated to football as he is. Now he sees you with the Viking Princess and does not like it."

"Well, he'd better get used to it."

*****

THOUGH ONLY A WEEK OLD, Fiona and Alexander had firmly established a morning habit of having coffee and tea together. Conveniently, their class schedules matched.

Monday morning, they met almost shyly. Fiona extended her hand, and Alexander touched it gently, saying softly, "You are so beautiful."

Fiona, her green eyes sparkling, whispered, "*Cuideigin a nì flatter.*" Their relationship had changed, and they both recognized the change.

A quiet moment later, Alexander said, "My parents called me last night. They saw your picture in the newspaper and wanted to know your name."

"What d'ye tell about me?"

"Your name, of course, and that we'd just met, and that I enjoyed being with you. They want you to autograph your picture."

"Oor picture."

"Well, everyone thinks of it as your picture. I know I do. I gave a copy to Donnie. He was disappointed you did not sign it 'Viking Princess.'"

"Viking Princess seems a bit of conceit but tell Donnie I'll add Viking Princess to his copy."

"Donnie showed me another version of your picture that includes Coach Guffy. He did not seem to be happy and was giving you a hard stare."

"I could feel his stare that night. He doesna like me. Perhaps he is jealous." Fiona blushed.

"Coach Guffy does not want his players to date during football season, but he cannot make that a requirement."

"Have we had a date?" Fiona teased. "Are we dating?"

"Certainly yesterday, but yes, every day since we met." Alexander's face was red.

"That's what I telt Auntie last night. Of course, she wants autographs too. Uncle wants ye to sign a football. He is a big fan of MU football and of ye."

"I'll be happy to sign your picture and a football."

Fiona seemed thoughtful. "What about Coach Guffy?"

"He's not said anything to me about our dating. I'm not opening the subject with him."

"But what if Coach Guffy tells ye to stay away from me?"

"I won't. That is, I won't stay away from you unless you tell me to. Please don't tell me."

"I willna." She smiled, green eyes wide and gleaming.

Fiona took a sip of tea and casually changed the subject. "A reporter from oor student newspaper has asked me for an interview. What should I do?"

"Oh, go along with the interview. I am interviewed all the time. Nothing to it; just be yourself and be truthful. You don't have to respond to every question. You can always say no comment or nothing at all. Don't worry about it; you'll be fine."

"He also wants some pictures."

"So do I!"

"I'm no accustomed to this level of attention."

"You should probably get used to it. I suspect you are well on your way to becoming a celebrity. You know, fifteen minutes of fame and all that stuff, but you will probably get over fifteen minutes."

"Only if I'm with ye."

"Next semester, you might take a media communications class. Many athletes take Communications 101 to learn how to handle the media. Some athletes even become the media themselves. When is the interview?"

"This morning at ten. The reporter wanted ye there as well, but I telt him ye had a class. He's on a tight schedule, so he agreed to interview only me."

"I have a ten o'clock class, in fact, a test today. I'd be glad to join you for an interview but can't do this one."

"I ken. I'm a wee bit nervous."

*****

SO, YOU ARE THE BEAUTIFUL BUT UNKNOWN ADMIRER of our star football player, Alexander Gordon?

Fiona was reading in the study area of the Student Union, and a short, overweight guy approached her. "Hello, I'm Harry Shattick, a reporter for our student newspaper. Thank you for agreeing to this interview on such short notice; my deadline is today. I'm surprised you were not identified--anyone could have given the photographer your name. I had no problem finding you and learning a little about you."

Fiona just smiled, as this was not a question. Fiona suspected the reporter had researched her background information and probably could have already written his story— and perhaps he had.

"Tell me about yourself, so I can confirm what I've found about you."

"I am Fiona MacDonald, a freshman majoring in music, vocals and dance with a minor in philosophy. I was born and raised in Scotland but am noo living with my aunt and uncle in Easton, Mississippi."

"How tall are you?"

"Taller than ye."

"How did you meet Alexander Gordon?"

"A mutual friend introduced us."

"When did you meet?"

"A week ago today."

"Are you a big football fan?"

"Nay. I'm from Scotland and dinna ken American football, but I am learning."

"Would you evaluate Alexander Gordon's last game?"

"I dinna ken enough to evaluate his performance properly, but everyone tells me it was fantastic, nearly unbelievable."

"And you are called the 'Viking Princess?'

"Some call me that, but I am no a Viking; I'm a Scot."

"People say you and Alexander spend a lot of time together. Would it be fair to describe you as Alexander Gordon's girlfriend?"

"Ye should ask him that question."

The reporter continued to probe from another angle. "Would it be fair to describe Alexander Gordon as your boyfriend?"

"Ye should ask him that question."

"Would it be fair to say you and Alexander Gordon are dating?"

"Aye."

"The photograph of you and Alexander is called 'The Look.'. Are you aware of this label? You appeared to be admiring him."

"Weel, I was admiring Alexander. He is that handsome, and he played a fantastic game of football."

"Some say you are the most beautiful girl on campus."

Fiona blushed. "That's what Alexander says. Och, I shouldn't have said that."

"Can I snap a few pictures?"

"What will ye do with them?"

"I will use them in our student newspaper and perhaps in the yearbook."

"If ye put that in writing and sign it, I will agree to your using the one photograph that I approve provided ye give me three 8x10 copies."

"Deal," and the reporter scribed out a short version of a model release.

*****

THE EDITOR OF THE STUDENT NEWSPAPER and his advisor reviewed the student reporter's draft of his article 'The Look.' The advisor commented, "This is well done and an interesting article, but too personal for our use. Remove the parts about girlfriend and boyfriend. Keep the fact that they are dating, but remove the information that they just met. The 'Viking Princess' bit is appropriate. You can describe her as beautiful but cannot write Alexander thinks she is the most beautiful girl on campus unless he tells you."

"I'll call him right now." He dialed his desk telephone.

Alexander's telephone rang, and he answered.

"Hello, I'm Harry Shattick, a reporter for our student newspaper. Is this Alexander Gordon?"

"Yes, this is Alexander. What can I do for you?"

"As I'm sure you are aware, I interviewed your girlfriend, Fiona MacDonald, today. It was a great interview; sorry you could not make it."

Alexander noted the term "girlfriend," but that was the way everyone was now describing their relationship, and he did not comment.

Harry continued, "I have one question for you, and then I'll leave you to your studies. Fiona is, of course, extraordinarily beautiful. Many say she is the most beautiful girl on campus. Would you agree with that judgment?"

Alexander answered, "Fiona MacDonald is not only and obviously the most beautiful girl on campus, but she is also the most beautiful and fascinating girl I've ever known."

"Thank you very much." Harry had his quote.

*****

TUESDAY EVENING IN FIONA'S ROOM, Fiona asserted to Mary and Anne, "This will be fun. I'm glad ye are coming." A concert and dance in the Student Union featured the Big Band Sound of the 1940s and merged into the Rock and Roll of the 1950s. Alexander had told Fiona he could dance to those musical genres. She expected him at the dormitory any minute.

The speaker in Fiona's room buzzed. "Fiona, your guest is here." Fiona, Mary and Anne went downstairs to meet Alexander.

As they walked to the Student Union, Fiona teased, "Ye said ye could dance. Now ye can prove it."

"Yes, I can dance, but I wish I were better. I suspect you dance like a professional. Still, I'm willing to try my hand—well, feet—at dancing together."

The sponsors had rearranged the largest room in the Student Union to include a stage for the band. An open space remained for dancing. Tables and chairs were for the non-dancers and listeners. Fiona and Alexander found an empty table; Mary and Anne joined them, then Alexander left to get sodas.

Mary nudged Fiona. Thomas Bennoitt approached Fiona's table, but he noticed Alexander and turned around and eased away.

Fiona thought, ... *and stay away.*

Alexander put the sodas on the table; Mary teased, "Can he talk?" Everyone laughed, even Alexander.

Alexander admitted, "I'll never live that one down."

Mary continued, "Nor should you be able to."

Fiona blushed and smiled at Alexander. She loved their introduction.

The band played music from the 1940s, and everyone was tapping their feet.

Fiona wanted to dance, but Alexander seemed hesitant. A few songs later, the band played "In the Mood."

Alexander ventured, "This is one of my favorite Big Band tunes. Would you try it with me?"

Fiona agreed. "One of my favorites as well. Let's try it." They stepped onto the dance floor, faced each other, held hands, and swung to find the beat.

Alexander confessed, "I'll be a little rusty. Take it easy on me." Together they found the beat and began a simple variation of Jitterbug. Alexander spun Fiona away, and she reversed the spin to come back into his arms. They increased their movements but maintained a sophisticated jitterbug. They returned to their table with deep smiles.

"Wow, I was afraid I'd forgotten how to do that stuff!"

Fiona gushed, "Ye might be the best dance partner I've ever had!"

"You mean you've danced with other men?" Everyone laughed.

The band continued to play songs from the 1940s, with Fiona and Alexander alternating between dancing and resting.

The song selections shifted into the 1950s and early Rock and Roll with "Rock Around the Clock."

"Shall we try this one?" Alexander asked Fiona.

"I'm ready. Let's give it a go." Fiona and Alexander stepped quickly onto the dance floor.

Fiona and Alexander were holding hands and laughing when they returned to their table. They sat and sipped on their sodas.

After a few more fast songs, the conductor announced, "This has been a short concert and dance, but it is time to close. Here's a nice slow song. Find your special partner and enjoy it."

"May I have this dance?" Alexander asked Fiona.

"I'd love to dance with ye," answered Fiona, green eyes wide and eager. They walked onto the floor hand in hand.

As the band began playing the introduction, Alexander took Fiona's right hand in his left and placed his right hand on the small of her back. Fiona put her left hand on the upper part of Alexander's muscular right arm. They swayed to the music while standing slightly apart in the classic waltz closed position.

Alexander smiled at Fiona. "I hope I don't step on your feet."

Fiona smiled back, "I have big feet, and they will be difficult for ye to avoid."

"Confucius said a woman with big feet will not blow over in a storm."

Fiona giggled. "What about a guy with big feet?"

"He may use them as an excuse for his dancing."

A singer came to the microphone and began a credible cover of the Platter's version of "Ebb Tide."

Fiona stepped closer to Alexander. "I like your English leather."

They began dancing.

Fiona moved even closer to Alexander and lay her right hand on his chest. He exuded warmth from jitterbugging. Alexander placed his left hand over her hand. She put her left hand around his neck and moved still closer.

The song ended, but Alexander objected, "I don't want this song to end."

"I dinna want this dance to end," Fiona added.

"Then we won't let it end." Without music, they continued dancing.

Mary jumped up and rushed to the conductor while making a circular motion with her hands to indicate that he should continue the song. At first, the conductor seemed puzzled, but then he understood and mouthed, "One more chorus." The band resumed playing.

Fiona stepped slightly away from Alexander, flipped her long auburn hair over his shoulder and embraced him with her face towards him, both arms around him. They were the only dancers.

The song ended again with Fiona's wide green eyes locked on Alexander and inviting him even closer. Their faces were coming together, but the Dean of Women, Dr. Crawford, reached them first and scolded, "All right, you two. That's enough."

With the concert and dance ended, Alexander walked Fiona, Mary, and Anne to their dormitory. Alexander and Fiona were nearly silent.

They were almost late getting to the dorm. Still, Alexander managed to ask, "Fiona, would you have coffee with me tomorrow morning?"

"I'd love to."

The Dorm Mother rushed the girls inside and locked the door behind them. The girls headed for Mary's room. A few other girls came in, and the discussion began about the concert and dance.

One girl complimented Fiona. "You are an excellent dancer."

"*Taing*. Dance is one of my majors. Besides, tonight I had a braw partner."

"We noticed!"

"How many hours of practice did it take to dance like that?"

"This was oor first time to dance together."

Mary snorted. "This may have been your first time to dance together, but a piece of tissue paper would not have fit between the two of you."

"Fiona," Anne teased, "did your dance lessons include how to flip your hair over his shoulder and wrap your arms around him."

"Och, did I do that?" Fiona blushed a deep red.

"I can't believe Dr. Crawford stopped you from kissing," Anne complained. "What is wrong with that woman?" She waved her hand in front of her face. "Whew, is it just me, or is this room heating up?"

*****

DONNIE WAS STUDYING IN THEIR DORM ROOM when Alexander came in quietly, sat on his cot, and stared at the wall, obviously lost in thought.

"You OK, man?"

"What? Oh, yeh, I'm OK. Why?"

"Are you lost? How was the concert?"

"What? Oh, good."

"You were with Fiona, of course?"

"Yes. We danced. Fiona is a wonderful dancer and kept her feet out from under mine."

"You've been seeing more and more of her lately."

"What? Oh, I suppose. She's interesting and fun to be around. We're having coffee tomorrow morning."

"You've had coffee with Fiona every morning since you met."

"I suppose so. Gets my day off to a good start."

"You realize it's all over for you, don't you?"

"What do you mean by 'all over?'"

"Your bachelor days are finished."

"How can you say that? I've only known Fiona a week."

"But I've known you a couple of years. You've never been captivated by a girl. Plus, you knew exactly who and what I was talking about."

"Maybe."
"No maybe to it. You're a goner."

Chapter 3: Ae Fond Kiss

For to see her was to love her
Love but her, and love for ever
— Robert Burns

FIONA AND ALEXANDER enjoyed their Wednesday morning coffee and relived the concert and dance from the previous night. Anne came to their table, waving the student newspaper. "Have you seen this?"

"Not yet."

"Here, I got a few extra copies." She put the newspapers on their table.

Featured on the front page was a beautiful portrait of Fiona with the headline "Viking Princess." Fiona complained, "They promised me approval rights." The brief article accompanying the picture read:

> The beautiful unknown admirer of Alexander Gordon—recently featured in a prize-winning photograph called 'The Look, is Fiona MacDonald, a freshman at MU known as the 'Viking Princess.' Fiona is majoring in music, vocals, and dance with a minor in philosophy. She was born and raised in Scotland and readily acknowledges that she does not know much about football. Perhaps Alexander can teach her! Of the Viking Princess, Alexander said, 'Fiona MacDonald is not only and obviously the most beautiful girl on campus, but she is also the most beautiful and fascinating girl I've ever known.'

A miniature version of the original 'The Look' picture also accompanied the article.

Alexander noted, "You can't buy that kind of publicity."

Fiona complained, "I dinna want publicity." Then she smiled at Alexander, "But *taing* for the compliment, ye flatterer!" She winked.

"I want an actual copy of your portrait."

"They've promised me three copies. One is for ye."

Alexander remarked, "You'd best get prepared to autograph more newspapers. Here they come."

*****

WEDNESDAY NIGHT, after football practice and supper with Fiona, Alexander returned to his dorm. To his surprise, Donnie was not at his desk studying. Instead, he was sitting at Alexander's desk and talking on the telephone.

As Alexander came in, Donnie said, "Uh, OK. See you tomorrow. Bye."

Alexander laughed. "Jane?"

Donnie's face turned red. "Yes. We're having lunch tomorrow."

"Do we need to have the telephone moved to your desk?" teased Alexander.

"No. You're still on it much more than I am." Donnie moved back to his own desk.

"Here's an autographed copy of today's student newspaper for you." Alexander handed Donnie the paper with Fiona's "Viking Princess" autograph.

"She is one beautiful girl." Donnie skimmed the article. "Apparently, you think so too."

"You were right about Coach Guffy," advised Alexander. "My dating Fiona caught him by surprise. He gave a lecture today about dedication to the season and leaving the girls alone. He was speaking to the entire team but stared at me most of the time. He is not happy."

"What are you going to do?"

"Nothing. No changes in my behavior, attention to Fiona, or dating Fiona. No changes at all. Guffy might make recommendations about dating, but he cannot make rules forbidding it. He would be in serious trouble if he made such a rule—not to mention the disastrous effect it would have on recruiting."

"Anyone ever say you are stubborn?"

"Seems like someone has said those words before. But I'm right, and you know it."

"But what if Guffy doesn't put you in the games?"

"He's the coach; that's his option. But, at the risk of tooting my own horn..."

Donnie interrupted, "Not exactly a new toot."

"He that tooteth not his own horn, the same shall remain untooted." Alexander grinned.

"Have you told Fiona about this?"

"No. She would be upset. Don't tell Jane either."

"OK, but I've got a bad feeling about this."

$$*****$$

ON THURSDAYS, ALEXANDER often practiced guitar while sitting on the steps to the main library. The location was convenient, and he liked the tones from his acoustic guitar in the open air.

Alexander's guitar was a beautiful Martin N-20 nylon-stringed classical made of Brazilian rosewood with a Sitka spruce top. Although acoustic, it included an electrical pickup that could be connected to an amplifier. No amplifier was used during his library practices.

During his Thursday guitar practice sessions—which was the way Alexander considered it—he did not sing; he just played guitar. Sometimes he would fingerpick a melody or accompaniment, and other times he simply strummed. A small crowd might appear for a few minutes, then gradually disperse, only to be replaced by another. On hearing a familiar melody, someone might break into song—which was fine with Alexander.

Today might be different; that is, if Fiona came. Fiona had never heard Alexander play guitar, but she was aware of his practicing on the steps of the library. Alexander had a song for her.

After Alexander strummed a few tunes, Fiona came into view. He continued strumming until she joined the small group of, perhaps, ten students. Alexander locked eyes with her, and she moved through the group to be closer to Alexander. A few more students joined the group. Something was about to happen.

With his eyes on Fiona, Alexander made known: "There has been a special change in my life, and today is a good day to sing about it." He played the introduction to "Perhaps Love" by John Denver and sang it to her, never taking his eyes away from Fiona.

Fiona came up the steps and stood by Alexander. He caught a whiff of her musky perfume and felt her nervousness. She made a slight motion with her hand to indicate Alexander should continue playing, and he did. Fiona sang the ending again while gazing into Alexander's eyes.

Alexander stood. Taking Fiona's warm hand in his, he raised their hands high in the air. "Ladies and Gentlemen, Miss Fiona MacDonald." Then, looking deeply into each other's eyes, Fiona and Alexander embraced and kissed with passion. The crowd, for now, it was a crowd, broke into applause.

The Dean of Women, Dr. Crawford, did not applaud. She had been walking past the library and witnessed Fiona and Alexander kiss. She hastened to the couple, still embracing, and commanded, "Fiona, come with me." Fiona and Alexander were startled. They separated as they attempted to understand. Dr.

Crawford commanded again, "Fiona, come with me," and walked away.

Fiona and Alexander followed Dr. Crawford, but Dr. Crawford stopped, glared at Alexander, and said sharply, "Young man, there is no need for you to come." Dr. Crawford walked on. Alexander said nothing but continued to accompany Fiona, and Dr. Crawford ignored him.

*****

THEY ENTERED DR. CRAWFORD'S OFFICE in the Main Administration Building. Dr. Crawford had foreseen this Public Display of Affection, especially since seeing them dance, but being so public and affectionate was not acceptable.

Ignoring Alexander, Dr. Crawford scolded, "Fiona, we have rules about Public Display of Affection. In case you are not aware, here is our rulebook." She reached into her desk, pulled out a thin pamphlet, and handed it to her. "Are you aware of our rules? Do you have a copy of our rulebook?"

"Aye. I do," said Fiona through quivering lips. She gnawed on her bottom lip.

"The punishment for a Public Display of Affection is Campused for two consecutive weekends. Also, a note of demerit will be placed in your personal file. Do you understand what this means?"

Fiona nodded, and her voice trembled, "I ken." Tears rolled down her cheeks.

"You can read the details in the rulebook," instructed Dr. Crawford. "But to be certain you understand, you may not leave the campus and must be in your dormitory by seven o'clock each night. Weekends included."

"Dr. Crawford," Alexander interjected, "this is all my fault, and I accept complete responsibility. I'm the one who should be punished, not Fiona. Please assign the punishment to me instead of her."

"Alexander, we, in particular I, do not punish the boys for participation in Public Display of Affection." Dr. Crawford fumed. "You boys would wear it like a badge of honor. We control Public Display of Affection by limiting the show of affection of the girls and punishing them for infractions."

"Yes, ma'am. I know the girl is always punished, but I hope you'll make a special case this time."

"No, I will not."

"Well, could I at least share the punishment? How about one week each of being Campused?"

"No. That is not done. You may not negotiate Fiona's punishment. Besides, you are committed to representing this university through your football extracurricular activity. Coach Guffy would protest and arrange for your punishment to be removed."

"In that case, I consider myself to be Campused in protest and empathy with Fiona."

Dr. Crawford picked up her telephone and dialed the extension of President Curry. "President Curry, this is Dr. Crawford. I have a major problem with two students. Could you come to my office right away? Good, thank you."

Fiona regarded Alexander with a mixture of disbelief, admiration, tears and smiling.

President Curry came into Dr. Crawford's office. "What is the problem, Dr. Crawford?"

Dr. Crawford explained the situation. "I observed these two students, Fiona and Alexander, involved in a Public Display of Affection in broad daylight in front of the library and a crowd. This violates our rules regarding a display of affection. The punishment is for the girl to be Campused for two consecutive weekends. However, Alexander insists he is responsible and the punishment should apply to him instead. I cannot do that. Alexander now insists he considers himself Campused in protest and empathy with Fiona."

"Is this correct?" President Curry asked Fiona and Alexander.

"Yes, sir," they answered together.

President Curry grimaced at Alexander and asked, "Alexander, does this mean you are threatening to not play in the next two football games?"

"This is not a threat. If Fiona was scheduled to play piano in a concert next week, would she be allowed?"

President Curry picked up Dr. Crawford's telephone and dialed it. "Coach Guffy? This is President Curry. We have a problem with one of your players, Alexander Gordon. Please come to Dr. Crawford's office at once. Thank you."

Coach Guffy arrived quickly. He greeted everyone but gave Fiona a hard stare that made her squirm in the seat.

President Curry asked Dr. Crawford to present her observations and Alexander's position. Coach Guffy was not pleased. He asked to meet privately with Alexander, and President Curry allowed them to use the conference room.

*****

MARY WAS AHEAD OF ANNE on the sidewalk and Anne ran to her. "Have you heard? Have you heard?"

"What?"

"Fiona and Alexander kissed! I watched them. It was beautiful."

"Well, it's about time. A bit of a Peeping Tom, eh?"

"No. they were standing on the steps of the library a few minutes ago. I was in the small crowd that witnessed them. Alexander sang a song to Fiona; she sang back to him, and then they kissed. It was the most romantic scene anyone could ever imagine. It brought tears to my eyes."

"Good, now the suspense is over."

"Well, there is a problem. The Dean of Women, Dr. Crawford, caught them kissing. She broke them up and led Fiona away. Alexander followed them. You know the punishment for PDA is to be Campused through two weekends."

"I've never had to worry about being punished for PDA myself, but I'm sure Alexander will never allow Fiona to be punished. He will consider her punishment a form of bullying, but I don't know how he can prevent it. Wonder what he will do? This is a dilemma. I hope their relationship can withstand whatever is about to happen next."

*****

THE CONFERENCE ROOM WAS PLAIN BUT FORMAL. Coach Guffy, a bulldog of a middle-aged man, wore his usual pullover polo shirt with "MU" insignia untucked. As always, he had his whistle around his neck as though it were a crucifix, and Alexander thought he was angry enough to blow it.

"What happened?"

Alexander admitted Dr. Crawford had stated the facts correctly. Coach Guffy pounded his fist on the conference table.

"Alexander, your the best football player I've ever knew. We're havin' a great season. Think careful 'bout what your sayin' you'll do. I'm afraid your about tuh make a terrible mistake, all for the sake of some girl. Ah warned ya yesterday. I seen it comin'. Ya know the rules. There's nothin' ya can do 'bout this. Let her take the punishment she deserves."

"Coach, I <u>have</u> been thinking this over. I cannot allow Fiona to be punished for something I arranged. This is my fault, and I'm the one that should be punished."

"Ya can be an All-Star professional football player. Don't throw it all away for this girl."

"I'll miss two games. That won't ruin my football career. Besides, I don't plan to play professional football.

Coach Guffy changed his manner of argument. "No, if ya miss practices and two games protestin', then your suspended for the rest of the season. That would be a black mark on your draft rankin'."

"Then so be it. None of this is fair to Fiona."

At this second use of Fiona's name, Coach Guffy grew red-in-the face and nearly shouted, "Ah know your running around with that red-headed bitch. Ever'body talkin' 'bout it. Don't let that bitch rule ya!"

"What? What did you say?"

"Ya heard me. Your the most popular man on campus. Ya could have any girl or girls ya want. In fact, Ah can get ya an off-campus apartment for, uh, datin'. Girls will be beating on your door. Ya can probably even keep that red-headed slut as well. Now let's go talk tuh Curry." He got up and stomped out of the conference room.

Alexander followed.

*****

PRESIDENT CURRY addressed Alexander in Dr. Crawford's office. "Have you made a decision?"

Alexander tried to remain calm but retorted, "Yes, indeed. Coach Guffy, you are a lucky man. You may despise women, but I wanted to hit you for cursing Fiona and questioning her virtues. I guess I'm a lucky man too. If I had hit you, you'd be in the hospital, but I'd be in jail."

Alexander's reproach was a complete surprise and shock to Coach Guffy. He reacted with, "Are ya threatenin' me?"

"No, sir. I was describing my feelings and bragging about controlling my temper," said Alexander. "I did not threaten you then, and I'm not threatening you now. However, I will have nothing to do with you again. Ever."

Coach Guffy attempted to recover. "If Ah said anythin' that offended anyone, Ah apologize."

Alexander exclaimed loudly and sharply, "IF? IF? That is not an apology!"

Alexander turned to President Curry. "President Curry, please ask Coach Guffy to leave the room and not return. I'm finished with him."

"You should leave now, Coach," said President Curry. "You and I can discuss this further tomorrow."

Fiona stopped crying and beamed at her hero.

President Curry turned to Fiona holding two files in his hand. After glancing at the files, he looked up. "Fiona, your guardians are Robert Johnston and Ellen Mackenzie, is that correct?"

Fiona nodded. "Yes, sir."

"Robert, Ellen and I, as well as my wife, Linda, were classmates here back in the day. I once knew them well. They are fine people."

President Curry turned to Alexander. "Alexander, you are named after your father, Alexander Malcolm Gordon?"

"Yes, sir. He speaks very favorably of you."

"Malcolm and I served in the National Guard together for many years. He was my First Lieutenant. Your mother is a splendid cook, among her other talents."

President Curry spoke to both Fiona and Alexander. "Here is my suggestion. Please telephone your guardians and parents and inform them of this situation. Ask them to come here to meet with Dr. Crawford and me to discuss your conduct and our disciplinary action. You may use the telephone in the conference room."

Fiona and Alexander gladly agreed. Fiona entered the conference room first.

*****

Fiona dialed the Johnston telephone. There was no way her aunt could anticipate this call.

"Auntie, it's Fiona. I'm in trouble. No, not that type of trouble, thank goodness. I have been Campused for PDA."

"With Alexander Gordon?"

"Of course, with Alexander. There is no one else. Can ye help me?"

"Of course, I'll try. What can I do?"

"President Curry says he knows ye and uncle. If ye come to campus for a conference with him, he might change oor punishment."

"Our?"

"Aye. Alexander is Campused as well."

"Guys are not Campused."

"I ken that, but Alexander insisted."

"What about football?"

"Alexander is off the team. Apparently, the coach said vulgar things about me, and Alexander will have nothing more to do with him."

"When are we needed on campus?"

"President Curry says to come Monday for a three o'clock meeting. Och, he reserved a room for you at the Alumni Inn."

"Robert and I will be there. Fiona, two things: One, this is a minor problem and disciplinary action; don't get depressed about it. Punishment for PDA is a carryover from the fifties. I'm surprised it is still used; it will not be around much longer. Two, I'm really looking forward to meeting your young man. He must be something else."

"Yes, ma'am; he is. *Moran taing.*"

Fiona smiled. *Ellen called Alexander her young man.*

*****

ALEXANDER'S QUIZICAL LOOK was answered by Fiona's smile as she came out of the conference room. "Auntie and Uncle will come."

Alexander entered the conference room, picked up the telephone and dialed his parents. "Dad, it's Alexander. I'm OK, but there is a problem."

"What happened?"

"Here's the short version. I met a girl I really like. Her name is Fiona. Well, we were caught kissing by the Dean of Women. The punishment is for the girl to be Campused for two weekends. I tried to negotiate with the Dean of Women, but she insisted that Fiona be punished, so I imposed the same punishment on myself. Coach Guffy found out, and he threw a fit. He called Fiona all kinds of vulgar names. I told him off, and now I'm not playing football anymore."

"Not playing football?"

"I'm not playing football or having anything to do with Coach Guffy."

"I'm disappointed to hear that."

"I was sure you would be, and I'm sorry to disappoint you. But I think you'll change your mind when you learn the complete story. President Curry hinted that if you and mom could come up here for a conference with him, our punishment might be reduced."

"Colonel Curry is involved? This must be a big deal."

"Yes, sir. It is to Fiona and me."

"Where and when?"

"Monday at three o'clock in President Curry's office. Oh, he said to tell you hello, and he has reserved a room for you at the Alumni Inn."

"We'll be there."

Alexander hung up and returned to Dr. Crawford's office.

* * * * *

PRESIDENT CURRY WAS PLEASED that Robert and Ellen, and Malcolm and Rachel, would meet with him and Dr. Crawford on Monday. "I will be delighted to see them again. It's been too long."

As Fiona and Alexander were about to leave, Fiona turned to Dr. Crawford and asked, "May we hold hands?"

Dr. Crawford smiled and answered, "Yes, you may. That is, provided you both want to."

"*Moran taing*," Fiona replied. "I need his hand in mine, right noo."

Fiona and Alexander left Dr. Crawford's office, and she turned to President Curry. "William, I wish I had not been present for their kiss, but I was. A small crowd saw me there. I had to separate them. There was no other choice."

"I understand. Thanks for telling me, Beth. These are fine young people—they are just in a bit over their heads right now."

"I agree."

"Let me suggest a plan for dealing with this situation. First, do not even bother putting a letter in their permanent record as it would soon be removed. Second, proceed with their being Campused this weekend but anticipate their punishment being commuted after our Monday conference. If necessary, you can blame me for overruling your disciplinary action."

"That sounds like an excellent plan. I agree."

Dr. Crawford added, "Oh, and William, Alexander is right about Coach Guffy, you know. That man is very unpopular with the girls and women on campus. Everyone says he loathes women. I suspect Alexander's description of his vulgar insults about Fiona is correct."

"There have been other, similar, complaints about Coach Guffy. My wife would agree with you; she is very uncomfortable

111

around him. I believe you are correct. His days here are probably limited. But there goes our football season."

*****

FIONA AND ALEXANDER left the Main Administration Building hand-in-hand and ambled towards Fiona's dormitory in silence. *What is wrong with me?* Alexander thought. *What have I done? How can I correct this mess?*

Several minutes passed before he broke their silence. "Fiona, I'm so sorry for getting you in trouble. I imagine you've never been in any kind of trouble before meeting me. I'm extremely sorry. I rarely get into trouble. I don't know what has come over me. I'm sorry about everything. This is all my fault."

"*Dinna fash yersel.* This is not your fault; I was a most willing participant." Fiona smiled at him. "Auntie said being Campused is a minor disciplinary action, and I should not get depressed about it. She's excited about meeting ye." *And I want her to meet ye as well.*

"I'll be glad to meet your aunt and uncle as well, but I wish the circumstances were better. This puts me off to a poor start with them."

"But, Alexander, I feel responsible that ye canna play football anymore. I'm deeply sorry about that. Perhaps if I talked to Coach Guffy..."

"No! This is between Guffy and me. Do not talk to him."

Alexander recognized, too late, the shock on Fiona's face at his harshness.

"So ye can defend me, but I canna defend ye? I dinna ken."

"I'm sorry, Fiona. I should not have been so sharp. Don't worry about football. I am staying away from Guffy, and I hope you do too—please? He made horribly vulgar remarks about you. Sure, I lost my temper, but you and I are OK. I just don't understand what has been going on with me lately."

"As long as we're together, we can handle anything."

Alexander abruptly stopped in his tracks. He gazed into Fiona's deep green eyes as though seeing them anew. "What am I talking about? Of course, I know what is happening to me. Fiona, I'm falling in love with you. What a strange and wonderful feeling—exciting and scary at the same time. Lord, have mercy on me."

Fiona's eyes opened even wider and welled with tears. "I ken exactly the way ye feel, *mo leannan.* I am falling in love with ye, Alexander Malcolm Gordon."

"And now, I can't even kiss you! But I promise you this. I will give you the most passionate kiss ever as soon as we are no longer Campused. Well, that is, if you want it."

"Ye are the current record holder, and I'm looking forward to ye breaking your own record."

*****

WORD GOT OUT about 'The Kiss,' and girls gathered excitedly in Mary's room that night to hear Fiona's version of the story. Fiona came in wearing a huge smile and blushing. The room became quiet in anticipation.

"So, how was your day?" Mary giggled. "Anything exciting happen?"

"Ye ken exactly the way of my day. I've been serenaded, kissed, Campused, and I'm falling in love. It's been a braw day."

All the girls joined the giggling. "Start from the beginning," Jane asked.

"I kent Alexander sometimes practiced guitar on the library steps, but I hadna heard him play. Today, I noticed him on the steps with a small crowd, so I walked over to listen. When he saw me, oor eyes locked, and I kent he wanted me to come closer. Everyone else could feel it as well, and they let me through."

Fiona sniffed, choked emotionally, and dabbed at the corner of her eyes with a tissue. She went on, "Alexander said, 'There has been a special change in my life, and today is a good day to sing about it.' He then played and sang 'Perhaps Love' by John Denver—it's one of my favorite songs—well, now it is my very favorite. I joined him in the last verse. He took my hand in his and raised them above oor heads.

"It was strange, but as though Alexander was introducing me, he said, 'Ladies and Gentlemen, Miss Fiona MacDonald.'"

"Fiona, he <u>was</u> introducing you," Mary interjected.

"I turned toward him, he lowered oor hands, put his arms around me, and we kissed. Everyone applauded."

"I was there," said Anne. "The simple word, 'kiss', is an inadequate description. A simple peck—even on the lips—might not have been cited as a PDA. Fiona, you had both arms—in fact, your entire body—wrapped around Alexander and were standing tiptoe on one foot just like in the movies." Anne fanned her face with her hand.

"Fiona popped her foot?" asked Jane.

"Och, did I? I didna kent. Ye ken he's that tall."

"Also, you can hold your breath for a long time!" Anne giggled. "It's a good thing that both of you do not have braces. If a photographer had been there, your picture would be in the newspaper again—and a copy would be in the MU rule book under 'Don't do this.'"

"I'll remember oor first kiss all my life," Fiona mused wistfully.

"First? So, you're already planning for another?" teased Jane.

"Aye. Indeed I am. More than one."

"Is that when Dr. Crawford showed up?"

"Aye, she wasna happy."

"And now you are Campused?"

"Aye, the kiss was well worth being Campused."

114

Fiona's smile disappeared. "Alexander is off the football team."

"What?"

Fiona related the actions of Coach Guffy and Alexander's response.

"Maybe they will patch things up, and Alexander will return to the team," suggested Jane.

"I doubt it," Fiona said.

Mary agreed. "You've had quite a day."

"Aye, and my aunt and uncle, as well as Alexander's parents, are coming on Monday."

"So, more to come…," Mary added.

*****

IN THEIR DORM ROOM THAT NIGHT, Donnie was incredulous as Alexander related the events of his day.

"I shouldn't be surprised. You've confirmed something I always suspected: you are a hopeless romantic. Why not wait until nighttime and go to a drive-in movie and smooch like everyone else does? No, no. Not you. You had to serenade Fiona in the middle of the afternoon and kiss her on the steps of the library where every student on campus could see. That is so you—it is almost the definition of you except for your stubbornness."

Like Mary, Donnie was not intimidated by Alexander.

"Speaking of stubbornness, why are you punishing yourself? You could have followed the existing rules, but, no, you had to do it your way, didn't you? It doesn't matter whether a math problem or a romance; it must be done your way. You tried to rewrite the rules, and what good did it do? Fiona's punishment did not change. If you'd gone along with the rules, Fiona would not have known the difference and, if she did, she'd have accepted it. She would gladly protect you from all this.

"And no football? The fans will not like that at all; in fact, they'll give you—and Fiona—a hard time. Your days as a big man on campus are over. Fiona will be accused of making you quit. Times are about to get tough."

"And I'd do it again. Tomorrow even."

"Only you, Alexander. Only you."

Donnie grinned. "All the same, congratulations! I hope that kiss was worth it!"

"It was, and now I get to meet her aunt and uncle."

"Oh, I'll just bet they will be happy to meet you, too." Donnie shook his head and laughed.

*****

FRIDAY MORNING, as Fiona was about to leave the dorm for breakfast with Alexander, Mary came into her room.

"Fiona, I have some profound things to say. When I first told you about Alexander, I did not mention how stubborn he can be——particularly if he believes he is right—and he usually is—or if he has taken a stand based on some principle or defending someone else. Not to mention his love for you. He will never change his mind about the PDA, Campused, or Coach Guffy, no matter how much it hurts him personally."

"I witnessed that stubbornness yesterday."

"Being Campused is nothing, but Alexander has never not played football. The football season was going great but now will probably fall apart—at least, that's what Hannah says. Many people, especially the guys, take it very seriously, as silly a game as football is. Alexander will not know what to do tomorrow during game time. On top of that, people will be upset, even angry, when they learn he is off the team. Some people will say you caused him to leave the team, and those people will be angry at you. He will be called a quitter, and you may be called even worse. You and Alexander need to stay together as much as

116

possible. He may need to protect you. You may need to protect him. You might consider cutting some classes just to be together."

"*Taing*, Mary. I hadn't considered those things. I'll discuss them with Alexander at breakfast."

*****

WORD ABOUT "THE KISS" and being Campused spread quickly. At breakfast, stares and whispers surrounded Fiona and Alexander. Alexander could feel himself going into protective mode, but what could he do?

"Apparently, our fifteen minutes of fame have ended. Now to get on with a normal life. We can do this—especially with each other's support."

"Mary suggested we stay together as much as possible for the next several days even if we must cut classes."

"Not a bad idea, but let's try our normal day first. If the situation gets terrible, then we can cut classes on Monday and face everything together. All this will blow over in a few days."

"Perhaps our meeting with President Curry on Monday will resolve harassment as well as punishment."

"My parents are looking forward to meeting you," Alexander informed her. "They still want your autograph. You are still a beautiful celebrity."

"I'm nervous about meeting your parents. What must they think of me?" Fiona twirled a strand of her long hair between her fingers. "What if they believe Coach Guffy?"

"I've explained the PDA and Coach Guffy to my parents. They believe me. Don't worry; they will love you but caution me to be more restrained."

"Auntie is eager to meet ye, but I must warn ye that Uncle Robert no longer wants ye to autograph a football. He is scunner."

"I was afraid of that," Alexander sighed. "Thinking of football, I must clean out my locker, but I'll catch up to you in a few minutes."

*****

THE STUDENT MANAGER, Pat, unlocked the locker room door and walked in with Alexander. *A locker room always smells like sweat,* Alexander thought, *no matter how much air freshener is applied.*

"Sorry, Alexander," Pat apologized, "but Coach Guffy ordered me to supervise you carefully and personally. I must remain with you."

"I understand. Not a problem. I'm glad it's you and not Guffy. I only need to get a few personal things from my locker." He was willing to lose the hairbrush, deodorant, and a few articles of clothing. However, Alexander would not give up the photograph Fiona had autographed, "Your Viking Princess." He put her framed photo between some clothing, placed it carefully into his gym bag, and added things until the bag was full. That was enough. He wanted out of there.

John came in. "I can't believe you are doing this, Alexander! Sure, Coach Guffy has a problem with women. It is well known he hates women, but why leave the team? Let that be his problem, not yours."

John was a senior. He had been around Coach Guffy for four years. "Coach Guffy was married briefly," John reminded him. "I suppose being married disagreed with him."

"It's simple, John. After what Guffy said about Fiona, I could not tolerate being around him. I could never forget his words."

"You're the best player and best person I've ever met, Alexander. I understand your position; in fact, I admire it. I wish you were still on the team, but I'm still your friend and will support and defend you."

"Thank you, John. Your support is important to me."

"But Alexander, many people will not support you in your decision. Be careful."

"I know that."

John added, "That Fiona must be something else!"

"She is, indeed. There is no one like her."

＊＊＊＊＊

ALEXANDER HAD GONE TO THE LOCKER ROOM, SO FIONA WALKED alone to her class. She wanted a normal day but feared it was not to be. Sure enough, Thomas Bennoitt sauntered to her wearing a big grin. She tried to avoid him by turning away, but he was not about to be avoided.

"Big Red!"

Fiona said nothing but tried to step around Thomas. He moved to the side to block her, his face damp with perspiration.

"So, your quitter of a boyfriend got you in trouble. You could have avoided all this by hooking up with me. I have an apartment, so we would not have to make out in the library."

"Thomas!" His rapid footsteps accompanied Alexander's exclamation. "You'd better leave and leave now."

"Or what? You're not frightening me." Thomas's bravado had returned. "You're not such a big man on campus anymore, are you? Touch me, and I'll see they expel you. In fact, I'm considering filing a complaint about that business at the 'Meet and Greet.' My complaint added to your being a quitter, and Campused might be enough reasons for expulsion. Of course, Big Red, you might get me to change my mind." Thomas yukked.

"Alexander, please, let's leave," urged Fiona.

Alexander growled, "Thomas, one day it's going to be just you and me."

As Fiona and Alexander moved away from Thomas, Alexander suggested, "I'll stay with you and audit your classes, and you can audit mine. Otherwise, we can cut classes as necessary." They remained together for the rest of the day.

Just before seven o'clock, following the Campused rules, Alexander accompanied Fiona to her dorm.

*****

"TOUGH DAY?" asked Mary. She had been waiting in her room, expecting Fiona.

"Aye," answered Fiona. "I've been called every name in the book and some new ones I dinna ken."

Fiona told Mary about the confrontation with Thomas Bennoitt.

Mary suggested, "You could and probably should file a complaint against Thomas, but I doubt it would do much good."

"Mary," asked Fiona, "Whit does it mean to say that someone is 'whipped'?"

"Where did you hear that?"

"Several people yelled 'Whipped' at Alexander and me as we were walking. They yelled while driving by. Alexander started to chase one of them but stopped."

"They were yelling at Alexander. They were saying you and Alexander have a sexual relationship, and he is interested in nothing else and will do anything to continue that sexual relationship."

"Well, we dinna."

"Usually, guys use 'whipped' to tease a friend who has just gotten married."

Mary pondered the situation for a few moments then sent out the word she wanted to talk to a group of her friends, including Fiona, in her room. Soon, perhaps twenty girls crowded into her room, wondering what Mary wanted to tell them.

"Thank you for coming. I need your help," began Mary. I'm sure you all know what has happened to our friend Fiona and her boyfriend, Alexander Gordon." Mary stopped speaking and turned to Fiona with a smile. "First time I've called Alexander your boyfriend. Is that OK?"

"Och, aye," Fiona said with a blush, "Alexander is *mo leannan*."

Mary continued, "And my best friend. Rumors and lies are circulating like wildfire, and we must put a stop to them. Let me tell you some truths and expose some lies.

"Fiona has not been expelled or even suspended. She has only been Campused for two weeks for PDA. I understand some of you have faced—or narrowly avoided—that same disciplinary action." Mary smiled.

"Fiona is not pregnant.

"Fiona is not quitting school. She is not returning to Scotland.

"Fiona did not ask, much less insist, that Alexander quit playing football. He quit after Coach Guffy rudely and vulgarly insulted Fiona. Alexander says he will never be involved with Coach Guffy again.

"Alexander is not transferring to another school to play football.

"Fiona and Alexander are not married; they are still dating.

"Now, what can we do? Here's what I'm asking you to do. If you hear the rumors and lies—whether from a guy or a girl—then immediately and forcefully correct them. Now be an evangelist, and let's aggressively stop these lies and rumors about our friends."

*****

ALEXANDER ENTERED his dorm room and threw his books on the bed. They bounced and scattered. He had never been so angry and frustrated in his life.

"Well, Donnie, how's life treating <u>you</u>?"

121

"I've got it with both hands on a downhill pull. But you seem troubled. How was your day?"

"Not good," Alexander told Donnie about encountering Thomas. "I should have beaten him to a pulp right then and there. I'd be expelled, of course, but it might be worth it."

"Not a good idea. Stay away from Thomas and avoid all confrontations."

"I'll try."

"Remember our first day at MU when the upperclassmen shaved our heads? I didn't know you then, but I could tell you were tempted to fight them. You didn't like it but got your head shaved anyway."

"That harassment is still stupid. I'll never take part in it."

"Even Mary said you were not cute with a shaved head and wearing the MU beanie."

"I hated that beanie."

"Your hair grew back. Don't worry, all this will blow over in less time than it took for your hair to grow back. Don't lose your beanie—keeps you humble."

Alexander rummaged around in his dresser drawer and pulled out his MU beanie. He put it over the miniature football helmet on his bookshelf.

"Well, I'd best make the most of an unpleasant situation and study for a while." Alexander removed an engineering book from the shelf, opened it, and sat down at his desk. Now, if only he could study.

*****

THEY STILL ATE BREAKFAST together. Saturday morning, in the main cafeteria, Fiona collected her thoughts and took a deep breath. *I hope he takes this the right way.* She suggested, "*Mo leannan,* let's watch the football game together on the telly in the lobby of my dorm."

122

Alexander made a "harrumph" noise in his throat. "So, I've gone from playing football to watching it from the lobby of the girls' dorm." He immediately added, "I'm sorry, Fiona. At least I'll be with you. You are right. The lobby of the girls' dorm is probably the quietest and safest place for me to watch the game. I'll be there."

Alexander walked Fiona to her dorm and declared, "I'll be back for the game."

Fiona proceeded to Mary's room. "Alexander agreed to watch the game from oor lobby. Thanks for the idea."

"It will be difficult for Alexander, but our lobby is the best place for him to be today."

Fiona agreed. "I ken people say his Viking Princess is protecting him, and perhaps that is true, but they dinna ken I am protecting them from Alexander. If people continue to insult us, someone is going to get hurt."

*****

ALEXANDER WAS MISERABLE sitting alone in the lobby of the girls' dormitory. He had never missed a football game he was supposed to play in. Yet, here he was, about to watch his former teammates play without him.

Fiona entered, quietly sat beside Alexander, and grasped his hand.

As part of the pre-game show, the announcer began, "Now, let us explain why Alexander Gordon is not playing today."

A second announcer reported, "Unexpectedly, Coach Guffy announced the star player and captain of the MU Landsharks has been suspended for missing practice and will not be playing today. We are scrambling, trying to learn more.

"Here is the background information," added the first announcer. "Just one week ago, Alexander Gordon was the star of the game and on his way to becoming a celebrity featured in a prize-winning photograph called 'The Look.' The picture of Fiona admiring Alexander came on-screen. The young lady in 'The Look' is a freshman at MU, Fiona MacDonald."

The second announcer came in, "Fiona MacDonald is called the 'Viking Princess' at MU." The MU student newspaper portrait of Fiona came on-screen. Apparently, Alexander serenaded the Viking Princess on Thursday before football practice, and they kissed. Unfortunately for them, this was witnessed by the MU Dean of Women, Dr. Crawford. At MU, kissing is a forbidden form of Public Display of Affection."

"The punishment for PDA is to be Campused," continued the first announcer. "This meant the Viking Princess must be in her dormitory every night by seven o'clock and cannot leave the campus on the weekends. Alexander Gordon strenuously objected to this punishment and offered to accept the punishment himself. However, at MU—as at many colleges—only girls are punished for a Public Display of Affection. Coach Guffy came into the discussion, but there is disagreement about subsequent events."

The second announcer admitted, "We could not question either Alexander Gordon or Coach Guffy. However, the word on campus is Alexander Gordon claims Coach Guffy insulted the Viking Princess and made sexually explicit and derogatory statements about her. Therefore, Alexander Gordon has refused to have anything to do with Coach Guffy, including playing football."

The first announcer concluded with, "We contacted the MU Athletic Director, and he said this incident will receive a thorough investigation."

"Well, at least they have the story correct," Alexander noted. "Let's hope it doesn't get stretched out of shape."

The second announcer teased conversationally, "So, kissing is not allowed at MU? Hmm."

The first announcer contended, "Without their captain and star player, the MU Landsharks will have a tough time today—not to mention the confusion they must be feeling. Plus, Alexander Gordon was almost a coach on the field. I predict a loss for the Landsharks."

As predicted by the announcers, the Landsharks were confused and played poorly. They lost by a score of 35 to 0.

Alexander became even more miserable. Fiona tried but could not console him.

"I don't care so much about Guffy," Alexander groaned, "but I've let down my teammates. They are good players and have practiced hard. I wanted to explain to them but Guffy said no."

"Coach Guffy would take ye back in an instant and I will underston ye returning. I wouldna like it but we could stay away from each other until next semester."

"No, I'm not giving in to Guffy. I could never forget him insulting you." Alexander smiled for the first time that day. "Besides, I'd be even more miserable without you—not to mention we'd have to go through this again next football season. No, I'm through with Guffy."

Fiona smiled when Alexander mentioned their relationship continuing.

Coach Guffy was furious, and his anger showed during his red-faced post-game interview. He talked about a lack of dedication to the game and how distractions could ruin potential professional careers. He decried the absence of concentration and communication. He promised to develop new players to fill positions that suddenly became available. However, he did not mention Alexander by name or respond to questions about him. No one dared mention the Viking Princess.

*****

SUNDAY, unable to leave campus, Fiona and Alexander attended a non-denominational service in the Chapel on Campus. They were aware of stares and whispers from the small congregation. Fiona was especially uncomfortable since she often played piano in the chapel. They left as soon as the service ended, grabbed a quick lunch at the small cafeteria, and retreated to the shelter of the lobby in Fiona's dorm.

"Perhaps a few songs on the piano will soothe you, *mo leannan*," Fiona suggested. She sat at the piano and played.

After a few minutes, Alexander said, "I'll get my guitar; the walk will do me good. Then I can accompany you."

"I'll go with ye." Fiona's concern showed in her voice. She wanted to make certain Alexander returned.

"Thank you. I'd appreciate the company, but I don't like the idea of you standing alone outside the boys' dorm while I get the guitar. I'll be right back." Alexander then left the girls' dorm.

As promised, Alexander quickly returned with his guitar. He opened the case and checked the tuning.

"Any problems along the way?"

"Couple of harassing insults, but I ignored them. Teach me a Scottish song."

Fiona thought only a moment before saying, "There's an appropriate song by Robert Burns you should learn: 'A Man's a Man for A' That.'" She played and sang

> Is there for honest Poverty
> That hings his head, an' a' that;
> The coward-slave, we pass him by,
> We dare be poor for a' that!

"Thank you, Fiona. Tomorrow may be a rough day, but I'm not hanging my head. We'll meet tomorrow together."

Chapter 4: Campused

We two have paddled in the stream,
from morning sun till dine;
But seas between us broad have roared
since days of long ago.
--Robert Burns

WITH THE FIRST WEEKEND behind them, Fiona prepared to face the new week. *Being Campused is not all that bad—just as Auntie said*, thought Fiona. The daytime routine was nearly normal, except she could not leave campus for anything. Alexander could have left campus but chose not to and stayed by her side. The worst part of being Campused was returning to the dorm by seven o'clock without Alexander. But the worst part of each day was the staring, pointing, whispering, heckling, and sometimes outright insults thrown their way.

On Monday, Fiona and Alexander cut all their classes and waited anxiously for her guardians and his parents to arrive. They did not want to separate and had asked everyone to meet at Fiona's dormitory.

"I must warn ye my uncle, Robert, is overly protective of me—as ye are," explained Fiona to Alexander. "My uncle willna like my being punished, and he will blame ye for it. He willna like that ye are not playing football. I ken this is inconsistent, but that's the way he will view it. My aunt is fun and will flirt with ye, but she is very straightforward. I call her Auntie. In Gaelic, she would be called *piuthat-mathar* because she is my mother's sister.

Auntie sometimes has the gift of second sight—she can predict the future. I wonder whit she will see in ye?"

"Now you have me worried."

"How will your parents take this?"

"My mother is a worrier and will be deeply concerned. My dad is disappointed I'm not playing football, but he will support me in any decision I make. They will both like you very much."

"I hope so. I'm a wee bit nervous but want to ken your parents."

"I'm certain you will like my parents but I'm concerned about your Uncle Robert."

*****

ROBERT JOHNSTON was not looking forward to the day. He did not like being away from the farm and could not enjoy the drive to MU. Fiona was in trouble, and Robert much preferred her to be studying instead of dating Alexander Gordon. Not only had Alexander caused problems for Fiona, but he had also messed up the MU football team and probably the entire season. Not even the prospect of seeing his old classmate, Bill Curry, cheered him up. Besides, Bill was sure to embarrass Robert—he knew and remembered too much.

Ellen and Robert arrived at Fiona's dormitory to find Fiona and Alexander in the lobby waiting for them. Fiona introduced Alexander to Ellen, and she immediately gave him a huge and lingering hug.

Ellen released Alexander, turned to Fiona, and laughed, "I just had to feel those muscles!"

"Auntie!"

Robert pumped Alexander's hand once and gave a gruff "Hello."

Ellen admired the lobby. "This is such a beautiful dormitory. They tore down my old dorm and built this new one right on top of it. You walk the same paths I did back in the day."

Rachel and Malcolm Gordon soon arrived, and all were introduced. Despite Ellen's smiling and occasionally laughing—especially with Alexander—the mood became solemn and business-like. They moved into a corner room off the lobby.

Robert Johnston took the lead. He demanded: "So, what is this all about? We've read the newspaper version and heard the reports on the sports shows. What is going on here?"

"What you've read and heard is substantially correct, Mr. Johnston," answered Alexander. "We've not made a statement to the media, but Coach Guffy insulted Fiona and made sexually explicit and derogatory statements about her. You may consider me foolish, but I will have nothing more to do with Coach Guffy—ever. The Athletic Director has informed us that our case and claims will be thoroughly investigated. Regarding the PDA, I accept complete responsibility. Any punishments should be applied to me."

"At least you are man enough to admit it. You took advantage of being a football hero and Big Man on Campus to entrap this young, inexperienced freshman girl. Now you've complicated the situation by forcing Coach Guffy to kick you off the team. The MU football season is ruined. You should be ashamed of yourself. Now, leave Fiona alone and allow her to overcome her embarrassment. I hope you learn a lesson from this incident."

"Och," Fiona objected, "I was a most willing participant in the PDA, and I'm no embarrassed." Ellen laughed out loud and Fiona blushed.

Malcolm Gordon seemed about to respond to Robert, but Rachel placed her hand on his arm to restrain him.

Alexander took a deep breath. "With all due respect," Alexander said calmly, "I did nothing of the kind, Mr. Johnston.

Fiona does not care about football or my social status. A mutual friend who thought we would like each other introduced us. She was correct. Fiona is not only the most beautiful girl I've ever seen, but she is also the most interesting and fascinating girl I've ever known. I want to know her better. I will not stay away from Fiona unless she asks me to do so. I am not ashamed of myself. Fiona and I have done nothing to be ashamed of or embarrassed about. I would do the same again." He took in Fiona's eyes. "Everything."

"Aye. Please dinna stay away, *mo leannan.*" Fiona had tears in her eyes but was smiling.

Malcolm Gordon chuckled, and Rachel just shook her head.

"Robert," said Ellen, "get control of yourself. Think about what you are saying. Don't make this situation worse."

Alexander continued, "Thank you for coming. We hope, after meeting with you, President Curry will show leniency. Like you, I don't want Fiona punished."

Malcolm Gordon assured, "Colonel Curry will do what is right."

Robert added, "I've known William for many years, and I agree with you, Malcolm. Let's see what his review has discovered and what he recommends."

On the way to their cars, Ellen whispered to Fiona, "I like your Alexander!"

"I kent ye would," she smiled at the thought, My Alexander.

They departed the girl's dormitory for the Main Administration Building.

*****

PRESIDENT CURRY INSTRUCTED HIS RECEPTIONIST to admit the Johnstons, Gordons, Fiona, and Alexander as soon as they arrived. "These are old friends," he added. "I'll be glad to see them again."

President Curry and his wife, Linda, received the visitors in his office. Linda had not met Fiona and Alexander, and they were introduced. Dr. Crawford arrived, and more introductions followed.

Chairs had been arranged around the President's desk. Fiona was careful to sit in a chair near the middle, and Alexander sat beside her. She took his hand.

President Curry addressed the group. "I am delighted to see you all. Thank you for coming. It has been far too many years since we have been together. I cannot believe I have not been a better friend. We must not remain apart for so long again. Now, to get to the business at hand, I'll ask Dr. Crawford to review the issues here."

Dr. Crawford gave her observations, summarized the Campused disciplinary action and noted they did not apply it to guys. She added she could not comment on the discussion between Alexander and Coach Guffy. She pointed out the Athletic Director was investigating the incident separately and noted Coach Guffy had not been invited to this meeting. Dr. Crawford concluded by saying, "We are here today only to review and discuss the PDA and Campused issue."

President Curry added, "First, I'd like a private discussion with the parents and guardians. Fiona and Alexander, would you please leave the room for a few minutes?" They did.

President Curry smiled and confided to the Johnstons and Gordons, "Ellen, Rachel, Robert, Malcolm. Allow me to be less formal and explain more."

"Fiona and Alexander are two of our most prized students. The issues of disciplinary action, demerits and letters in their permanent record were effectively resolved as soon as you agreed to stand for them. They are no longer Campused."

Robert asked, "So, they are not in trouble?"

"No, Robert, Fiona and Alexander are not in trouble," President Curry replied, "and, in fact, were never in as much trouble as Ellen and you were." He grinned at Ellen and Robert.

Ellen jumped up. "I knew you were going to bring that up!" She turned to Rachel and Malcolm. "Robert and I, uh, eloped three months after we met. We returned to school with great difficulty but have been fine ever since." She smiled. "As hard as it may seem to believe, Robert was once young and foolish too."

Malcolm responded, "I knew you'd handle this, Colonel. Thank you."

Rachel added, "Yes, thank you very much. We trust you."

Robert asked, "But isn't there some way you can keep him away from Fiona?"

"You old fool! Are you blind?" ridiculed Ellen. "An army could not keep them separated."

Linda noted, "Ellen, your tongue has not lost its edge, nor have your powers of observation diminished."

President Curry addressed Malcolm, "I wish Alexander was still playing football, but I suspect he will not change his mind. Malcolm, is your son as hard-headed as you were?"

"I'm afraid so, Colonel. Maybe more, especially when he is defending someone based on principle. It would be a character flaw, except he is usually correct."

"In any case, that is another issue. Let us get Fiona and Alexander in here for the good news."

*****

FIONA AND ALEXANDER strolled into President Curry's office, and Alexander pulled their chairs back a few feet from the others. Before anyone could speak, Alexander addressed the group, "We want to reenact this to show you exactly what happened." He and Fiona sat. He strummed his guitar.

132

"On Thursdays, I often practice guitar while sitting on the steps to the main library. It's convenient, and I like the way the guitar sounds outdoors. Sometimes people come and listen for a while. Occasionally, someone will sing. I had not sung until that day, but I learned a new song to sing to Fiona if she came. Now, why an engineer would choose to sing to a music major is another question." He laughed.

"Fiona had never heard me play guitar. After strumming a few songs, I saw Fiona approaching. You might be surprised, but there are not many beautiful six-foot one-inch-tall girls with auburn hair on campus, so I was certain it was Fiona. Some of the crowd stepped aside to allow Fiona to get near." He cleared his throat emotionally.

"There has been a special change in my life, and today is a good day to sing about it.'"

Alexander played the introduction to "Perhaps Love" and, never taking his gaze away from Fiona, sang the first verse. Fiona sang the second verse. They closed the song together.

Alexander and Fiona stood. Taking Fiona's hand in his, Alexander raised their hands high in the air. "Ladies and Gentlemen, Miss Fiona MacDonald." Gazing deeply into each other's eyes, Fiona and Alexander embraced and kissed—feeling this might be their last opportunity for at least two weeks.

Ellen, Rachel, and Linda had tears in their eyes.

Robert coughed loudly, "Ahem!"

Separating from Fiona, Alexander concluded, "That's the way it happened."

"Aye."

President Curry commented, "Thank you for the reenactment, but it was not necessary. You are no longer Campused, and no letters will be placed in your files."

President Curry scrutinized Dr. Crawford and said, pointedly, "Dr. Crawford, since their parents and guardians were present, I suggest their kiss be conveniently overlooked."

Dr. Crawford replied, "What kiss?"

"Linda and I would like to invite everyone to our house for supper tonight," invited President Curry. "I've already arranged for you to stay in our Alumni Inn. Fiona and Alexander, you may spend the night with your parents and guardians. Now is a good time for you to drive to the Alumni Inn and get settled. Supper is at six."

Robert said to Malcolm, "Follow me to the Alumni Inn. We stay there whenever we visit MU."

*****

BUILT ONLY TWO YEARS PREVIOUSLY, the Alumni Inn and Conference Center was one of the premier alumni centers in the nation. Besides conference rooms, the Inn included a hundred bedrooms, with half being luxury suites. The Inn had its own luxury restaurant and swimming pool.

"I'll show you to your suite," Ellen said. "Ours is similar and just down the hall. Robert, would you take our luggage to our suite?"

"I'll help you, sir," Alexander volunteered.

The Gordons had never been to the Alumni Inn and were impressed by their suite and facilities. Ellen opened the curtains and exclaimed, "What a beautiful view. I love the lake!"

Everyone freshened up and returned to their cars. Ellen noticed Alexander and Fiona hand-in-hand and obviously wanting to stay together. "Alexander, why don't you ride with us?" she invited.

Fiona thanked Ellen with her eyes and smile. Robert was not pleased but remained silent as he led the way to the Curry's house. Rachel and Malcolm followed.

The Gordons and Johnstons parked in a small parking lot in front of the house. They stepped onto the large front porch where William and Linda Curry met them at the door.

*****

"WELCOME TO OUR HOME," said President Curry. "Please come in."

"Colonel," said Malcolm. "Your house reminds me of an antebellum mansion in Natchez."

"Only a reproduction—like the furniture you used to build. Do you still enjoy woodworking?"

"Yes, sir. I still tinker with it."

"We do a lot of entertaining, and this house provides the atmosphere and the size. Would you care for a drink before supper?"

"Perhaps a little wine," said Malcolm. "Not like in the old days, Colonel."

Colonel Curry grinned and admitted, "I have cut back as well."

The dining room was spacious, but they had shortened the table to accommodate eight. A server appeared with a bottle of wine and poured a glass for everyone except Fiona and Alexander, who politely declined.

Supper was a gourmet meal featuring grilled catfish fillets. President Curry explained MU was a major researcher and developer in farm-raised catfish. "Also, I know you like it."

The appetizer was a shrimp cocktail with lump crabmeat. A baked potato and asparagus on the side provided the main course. President Curry noted all were grown on the MU farms, except the shrimp and crab were from Oceanport.

Fiona questioned, "This is a fine gourmet meal, but how is it called supper?" Her question launched a discussion about the names used for meals.

Rachel answered, "I was raised poor, and we called the meals breakfast, dinner and supper."

Robert added, "On the farm, the noon meal is the biggest meal of the day, so it is called dinner."

President Curry countered with, "In the military, the noon meal is often the lightest and most quickly prepared meal, so it is called lunch. The evening meal is called dinner."

Malcolm said, "They have always been breakfast, dinner, and supper to me. However, it is my lunch—usually a sandwich— that I take to work.

Ellen explained, "In Scotland, the evening meal is called 'tea' or sometimes 'high tea' if it is more substantial. 'Supper' is more of a late evening snack or takeout meal like fish and chips."

Linda added, "During my visits to England, I learned that meals are breakfast, dinner and tea."

Fiona agreed, "My parents always served breakfast, dinner and tea."

Alexander observed, "When I'm hungry, which is often, I go to the lunch hall where I eat at a dinner table." Everyone laughed.

Fiona said to Alexander, "Ye would love the full Scottish breakfast. It includes eggs, bacon, link sausage, buttered toast, baked beans, tattie scones, porridge, and tea or coffee."

"Sounds great to me! Where can I get it."

"I'll fix it for you someday." Ellen volunteered with a smile.

"Our desert is ice cream," said President Curry. "We are very proud to make ice cream on campus using milk from the MU dairy herd."

✳✳✳✳✳

"BUT DON'T WE HAVE TO BE CAREFUL WITH THE ICE CREAM?" Alexander began with a straight face, "Back in my younger days, "the school cafeteria always served fish on Fridays since Catholics couldn't eat meat on Friday. However, this menu created a problem. It was common knowledge that drinking milk and eating fish created a 'poison' in the stomach. Therefore, each Friday, we had to choose between eating fish and drinking milk! So, the daily bartering during lunch included the fish for milk exchange on

Fridays. Some kids had two pieces of fish; others, two half-pints of milk."

Fiona chuckled. She was becoming familiar with Alexander's sometimes strange sense of humor and deadpan manner of speaking. But Linda asked, "Where in the world did you hear that mixing fish and milk created a poison?"

"Oh, this was one of the many things I learned on the elementary school playground."

Rachel chimed in, "You'd be surprised at how many people seriously believe this. I think it is a carryover from the days without refrigeration."

The supper discussion shifted topics as the older people reminisced about the good old days in the military and college at MU. Fiona and Alexander listened attentively.

*****

AFTER DESSERT, Fiona entertained by playing the piano and singing Scottish ballads.

President Curry teased, "If only Alexander had his guitar, we could have another reenactment! You kids are smart; I give you credit for coming up with the reenactment idea."

Fiona and Alexander were red but smiling at each other.

Linda surmised, "I wish I had been there for the original performance. It must have been beautiful. Those who were there—and by now many claim to have been present—say it was the most romantic scene they had ever witnessed—better than a movie even.

Fiona and Alexander were both red-faced but smiling at each other.

Alexander explained, "I first sang a solo to Fiona. I was tempted to claim I had written the song—good thing I did not because Fiona already knew it. I was lucky—it was one of her favorite songs. Later, she rearranged the song to become a true duet, and we practiced it a few times—minus the finale, of course."

"Actually, I first sang to Alexander at oor Meet and Greet Social," Fiona said with a smile. "But I dinna think he realized it." She played and sang "My Love is Like a Red, Red Rose."

At the mention of the Meet and Greet, Alexander turned scarlet. He smiled through his redness at Fiona and mouthed, "Thank you."

*****

DESPITE THE REUNION ATMOSPHERE and problems solved, Robert had such a strained and severe expression that President Curry pulled him aside. "Robert, ease up. Alexander is a fine young man. You should be pleased he and Fiona are interested in each other."

"Fiona is so young and inexperienced. She lost both parents only three years ago. With no children of my own and having made my share of mistakes, I just want the best for Fiona."

"Then you want Alexander Gordon. If you do not believe me, ask Ellen."

They spotted Ellen in animated conversation and laughing with Alexander and Fiona as Linda and the Gordons looked on. Alexander was saying, "... well, I was stunned..."

"I don't know, Bill," said Robert. "This is all happening so quickly. I just can't get comfortable with it."

"Relax. You were young once yourself."

"I know—that's why I'm worried."

"Forgive me, Robert, but I remember you well, and although Alexander matches your youthful stubbornness, he is more mature and considerate. Give him a chance."

Linda laughed her way over to William and Robert. "I just heard the funniest story about when Fiona and Alexander first met. I love it! What a couple!"

About nine o'clock, Rachel suggested, "It's getting late, and we should return to our room. Fiona, you and Alexander can ride with us on the return."

*****

MALCOLM TURNED TO ROBERT IN THE ALUMNI INN'S ELEVATOR, "Robert, how about a nightcap?".

"Sounds good to me. It's been a long day."

"It began a little rocky but is smooth now. Let's relax."

In his built-in kitchen, Malcolm took out a bottle of Jack Daniel's bourbon, six glasses and soda.

"Ellen drinks only Scotch," said Robert with a grin.

"Mackenzie Scotch," corrected Ellen.

"Ellen's grandfather founded a distillery near Inverness to make what you call Scotch, but they call Scotch whisky—that's spelled 'w h I s k y' without an 'e.' Scots call it the 'water of life.'"

"My brother manages the distillery now," Ellen added.

"I think I worked there as a child," Fiona said.

"I don't care for Scotch," replied Malcolm. "Plus, it is very expensive."

"I'll get you some Mackenzie Scotch," offered Ellen. "Tonight, I'll have a glass of wine."

"I'm not too proud to drink bourbon," laughed Robert.

Alexander asked Fiona with his eyes and she shook her head. "Just soda for us, Dad."

While the Johnstons and Gordons sat around the table drinking, Fiona and Alexander were on the couch. Alexander sat on the right-hand side of the sofa with Fiona near him towards the middle. He put his left arm around Fiona's shoulder. A delicate hint of her perfume remained. The Johnstons and Gordons relived the day with occasional references to their own younger days. Fiona was behind Robert and in the corner of Ellen's eye.

Fiona murmured to Alexander, "I feel relieved, noo. Safe. Secure. At peace." She leaned against him, her eyes sleepily closing.

As they finished their drinks, Robert said, "I've enjoyed meeting you. Thank you for the drinks. We should go to our own room."

Almost unwilling to wake her, Ellen spoke softly, "Fiona, we must leave now."

Fiona dreamily responded, "Good night. See ye in the morn." She turned toward Alexander and put her left arm over his chest. She rolled even more towards him and put her left leg partially over his while purring, "Mmmm."

Robert said abruptly, "Fiona, you can't stay here. Come with us." Ellen was trying not to laugh but had to turn away.

Startled, Fiona jumped up and surveyed the room. "Och, I'm sorry. I must have dozed off. I dinna ken."

"I'll walk you down the hall," Alexander offered as the Johnstons left Gordon's room.

Robert blurted, "That will not be necessary," but Alexander accompanied Fiona all the same. They entered the Johnston's suite.

Ellen spoke knowingly to Robert, "You should come to bed now." He hesitated but sulked into their bedroom, leaving Fiona with Alexander.

Alexander whispered to Fiona, "Do you recall my promise to you a few days ago?"

Fiona fixed her eyes on Alexander in anticipation. "I do indeed."

"Do you want to take me up on it?"

"I do indeed." She stepped close to Alexander. She was wide awake now, her green eyes sparkled, and she radiated heat.

"In sports, I learned that, before attempting to break a record, one should get properly warmed up." Alexander kissed

Fiona on the cheek, then tasted her long neck, then kissed her cheek again before their lips met.

*****

THE NEXT MORNING, before joining the Gordons for breakfast and departing for home, Ellen slipped quietly into Fiona's bedroom. Fiona was touching up her makeup. *For Alexander,* Ellen thought. *What a difference he has already made in her life. Well, I must ask her.*

"Fiona, last night, did you intend to spend the entire night with Alexander?"

"No, ma'am, I didna <u>plan</u> to. It was just that, for the first time in several days, I wasna stressed out. I dinna ken whit came over me, but, aye, I would have stayed. There's no point in denying it. I hope his parents dinna think badly of me."

"Alexander's parents love you. Don't worry. We all realized what was happening—well, maybe not your uncle. Come, let's join the others for breakfast."

*****

ALEXANDER PACKED HIS PARENT'S CAR for their drive home and then joined everyone for breakfast. The aroma of bacon and coffee dominated the restaurant atmosphere.

Alexander was starving and ate a huge breakfast of pancakes, a western omelet, bacon, grits, and biscuits, along with orange juice and coffee. On realizing his appetite, he remarked, "I feel like I haven't eaten in days, and this is much better than our usual cafeteria food."

Fiona smiled at Alexander. "It must take a lot of energy to break a record."

Alexander reddened at their inside joke and winked at Fiona.

141

Fiona turned to Alexander's dad and changed the subject. "Alexander telt me your grandmother named you after her Scottish ancestors. Are you a genealogist?"

Malcolm replied, "Just beginning the hobby. My uncle drew a remarkable family tree after he retired from the telephone company. I became custodian of his charts and am now attempting to extend them. The Gordons came to America after being defeated at Culloden. I have information on them and their descendants but not much information on the Gordon family before they came to America."

"Clan Gordon was a proud and fierce Highlander Clan," Fiona noted. "I'll see if I can find more information for ye."

"Thank you. I'm new to this, and getting information from Scotland is difficult."

Their breakfast over, Rachel and Malcolm excused themselves to begin their homeward travels.

"I've so enjoyed meeting ye," Fiona said to Rachel and Malcolm. "*Moran taing* for coming and helping us. Ye've even helped me underston Alexander a wee bit." She blushed and giggled.

"Pleased to have met you," Robert said to the Gordons. "Have a good trip home."

Ellen said to Rachel, "You must be enormously proud of Alexander. He is a wonderful young man. I'm pleased he and Fiona are fond of each other. I'm delighted to have met you and expect we will spend time together in the future."

Rachel agreed, "I'm glad we've met. Fiona is a beautiful and wonderful girl. I really like her. I'm glad they are dating."

Alongside his dad on their way to his car, Alexander said, "Thanks for coming, Dad. Your being here solved a major problem for Fiona and me. Also, I enjoyed meeting President Curry. He is a fine man—as you've always said."

"Do you think you'll ever play football again?"

"Not for Guffy, and I'm not transferring as long as Fiona is here."

"I understand. Fiona certainly is a beautiful girl—in every way. I'm glad to have met her. Now, you know your sisters, I must ask, is it OK to call Fiona your girlfriend?"

Alexander stopped. He had never called any of his dates "girlfriend" but everyone referred to Fiona that way. *What do Fiona's friends call me?* He began walking again. "Yes, sir. Fiona is my girlfriend."

*****

THE GORDONS DROVE AWAY. Fiona, Alexander and the Johnstons returned to their breakfast table. Alexander eyed the last biscuit.

"Auntie," asked Fiona, "I need to go to oor room and freshen up before class. Can I put my things in your car?"

"I'll help you," Alexander volunteered and left the biscuit untouched.

"Robert, let's drink another cup of coffee," Ellen smiled. "You can finish reading your paper down here."

Robert grunted but returned to their table.

Once inside the Johnston's room, Fiona gazed deeply into Alexander's eyes and cooed, "Do ye have enough energy noo for another attempt at a record?"

He did.

Fiona and Alexander returned to the breakfast table just in time to hear Robert ask Ellen, "Where are those kids? It doesn't take that long to pack the car."

"Don't worry. They'll be here soon enough." Ellen smiled knowingly.

Fiona rushed to them and apologized through her blush. "Sorry for the delay. We've put my things into the car. Would ye drop them off at my dorm? *Moran taing*! You've turned oor punishment into a wonderful time."

Alexander extended his hand to Robert. "I'm pleased to have met you, Mr. Johnston. I hope we will meet again soon and become better acquainted."

Robert shook Alexander's hand briefly and said, "Good to have met you."

Alexander turned to Ellen. "I'm so pleased to have met you, Mrs. Johnston, and to discover all the wonderful things Fiona said about you are true. I hope to see you again soon."

Ellen agreed with Alexander, "I'm sure we will see more of each other." She hugged Alexander, choked, and whispered in his ear, "Take care of Fiona."

"I will," he whispered in return.

Robert said to Ellen, "I'm going to talk to Coach Guffy."

"You be careful, Robert. Don't cause any additional trouble. I want to visit my friend Betty at the Chapel on Campus."

Fiona gave her aunt and uncle a goodbye hug. "Alexander will walk me to class."

*****

AT THE CHAPEL ON CAMPUS, Ellen knocked on the door showing the title "Chapel Manager" and peeked inside. "Betty?"

"Ellen!"

They hugged as old friends do who haven't seen one another in a long time.

"Betty, you look wonderful. How are you?"

"I'm doing well. I like my job very much and before I forget, thank you for your support. Your donations helped us to not only keep the doors open but to renovate a bit. I'll show you. But first, what brings you here?"

"My niece, Fiona."

"Oh, I've met her. Your niece is beautiful and talented. She sings and plays for us sometimes. She favors you, only taller."

"Thank you; that's quite a compliment. Fiona looks almost exactly like my sister, Aileen, her mother. Aileen was killed in an automobile accident three years ago. She was gorgeous and only a little shorter than Fiona. I promise you, if it were possible for Aileen and Fiona to enter a room together now, all male activity in that room would cease."

Betty laughed. "What can I do for you and Fiona?"

"I want to reserve the chapel for a late June wedding."

"A wedding? How wonderful! I suppose I've seen Fiona with her fiancée but didn't realize it. He is handsome and popular. They are a beautiful couple. When did they become engaged?"

"They're not engaged—yet. In fact, they've only known each other for two weeks. I just hope they don't elope before June." Ellen laughed and blushed.

Betty remembered Ellen's elopement and giggled. "Ellen, you have always been amazingly prescient, but you will have outdone yourself if you are this correct. I don't know how you do it, but I have great faith in you. Let's check what's available."

Betty took out her planner for the Chapel. "How about June 28th?"

Ellen choked. "That is perfect. June 28th was her mother's wedding date. Please reserve it and don't tell anyone I've done this—especially Fiona. You may tell Fiona only when she personally comes to see you to schedule her wedding."

"Consider it done."

Ellen continued, "I'll give you a deposit."

Betty laughed. "You've donated so much that a deposit is not required. Now let me show you around the chapel."

*****

AT THE MU SPORTS COMPLEX, ROBERT introduced himself to the receptionist and asked to see Coach Guffy. She disappeared for a moment before returning. "I'm sorry. Coach Guffy is a very busy man and cannot see you now."

Robert said gruffly, "Tell that sorry SOB I am Fiona MacDonald's uncle."

The receptionist disappeared again, returned, and said, "Please come in."

Coach Guffy stood to shake Robert's hand, but Robert did not grasp it.

Guffy began, "Obvious, ya are upset with me, but Ah am upset too. Ah'm sorry to say this, but Ah don't have a good opinion 'bout ya niece. She cost me the bes' player Ah ever had and probably the best season Ah could've. She cost Alexander Gordon a high-paying career in pro football. This shouldn't surpris' ya. Ah expect she caused ya other problems as well. Alexander probably was gettin' much more than that kiss ever'one is talkin' about."

"I wanted to see you personally and verify what Fiona and Alexander told me," Robert retorted. "I want you to know I will do my best to have you fired—and soon." Robert left the building fuming and making plans.

Chapter 5: Getting Away

Some hae meat and canna eat,
And some wad eat that want it.
But we hae meat, and we can eat,
Sae let the Lord be thankit.
--Robert Burns

AT THE WORKBENCH in Dr. Southern's handicraft shop, Alexander Gordon carefully bent the jump rings into place on each side of the pendant. It was a simple gold necklace with a dainty curb-style chain and spring-ring clasp. The pendant had intertwined letters "AF" which Alexander had formed from gold wire as instructed by Dr. Southern. Alexander considered his subtle but meaningful message. *If she declines it, then at least I'll know.*

"Thank you, Dr. Southern, for helping with my little project."

Dr. Tom Southern was a Professor of Industrial Engineering but also taught handicrafts, especially intricate details. He had previously helped Alexander with one of his inventions.

"Anytime, Alexander. Here, put it in this flat rectangular box and give me that ring box. I'm sure your girlfriend will love it, but you don't want to give her the wrong idea." He grinned.

Alexander placed the necklace in the rectangular box and put the box in his pocket. *Be patient and wait for the right opportunity.*

* * * * *

ELLEN JOHNSTON'S PHONE RANG, and she took the call in her kitchen.

"Auntie? It's Fiona."

"Well, hello, Honey. Are you OK?" *Fiona sounded worried. Something was about to happen or change.*

"Aye, everything is getting better here. Not back to normal, but better."

Ellen breathed a sigh of relief. So much was going on in her young niece's life. Ellen recalled the stress of her early days with Robert and shook her head to clear it.

"Auntie, can I come home for the weekend?"

"Of course. Is there a problem with Alexander?"

"No, we're fine. I feel the need to get away from campus, but not from Alexander. In fact, I want to bring him with me. There is a home football game, and he would be better off not being on campus. Can he come with me?"

"Of course. I'll be glad to see Alexander again. Maybe Robert will be a little more accepting." *Or at least begin to accept.*

"We'll be there Friday night after supper."

"I'll prepare the spare bedroom," Ellen smirked, but Fiona did not comment.

Ellen entered their living room. "Robert, Fiona is coming home for the weekend. She said the situation at MU is improving but she still needed a break from the harassment."

"Good. Being here will also get her away from that Alexander guy."

"Fiona is bringing Alexander with her."

Robert muttered, "I'm the one that needs a break."

*****

AFTER HANGING UP HER PHONE, Fiona pulled her suitcase from beneath her bed, placed it on the bed, and began packing. Jane came in and gave her a quizzical look.

148

"Jane, I'm going home for the weekend," Fiona explained. "I need to get away for a few days. I'll be back late Sunday."

"Who are you riding with?"

Freshmen could not have cars on campus.

"Alexander is taking me. He will spend the weekend on the farm." Fiona understood the reason for Jane's question.

"So, taking the boyfriend home to meet the family?" Jane teased. "Sounds serious."

Fiona smiled at the 'boyfriend' word. She liked that people recognized Alexander her boyfriend. *What did he call her?*

"Ye ken they've already met."

"Yes, but that was different. A girl should not invite her boyfriend to meet her parents until they've been dating for at least five or six months. You've begun a new chapter in your life, and you know it."

"Maybe. We'll see."

"Well, I can see, and I think you can too!"

The speaker in Fiona's room crackled. "Fiona, your ride is here. Be sure to sign out."

Fiona smiled. She loved Alexander's customized truck, and now they would spend the weekend together.

"I'll be back late Sunday, Jane. Enjoy your weekend."

"And you."

*****

ALEXANDER ENTERED THEIR ROOM to find Donnie lying in bed reading a hunting magazine. "Shouldn't you be studying?" Alexander teased.

"Man does not live by study alone," Donnie misquoted. "I'm getting psyched up for deer season."

"Where would we put it if you killed one?"

"The antlers could go over Farrah's poster. I bet she'd like that."

Alexander got his suitcase from beneath his bed and began putting in clothes and personal effects.

"Heading out?" asked Donnie.

"I'm getting away for the weekend. Fiona invited me to spend the weekend at her aunt and uncle's farm. It should be a good break."

"I'll bet that makes her uncle happy."

"Well, at least this is my chance to win him over—I hope." Alexander carefully placed his guitar in its case.

"More serenading?" Donnie teased. "Didn't learn your lesson?"

"Fiona likes my playing and singing. Maybe we'll learn a duet."

"Isn't it a little soon to be spending the weekend with the girlfriend's parents?"

Alexander would have denied the "girlfriend" tag, but the 'AF' necklace was burning a hole in his pocket. Besides, Donnie would ridicule him even without being aware of the necklace.

"They are her guardians."

"Well, they'd better guard her against you. Say, if you don't come back, can I have your pocket slide rule?"

"See you Sunday night."

"Unless her old man kills you."

*****

INSIDE HIS TRUCK WITH FIONA, Alexander conceded, "This is a good idea. I hadn't realized how much I needed to get away until now." *Boy, do I!*

"I needed to get away from campus but not from ye."

"And I'm glad to be away from the game tomorrow."

"I thought ye would be."

"Since the game is not being televised, I won't be tempted to watch it." *Not even a little bit.*

"Uncle will have it tuned in on the radio."

"Speaking of your uncle, we have a couple of hours for you to tell me more about him. I know he doesn't like me, and I need to win him over."

"Uncle Robert is a genuinely nice man and an exceptionally good man. It's no that he doesna like ye, having no children of his own, he is overly protective of me and, for that matter, Auntie. He majored in agriculture at MU..."

During their drive, Alexander also learned more about Fiona's ancestors in Scotland. Her maternal grandfather had an estate east of Aberdeen. The MacKenzie Estate was deteriorating, and the land was now being leased for grazing sheep. Fiona smiled as she recalled the old house and hiking around the estate. She spoke of having "bagged" several nearby Munros—Scottish mountains—and explained she had climbed them.

Fiona's maternal great-grandfather had founded the whiskey distillery near Inverness. Her uncle, James, managed the distillery. Fiona laughed. "I worked in the distillery. As a child, I turned the germinated barley."

Fiona's family was wealthy. How would this affect their relationship?

*****

ARRIVING AT THE JOHNSTON FARM, Alexander heard the dog before seeing the tan and white furry blur race around his truck. He jammed on the brakes. The wheels had scarcely stopped turning before Fiona squealed, "Burnsie!" and jumped out. The dog was quickly in her arms.

Alexander hesitated a bit in the safety of his truck, then got out slowly and cautiously crossed over to the passenger side, where Fiona was petting, hugging, and kissing the dog. "Oh, Burnsie, Burnsie! How I've missed ye." The dog was peering over Fiona's shoulder and through her hair while evaluating Alexander.

Alexander thought the dog was gloating at him, and pangs stirred inside. *Was this jealousy?*

"Come, Burnsie and I'll introduce ye to Alexander."

"I didn't know your aunt and uncle had a dog. Natural, I suppose, on a farm."

"Burnsie is mine—all mine, aren't ye, Burnsie? Oh, I'm so glad to hold ye again. I love ye that much."

"Burnsie, this is Alexander. He is my, um, friend. Say hello."

Burnsie barked once, sat up, and held out his paw.

Alexander squatted, took Burnsie's paw, and said, "Hello, Burnsie. Nice to meet you." *I'm talking to a dog!*

"Burnsie is a Sheltie—a sheepdog from the Shetland Islands off the coast of Scotland. I got him a few weeks after arriving in the States. He was a tiny puppy but waddled right up to me at the kennel. I was so sad and lonely until I got Burnsie. I've missed him so much!"

"Burnsie? That's a new name to me."

"His registered name is 'The Poet Robert Burns' after the Scottish poet."

"Ah, makes sense." *Of course, a Scottish dog and Scottish poet.*

"Burnsie is very protective. Best to let him smell your hand now."

Alexander slowly placed his hand near Burnsie's nose. Burnsie sniffed, then licked Alexander's hand and peered up at Fiona.

"He likes ye! Och, I'm so glad. I thought he would like ye, but I didna ken."

Alexander wondered about his status should Burnsie not have liked him. *I'd probably be on my way back to MU.* He carefully stroked Burnsie's head. "Good dog."

"He doesna like to be called a dog. Call him Burnsie."

Alexander lifted Fiona's suitcase from the truck bed. They stepped onto the porch and up to the door with Burnsie close behind. Fiona opened the door and called out, "Auntie! Uncle!" Ellen and Robert quickly appeared, and Fiona hugged them. Ellen hugged Alexander; Robert gave his hand a quick shake.

Fiona suggested, "We've already had supper. Let us get settled, and then we'll tell you all about the rest of last week." Alexander picked up Fiona's suitcase and followed her.

As Alexander guessed, Fiona's bedroom was extraordinarily feminine—pink, frilly, and fluffy, with floral perfume. Pictures of Scotland, a portrait of Robert Burns and quotes from his poems lined the walls.

"Is this a picture of you as a baby?"

"Yes, and that's Mum holding me."

"Of course it is. You look just like her. She's beautiful."

"*Cuideigin a nì flatter!*" Fiona smiled and squeezed his arm.

Alexander deposited Fiona's luggage in her room, returned to his truck, and retrieved his suitcase and guitar.

"I'm so glad to see you," Ellen said. "Let me show you to your room."

Alexander found that to get from his bedroom to Fiona's bedroom, he would have to pass through the living room and the kitchen and go past Ellen and Robert's bedroom. He and Fiona were on opposite sides of the house.

Back in the living room, Robert updated Alexander. "Before leaving the campus on Monday, I visited Coach Guffy. I now accept your description of Guffy's words and your evaluation of Guffy. Others have concurred. Just wanted you to know."

"Thank you, sir." *Well, there's the first step.*

Ellen added, "I toured the Chapel on Campus. The renovations have restored it to its original beauty."

Fiona updated her aunt and uncle regarding the harassment they were being subjected to on campus. "It's awful—for Alexander and for me. The name-calling, the stares, the whispers. I can only imagine whit Alexander must go through. He won't tell me."

"Pretty tough, some days," Alexander acknowledged. "But people will tire of it, and we'll be OK, eventually. Our friends are supporting us and contradicting the rumors and outright lies."

A little later, Fiona said, "*It's a braw bricht moonlit nicht the nicht.*"

Alexander raised his eyebrows for an interpretation.

"It's a brilliant, moonlight night tonight. Let's go out on the porch and sit in the swing."

"Let me get my guitar."

"Robert, it is past our bedtime," said Ellen. Let's leave these young folks to themselves."

Sitting in the swing with Fiona near, Alexander was intimately aware of her flowery perfume blending with the aroma of the rural night. "I can't begin to tell you how happy I am to have met you," he began, "and how pleased I am to be here—or anywhere—with you. But let me try this:"

Alexander strummed his guitar a few strokes, then sang, "I'll have to say I love you in a song." "I love you, Fiona. Simple, but there's no other way to say it. I love you."

Teary-eyed, Fiona answered, "I love you, Alexander Malcolm Gordon." She leaned into him, and they kissed tenderly.

*****

AT BREAKFAST THE NEXT DAY, Ellen commented, "Alexander, I know how much you love a big breakfast. I've put together the best Americanized version of a full Scottish breakfast I could manage. Here's your coffee. Start with scones and parritch.

"Parritch?" questioned Alexander.

"Oatmeal. In Gaelic it is *leite.*" answered Fiona. "I eat parritch every morning but must make it with rolled oats instead of Scottish oats. *Ith do leor!*—eat your fill."

"I didn't think you could cook in your room."

"I canna. I soak the oats overnight in water and eat it cold with fruit. Without soaking overnight, oats and cold water is called drammach. I prefer to soak it."

There followed eggs, bacon, square-shaped sausage patties, buttered toast, and baked beans.

Finally finished, Alexander groaned, "I'm stuffed. Mr. Johnston, does she do this every morning?"

"Most mornings I have cereal, toast and coffee, which I make for myself while Ellen and Fiona are sleeping."

Alexander laughed.

Robert continued, "Since you are here, could you help me with a few chores on the farm? I need some additional muscle."

"I'll be happy to help and earn my keep, but you may have to show me what to do."

Alexander followed Robert outside while Fiona helped her aunt clear the table and clean the dishes. Ellen smiled as she said, "You know, Fiona, that the way to a man's heart is through his stomach. Of course, there are other ways as well!"

"Auntie!"

"Well, it's true. Now tell me more about your young man."

"Auntie, he's not my young man."

"Fiona, I've seen the way he looks at you, and I've seen the way you look at him. He's yours all right, and you are his. Now tell me more about Alexander."

"Last night," Fiona smiled, "Alexander telt me he loved me."

"And?"

"I telt him I love him—and I do."

With tears in her eyes, Ellen opened her arms to Fiona and hugged her.

*****

IN THE WOODYARD, ROBERT ASKED ALEXANDER, "Do you know how to use an axe?" and handed him one.

Alexander recognized it as a splitting maul and was glad to have used one on his aunt's farm. "A little, but show me the best way."

Robert instructed, "First, put on these gloves and safety glasses. Put one of these short logs vertically on the chopping block—not on the ground. Hold the axe with your left hand near the bottom and your right hand near the middle. Allow your right hand to slide down the handle as you swing the axe. Put your feet apart and swing so that if you miss, you won't hit your leg. Gauge your distance to the log by extending your arm and axe before you swing. If there is already some kind of crack in the log, try to hit it. I'll show you." Robert split a log into two pieces and then split each half again. "Here, your turn." He handed the maul to Alexander.

Alexander followed Robert's instructions and successfully split a log—as he knew he could.

Robert congratulated him, "Good. You've got it. Now get to work on that pile of logs while I check on a few other chores."

Robert returned an hour later. Alexander was sweating, but he enjoyed splitting the logs—he worked out his frustrations on them.

Robert asked Alexander, "Ever use a posthole digger?"

"Yes, sir. Not a lot, but I have used one."

"There are a few holes I need dug." He led Alexander to a fence that needed repair and handed him a post-hole digger. "I've already marked the locations of the holes. Make the holes about two feet deep. I'll be back after a while."

Alexander moved to the location of the first hole. He stood directly over the hole location with his feet spread apart the width of his shoulders. He squeezed the two handles together to open the blades. Raising the digger high, he drove the blades down into the dirt. He pulled the handles apart to close the blades and capture the dirt. He lifted the digger out of the hole with the dirt between the closed blades. Moving the digger to the side of the hole, Alexander opened the blades by pushing the handles together, and the dirt dropped out. He repeated the process until the hole was about two feet deep. Another workout.

Robert returned, inspected the holes, and congratulated Alexander. "Good work. How about a little fun? Can you shoot a gun?"

"Yes, sir. I enjoy target shooting."

"Well, let's see how good you are." Robert led Alexander to an old Jeep.

They got in, and Robert drove about a quarter of a mile away to the entrance of a gully.

"We can shoot inside that gully." Robert placed a few tin cans on top of a wooden rail and returned to the truck. He reached into a gun bag and handed Alexander a Colt 1911 semi-automatic pistol.

Alexander performed a quick safety check of the pistol, then noted, "My dad has a 1911A like this. In World War II, while stationed on a small island, he had the only 45 ACP, but every month, a case of ammunition arrived. He learned to shoot with either hand. He's a good shot and taught me."

Robert handed Alexander a magazine and challenged, "See if you can hit one of those cans."

Alexander racked the slide, aimed at a can, shot it, and then rapidly shot and hit a second can. More carefully, he aimed at the third can, shot and hit it, then quickly shot it again as it rolled on the ground. Alexander put the pistol on safety, smiled at Robert and remarked, "Your turn."

"No, you can finish that magazine." Alexander quickly and accurately fired the pistol at the last three cans.

Robert complimented, "That was some fine shooting."

"Thank you, sir. I enjoy shooting but have not had the opportunity for a while."

"How long have you been shooting?"

"The first time I ever shot a gun was at my aunt's farm. I was two years old. The men had been out hunting and leaned their shotguns against the wall when they returned. The safety was off on one of the double-barreled 12 gauge shotguns, and I pulled both triggers. Needless to say, this blew a huge hole into the wall. I strutted into the kitchen and proudly bragged, 'Me tot ta totgun!' Of course, I don't remember this at all, but it has become family lore."

"You were lucky!"

"I'll say!"

They got into the Jeep and returned to the house.

Alexander thought, *I'm making progress!*

✶✶✶✶✶

THE MEN CAME IN for the mid-day meal, and Ellen remarked, "You've been working hard, so Fiona and I made a large <u>dinner</u>." She asserted, "Fiona is well on her way to becoming an excellent cook." Fiona flushed at the obvious implication of her aunt's compliment.

The warm aroma of a workingman's meal filled the dining room: meatloaf, mashed potatoes, lima beans, and yeast rolls with lots of iced tea to drink and apple pie to top it off. Burnsie's tongue was hanging out in anticipation of getting his share.

They had just begun eating when Robert advised, "You've both talked about how much stress you are feeling. Here are some suggestions that might help. Alexander, I know how much you love football and that you could be a successful professional—not to mention how much money you might earn. Ellen and I are MU alumni, and we love MU. However, suppose you transfer to another university? In that case, you could still play football and also get away from Guffy and the heckling at MU."

Robert turned to Fiona. "Fiona, you could get away from the heckling and stress at MU by transferring to another university too. I know how much you love Scotland. I would miss you, but you might even return to Scotland."

Ellen scowled at Robert in disbelief, but before she could say anything, Fiona sprang to her feet. Giving Robert a stern face, she exploded, "Uncle Robert, ye ken how much I love ye and appreciate everything ye do for me. Ye not only took me in, but sheltered and loved me. I ken ye think ye have my best interests at heart. But ye are wrong, *bràthair màthaireil*."

Alexander had never seen Fiona angry, but she clearly was. Her face was flushed and glistening. Tears dripped from her cheeks and splattered on the tablecloth.

Fiona continued, her voice rising, "If Alexander transfers to play football or for any other reason, I will go with him. If I am forced to transfer or return to Scotland, I will ask Alexander to come with me."

Alexander interjected, "You don't even need to ask."

Fiona's voice cracked as she demanded, "Am I making myself perfectly clear?" She gasped, "Och, och," more tears flowed, and she stomped out. Burnsie followed.

Alexander rose and glanced at Ellen. She nodded, and he left the dining table to find Fiona.

In the dining room, Ellen shook her head and angrily addressed Robert, "You old fool. Are you trying to get rid of Fiona? That is what you are doing. They are in love, and they will find a way to stay together."

Robert objected, "They are too young and haven't known each other long enough."

".... says the man who asked me for a date an hour after we met and then proposed three months later."

"We were older and more mature."

"We were the same age and only thought we were mature."

"Well, it's worked out well for us."

"... and it will work out well for Fiona and Alexander as well. Give them some time, or they will take it."

"On Monday, William Curry recommended I ease up on Alexander. I told him I only wanted the best for Fiona. He said that meant Alexander, and if I didn't believe him, I should ask you. What is your opinion?"

"They are meant for each other."

"Ellen, I love you very much."

"And I love you too, Robert—even though you are still an old fool."

*****

ALEXANDER FOUND FIONA SOBBING in the kitchen with Burnsie whining in sympathy. He gently placed his arms around her. "Fiona."

Fiona was trembling. Between sobs, she fumed, "I canna believe whit I just did. I've not only made a fool of myself, but I've made a fool of myself in front of ye."

Alexander assured her, "You're no fool. I love you very much."

"And I love ye, *mo leannan*."

"Let's consider our options," Alexander suggested. "We can leave here right now and go anywhere you want—together. Another school, Scotland—anywhere. Or I can leave and let you patch things up with your uncle without me; we'll see each other again Sunday night. Or we can go back into the dining room together, and you can apologize—if that's what you want—to your uncle."

"Engineers and logic! Och, Aye, let's return to the dining room."

Alexander put his arm around Fiona, and they returned to the dining room. Burnsie followed.

Fiona was about to speak as they entered the dining room, but Robert interrupted, "Me first. I apologize to everyone. I'm terribly sorry for what I said. As Ellen reminded me, I am indeed an old fool. Please forget all those stupid things I said and forgive me."

Fiona stepped around the table and hugged her uncle.

Ellen recommended, "Let's eat before dinner gets cold."

*****

AS THEY WERE EATING APPLE PIE, Alexander said, "While we're together, there is something I should share. Fiona, you don't know about this but don't worry, it's a good thing. I hope I can explain without bragging too much." Alexander took a deep breath and continued, "Although I live modestly, I have a good income and money in the bank."

Fiona smiled at him. "Alexander, I ken ye have money."

"How? Mary?"

"Mary did not need to tell me. It's obvious. Aye, ye live in an auld dormitory and eat in the cafeteria, but look at ye. The watch ye wear. Your 'auld' truck probably cost more than a new luxury car. Your clothes are tailored to fit those muscles." Fiona's cheeks were rosy. "I dinna think I've spent a dime since we met. Ye are always picking up the tab, not just for me but for everyone."

"So, you knew?"

"I learnt quickly, but it doesna matter to me. I love ye despite your money, not because of it."

The significance of Fiona's profession did not occur to Robert until much later, but Ellen caught it immediately, and Alexander beamed.

"You've caught me living a lie!" Alexander laughed. "I might as well confess."

"I like science fiction, especially time travel stories. While in high school, I wrote a series of short stories about time travel. Although the stories were simple and the writing sophomoric, my stories were just right for television. A TV producer bought my stories, and they are now running on television. You may have seen the TV series 'Travels to History.' It is about the invention of a time machine and a group of historians and scientists who use it to go back in time and adjust to improve the future."

"I've seen it," acknowledged Robert. "It's a good show."

"Thank you. Anyway, I sold those stories and get a regular royalty from the TV series. That royalty should continue for several years and perhaps more if the series goes into syndication."

Alexander continued, "But my goal is to be an inventor and have my own research company. I recently got a patent on a mechanical seal similar to an automobile water pump seal except made from thin metal sheets. My latest and most lucrative project is ultrasonic atomization. Ultrasonic atomization uses high-frequency sound to vaporize liquids. I can apply ultrasonic atomization in the carburetor of a gasoline engine."

In a strong accent, Ellen interjected, "Ma heid's mince."

Alexander turned questioningly to Fiona, who explained, "She is saying this is confusing."

Alexander chuckled. "Don't worry, I won't describe the details. My device improves both the power and efficiency of an automobile engine. In particular, gas mileage increases by about 30%. I got a patent and licensed a manufacturer. Installation kits are selling, and Ford has bought a license to use my device next year. My ultrasonic atomizer has generated a nice down payment and an ongoing royalty."

Robert responded, somewhat sarcastically, "Sounds like you are well on your way to becoming a millionaire."

"I already am a millionaire, sir."

Fiona, her eyes gleaming with pride, said, "This is like the goals ye described the day we met."

"It was so easy to talk to you. I surprised myself by telling you those things—goals I'd never expressed to anyone else."

"At any rate, Mr. Johnston, what I'm coming to is that I've not wanted to be a professional athlete since about ninth grade even though I sincerely love competitive sports."

"Thank you for sharing this," replied Robert. "Now I can better grasp your situation and goals."

Alexander concluded, "Mrs. Johnston and Fiona, that was a fabulous meal. Thank you. Now, allow me to clear the table and do the dishes."

Fiona said, "Ye dinna ken where things are located. I'll help ye. Auntie, ye can rest."

Ellen smiled.

Robert added, "Nap time for me." He and Ellen moved into the living room.

*****

AFTER A FEW MINUTES, Robert pointed out to Ellen, "No dishes rattling around in there. I better go check on them." He stood up.

"Don't you dare, Robert Johnston. I'll check." Ellen stepped to the kitchen doorway to see Fiona and Alexander locked in an embrace. Ellen returned to the living room, smiling.

"They're fine. Go back to sleep."

"Are you sure? What if..."

"I'm sure, you old fool." Ellen grinned. "I remember when you were a young fool. Do you?"

"Yes, I remember all too well, and that's what troubles me." Robert laughed despite himself.

"Go back to sleep," Ellen repeated.

A dish rattled in the kitchen, and Robert relaxed.

*****

IN THE KITCHEN, FIONA TWIRLED THE PLATE AGAIN. She laughed at it rattling on the countertop and returned to Alexander's arms.

With the dishes finally in the dishwasher, Fiona and Alexander returned to the living room. Robert was napping. Ellen suggested, "Fiona, why don't you take the Jeep and show Alexander the farm. I suspect Robert did nothing but work him hard this morning."

Fiona took the Jeep keys off the hanger on the wall. "Follow me." She handed the keys to Alexander when they reached the old Jeep. "Ye drive. I'll give directions and point out the scenery."

Burnsie jumped in the back seat and barked that he was ready to depart.

"Whit did my uncle have ye doing this morning?"

"I was glad to have the chance to be with him and get to know him better. I even hoped he might see me in a better light. First, he gave me a splitting maul and had me splitting wood."

"He has a machine for splitting wood!"

Alexander grinned. "I know. He wanted to see if I could use the splitting maul."

"Whit else?"

"Next, he had me using a posthole digger to repair a fence."

"Uncle has a machine for that as well."

Alexander's grin widened. "I know, I saw it. I think he was trying to wear me out."

"And did he?"

Alexander stopped the Jeep on top of a small hill, leaned over to Fiona, and kissed her. "Not as much as he wanted."

"Ruff!"

"Burnsie doesna underston."

"Ha! He understands, and he's jealous."

They got out of the Jeep and strolled. Burnsie followed. Alexander reached into his pocket and took out the box containing the necklace. "I made something for you," and handed Fiona the box. She opened it and gasped.

"You made this? It is braw."

She removed the necklace and admired the "AF" pendant. Alexander said, "AF is not an abbreviation for 'A Friend.' I love you very much."

"I will wear it always. Please put it on me." He did—in more ways than one.

Eventually, they continued their tour. Fiona showed Alexander things she had described during their drive from MU. The "farm" was no longer a farm, although it had a vegetable garden. Most of the acreage was timberland and a small lake. There were a few deer and turkey in the timberland sections; Robert and his friends liked to hunt there. They leased one section of pasture for grazing cattle. A gas production well was inside a small fenced-off area.

Fiona explained, "The farm includes several of these gas wells. That's where the rotten egg smell comes from. Auntie and Uncle dinna like them, but the gas wells provide their income."

Fiona's tour of the farm was lengthy, and she seemed in no hurry. Alexander understood he was missing the broadcast of the football game but accepted absence was probably best.

As they returned to the farmhouse, Alexander asked Fiona, "Is there a place we can go tonight for entertainment?"

"Aye. There's a dance hall. Ye won't believe this, but it is actually called the 'Do Drop Inn.'"

Alexander chuckled.

"My friends say it is the definition of a country honkytonk bar. I've never been there, but I'm curious about it."

"Then let's try the Do Drop Inn."

*****

ROBERT LISTENED TO THE RADIO BROADCAST of the MU football game from his den. He did not like what he heard. During the pre-game program, the radio announcer reported, "Here's an update on why Alexander Gordon is not playing football. You are probably already aware Alexander Gordon was the star of the MU Landsharks. He and his supposedly unknown admirer became celebrities in a prize-winning photograph dubbed 'The Look.' The young lady in 'The Look' is a freshman at MU, Fiona MacDonald. She is called the 'Viking Princess.'

"Apparently, Alexander serenaded and kissed the Viking Princess. Unfortunately for them, the MU Dean of Women witnessed this, and they were disciplined by 'being Campused.' At that point, Coach Guffy came into the issue.

"The MU Athletic Director has acknowledged Alexander Gordon has refused to have anything to do with Coach Guffy, including playing football. He also confirmed Alexander Gordon and his Viking Princess are no longer Campused. The Athletic Director has stated this incident continues to be investigated.

"Without their captain and star player, who often seemed to be an on-field coach, the MU Landsharks suffered an embarrassing defeat last week. They are not expected to do much better today."

Robert listened to the radio broadcast in dismay as MU lost once again. He did not like Coach Guffy, but he was still an MU alumni and football fan. *Why couldn't Alexander play football and date Fiona? It seemed so simple.*

Frustrated, Robert gave up on the football game. "Ellen," he said loudly, "I have some errands to run. Be back in a little while."

*****

FIONA was getting prepared for a night at the Do Drop Inn. What would it be like? How should she dress? Casual? Rough? In any case, she wanted to curl her hair and her curler box was falling apart. She came into the den with the box in her hands. "Where's Uncle?"

Ellen answered, "He had to run an errand; why?"

"This box for my curlers is falling apart. I was hoping Uncle could repair it."

"Can I try?" asked Alexander.

"Sure. Here it is." Fiona handed Alexander a small, empty plastic box. The lid was loose.

Alexander glanced at the box, reached into his pocket, and pulled out his Swiss Army Knife. He opened the Phillips head screwdriver blade and tightened all the screws on the box. He handed the box back to Fiona and smiled.

"I should have known!" Fiona beamed. "But whit kind of penknife is that?"

"It's called a Swiss Army Knife. There are many variations, but I always carry this small version." He opened all the blades to show them off. "It even has a flashlight and ballpoint pen."

Alexander continued, "With my Swiss Army Knife, a can of WD-40 and a roll of Duck Tape, I'm prepared for just about any emergency."

"Whit is WD-40?"

"WD-40 is a universal spray-on lubricant. If something is stuck or squeaks, the first attempt to free it usually involves WD-40."

"Whit is Duck Tape."

"Duck Tape is a thick, strong sticky tape. It is usually black or grey. If the lid had broken off the box, I'd have repaired it with Duck Tape."

"I've seen that type of tape on things Uncle has repaired."

"Thank you for the lessons and for repairing my curler box." Fiona gave Alexander a light kiss on his cheek. Her glance at Ellen so clearly said, *"He can do anything,"* that Ellen smiled.

Ellen was glad she had reserved the Chapel on Campus and wondered if Fiona and Alexander could wait until June.

"Anything else I can repair?" Alexander grinned.

Sandlin

Chapter 6: Do Drop Inn

My heart's in the Highlands, my heart is not here;
My heart's in the Highlands a-chasing the deer;
A-chasing the wild-deer, and following the roe,
My heart's in the Highlands wherever I go.
--Robert Burns

FIONA AND ALEXANDER arrived at The Do Drop Inn about nine o'clock. It was rough and ramshackle from the outside and not much better inside, but it had a dance floor and a band. The band played from behind a screen made of chicken wire. A sawdust-covered dance floor was next to the bandstand. The band faced the long bar, which had no stools. Tables separated the dance floor from the bar.

Fiona drew many admiring glances and some outright stares. Alexander ordered sodas and thought, *I'm staying close to Fiona, and we'll not be here long.* They sipped on their sodas and listened to the mediocre band.

Fiona whispered, "I hope ye ken, but I dinna want to dance here."

"I understand. Good decision. Let's drink our sodas and leave." He was very conscious of being an outsider.

They were listening to the band when a concerned expression appeared on Fiona's face. She advised, "I canna believe! Here comes Thomas Bennoitt."

Alexander turned to his left, and, sure enough, Thomas Bennoitt and two other guys were approaching their table. Thomas was staggering and swaggering. This was not good.

Fiona said, "One of those guys is Rab Jansen. He was two years ahead of me at my high school. Rab was the ringleader of the guys who harassed me when ye saved me. I think he is in Thomas' fraternity. I dinna ken the other, probably another fraternity brother."

Thomas reached their table with Rab Jansen beside him. They reeked of whiskey. A third guy was behind Thomas with his hand in his pocket. "Big Red!" Thomas exclaimed. "I can't believe my good luck. Rab, Tim and I are taking a tour of honkytonks, and Rab here suggested that the Do Drop Inn should be first. Never in my wildest dreams did I think you'd be here."

Rab bragged, "I wanted to bring Fiona here a couple of years ago."

Fiona interrupted, "I was too young. But I would not have gone here or anywhere with ye, Rab Jansen!"

"She was saving herself for me, Rab," Thomas claimed. "Now I'm here, and the band is playing a good slow song. We'll have our dance, and I'll show you how a real man holds you close." He put his hand on Fiona's shoulder. She shuttered.

Alexander stood but said nothing. Thomas taunted, "Well, if it isn't the coward and quitter! I may have riled him into action."

Thomas turned around to his accomplices and added, "He's a big one, but we can take him."

Alexander noted the use of "we" and prepared himself for an attack.

Rab's eyes abruptly revealed recognition. "Hey, aren't you the one..."

Thomas spun quickly and threw a sucker punch at Alexander's face, but Alexander had anticipated his move. He stepped aside, grabbed Thomas' wrist with one hand, twisted Thomas' arm severely and brought it down violently upon his own knee. Alexander drove his free but fisted hand deep into Thomas' stomach. He released Thomas' wrist and hit Thomas in the jaw with a tremendous uppercut that lifted him off the floor and followed it with a powerful blow to his face. Thomas collapsed into an unconscious heap in the sawdust, blood flowing from his face. All this took only a few seconds.

Rab Jansen was coming at Alexander with his fists raised high. Alexander employed a roundhouse kick to break Rab's knee and then hit him in the face with hard hooks to his nose and jaw. Rab fell to the floor, writhing in pain and moaning.

Tim, the third guy, had taken his hand out of his pocket and waved a blackjack threateningly. Alexander kicked through the blackjack into Tim's face, and Tim dropped with a thud, his face a bloody mess.

Alexander stood with his hands by his side but made into fists. He examined the room as if to say, "Anyone else?"

The bouncer came to their table and stated, "Sorry, but I came over as fast as I could. That was quick. I witnessed everything. I've never seen anything like that."

The bartender and owner came to them. "I've called the Sheriff and ambulance. Are you OK?"

Fiona was too scared and shocked to speak, but she nodded.

People from nearby tables assured Alexander that they would be witnesses to the attack by Thomas and his accomplices.

The Sheriff and a deputy arrived about the same time as the ambulance; he took statements from everyone.

Fiona and Alexander got into his truck. They rode home in silence except for an occasional gasp and sob from Fiona. Inside the farmhouse, they entered the living room and sat on the couch. Alexander put his arm around Fiona as she shook between sobs. Her salty tears flowed in both fright and relief.

Ellen came into the living room in her night robe. "What's wrong? What happened?"

Alexander explained, "There was a fight at the Do Drop Inn."

Ellen interrupted, "I'll get Robert." She left the room and returned with Robert in his robe.

Robert glared at Alexander and demanded, "What did you do to her?"

Fiona composed herself enough to say, "Alexander did nothing to me. He was attacked at the Do Drop Inn."

"I'll call Sheriff Leo. He's a good friend and will find and arrest the attackers."

Fiona continued, "It was Rab Jansen and two others. Sheriff Leo has already arrested them."

Robert swore, "That SOB. I'll go to the jail and prefer charges."

Fiona, remembering, dabbed at her teary eyes. Ellen handed her a box of tissues.

Alexander informed Robert, "They're not at the jail. They're in the hospital."

"All three of them?"

"Yes, sir."

"Wait a minute. You're telling me you fought and injured Rab Jansen so badly he is in the hospital along with two of his friends?"

"Yes, sir. One attacker, in fact, the instigator, was Thomas Bennoitt, a student at MU. He had harassed Fiona before and was doing it again tonight. The other guy was named Tim."

Robert asked, "Fiona, were you harmed in any way?"

"No, sir. I'm fine."

Robert asked Alexander, "Are you hurt?"

"No, sir. My hand is bruised, but I don't think it is broken."

Ellen responded, "Let me see your hand." Alexander held out his bruised and swollen hand. Fiona gasped. Ellen applied ice and towels.

Fiona choked and sobbed. "I've never been so frightened in my entire life. They could have injured Alexander before the bouncer and Sheriff arrived."

Robert stepped into the kitchen. They could hear him talking on the phone but could not understand the conversation. After a few minutes, he returned.

Robert said, "Sheriff Leo vouched for everything. Those three guys are badly injured and will be in the hospital for some time. Leo said the witnesses agreed with your story. The witnesses and bouncer agreed they had never seen anything like your defense, and the fight was over in fewer than fifteen seconds."

Fiona appealed to Ellen and Robert, "I need to be with Alexander for a while longer and try to recover."

*****

ELLEN AND ROBERT returned to their bedroom. About three a.m. Ellen peeked into the living room. Fiona and Alexander were still on the couch in the living room. Alexander had his arm around Fiona; she was asleep and curled up against him. Ellen returned to bed.

The following morning, Ellen was up early. She confirmed Fiona and Alexander were still asleep on the couch; they had not moved at all. She moved to the kitchen and prepared breakfast. A few minutes later, Alexander appeared in the doorway. "Thank you for your trust."

Ellen responded, "Thank you for defending Fiona."

"We should not have gone to that joint. I should have known better." Alexander shook his head at his mistake.

"It's not your fault they attacked you. Now, let me see your hand. Can you move your fingers?"

"My hand is sore, but it will be OK in a few days."

Ellen asked, "Where is Fiona? How is she?"

"She is in her bedroom changing clothes. She's feeling much better."

Robert came into the kitchen. "Thank you for protecting Fiona last night."

Alexander replied, "I will never allow anyone to harm Fiona. Never."

"It's still difficult to believe you put those three guys in the hospital."

Fiona came into the kitchen. Alexander moved to her side, observing, "You are incredibly beautiful."

Fiona disagreed, "Not this morning, but *taing*." Then she added, "Flatterer!"

Ellen invited, "Let's eat breakfast before we go to church. Alexander deserves a full Scottish breakfast, and I've done the best I can with what I had."

*****

AFTER CHURCH, ROBERT TALKED to his friends, including the sheriff. Robert left the group and approached Alexander. "Here's an update for you. Sheriff Leo says the three guys who attacked you are severely injured with some internal injuries. They will be hospitalized for days, perhaps a week or even more. Thomas's father is a physician and has arranged for reconstructive surgery in a Jackson hospital. Sheriff Leo's guess is that Rab and Tim, who were already on parole for other offensives, will spend time in jail. In any case, Rab cannot walk well enough to return to MU now. Thomas may not be permitted to return to MU if he is found guilty of attacking you, but Leo is not positive. However, he suspects Thomas will choose not to return to MU."

"I hope not. Thomas has been nothing but trouble for Fiona."

Robert continued, "Sheriff Leo still cannot believe you could dispatch those three guys so quickly. You are free to return to MU. If anything new comes up, Leo will contact me."

"Thank you, sir."

Alexander invited everyone to dinner, and Ellen recommended her favorite restaurant. Alexander repeated his joke about church service schedules and restaurants. "By law, Protestant church services begin and end on the hour, whereas Catholic services begin and end on the half-hour. This assures restaurants do not get overcrowded." Fiona groaned, but Ellen laughed.

*****

ELLEN AND FIONA EXCUSED THEMSELVES for the Lady's Room.

"Auntie, I want to get Alexander a present."

"What are you considering?"

"A gold choker with my name on it." Fiona blushed. "I want my name to be like my signature."

"I'll talk to Mr. Patterson and see what he can do."

"I ken a custom gold neck chain might be expensive. Can I afford it?"

"Honey, you can afford it. In fact, this is a reminder that we need to meet with my brother, James, to discuss your finances. You'll be wanting and needing to take over those responsibilities. Of course, James will always be available to advise you."

"I almost feel like some kind of airhead when it comes to my finances, but I dinna like thinking about that money. To me, it represents the death of my parents. I'll be taking a business class next semester; perhaps that will help."

"Probably."

"Do I have as much money as Alexander?"

"Honey, we don't know how much money Alexander has, but you probably have more."

175

Fiona smiled. "Good."

*****

SUNDAY AFTERNOON, ABOUT TO LEAVE THE FARM, Alexander said, "Thank you, Mr. Johnston, for allowing me to visit your farm. It's quite a place, and I know you are proud of it. I enjoyed being here."

Robert replied, "Anytime."

Alexander turned to Ellen. "Thank you, Mrs. Johnston, for everything. Except for the fight, I had a wonderful weekend."

Ellen smiled. "Please call me Auntie."

Alexander complied, "Thank you, Auntie."

Emotional now, Ellen urged, "Haste ye back!"

As Fiona and Alexander drove away, Robert asked Ellen, "Why did you tell him to call you Auntie?"

"Because, you old fool, he's going to be our son-in-law. Can't you tell?"

Bewildered, Robert shook his head.

*****

DURING THEIR RETURN TO MU, Alexander asked, "How would you feel about my trying out for basketball? I think I could make the team. I'm a bit rusty, but I was a good basketball player in high school."

"I would be jealous of the time ye spend on the court, but I'm not surprised ye are considering it. In fact, I would be more surprised if ye gave up all sports."

"If nothing else, I need the exercise. I'll talk to Coach Robinson tomorrow."

Alexander and Fiona continued to muse about meeting each other, the Meet and Greet, the Look, the Kiss, Campused, being heckled, the fight and other complications in their lives.

Alexander noted, "You know, Fiona, you and I are not exactly inconspicuous. Besides being the tallest, you are always the most beautiful girl in the room. The guys admire you and want to meet you and be with you. The girls are likely to be jealous. Even your accent makes you stand out. Your word choices mark you as different. It must not be easy being a Viking Princess."

"Whit about being ye? Ye are always the biggest and strongest guy in the room. Most handsome too. Obviously, the leader wherever ye are. The lassies want to meet ye, and I ken the guys want to beat ye, but they canna."

"Especially when we are together, there seem to be problems—not between you and me, but with others. We've got to learn to live with and manage these situations. But how?"

"Maybe Mary can help. Let's discuss this with her tomorrow."

"Good idea."

$$*****$$

FIONA CARRIED HER SUITCASE into her dormitory room and swung it onto her bed. "Whew, whit a weekend!"

Jane peeked up from her studies. "Good or bad?"

"Both."

"Tell me about it. Wait, first tell me about your necklace. It looks new." She stood and stepped over to Fiona. "Lovely. Hmm, 'AF.' What could that stand for?"

"Alexander made it himself."

"He made this necklace? I'm impressed."

"Alexander said he loved me."

"Wow! He told you he loved you and gave you this necklace? He is romantic, isn't he?"

Fiona blushed. "Actually, he sang that he loved me on Friday night and gave me the necklace on Saturday."

"Alexander sings to you often."

"He is my favorite singer."

177

"All this sounds wonderful. I hate to ask, but what was the bad part?"

"Well, I had an argument with my uncle, and Alexander was attacked on Saturday night in a honkytonk joint."

"Fiona, your life and weekends are more exciting and interesting than any television show. Tell me more."

Fiona suggested, "It is a long story. First, tell me about your weekend."

"I had a nice dinner date with Donnie and did lots of studying. Now go on with your story."

"Friday night, we were sitting on the porch, and Alexander played his guitar..."

*****

FINALLY IN HIS DORM, Alexander, deep in thought, unpacked.

Donnie came in. "Get any studying done?" he asked.

"No, how about you?"

"Well, I didn't study much but I learned that Jane can drink three beers without getting drunk or going to the bathroom. She must have a hollow leg—couldn't fit a bladder that big in her small waist."

Alexander snorted. "Were you trying to get her drunk?"

"No, we had steaks and beer at Lou's then went to the Dance Room."

"You danced? Didn't know you could."

"I can't but Jane wanted me to try. How about you?"

"I learned a lot as well."

"Like what?"

"For starters, I'm in love with Fiona." *There, he'd said it.*

"Mary told me that two weeks ago." Donnie laughed. "What else is new?"

"Thomas Bennoitt and two of his hoodlum buddies attacked me in a honkytonk joint where Fiona and I were."

"You don't seem hurt."

"I'm not, but they are in the hospital."

"All three of them?"

"Right. Donnie, how do I get in these situations?"

"I'm not sure. You are a target for some people, and Thomas is one of them."

"Thomas probably will not return to MU after he heals."

"Good. How did you get along with Fiona's aunt and uncle?"

"Her aunt asked me to call her 'Auntie' like Fiona does."

"Uh oh."

"Her dog likes me—at least that's what Fiona said."

"What about her uncle?"

"On Saturday, before the fight, he suggested I transfer to another school. Fiona was furious with him. She told him that if I transferred to another school, she would follow me. Her uncle was not ready for that, but they patched things up. Her uncle is still very protective of Fiona but eased up on me after the fight. We'll eventually be OK."

"If he is trying to separate you and Fiona, why doesn't he send Fiona to another school?"

Alexander hesitated, then replied, "In fact, he suggested that."

"And?"

"Fiona said if they forced her to transfer to another school or go back to Scotland, she would ask me to go with her."

"Wow! She really said that? Would you go?"

"I'd follow Fiona even if she did not ask."

"You've got it bad." Donnie waved his hands around their room. "You'd leave all this—and me—for Fiona?"

Alexander grinned.

Donnie changed subjects. "What did you do on the farm?"

"Chopped wood, dug a few postholes, had a tour of the farm, and took a little target practice."

"Sounds like her old man wanted you to know he had a shotgun!"

"I suspect you are correct, but in fact, it was a pistol. A Colt 1911 like the one my dad has.

Donnie teased, "Sounds like I need to find another roommate."

"Fiona and I are not leaving MU."

"That's not what I'm talking about."

Confused, Alexander asked, "Well, what are you trying to say?"

"My fiercely independent roomie has been roped and hog tied by the Viking Princess. His dormitory days are ending. Next year, I'll have a different roomie." He laughed. "You will too!"

*****

MARY JOINED ALEXANDER AND FIONA in the coffee shop. Alexander confided, "Mary, I'm glad to see you. Fiona and I need some counseling and advice."

"I won't be a psychologist for many more years."

"You've always been a psychologist. Please listen. Fiona and I are not seekers of fame, much less troublemakers. But when we are together, things seem to happen—sometimes fantastic things, sometimes not so good. What can we do?"

"Alexander, you've always had this problem and, mostly, you've learned to manage it. Fiona, I suspect you too have always had this problem, certainly for the past several years as you've matured. You compound the situation when you are together. I'm afraid you'll have to learn to live with it. In other words, there's nothing you can do to change the actions of others; you must change yourselves."

Fiona and Alexander glanced at each other. This was not what they expected to hear.

Mary continued, "Even if you did nothing noteworthy the rest of your lives—which is unlikely—you'd still attract attention in a restaurant, a theatre, church—anywhere you go. For one thing, you are a beautiful couple, and that's not even considering your talents and leadership. You are doomed to be celebrities, if not internationally, then nationally or certainly locally. It is your curse, and you must accept it and adapt.

"Emerson said, 'To be great is to be misunderstood.' I would add 'and to be criticized and even harassed.'"

Mary closed with, "That will be five cents, please."

Alexander snickered, "Thank you, Lucy," and gave Mary a nickel.

*****

ALEXANDER KNOCKED ON THE DOOR to Coach Robinson's office and was invited in. He introduced himself and reminded Coach Robinson they had met when Alexander was in high school. Coach Robinson smiled. "I remember you well, Alexander. You were an extraordinary basketball player, and I wanted you to come to MU and play basketball here."

"Thank you, sir. In fact, that's what I'm here about. I'm no longer playing football. Is there a way I could try out for the basketball team? There would be no need for a scholarship. I'd be happy to be a practice player. I need the activity and exercise."

"I heard you were not playing football and, given the explanation, I wondered if you might try basketball, but I could not contact you directly about it. I hoped you'd ask about playing basketball. You can certainly be a practice player and perhaps more. I'll have to check into the details of the rules and regulations, but I think you can become a full member of the team." He picked up the telephone and said, "Greg, I'm sending Alexander Gordon to the locker room. Please help him get equipped to play basketball."

"Thank you, sir. I'll do my best to convince you this is a good decision."

*****

AFTER TWO BASKETBALL PRACTICES, Coach Robinson called Alexander aside. "I'm sorry, Alexander, but you can only be a practice player. Coach Guffy formally suspended you, which means you cannot take part in other sports this semester. I do hope you will continue to practice with the team, though."

"I'm not surprised. Coach Guffy really has it in for me. But I will continue as a practice-only player."

Coach Robinson hinted, "Practice now will make you a better player for next year."

Alexander returned to the basketball floor, picked up a ball and continued taking warmup shots. Guffy had really messed over him.

*****

COACH GUFFY HAD BEEN SUMMONED to the office of the Athletic Director. He knew what was coming. Without Alexander Gordon, the Landsharks had not won a game. President Curry was also in the Athletic Director's office, along with a security officer.

The Athletic Director confirmed Coach Guffy's fears. "Coach, there should be no need to beat around the bush. Your services are no longer needed or wanted at MU. You are fired but will be compensated according to your contract.

Coach Guffy responded angrily, "This is all the fault of that red-headed bitch!"

President Curry objected. "Mr. Guffy, if I ever had any doubt of your conduct regarding Miss MacDonald, you have confirmed those accusations. You are indeed a lucky man, Mr. Guffy. If

Alexander Gordon were in this office, he might not restrain himself, and I might be inclined to look the other way."

The Athletic Director warned, "Mr. Guffy, the official reason you are being fired is you did not win enough football games this year, and my evaluation is you would not win enough games next year either. However, if you wish for us to include additional charges, that can be easily arranged.

"Mr. Guffy, your office has been cleared of your belongings. This security officer will escort you to your car."

*****

DURING SUPPER IN THE CAFETERIA, Fiona listened thoughtfully as Alexander told her Coach Guffy had been fired, but he still could not play basketball.

"Ye've been forced to make many adjustments because of me."

"You're worth it," Alexander assured. "You've had to adjust as well. Tell me about the differences between Scotland and America. What were the most difficult adjustments you had to make?"

Fiona considered for a moment. "In my mid-teens, I was having an awkward time, even in Scotland. I was skinny and tall with braces and red hair and freckles."

"I love your hair color."

"*Moran taing*! As ye probably ken, Scotland has the highest percentage of red-haired people anywhere. But in America, some still think it is unlucky or even a curse."

"Only a few ignorant ones."

Fiona continued, "My parents sheltered me and assured me everything would be alright. Then they were killed." A tear formed and ran down Fiona's cheek. "I was a depressed teenager on top of everything else when I first came to America. Being a Scot but having lived in America for many years, Auntie helped me adjust to living in America. She was terrific to me, but I was still a city lassie living in the country.

"School was the most challenging change I had to face. Many of the school kids, especially the football players, teased and taunted me. I learnt to keep to myself and study. I kent almost nothing about America but had to learn Mississippi history and the way of writing in American English. I did no date, except group dates. In my senior year, my freckles nearly disappeared, my braces were removed, and I gained a wee bit of weight. By then, I was no interested in any of my guy classmates. I invited a boy who had Down's Syndrome to the Senior Prom."

"I'm getting upset with your classmates."

"*Dinna fash yersel.* That part of my life is over, and I love the life I'm living noo. Ye asked about differences, here are some:

"In Scotland, whit America calls pants are called trousers, and the word pants means underwear. There is a joke about an American woman wearing a dress and saying, 'I didn't feel like wearing pants today.'

"Many Scots still speak Gaelic. I can. *A bheil thu a 'bruidhinn gaelic?* That means 'Can you speak Gaelic?'

Alexander shook his head.

"As ye've no doubt noticed, I like to throw in a few Gaelic words every now and then. Sometimes I do it intentionally, but most of the time, I use Gaelic out of habit."

Alexander praised her. "I must say you have adapted extraordinarily well."

"The holidays will be a perfect time for us to teach and share customs," she hinted.

*****

Chapter 7: Holidays

For auld lang syne, my jo,
For auld lang syne,
We'll tak a cup o' kindness yet
For auld lang syne.
--Robert Burns

"WHIT A WONDERFUL AFTERNOON to travel!" exclaimed Fiona. "The temperature is right, the sun is bright, the sky is blue, and I'm with you!"

"I like your poetry," teased Alexander. "Think we can stand each other for ten days?"

"Well, if we canna, then we will find out. But I'm sure we can manage."

Planning for Thanksgiving had been awkward. Alexander wanted time with his parents, and Fiona wanted time with her aunt and uncle. They also wanted to be together. The traditional Thanksgiving meal complicated the situation even more: Where would they eat Thanksgiving dinner?

Since Fiona had not visited Alexander's parents in Oceanport, they would stay there first. They would have Thanksgiving dinner with the Gordons, then go to the Johnston's farm the next day before returning to MU. Ellen had graciously delayed her Thanksgiving dinner until the day after Thanksgiving.

"It will thrill my parents to see you again. In fact, they're a little miffed that I've not brought you home sooner. You'll meet my sisters and some of my good friends from high school."

"And auld girlfriends?" Fiona was very curious about this.

"Not if I can prevent it!"

"Too bad. I want to check them out and see whit I can learn." Fiona giggled.

Alexander changed the subject and named and described some of his high school classmates.

*****

ALEXANDER TURNED HIS TRUCK into the driveway of the single-story ranch-style house and parked behind his dad's truck in the carport. "Let's go inside. I'll come back for the luggage."

Malcolm, Rachel, and Alexander's sisters, Caroline and Liz, met them at the front door of the yellow brick house. After hugs and introductions, Alexander returned to the truck for their luggage while everyone got acquainted in the den. Alexander put his suitcase in the enclosed patio.

"Fiona, let me show you your room." She followed him. "This is my room, but it is the best place for you. I'll be sleeping on the couch in the patio."

"So, I'll be sleeping in your bed?" Fiona teased. "I'll have to think about the way I say that to my friends." They returned to the den.

Caroline probed, "Mom and Dad told us some things about you, Fiona, but please tell us about yourself." Caroline was three years younger than Alexander, and Liz was six years younger than Alexander.

Fiona began, "I expect ye already ken me, but to be sure, here is the short version. I was born and raised in Scotland. My father and mother were killed in an automobile accident three years ago. I needed to get away, so I moved to the United States to be with my aunt and uncle. They own a large farm in East Mississippi.

Another uncle, the brother of my aunt in Mississippi, still lives in Scotland. My ancestors have lived in Scotland for hundreds of years."

Caroline interrupted, "Do you think you'll return to Scotland?"

Fiona glanced at Alexander. "I'll revisit Scotland someday."

Fiona continued, "At MU, my major is music, especially classical music and voice. I play several instruments, especially the piano. I'm also majoring in philosophy—I'm Presbyterian. I speak Scottish Gaelic, French and Italian. So, that's the short version. Noo tell me about yourselves."

Caroline summarized, "I'm a Junior in high school. I play basketball and softball. I plan to become an elementary school teacher."

Liz offered, "I'm in the eighth grade. I'm in the band. I'll probably become a kindergarten teacher like Mom."

Fiona sympathized with Liz. "In eighth grade, I did not know whit I'd become. Perhaps still I dinna ken."

Liz complimented Fiona, "Well, you've certainly become beautiful!"

"*Moran taing*. Ye will too."

*****

MALCOLM INVITED FIONA to visit his workshop behind the house, and Alexander joined them. His small workshop was crammed with wood and woodworking tools. The aroma of cedar filled it, and there were pieces of cedar on his workbench. "Woodworking is my hobby, and I'm out here piddling on something every chance I get. My current project is to build a cedar chest for Liz. Some call it a Hope Chest. Do you know what a Hope Chest is?"

"Aye, I have my mother's Hope Chest with my things in Scotland. She called it a Trousseau Chest, but that's the same thing. Hers is made of Scottish oak."

187

Malcolm pointed to an adjoining room. "That is Rachel's studio where she paints and does arts and crafts projects."

Fiona stepped into the studio and the odor of oil paint. A painting of a beach scene, including a shrimp boat, was in progress.

Returning to the patio, Fiona remarked to Alexander, "Your parents certainly are creative!"

"Yes indeed. They are planning to open an arts and crafts store in a few years."

"Did ye and your sisters inherit their skills?"

"I don't know about inherit, but since we've always been exposed to their work, it seems natural to us. After growing up during the depression, they throw nothing away and are constantly finding new uses for old things."

"Sounds that Scottish to me!"

Fiona approached Rachel with a compliment. "I was admiring the paintings in your studio. Ye are quite an artist."

"Thank you. I truly enjoy painting; it relaxes me. I even give painting lessons."

"I'm studying art and hope to improve my painting skills."

"Perhaps I can give you a few tips while you are here."

"I'd like that."

*****

FIONA AND ALEXANDER joined everyone in the den and sat on Malcolm's reproduction of an antique couch. Malcolm set up his movie projector on a homemade coffee table and aimed it at the screen. Rachel brought in popcorn. Alexander groaned.

Malcolm joked, "What's the use of having a son if you can't embarrass him?" and turned on the projector.

After nine 8mm silent movies, the mechanical clock gonged, and even Malcolm had seen enough. "Time for bed," he announced.

Fiona giggled at Alexander. "Ye were a cute wee bairn, *mo leannan,* but ye sure were skinny!"

With sleeping arrangements made, all went to their bedrooms except Fiona and Alexander, who remained in the den on the couch watching a talk show on television. Alexander put his arm around Fiona and kissed her softly. She snuggled close to him and whispered, "If I had my way..."

Later, lying in Alexander's bed, Fiona enjoyed a faint remnant of Alexander's scent as she fell peacefully asleep.

*****

THE NEXT MORNING, Alexander was already in the kitchen sipping coffee when Fiona entered. Rachel had got up early and made a huge breakfast. The aromas of ham, eggs, grits, biscuits, coffee, and orange juice mixed deliciously in the kitchen.

Fiona gave Alexander a peck on the cheek. "D'ye ken ye are spoiled, *mo leannan*?"

"Firstborn, the only son!"

"Would you like coffee?" Rachel asked Fiona.

"Mom, Fiona drinks tea with lemon, not coffee."

"I brought my favorite tea from Scotland," Fiona explained. "Do ye have hot water and a lemon?"

Later, Fiona quipped to Alexander, "Your mother must wonder whit kind of uppity ye are dating who must have tea instead of coffee and carries her own special tea?"

"She is wondering no such thing. But I promise you, she will buy that tea today, and tomorrow morning your special tea will already be prepared when you come to breakfast. She will spoil you, too."

"I will buy your mother a proper teapot and show her the way of making tea in Scotland."

"Well, perhaps you <u>are</u> a bit uppity!"

Fiona laughed and poked Alexander in the ribs. "Americans dinna ken the way of taking tea properly."

*****

FIONA COULD SENSE JEALOUSY as she was introduced to the girls in Alexander's Sunday School class. Several girls admired and remarked on her "AF" necklace; Fiona thanked them and smiled. The guys practically beat Alexander on the back in congratulations for having such a beautiful girlfriend and in thanks for bringing her to church.

Fiona introduced herself using the "short version" she had composed. Someone recognized her from "The Look" photograph, and Fiona confirmed that, aye, people called her the "Viking Princess." She was eager to change the topic to the Bible lesson.

When asked why he was no longer playing football, Alexander repeated the brief statement he regularly used. "Coach Guffy vulgarly insulted Fiona, and I could no longer stand to be around him. In a nutshell, that's it." Everyone knew the story anyway, and Alexander confirmed it.

After an introductory prayer and song, the group separated into girls' and boys' classes for discussion. After the discussion and lesson, as they left Sunday School, Fiona whispered to Alexander, "Just exactly how many of your ex-girlfriends were in Sunday School today?" Alexander turned red but said nothing.

During Worship Service, as Fiona sang, people in front turned around to locate her dulcet voice. Many of the congregation commented later on how much they enjoyed the concert.

After the Worship Service, the Gordons and Fiona regrouped and Malcolm suggested a restaurant for dinner. "Rachel is about to start cooking tomorrow for Thanksgiving. I want to give her the day off today."

As they were eating, Caroline suddenly exclaimed, "Since when did you hold your fork upside down? Is this something they teach in college?"

Alexander laughed. "Fiona is teaching me the European style of using utensils."

"Forks," smiled Fiona, "were invented in Egypt but used only for cooking. Modern forks were developed in Europe but had only two tines and were flat. Those flat forks could only be used for spearing. Curved tines face downward for spearing—not up for scooping. The European style keeps the fork in the left hand and the knife in the right hand. We don't swap the fork between the left and right hands. Try it."

Everyone tried using their fork in their left hand, but finally, Mr. Gordon said, "I think I'll stay with the American style."

*****

"DO YOU KNOW HOW to cook?" Rachel asked Fiona the next day.

"Some. I helped my mother in Scotland, so I ken a wee bit about cooking Scottish foods. Of course, the foods are different, especially haggis, salmon, bannocks, scones, and shortbread. Noo, I help Auntie cook Southern foods, which she learnt after moving to Mississippi many years ago. But there is much to learn. I may take a cooking course next semester." Fiona blushed.

Rachel did not comment about Fiona's embarrassment. Instead, she suggested, "Let me show you how to prepare a quick and simple dish, which happens to be one of Alexander's favorites. It's called "Peas and Cornbread."

"Please show me the way of it."

"I'm going to fix it the easy way using semi-prepared ingredients in the slow cooker. First, pour in a bag of frozen purple hulled peas. Next, we'll put in chopped onions—about one-fourth the amount of the peas. Next, add a couple of slices of ham. Whenever we have ham, I always save a few pieces, or even

191

the bone, to use as flavoring. Finally, toss in a bay leaf and then add enough water to cover everything. That's it. The exact amounts and proportions aren't particularly important. Now set the slow cooker to a medium temperature and let it cook for eight or ten hours. We'll make cornbread before serving the peas."

"So simple. *Moran taing!*"

"There is nothing like a traditional Southern meal, and this one is also economical. I was raised in a poor family and had many meals of peas and cornbread. You put the peas on top of crumbled cornbread and sprinkle chopped onion on top. Peas and cornbread were Alexander's introduction to onions."

"He certainly likes onions now."

Rachel continued, "Until he was about ten or twelve years old, he did not eat raw onion. One autumn, while at my sister's farm, Alexander's cousins used a knife to cross hatch an onion and slice a layer of the pieces to put on their peas and cornbread. He wanted to use the knife and do the same, and we let him, but then he had to eat the onion pieces. He was surprised to discover he liked it!"

"I struggle to think of Alexander as a small boy. Ye must have many good stories about him."

"I sure do, and I'm afraid you will have to listen to them."

Fiona laughed. "I want to hear them!"

"Next time, I'll show you how to make a roux."

"A roux? There is a famous chef named Albert Roux in Scotland, but I think he was born in France."

"That sounds about right. I only know how to make a roux the way the Cajun French do."

Liz came in holding a photograph album and asked Fiona, "Would you like to see some old pictures of Alexander?" Fiona joined her as she flipped through page after page of Alexander's baby and child photographs. After fifteen minutes, Alexander interrupted and invited Fiona, "Let's go visit my friend, David."

* * * * *

ONCE IN HIS TRUCK, Alexander explained, "David and I were very close, especially in high school. We played football, worked on cars, and even played in a rock and roll band. David still has his own rock band. You'll like him. He goes to a Community College now, and I don't get to see him as often. In fact, I haven't seen David since meeting you."

Alexander rang the doorbell of David's parents' house, and David yelled, "Come on in. I'm in the game room."

Alexander and Fiona stepped into the game room, and David exclaimed, "Alexander!" They shook hands and then hugged. David admired Fiona and quipped, "This must be your beautiful girlfriend, but you said she was a short brunette?"

Alexander groaned, "Come on, man! Give me a break." They both cackled.

"Fiona, I'd like to introduce my good friend David."

"Fiona, I'm very pleased to meet you. I only hope you can keep my good friend here on the straight and narrow path."

"I try, but he can be that stubborn."

Alexander laughed and assessed the room. "What's happening, David?"

"We're about to have a jam session in a couple of hours. Care to join us?"

"We can't. We're on our way to see Mary. Only a quick visit this time. Maybe some other time."

"How about one song? Fiona, Alexander said you are a talented pianist. Can you manage a song on that keyboard? Anything you'd like."

"I'll try."

Alexander returned to his truck and retrieved his guitar.

Fiona sat at the keyboard and began playing "What'd I Say." David joined on drums. Eight bars later, Alexander came in with

193

the guitar accompaniment. Another eight bars and David hit the drum with a rim shot and shouted

"Hey mama, don't you treat me wrong
Come and love your daddy all night long."

Startled, Fiona missed a beat. Their timing became jumbled. They stopped playing and laughed hysterically.

Fiona declared, "Guess I need more practice on that song."

David countered, "You can be in my band anytime."

Alexander said, "We really must go, David."

David responded, "Fiona, I'm happy to have met you. Please take care of my friend."

"I try but canna guarantee."

David shook Alexander's hand and smiled knowingly. "It's been great knowing you."

Back in the truck, Fiona scolded, "You guys are tough on each other."

"That's just the way it is."

Fiona ventured, "Ye ken your friend canna sing?"

"But <u>he</u> thinks he can, and he loves it."

"How did David say, 'It's been great knowing ye? Is he ill or going somewhere.?"

"No, David's fine. He thinks he will not be seeing much of me anymore.

Fiona did not comment except to ask, "Where to next?"

*****

"THIS IS THE WAY to Mary's house. They are having a shrimp boil for us." Alexander turned onto a small gravel road.

"How nice! I love boiled shrimp. I'm eager to see Mary and meet her parents. She has been extremely important to me—and to us."

194

"Please don't read me wrong on what I'm about to say. I may sound like a snob. You know how I love Mary—she is my best friend.

"Mary's parents are not poor, but they have little money and no extra money. Mary got a full scholarship to MU based on her excellent academic skills and her financial need."

"I ken. Mary telt me herself."

"Her parents did not graduate from high school—they are not dumb, just not well educated. Her father is a fisherman and shrimper; in fact, Dad bought our shrimp and crabs from him today. Her mother works in a seafood factory. They live in a small wood-framed house in a deteriorating neighborhood."

"*Taing* for advising me. I have been blessed beyond all measure through no actions of my own. I dinna want to appear to be a snob either. Whit has Mary telt her parents about me?"

Alexander stopped his truck. "Here we are. The house next door on the left is where we lived for the first twelve years of my life. My dad received a nice promotion, and we moved to the house they have now."

Alexander and Fiona walked up the steps to the small front porch and knocked on Mary's door. She had been waiting and welcomed them, hugging first Fiona and then Alexander.

"I'm so glad you are here!. Please come in. Fiona, I want you to meet my parents. They are eager to meet you."

"Mrs. Callahan, how good to see you again!"

Mary's mother greeted Alexander with, "My goodness, Alexander, you've gotten even bigger!" and gave him a warm hug.

Alexander gave Mary's father's hand a firm shake. "Mr. Callahan, I'm pleased to see you. Thank you for the shrimp and crabs. My mom will make gumbo tomorrow."

"Mama, Papa, this is my very good friend, Fiona."

Mrs. Callahan gushed, "I finally get to meet you! My word, you are beautiful!"

Fiona blushed.

Mr. Callahan agreed with his wife. "Welcome to our home. So, you are the Viking Princess we've heard so much about!"

Mary continued, "Fiona and Alexander are dating."

Mrs. Callahan replied, "Of course they are. Anyone could tell."

"I introduced them."

"Alexander, I believe you are deeply in debt to Mary."

Alexander agreed. "I am indeed. I'll never be able to repay her. Has Mary told you her story about introducing us?"

"Yes, she has. It is a funny story."

"She has embellished her story so much it is almost unrecognizable to me, and I was there."

Fiona smiled. "I was there as well. It was the most memorable introduction I've ever had."

"Fiona, we know Alexander. Please tell us about yourself. But first, tell us Mary is behaving and studying."

Fiona repeated the description of herself she had given to the Gordons and not the shorter version she had used in Sunday School.

Fiona turned to Mr. Callahan and asked, "Isn't Callahan an Irish name?"

Mr. Callahan nodded eagerly. "Yes, it is. It was my grandparents who came to America from Ireland."

Fiona responded, "Ireland is a beautiful place."

"So, you've been to Ireland?"

"Aye, it is a quick trip from Scotland to Ireland. I've been there many times."

Mrs. Callahan interjected, "My family is from France and came to America before his! Now we are known as Cajuns."

Fiona said, "*Je suis aussi allé plusieurs fois en France.*

Mrs. Callahan was delighted and replied, "*J'espère y aller un jour.*"

Fiona changed back to English, "Mrs. Gordon telt me she would teach me the way of making a Cajun roux."

"I'm the one who taught Rachel!"

"Speaking of cooking," said Mrs. Callahan, "We have fresh shrimp ready for boiling. Harry caught them this morning. Let's go to the picnic table in the backyard."

"I'll get the newspapers," said Mary, her eyes twinkling. "Alexander, bring those paper plates and paper towels. The beer is already out there in the cooler."

Mary dropped her bundle of newspapers on the picnic table. "Fiona, help me spread newspaper on the table. Use cans of beer to weigh them down."

Fiona seemed bewildered but began spreading newspapers.

Mr. Callahan stood over a pot of water boiling on a propane burner. He removed a basket and showed Fiona the small whole potatoes, corn on the cob, slices of sausage, and quarters of onions and lemons. "Mrs. Callahan makes the seasoning, and I boil everything in one pot." He lowered the basket back into the boiling water and poured in several pounds of whole raw shrimp. "Only a couple of minutes now. Better find yourself a place at the table."

Fiona sat down by Alexander. A moment later, Mr. Callahan dumped the basket of steaming hot shrimp and accompaniments in the center of the newspapers. Startled, Fiona jumped.

"Dig in," said Mr. Callahan, proud of his cooking, and sat down to join them.

Mary's focus traveled from the mountain of food to Fiona, who clearly did not know what to do. She laughed. "Help yourself, Fiona," then she demonstrated by grabbing a handful of shrimp, a few pieces of sausage, a potato, and a piece of corn and putting them on her paper plate. She popped the top on her can of beer and took a swig.

Fiona eyed her paper plate with aversion, gingerly picked up a shrimp from the pile, and placed it on her plate. Despairing, she searched unsuccessfully for a fork. Fiona appealed to Alexander with her eyes but said nothing.

"I'll show you how to peel your shrimp." Alexander took the hint. "Watch." He removed the head and peeled the shell away. He placed the peeled shrimp on Fiona's paper plate and the shrimp head and shell off to one side on the newspaper.

Fiona still seemed uneasy.

Alexander said, "I'll be right back," and disappeared into the house. He returned with a china plate and a stainless steel knife and fork and placed them in front of Fiona. He transferred the single peeled shrimp to the china plate.

Alexander reached to open Fiona's beer but instead said, "Excuse me again," and once again disappeared into the house. He returned with a glass mug and placed it near Fiona's plate. He opened her can of beer and slowly poured a small amount into the mug.

Fiona smiled a relieved and grateful smile at Alexander. He filled his plate, then began peeling shrimp and putting them on Fiona's plate. Fiona, fork in her left hand, speared a shrimp. She carefully cut off a tiny piece using the knife in her right hand and delicately put it in her mouth. Fiona turned to Mr. Callahan, "Och, this is that delicious! *Moran taing*!"

Mr. and Mrs. Callahan watched their proceedings in amazement. Mary giggled and shook her head.

"Try a potato and piece of corn," suggested Alexander. "And also some of Mrs. Callahan's famous dipping sauce." He put these on Fiona's plate.

Fiona cut away a small piece of potato and tasted it. "Mmm, it is that spicy. I like it." However, she stared helplessly at the corn on the cob.

Alexander opened his Swiss Army Knife and dipped the cutting blade into the boiling water. He sliced kernels of corn off the cob and scraped them onto Fiona's plate. She smiled in appreciation. Mary watched in amazement, struggling to not guffaw.

With Fiona's plate served, Alexander began peeling shrimp for himself. He was hungry.

The shrimp boil continued with many tales of Mary and Alexander growing up. Fiona laughed and laughed.

Eventually, Alexander said, "This has been a great visit. We thank you for the shrimp boil. Let us help clean up, but we should leave soon."

Cleaning up was quick and easy. Fiona and Alexander were soon in his truck.

"Och, whit a braw experience! I loved it. *Taing* that much for helping me." Fiona leaned over and kissed Alexander on the cheek. "I didna ken whit to do, *mo leannan.* The food was delicious; I've had nothing like it."

"And now Mary has another story to tell. Don't worry, her story will be told to embarrass me—not you." He laughed.

"Next time, I will learn to peel my own shrimp!"

As they drove away, Fiona carefully examined the neighborhood. She shuddered. "This seems such a rough neighborhood," and locked her door.

"The neighborhood has definitely gone down since I lived here, but it was a tough place to grow up even then. Growing up on this street was wonderful. Some lots were empty and wooded back then. We built clubhouses in the woods. All the kids played baseball and football in the vacant lots."

"Did Mary play baseball and football?" Fiona asked incredulously.

"Everyone played, even Mary," Alexander smiled. "She was not good, but she played. Don't tell her I said that. See that drainage ditch? Neighborhood kids called it a creek and built dams on it. We learned about minnows, tadpoles, frogs, turtles, and snakes in that creek. The bayou was for swimming, fishing, and boating. Mr. Callahan taught me how to catch shrimp and oysters; he showed me how to throw a cast net for mullet."

"Is this where ye learnt the way of kick fighting?"

"No, but it is where I learned to stand up for myself."

"Moran taing for showing and telling me this. I can better underston ye now, but I'm glad your parents have moved to a better place. Thinking of your parents, I promised to help your mom with preparations for Thanksgiving."

"We're on our way home now."

$$*****$$

RACHEL WAS TELLING FIONA about the upcoming Thanksgiving Dinner. "I talked to Ellen. She is planning a traditional roast turkey. Malcolm will cook our turducken in his smoker overnight."

"*Gabh mo leisgeul,*" Fiona interjected. "Whit is a turducken?"

"A turducken is a deboned turkey that is stuffed with a deboned duck. The duck is stuffed with a deboned chicken. The chicken is stuffed with shrimp and cornbread dressing. Malcolm injects the turducken with a marinade that I make."

"Och, that sounds delicious—and quite a lot to eat."

"You've seen Alexander eat," Rachel laughed. "We'll also have seafood gumbo, cornbread dressing and a salad. For dessert, we'll have pecan pie and ice cream. Come into the kitchen, and I'll show you how to make a roux for the gumbo. We'll make enough gumbo that you can take some to Ellen and Robert."

"First, we'll put bacon grease in this cast-iron skillet. I always save the grease from bacon. A cast-iron skillet works best."

Fiona smiled. "Auntie says all southern recipes begin with 'fry some bacon.'"

"Now that the bacon grease is hot, gradually whisk in some flour. This is the tedious part; you must constantly whisk until the mixture turns a reddish-brown color. Turn the flame to a medium setting when the mixture bubbles. Keep whisking. This process will take about 20 minutes—more if you want a dark roux. Don't let the roux burn. Keep whisking.

"While you are whisking, I'll chop the vegetables—onion, celery and green pepper. This mix is called the Cajun trinity. Cajuns use it in almost everything."

The scent of chopped onions filled the kitchen, and Rachel said, "The roux is ready. Let's pour it into this large cast-iron pot and then sauté the Cajun trinity." They did and then put the sautéed vegetables in the roux.

"Malcolm bought and cleaned some fresh shrimp and crabs from Mr. Callahan. He made a seafood stock to dilute the roux. Sometimes we use chicken stock." She smiled. "But I want this gumbo to be special. The shrimp and crab meat goes in last. We'll let it sit overnight. It is always better the next day."

Fiona noted, "You put a lot of effort into your gumbo!"

Outside the kitchen, Malcolm fired up his charcoal smoker and prepared to cook the turducken through the night. The fragrant aroma of mesquite-smoked turducken seeped through the patio and into the kitchen.

*****

THE DAY AFTER THANKSGIVING, AS FIONA AND ALEXANDER were about to leave for the Johnston's farm, Mrs. Gordon said, "Take this gumbo with you for Ellen and Robert." She gave Fiona a large, sealed container of gumbo.

Mrs. Gordon invited Fiona, "We've enjoyed having you. I hope we'll see you again for Christmas."

"I hope so as well."

A few minutes into their trip, Fiona mused, "Whit a wonderful family ye have, *mo leannan*! Truly a family to be thankful for!" She dabbed at her eyes. "They made me feel part of the family. I just love them."

"They certainly love you—just as I knew they would."

"And dinner was braw. I especially liked the gumbo. This was the first time I've eaten smoked turducken—it was delicious. No wonder everyone overeats!"

"You didn't overeat! You took only a bite or two of everything."

"I willna gain the freshman fifteen. I'm glad ye didna watch professional football on television and fall asleep."

"Parking on the beach with you and watching the sunset was much better. Those clouds in the sunset matched the color of your hair."

"Do ye realize we've only known each other for two months?"

Alexander teased, "It could have been longer if only you had accepted Mary's first invitation to meet me."

"By only a few days."

"I ken this: These two months have been wonderful, and I want many more."

"Me too."

*****

AT THE JOHNSTON FARM, Burnsie greeted the truck expectantly. Fiona jumped out and hugged him. "Burnsie! We're back. How have ye been?"

"Ruff!"

"I've missed ye too. Do ye remember Alexander? Say hello."

"Ruff!" Burnsie sat and raised his paw.

"Hello again, Burnsie. Yep, I'm back. Still hangin' in there."

Fiona laughed. "Ye are silly."

Alexander added, "Aaand, here we are for our second Thanksgiving Dinner!"

Fiona predicted, "And I'll bet ye eat it as well!"

"I intend to!"

"Two of my high school girlfriends will join us. I haven't seen Joan and Sandra since college started. They are day students at the local community college."

Ellen and Robert met Fiona and Alexander at the front door.

Ellen hugged Fiona tightly. "I'm so glad you are home. I miss having you to talk to. Robert doesn't talk much. There is much to catch up on."

While Robert was hugging Fiona, Ellen hugged Alexander, and he ventured, "I'm glad to see you again, Auntie." She smiled a warm and welcoming smile.

Robert shook Alexander's hand and said, "Welcome, welcome."

Ellen announced, "Dinner will be in a couple of hours. Fiona, can you help me?"

Fiona answered, "Let us get oor luggage from the truck." She and Alexander returned to the truck, and he retrieved their luggage. Fiona picked up the container of gumbo and brought it to the kitchen.

Fiona handed the gumbo to her aunt. "Mrs. Gordon sent ye some seafood gumbo." She added proudly, "I helped make it."

"Wonderful!"

$$*****$$

FIONA'S FRIENDS, Joan and Sandra, arrived shortly before dinner. After introductions all around, they entered the kitchen for final preparations.

Joan stepped back from Fiona, admired her and said, "Fiona, you are so beautiful—just as I always knew you would be. Plus, MU must agree with you. I do believe you've filled out a bit."

Fiona glowed. "At MU, I walk a lot. Also, I've taken up Jazzercise."

Sandra teased, "Well, Fiona, you may not have dated in high school, but you certainly are making up for it now!"

Joan agreed, "I'll say! When did you meet Alexander?"

"Two months ago, today."

"And how long have you been dating?"

"Two months today." Fiona smiled. Joan and Sandra giggled.

"Isn't this a bit soon to be inviting the boyfriend to your home?"

"Not in oor case."

Ellen was beaming. "Let's go to the table."

The girls got caught up with rapid back-and-forth bantering, giggling, and laughing. Alexander listened as he ate.

"Auntie, this is delicious," Alexander said. "Now I've had both the southern Mississippi and northern Mississippi versions of Thanksgiving Dinner."

"I wanted ours to be a little different, so I included a bit of Scotland as well. But I loved the delicious gumbo. Now for some pumpkin pie."

While eating her pie, Sandra grinned, "Fiona, so tell us how you met Alexander?"

Alexander pushed back from the table and declared, "That is my clue to excuse myself. Thank you, Auntie, for a wonderful dinner."

"I wish my friend Mary was here to tell the story," Fiona giggled. "Mary introduced us. I'll do the best I can."

Alexander turned to Robert. "Mr. Johnston, could I borrow your pistol to get in a little target practice?"

"Of course. I'll get it for you. Do you remember how to get to the shooting range? I'll stay inside and take a nap."

"I think I can find it. If not, I'll just walk."

Alexander hesitated a split second, then leaned over and gave Fiona a brief peck on her lips. He was rewarded with a reminder of the pumpkin pie.

Fiona's color brightened. Joan and Sandra giggled.

As Alexander eased away, Fiona began, "Mary wanted to introduce her friend to me but I..."

*****

THE GIRLS WERE WAITING for him when Alexander returned. They each had a copy of "The Look" picture. Fiona had already autographed the pictures, and the girls wanted Alexander's autograph as well. He obliged.

Ellen called Fiona for help, to leave Alexander with Joan and Sandra. Sandra whispered to Alexander. "I wanted to tell you quickly about Fiona in high school. She did not fit in well. She was too foreign, too tall, too skinny, too sophisticated, too smart, and too rich. She wore braces and had freckles. She was depressed about the death of her parents. Plus, she was shy. She did not have a good social life at all. She was a city girl in the country. Some people made fun of her, especially the football players. These are part of the reasons she chose MU instead of the community college. Fiona wanted to get away and start over."

"Thank you for telling me this. Fiona told me a little of it. I believe you, but it's almost impossible to imagine."

"I know. When Sandra and I first met Fiona, one of our first comments was she would be a raving beauty in a few years."

"Wherever we go, to a restaurant, store, church, even walking on campus, Fiona immediately attracts attention. She is so unbelievably beautiful that people want to see her for themselves. She is always the most beautiful girl in the room. It must be difficult for her sometimes."

"Did you ever think you might be one reason for attracting attention? Not to mention the sight of the two of you together!"

"Fiona has already changed very much since high school. Some of that credit must go to you. We're glad you two are dating. Please be careful. Please don't hurt her. She obviously loves you."

"I thank God every day for Fiona. I love her very much."

"Oh, do me a favor and show Fiona's picture to the boys who were giving her a hard time. Tell them they were stupid."

"Believe me, they already know."

*****

HAVING RETURNED to the MU campus, the girls were in Mary's room reliving their Thanksgiving holiday. All agreed they had overeaten, and they laughed about men falling asleep while watching one football game after another.

Fiona admitted, "Alexander and I had <u>two</u> Thanksgiving dinners!" and explained how that came to be. She described the Gordons and her time at their house, slyly adding, "I slept in Alexander's bed," which caused much giggling.

"Fiona learned how to peel shrimp," teased Mary. "She just sits by Alexander, and peeled shrimp appear on her plate."

Fiona blushed. "I loved meeting your parents, and the shrimp boil was a unique experience. The shrimp were wonderful!"

"My parents were impressed with you as well. They said they've never met anyone like you. My mom was especially impressed at the way Alexander attended you." Mary smiled.

"How about you, Jane?" asked Fiona. "You are very quiet."

"I had a good Thanksgiving with my family," Jane began, then choked. "I went out with my old high school boyfriend. He flunked out of junior college and is joining the Navy. He, uh, wants us to get back together before he ships out. I'm not so sure."

"Wait a minute!" said Anne. "Is that a hickey?"

"I didn't say I didn't like him, I just don't want to be as, uh, involved as he wants."

"Does it hurt?" Fiona asked as she rubbed her neck.

"No, it doesn't hurt, but probably will take a week to disappear. Guess I'd better put a little more makeup on it."

"Do guys get hickeys?" Fiona was intrigued.

"They can. Are you planning to mark Alexander with a hickey? You can practice on your arm but, believe me, everyone already knows he is yours."

"I thought you liked Donnie," Fiona said, changing the subject.

"I do and Donnie is a much better prospect."

"Have you told Donnie about this?"

"No, and there probably is no need to. I just need to think this through. I'm not ready to go steady with anyone. I'm having too much fun." Jane turned to Fiona. "Please don't say anything about this to Alexander or Donnie."

"I willna."

Later, alone with Mary, Fiona asked, "How many girlfriends did Alexander have?" She told Mary about meeting the girls at his Sunday School.

"Alexander dated several girls, but I wouldn't call any of them his girlfriend. Alexander has dated you for longer and more often than anyone ever. He's never brought a girl home to meet his parents, nor has he visited a date's parents. Don't worry, Fiona. Alexander is yours."

"That's whit Auntie says, too."

"And you are his."

"I ken."

*****

AS FIONA AND ALEXANDER ambled towards class the week before final exams, a well-dressed man in his middle forties approached them. "Alexander Malcolm Gordon?" he asked.

"Yes, sir. What can I do for you?"

The man handed Alexander a thick sealed envelope. "This is a summons to appear in court in Jackson next week."

"But I have finals next week. What's this all about?"

"I'm only the process server. I do not know the details. Just be in court next week. Sign here."

"What if I don't sign?"

"Then you are in contempt of court."

Alexander signed.

"Whit could this be about?" asked Fiona.

"I've got to call my lawyer right away. I don't know if I should open the envelope or not. Let me walk you to your class, then I'll go to my dorm and call my lawyer in privacy." They moved on.

Alone in his dorm room, Alexander called his lawyer, Bill Tees, in Oceanport.

"Hello, Alexander. Another invention?"

"I wish. There might be a legal problem. I don't know."

"You, a legal problem? I can't believe it. Tell me more."

"A process server gave me a summons today to appear in court in Jackson next week. I have finals next week."

"What does the summons say or claim?"

"I've not opened it. I wondered if I should give it to you first."

"No, open it. Read it to me."

After several minutes of reading legalese over the phone, Bill Tees interrupted Alexander.

"This is a trivial lawsuit—more harassment than anything else. It is likely to be quickly dismissed; however, it must be addressed. Who is Dr. Thomas Bennoitt Sr.?"

"Dr. Thomas Bennoitt must be the father of the guy who attacked me in a honkytonk bar."

"Ah, yes. I remember. Now he claims you attacked his son and is suing for medical costs plus damages and legal fees. He is also asking for a restraining order to keep you away from his son. He says his son will attend MU, and therefore you should not be allowed there."

"But Thomas was found guilty of attacking <u>me</u>."

"That was in criminal court. This is a civil suit."

"What do I do?"

"I need to see the full summons and review the charges and the criminal case. Can you meet me in Jackson tomorrow? I have a partner there who is better at this sort of case than I am. We will first file for a delay so you can take your finals and finish the semester. Then we will file a countersuit based on harassment and ask for dismissal and legal fees."

"I'll be there. See you tomorrow."

Alexander rushed to Fiona's classroom and arrived as she was leaving. He gave her the grim news.

"I'll ride to Jackson with ye."

"No, you need to prepare for finals."

"Ye need company and support. I'm going with ye."

Alexander was about to say he could handle this problem himself, but the determined expression on Fiona's face advised him otherwise. Besides, he really was happy to have her company on the drive to Jackson.

*****

TWO DAYS LATER, as Fiona and Alexander walked to class, the same process server approached.

"Mr. Gordon, sorry to be the bearer of bad news, but it's my job. This is a summons to appear in the local court."

Alexander signed the receipt, accepted the envelope, and opened it. He read the first page, skimmed the second, shook his head in disbelief, and said, "Coach Guffy is suing me for libel. He claims I got him fired and wants me to pay his contractual salary plus damages and court costs."

*****

THE FOLLOWING DAY, the same process server approached Fiona and Alexander, but this time he asked, "Miss Fiona MacDonald?"

Fiona, her voice quivering, replied, "Aye."

"This is a registered letter from the U.S. Citizenship and Immigration Services. Please sign here."

Fiona signed, opened the letter, and read. She turned to Alexander with tears in her eyes. "I must refile for my student visa to study in the United States."

*****

THE NEXT DAY WAS ALEXANDER'S TURN AGAIN. This time the registered letter was from his draft board asking that he prove he was a student in good standing. He said, "I'm going to President Curry. Someone is after me."

"I'll go with ye. Dinna keek at me that way. They are after me, too. Dinna allow this harassment to drive a wedge between us, Alexander Gordon. I love ye."

They hurried to the Main Administration building, entered the president's chamber, and asked the receptionist for an appointment. She recognized them and entered President Curry's office. The receptionist quickly returned and motioned them into President Curry's office.

"Fiona! Alexander! How good to see you again. What can I do for you?"

Alexander explained the current situation and showed President Curry the letter from his draft board.

President Curry studied the letter. "I will handle the draft board letter personally. I know the chairman of your draft board; he was one of my men. He knows your father as well. This does not feel right. In fact, all the events you have described appear to be harassment. Here is how I can help.

"Fiona, Dr. Crawford will handle your student visa letter and request for renewal. I expect that issue to be quickly resolved.

"Alexander, I will contact the MU legal department about Coach Guffy's libel suit. The Athletic Director, a security guard, and I were witnesses to his damaging statements when we fired him. I suspect we can get additional supporting affidavits as well. I expect Coach Guffy's suit to be quickly dropped.

"As to Dr. Thomas Bennoitt's suit, that is a different matter, but I am sure we can help you. Dr. Bennoitt is a well-connected and formidable foe. However, his son is not in good standing with MU and will not be permitted to register."

"My lawyers have asked for a delay so I can take my final exams," said Alexander. "They are also organizing and filing a countersuit."

President Curry handed Fiona and Alexander business cards. "Have your parents and lawyers contact the MU legal department for their help."

President Curry smiled at Fiona. "Tell Robert to restrain himself and not make the situation worse."

*****

IN HIS DORM ROOM, Alexander answered the phone with reluctance. It was his personal lawyer, Bill Tees.

"Hello, Alexander. Let me give you some updates."

"Please let it be good news. I need it."

"OK. They have granted us a delay in the Bennoitt suit so you can study and take your final exams unrestrained next week. We've also filed a countersuit. That's the good news. However, an unexpected situation is developing around your ultrasonic atomization patent."

"Tell me."

"General Motors has objected to your patent. They claim a patent issued to S. K. Hughes predates your patent."

"This explains why GM has not bought my device. I'm familiar with the Hughes patent. The device it describes will not work. I know because I tested it. Tell GM they better build the Hughes device and test it before they put it into production. This can be a good thing for me and my device."

"How about your other situations?"

"Fiona's student visa problem with U.S. Citizenship and Immigration Services was easily cleared. They acknowledged their mistake.

Alexander continued, "My draft board problem has been resolved. Someone had a clerk send me a form letter. The chairman of my draft board was not aware of the request and is investigating it."

"And Guffy?"

"The MU legal department is dealing with him. They expect him to drop his suit."

"Sounds like your situation is improving. Don't worry about the Bennoitt suit; we'll win. Good luck with your finals."

Donnie said, "I know I was eavesdropping, but please give me the other half of the conversation and tell me everything has been resolved."

"I wish, but the Bennoitt suit is ongoing. I need to call Fiona and give her the latest news. Just listen, and you'll get the update too."

*****

WITH THE FALL SEMESTER completed and their harassment issues mostly resolved, Fiona and Alexander had three weeks away from campus before beginning the spring semester. They developed a travel plan allowing them to stay together. The first stop would be the Johnston's farm, then the Gordons. They would return to MU via the farm. They jam-packed Alexander's truck with luggage, winter clothes, his guitar, and Christmas presents.

Alexander had bought an expensive pendant necklace for Fiona for Christmas. The gold heart pendant was lined with diamonds. The gold chain was longer and heavier than the "AF" necklace, and it might be possible to wear both simultaneously. Alexander wondered how Fiona would wear them.

As he drove towards the Johnston's farm, Alexander asked Fiona, "Can you talk about your mom and dad now?"

"To ye, I can. Ye would have liked my parents, and they certainly would have liked ye. If only she could have met ye, my mum, *mathair* in Gaelic, would have checked off a box on her list of wishes."

"My mother's full name was Aileen Fiona MacKenzie. I called her Mum. She was the middle child. She was a bonnie lass and smart." Fiona beamed and continued, "Everyone says I look exactly like her but a wee bit taller."

Alexander interrupted, "Remember, I saw the picture of your mother holding you as a baby. Like you, your mother was incredibly beautiful."

"Cuideigin a nì flatter!" I love it—and you.

"Mum played piano and sung every day. I can almost hear her playing and singing in oor house noo. She taught me to play piano and sing." Misty-eyed, Fiona muttered, "Excuse me a moment." She dabbed at her eyes with a tissue.

"She was a stay-at-home mum. As far as I ken, she never worked a paying job, but she occasionally attended conferences at the MacKenzie Distillery. She probably inherited some of it. Hmm, I wonder whit happened to her shares? Anyway, she loved church and charity work. I attended a private school and had tutors, but otherwise, Mum and I did everything together: museums, concerts, church, movies, shopping—everything."

"My father, *athair* in Gaelic, was Daniel Alastair MacDonald. I called him Da. He was an only child and was born in Texas, so was a full U. S. citizen. He was tall—but not as tall as ye—and slim. Dad was handsome, and everyone always remarked on whit a beautiful couple he and Mum made. He studied business in college and expanded a small inheritance from his father."

"We had an immense house in an exclusive neighborhood. My mum enjoyed cooking, but we had a maid who did most of it. Mum did not like housecleaning, so the maid also kept the house clean. Mum had a gorgeous garden; she loved flowers. Da did not like gardening or yard work; he used landscaping services.

"My parents pampered me," Fiona admitted. "Compared to Mum, Da was frugal, but he also spoiled me the most." She laughed. "Da did not like shopping, but he would take me when I asked. Once, when I was a wee bairn, I wanted a new dress. I held up two dresses to show Da and asked him which one I should get. He only wanted to get out of that dress shop, so he said, 'Just get both of them and let's go.' I learnt from that!"

Alexander asked, "Did your dad like sports?"

"He played soccer as a youngster, but I never watched him play soccer except to kick the ball with me. He liked golf, but only played occasionally. I suppose you play golf?"

"Yes, I play golf sometimes."

"Of course, ye do."

"You had a wonderful childhood." Alexander reminded her.

"Aye, but it all ended." Fiona wept and sniffled.

*****

BURNSIE SEEMED TO BE WAITING for them at the farm. "Shelties are highly intelligent." Fiona laughed. "But I don't think he can read a calendar."

"He must have exceptional hearing," said Alexander.

Ellen and Robert greeted them eagerly on the porch.

"I contacted the MU legal department," Robert advised, "and told them what that SOB Gully said during my visit. They were appalled and wrote an affidavit which I signed, and they will use it in your defense and countersuit."

Ellen interceded. "Enough of this kind of talk. This is Christmas. Let's make it a merry one."

The Johnston house was decorated tastefully with a Christmas theme. The warm fragrance of cookies spilled from the kitchen into the den. A real Christmas tree, beautifully decorated, stood proudly in the den.

Fiona was beaming. "I'm so glad to be home." She hugged Alexander. "And so glad ye're with me."

Alexander retrieved their luggage from his truck and added their presents to those already under the Christmas tree.

*****

CHRISTMAS EVE night after returning from church service, Fiona suggested to Alexander that they go to the porch swing. This was fine with Alexander, even though the night air was cool. He casually picked up a small package from beneath the Christmas tree as he passed it. Seated next to Alexander on the porch swing with Burnsie at her feet, Fiona whispered, "I want to give ye your Christmas present noo."

Alexander thought she was referring to a kiss, but Fiona reached into her coat pocket and removed a small package in Christmas wrapping. Almost shyly, she handed the box to Alexander and whispered, "I love ye that much."

Alexander opened the package to find the 'Fiona' neck chain she had designed. He choked, "It's beautiful—as you are."

"*Cuideigin a nì flatter!*"

"Would you put it on me?" Fiona gave Alexander a long, wet kiss. "I meant the neck chain," grinned Alexander, "but that was even better."

Fiona put the neck chain on Alexander and stepped back to admire him wearing it. Alexander grinned, "You might as well have used the possessive case and written 'Fiona's' on the chain."

"I considered it! But my name is to remind ye of me and not as a warning to other lassies."

"Now my turn." Alexander removed Fiona's gift from his pocket and handed it to her. "Fiona, I love you more than I can say—especially without my guitar handy. Merry Christmas."

Fiona unwrapped the diamond heart pendant necklace and gasped, "It is exquisite! Alexander, ye shouldn't have! But put it on me." He did and then put the necklace around Fiona's neck.

They remained on the porch for some time until even their combined body heat could not overcome the coolness of the night, and they were forced into the house.

*****

CHRISTMAS MORNING, Alexander could not decide whether to shave with or without his 'Fiona' necklace. He had never worn a necklace but liked the looks and meaning of this one. He left it on and picked up his razor.

At the customarily large breakfast whenever Alexander visited, Ellen remarked, "Nice neck chain." Alexander beamed. Robert stared at the 'Fiona' neck chain but did not comment.

Fiona asked Ellen, "Is wearing a diamond necklace too formal for breakfast?" She was wearing a low-cut blouse, and her necklace was brilliantly reflecting her auburn hair.

Ellen gasped, "Oh, let me see!" and quickly stepped over to admire Fiona's necklace.

That afternoon, Joan and Sandra dropped in to visit Fiona. She met them at the door. They pointed to Alexander's customized truck and remarked, "So, you've lasted another month!"

"Aye, we have! Every day is a record!"

"Oh my," exclaimed Joan. "What a beautiful necklace."

"From Alexander," smiled Fiona.

"Of course." Sandra grinned and twisted a ring on her finger. "We wondered what he might give you."

Fiona blushed and shook her head.

Alexander came in with an armload of wood and placed it near the fireplace. He turned and greeted Joan and Sandra.

Sandra teased, "Does someone have a new neck chain?"

Alexander grinned. "Better than a branding iron."

*****

ALONE WITH ELLEN in the kitchen after supper, Fiona ventured, "Auntie, is it really true ye and Uncle eloped three months after meeting?"

Ellen hesitated. She had been expecting this conversation but did not relish it. "Yes, Honey. It's true. Let me be the first to admit we were too young, and we were foolish, but we were deeply in love. Fortunately, and luckily, our marriage survived the problems that followed. Everyone thought I was pregnant, but, of course, I was not. Our parents disapproved, and their disapproval lasted several years. MU did not allow us to return as a married couple until the next semester. Even Robert and I agreed we'd made a mistake; however, we remained in love and together. And still are."

Fiona had been unaware of these details of Ellen's elopement.

Ellen continued, "You and Alexander met three months ago, is that correct?"

"Yes, ma'am."

"Forgive me, but I must ask. Are you pregnant?"

"No, certainly not."

"Are you considering eloping?"

"No, ma'am. I love Alexander that much, and I ken he loves me. I'm certain he will propose. It's just that oor relationship is in a strange phase noo. Although he hasna proposed, we sometimes talk about oor future together. It is almost as though we are each taking the other for granted."

"Your situation is simply that you are young, inexperienced, often meet new people, and neither of you knows what to do. Be patient and continue to learn about each other. It will all work out.

"Your girlfriends are aware of your love for Alexander. They assume you will marry, and they are happy for you and are encouraging you, is that correct?"

"Och, aye, Auntie."

"Do you realize Alexander's guy friends are harassing him about giving up his independence and even freedom? They are telling him his income is about to be cut in half."

"I hadna considered that."

"Well, they are—and more, including the infamous 'why buy the cow when you can get the milk for free.'"

"Auntie!"

*****

THE DAY AFTER CHRISTMAS, Fiona and Alexander drove to Oceanport to visit and stay with Alexander's parents. Mr. and Mrs. Gordon had been waiting impatiently for them.

"We've saved Christmas dinner for tonight," Rachel explained. "We're having ham and the trimmings."

Caroline exclaimed, "Necklaces!" and came over to admire them. Liz followed.

The house looked and smelled Christmasy. Alexander unloaded his truck while Rachel showed off her Christmas-themed arts and crafts, including several hand-painted nativity scenes.

"Och, that sleigh," admired Fiona. "Can I hold it?"

"Yes," answered Rachel. "I made it from the breastbone of a turkey."

"How clever!" praised Fiona.

Fiona continued touring the Christmas decorations. "I really like your house. It is so <u>ye</u> and just perfect for ye with the studio and workshop."

Malcolm agreed. "We like this house, but we will move to a new and better place on twenty acres of land in a few months."

Caroline and Liz had invited a friend each for the delayed Christmas dinner. They all moved to the dining room after their friends arrived.

After dinner, they exchanged gifts. On learning Mr. Gordon collected knives, Fiona bought him an authentic Scottish dirk. She gave Mrs. Gordon a teapot as she promised. Fiona gave Caroline a Scottish thistle heart necklace and Liz a heather heart pendant.

Fiona put a large, fancy box on the table near Mr. Gordon. "From Auntie," she said. He unwrapped the box to discover a bottle of Mackenzie Scotch Whisky.

"Now I can try good Scotch," he smiled.

Mrs. Gordon had made Fiona a Scottish shawl using the MacDonald tartan pattern. A brooch pin, homemade by Mr. Gordon, completed the outfit. Fiona was thrilled and emotional.

"I'm no genealogist," said Fiona, "but I found information on your Clan Gordon at MU. They had little data but whit I found was interesting." She laid a thick file folder next to the bottle of Mackenzie Scotch Whisky. "The name 'Alexander' comes up often."

"Thank you, Fiona," said Malcolm. "My grandmother told me that Alexander was a celebrated name in the family."

Caroline, Liz, their friends, and Fiona went to the enclosed patio to discuss school, Scotland, and boys.

*****

IN THE KITCHEN, Malcolm said, "I hate to bring up a sore subject, son, but please update us on your legal problems."

"The lawsuits are still not resolved, but the outcomes will probably be favorable," Alexander said. "We think Coach Guffy will drop his suit soon. Fiona's student visa problem has been cleared. The draft board has okayed another student deferment for me. President Curry was most helpful in clearing up those issues.

"The Bennoitt lawsuit is the most bothersome, but my lawyers have filed a countersuit. They think—as I do—that Dr. Bennoitt is behind all this harassment to Fiona and me.

"On the bright side, General Motors is reconsidering using my ultrasonic emission device and probably will license it."

Malcolm asked, "Son, does Fiona know about your money?"

"Yes, sir. I told her, and she said she had already figured that out, and it did not matter to her."

Rachel asked, "What else did she say?"

"Fiona said she loved me despite my money and not because of it."

Rachel added, "All the same, she seems to be someone who grew up around money."

"You are probably correct."

"If your money does not matter to her, then she probably has money of her own."

"Her aunt and uncle are well off, and Fiona was the beneficiary of her parents' life insurance policies. Those policies remind her of her parent's death. We rarely discuss money."

*****

"HEY MAN, it's David."

"What's up?"

"I've got a good gig for New Year's Eve, and I want to invite you and Fiona."

"Thanks, David, but Fiona does not fit in well at honkytonks."

"I heard about that. But this is a private club. It will be nice, maybe even sophisticated; however, there's a catch."

"Tell me about it."

"You'll have to sing for your supper but only a few songs."

"Let me check with Fiona."

"I want her to play and sing as well. We can practice a couple of days before the party."

"Come on over. Let's talk about it.

On their way to David's house, Fiona ventured, "Ye are buying that land and house for your parents, aren't ye?"

"Yes, I am," Alexander responded. "They deserve it, and I'm more than happy to help them get it."

Fiona placed her hand on Alexander's arm and squeezed it gently.

Alexander rang the doorbell at David's house and heard David say, "I'm in the game room." He was sitting at his drums.

Alexander asked, "What do you have in mind?"

David explained he wanted Alexander and Fiona to help by stretching out the break for the band. "I'll let two people go on break, and you two can replace them for a couple of songs. Then the rest of the band can go on break, and you can sing a duet or two."

"Sounds good to me. You already know Fiona can play 'What'd I say.' How about 'Johnny B. Goode'? We already have a duet we can sing."

"Let's practice."

After practice ended, David asked Fiona about New Year's Eve in Scotland.

Fiona explained that, in Scotland, the last day of the year was called "Hogmanay" instead of New Year's Eve. "Oor famous poet, Robert Burns wrote 'Auld Lang Syne'. 'Auld Lang Syne' means something like 'auld long since' or 'for the sake of auld times.' In Gaelic, we might say *seann fhada on uair sin.*'"

"Can you introduce 'Auld Lang Syne' just before midnight?"

"I'd be honored to."

*****

THE ELK'S CLUB sponsored The New Year's Eve party in downtown Oceanport. To Alexander's relief, the floor had no sawdust, and the attendees were well-dressed. Most people were older than Alexander.

Fiona had bought a new off-the-shoulder gown and was gorgeous. Men's eyes followed her everywhere. Since she was with Alexander, she was wearing high heels and towered over everyone except Alexander.

Fiona admired Alexander's tuxedo. "In Scotland," she informed him, "Ye'd be wearing a kilt of the Gordon tartan and probably carrying a dirk."

David's band began with a few old standards and did a credible job. Fiona and Alexander sat quietly at a small table, sipping on sodas, and holding hands.

After about an hour, David announced, "The band will ease into a break now, but I have some replacements I'm sure you will enjoy. Please welcome Fiona and Alexander."

The keyboard player and a guitar player left the stage as Fiona and Alexander came on. Alexander was holding Fiona's hand. Whistles greeted Fiona. Alexander picked up his guitar, stepped to the microphone and grinned, "Eat your hearts out!"

Fiona blushed but began the introduction to "What'd I Say." David joined in and then Alexander. This time, David shouting the words did not surprise Fiona, although she smiled. A crowd gathered near the stage as they played. At the end of "What'd I Say," the crowd applauded.

Alexander played the introduction to "Johnny B. Goode" and then launched into the lyrics with Fiona's accompaniment. At the end of "Johnny B. Goode," the rest of the band slipped away. Alexander announced, "Here's a song that is particularly important to Fiona and me." Fiona joined Alexander at the microphone. Alexander played the introduction to "Perhaps Love" and then, never taking his eyes away from Fiona, began their duet.

Everyone enthusiastically applauded their duet, and women were misty-eyed.

When he returned to the stage, David commented, "This is supposed to be a dance, but you are turning it into a concert!" He smiled at Fiona.

Just before midnight, Alexander said, "Let's end the year with a kiss," and caressed Fiona in his arms.

Fiona approached the microphone. "'Auld Lang Syne' was written by the famous Scottish poet Robert Burns. In Scotland, the last day of the year is called "Hogmanay" instead of New Year's Eve. 'Auld Lang Syne' means something like 'auld long since' or 'for the sake of auld times.' In Gaelic, we might say 'seann fhada on uair sin.'"

At the stroke of midnight, in a heavy Scottish accent, Fiona sang

Shid ald akwentans bee firgot,
an nivir brocht ti mynd?
Shid ald akwentans bee firgot,
an ald lang syn?

Everyone joined in the singing.

"And now, let's begin the New Year with a kiss," Alexander invited. They did.

*****

"HAVE YOU EVER HAD A PO'BOY?" Alexander asked Fiona.

"I dinna ken. Whit is a po'boy?"

"Ah, so you've not eaten one. Let's go get some."

"I'm willing to try. After all, I went to a shrimp boil."

"Dad," Alexander called out, "Fiona and I are going to Rose's for po'boys. Should I bring some home?"

"Please. That will be a great supper for us."

In his truck, Alexander explained to Fiona that a po'boy was an inexpensive sandwich developed in New Orleans during the depression for poor laborers. The original po'boys were mostly bread, but they had since become a delicacy.

"Rose has the best po'boys in Oceanport. She features roast beef, shrimp, and crab—all fully dressed."

"Dressed?"

"Yes, shredded lettuce, tomatoes, pickles on homemade mayonnaise spread. Rose makes her own tartar sauce for the shrimp and crab po'boys. I like to add cheese to the crab po'boy—that makes it a Rose's Special."

"Sounds delicious. I willna have to peel the crab, will I?"

"No," Alexander laughed. "It will come as a crab cake."

Alexander parked his truck next to an old, dilapidated framed building whose flaking white paint needed attention. A hand-painted sign over the entrance door read 'Rose's Place.' "I know it doesn't seem like much," he explained, "but the po'boys are amazing."

They walked to the entrance hand-in-hand. Fiona stopped, and Alexander pulled the tattered screen door open, then stretched and pushed the wooden door open. Fiona stepped through, and Alexander followed.

Alexander found a table and pulled out a wooden chair for Fiona. He sat by her side, wondering what she thought of the restaurant. A red and white vinyl checkered table cloth covered the table. Salt, pepper, and a shaker of Ms. Rose's famous seasoning sat in the middle of the table near a roll of paper towels. Alexander felt certain Fiona had never been in a place like Rose's.

"Well, look what the cat drug in!" A tall waitress approached their table. She was shapely, with long straight platinum blonde hair and bright red lipstick. Her miniskirt and low-cut blouse accentuated her figure.

"Maude?" asked Alexander.

"Who else? Is Red here your latest new girlfriend?"

"I didn't recognize you as a blonde, Maude, and didn't know you worked here."

"I work for Rose during the week and holidays. I dance on the weekends."

"I'm majoring in dance," Fiona interjected. "Whit kind of dance do you do?"

Maude gave Fiona a hard stare. "Go-go, not lap."

"Fiona, allow me to introduce you to Maude. Maude and I were classmates in high school."

"*Madainn mhath*, Maude. I'm pleased to meet ye."

"I just bet you are, Red." Maude turned to Alexander. "Where'd you find her?"

"Fiona is from Scotland," Alexander explained. "She is a freshman at MU."

"How nice," Maude said. "Not everyone can afford to go to MU. I'm enrolled in the community college for now, but I hope eventually to go to MU. Maybe I'll see you there." She winked at Alexander.

"Perhaps," answered Fiona. "I can show you the campus."

"I was talking to Alexander, Red. Meanwhile, what can I get you?"

"We'll have three small po'boys to eat here: roast beef, shrimp and Rose's Special crab," answered Alexander. "Add onion rings and root beer. Then give us two small roast beef, one shrimp, and one Rose's Special crab to go. And please tell Ms. Rose hello for me."

"Think Ms. Rose will treat you special? Everyone else does."

"No," Alexander smiled. "I just want to tell her hello."

"And what for you, Red?"

"I ordered for Fiona," Alexander said.

"OK, you must not be hungry." Maude left their table and entered the kitchen.

"Whit is wrong with her?" asked Fiona.

225

"That's just the way she is—especially around me."

The kitchen door opened, and a rotund woman came out. "Alexander!" she cried. "Where have you been? I've missed you. What have you been up to?"

Alexander stood and hugged Ms. Rose, but even his long arms were too short. She noticed Alexander's 'Fiona' necklace and scrutinized Fiona. "Ah, I see what you've been up to!"

"Ms. Rose, allow me to introduce Fiona. Fiona is a freshman at MU and is in Oceanport with me visiting my parents." Alexander felt his cheeks glow as Ms. Rose smiled. He turned to Fiona. "Ms. Rose makes the best po'boys in town."

"*Madainn mhath*, Ms. Rose. I'm pleased to meet ye."

"What a lovely voice. Scottish, is it? Come, give us a hug." Fiona attempted to hug Ms. Rose.

"*Ma Cherie*," Ms. Rose teased. "You are beautiful but too skinny. You need some of my red beans and rice to give Alexander something to hold. I'll send some out."

Fiona blushed but laughed. "*Taing*. Only a small dish, please."

"Well, I have po'boys to make." Ms. Rose returned to her kitchen.

"I like her," Fiona noted. "I ken she is fun to be around."

Maude returned with a pitcher of root beer, two glasses, and a small bowl of red beans and rice with sausage. She plunked the bowl in front of Fiona and left.

"Ms. Rose makes her own root beer," Alexander said as he poured Fiona's glass. "It's delicious. You won't find anything like it anywhere else."

Fiona was delicately eating red beans and rice with her plastic fork in her left hand, tines down, when Maude returned with a basket of fried onion rings.

"Um, Maude, would you bring a plate for Fiona? A real plate, not paper. Oh, and a metal knife and fork."

"Of course, wouldn't want her to eat with her fingers, would we?" Maude swaggered away but quickly returned with a flourish and plunked a plate in front of Fiona.

Fiona speared an onion ring from the basket, placed it on her plate, and cut off a tiny bit. "Och, these are delicious!"

"Would you like some ketchup?"

"Nay, I want them to taste like onions, not ketchup. In Scotland, we sprinkle a wee bit of vinegar on fried foods. It is a lighter touch than ketchup."

"I'll try vinegar some time."

Maude returned with three po'boys wrapped in paper. "Which one is for Red?"

"I'll take care of it, thanks Maude."

The po'boys were already cut into two pieces each. Alexander opened each po'boy, cut one piece in half, and placed the quartered po'boy on Fiona's plate. He then slid the paper wrapping to his place. He grabbed a handful of onion rings, put them on top of his paper wrapping, and squirted ketchup on the side.

Alexander took a big bite of his roast beef po'boy and felt gravy drip down his chin. He glanced at his hands. Yes, gravy on his hands as well. Embarrassed, he glanced at Fiona.

Fiona had removed the top piece of bread from her quartered po'boys and treated the rest as open-faced sandwiches. She cut off a tiny bit of roast beef po'boy and tasted it. "Och, delicious as ye said."

Alexander tore off a section of paper towel from the roll on the table and wiped his chin and hands. "They say the measure of a roast beef po'boy is how many paper towels are needed to wipe up the gravy. This is a very good po'boy." He folded a few sheets of paper towels and handed them to Fiona.

Fiona had a bite of the shrimp and then the crab po'boy. "Och, they are all that good, but I dinna think I can eat everything."

"Well, Ms. Rose will come to check on us, and she will fuss. At least be prepared to tell her which one you liked best."

"I like the crab best. I've not had crab with cheese in a sandwich before, and that spread really brings out the taste."

"I'll finish your po'boys."

Maude came out with the to-go part of their order as Alexander finished Fiona's uneaten po'boy quarters. "So you still have an appetite after all!" She handed Alexander the bag of po'boys and the bill.

Alexander glanced at the bill, added a generous tip, and handed Maude the cash payment. "Keep the change."

"Thanks," Maude said and handed Alexander a business card. "Call me sometime."

In his truck, Alexander said, "Fiona, I owe you an apology and an explanation. I apologize on behalf of Maude. I did not know she worked at Rose's Place, or I would not have brought you here. Maude transferred to my high school as a sophomore. She's always been a bit rude—especially when I'm around. She has never liked me and still doesn't."

"Och, she likes ye all right—she just doesna <u>have</u> ye."

"You're a good judge of people, but you are wrong this time."

"Can I see the card she gave ye?"

Alexander handed Fiona the business card from Maude. It was from the Festival Night Club. 'Fancy' and 'Exotic Dancer' were printed on the front. Fiona flipped the card over. The back of the card contained 'Maude' and a telephone number written by a ballpoint pen with blue ink.

Fiona did not hesitate. She ripped Maude's card in half and then ripped the halves into smaller pieces. She dropped the pieces into her purse. "Ye dinna need that card."

No, I don't, thought Alexander. *I really don't.* He tried to hide his smile.

Part 2

Spring Semester

1971

Chapter 8: Spring Semester

The smiling Spring comes in rejoicing,
And surly Winter grimly flies;
Now crystal clear are the falling waters,
And bonie blue are the sunny skies.
Fresh o'er the mountains breaks forth the morning,
The ev'ning gilds the ocean's swell;
All creatures joy in the sun's returning,
And I rejoice in my bonie Bell.
--Robert Burns

THE MU CAMPUS, virtually empty over the extended Christmas and New Year's holiday, was filling up and returning to normal.

As usual, the girls congregated in Mary's room to relive their holiday adventures. Fiona intentionally wore the diamond necklace Alexander gave her, but she knew everyone would inspect her ring finger.

"That's a beautiful necklace," Anne said. "What did you give Alexander?"

"A choker with my signature."

"It chokes him if he looks at other girls," Mary laughed. "Sorry, could not resist."

Everyone laughed, even Fiona.

Jane came in, a tear in her eye. "I broke it off with my old boyfriend," she said. "He's in the Navy now—without me. I couldn't marry him and I couldn't wait for him—and not just because of Donnie. I don't love him anymore, perhaps never did.

Anyway, it is a new year and a new semester. Who knows what will happen?"

Fiona hugged Jane. "We're here for ye," she said.

Later, alone with Mary, Fiona said, "I met Maude."

"Oh, where?"

"We went to Rose's for poor boys. She is a waitress there. Alexander didna ken she worked at Rose's and did not recognize her at first. Her hair is bleached platinum blonde and is long and straight. I think she irons it. The poor boys were delicious, but I wouldna go there again if Maude was there. Alexander apologized over and over because of the way she treated me."

"She's OK. You just saw her bad side since you were with Alexander."

"Aye, Alexander told me they had never got along, and she still didna like him, but that's not the way I read it."

"You read it correctly. Guys are blind. Let me give you some background on Maude."

"Alexander said that she came to your school as a sophomore."

"Right. Maude's family moved to Oceanport from New Jersey. Her dad had been out of work for months. He found a job at the shipyard as a welder. As a Yankee, Maude did not fit in well. You probably know something about that."

"Aye."

"She was an excellent basketball player. In fact, Maude led the basketball team to a conference championship and was on the all-star team. She was tough.

"Maude was attracted to Alexander and saw how all the girls fawned over him. She took a different approach and played hard to get, but she overdid it, and it backfired on her. They never had a date. Her hard-to-get approach became a bad attitude whenever Alexander was around. Sounds like she still has that problem.

"In the summer before our senior year, Maude's dad had a heart attack and died. They had been recovering financially, but this set them back. Maude stayed in school but quit basketball to work as a cashier. So now, she's a waitress?"

"Aye, and she goes to the community college. She is a go-go dancer on the weekends. She gave Alexander her business card. It said she was an exotic dancer named 'Fancy.'"

"Maude never did like her name."

"She wrote her telephone number on the back of the card. As soon as we got back in the truck, I tore up the card."

Mary laughed and slapped her knee. "Did you really?"

"Aye. Alexander did not need that card."

"What did he say?"

"Nothing, but I noticed he was trying to hold back a smile."

"So that's Maude. She is smart and a very hard worker."

"Ye painted a different picture than I expected."

"I'm not saying you and Maude would be close friends—even disregarding Alexander. I'm just saying the real Maude is different from the person you met."

"I ken. Still, if she comes to MU, I willna go out of my way to meet her."

"Maude is using her looks and skills to gain experience and make her way in this world. Imagine what you would do if you suddenly were entirely on your own."

"Alexander would take care of me."

"Of course he would. But suppose he was not around or could not do so. What would you do?"

"I dinna ken." Fiona dabbed at her eye. "I'm not lazy. I'm not afraid, ye ken. I would find a job somehow, somewhere. I dinna like the idea of being without Alexander."

*****

THE NEXT MORNING, Fiona stepped tentatively on the scales in the dormitory exercise room. "Whew! I gained only five pounds of the dreaded freshman fifteen. And that's after two Christmas dinners!"

Jane complimented her. "Jazzercise is working for you. Believe me, those five pounds are well distributed!"

"I'm taking an introductory course in home economics that includes cooking. My diet may be about to change, so I must continue to exercise."

"What other courses are you taking?"

"The usual music and dance courses, but I've added a course in creative writing that I'm really looking forward to. How about ye?"

"Boring business classes, I'm afraid. Your classes seem much more interesting than mine."

"Well, ye can always change majors."

"No, I know my talents and my role in life."

"Wish I kent my role in life."

"Fiona," Jane smirked, "Your role in life is being defined."

Fiona blushed. Jane was referring to her relationship with Alexander, but what about a vocation? *Poet? Singer/songwriter? Musician? What contribution could she make to society? How would she earn a living? Perhaps she would discover herself this semester.*

*****

A FEW DAYS AFTER REGISTRATION, FIONA joined Alexander, Donnie, and Jane for morning coffee in the Student Union snack room. "I have an announcement!" Fiona was excited. "I have decided to become a United States Citizen!"

"I'm surprised. I know how much you love Scotland," said Jane. "Can you have dual citizenship?"

"Yes, in fact, my dad held dual citizenship. He was born in the USA. My paternal grandfather was on a military training assignment in Texas, where my dad was born.

"Wait a minute," Donnie teased. "So, you're not the pure Scot you claim to be. You're part Texan?"

"No, both my mom and dad were pure Scots. My dad was born on an army base in Texas. That meant he could be a US citizen and his parents followed through with the paperwork and procedures in case it might come in handy someday—and it has.

"This is terrific news," beamed Alexander. Fiona would remain in the States longer.

"Anyway, I'm eligible, and I've applied for naturalization. I've not been a permanent resident for a full five years, so I must apply for a special exemption. My counselor believes my application will be approved. There is an English test and a Civics test, but I can pass them."

That night in their dorm room, Jane commented, "I thought a non-citizen could become a citizen by marrying a citizen."

Fiona's cheeks were warm and rosy. "Many people believe that, but it is not correct. I checked."

"Oh."

*****

THE HIPPIE STANDING AT THE BASE of the Student Union steps was obviously waiting for Alexander. Alexander continued down the steps toward him. The hippie, backpack in place, watched him with a broad grin.

He probably wants money, thought Alexander. *If he's sober, I'll give him a few dollars. He needs to eat and wash those clothes.*

"Alexander," said the hippie. "Great to see you again."

Alexander was not surprised the hippie knew his name—most students did. However, he could not remember having met him previously and did not recognize him. Who could this be?

The hippie laughed; his eyes crinkled behind thick, round glasses. He extended his hand. "Jerry Owens. Now, do you remember?"

Alexander studied the hippie's face and tried to remove his scraggly beard and long, curly hair without success. "Of course, Jerry," he finally grinned in recognition. "It's just that you've changed a bit." He grasped Jerry's hand and shook it. Then they hugged.

Jerry Owens had been a year behind Alexander in high school and played football with him. Despite his limited size, Jerry was a fierce linebacker. He was also a gifted student and, like Alexander, Valedictorian of his class.

Alexander stepped back and, once again, took in the unkempt hippie standing in front of him. "In costume, or has the co-op program relaxed its dress code?" After graduating from high school, Jerry had joined the Cooperative Education program at MU as an aerospace engineering student. They had assigned him a lucrative student engineering job in Texas.

"I'm not a co-op student anymore. I'm tired of rules, regulations, and anything that attempts to limit my rights and freedoms. I am reinventing myself as a poet. Are you still in engineering?"

"Still majoring in mechanical engineering but also taking photography and music theory this semester. Are you enrolled at MU?"

"Yes, for the time being. I may not complete a degree program, though."

"Well, you look like you could use a meal. I'm going to the cafeteria to meet my girlfriend for supper. Come with me. I'll introduce you to Fiona and buy your supper."

"Best offer I've had today."

They walked to the cafeteria. "Let's wait. Fiona will be here in a few minutes." Alexander said, "I always try to be a little early, so she doesn't have to wait by herself."

Fiona soon arrived, a puzzled expression on her face at seeing Alexander with Jerry.

"Fiona, allow me to introduce Jerry Owens. Jerry attended the same high school as I did, and we played football together."

Fiona extended her hand, "Hello, Jerry." Jerry gently touched her hand.

"I've invited Jerry to have supper with us. Shall we go in and continue the conversation inside where it is warmer?" They entered the cafeteria.

Once seated at a table, Alexander opened the conversation with "Jerry began his studies as an aerospace engineer, but he tells me he now wants to become a poet."

"He already is a poet," Fiona replied. "Jerry is in my creative writing class. The professor often praises his work and sometimes reads his poems to the class as an example."

"As he does yours," Jerry added. "I recognize you from the class and am pleased to meet you. Your poetry is beautiful—as are you."

"*Moran taing,*" Fiona blushed.

Wanting to change the subject, Alexander asked, "When did you become a hippie?"

"Partway into my first work semester, I discovered I did not want to be an engineer. I've always liked the music of the Beatles, Bob Dylan, and Joan Baez, and I listened more carefully to the words. As I came to understand, I objected to and protested the Vietnam War and the draft. These are the major origins and foundation of the hippie movement."

"How do you feel about the war?" Jerry challenged Alexander. "What are you doing about it?"

"I don't like the war. The government misled us and probably lied to us about getting into it. So I vote against the war but do not take part in demonstrations and protests. I have, however, donated blood."

"So while I am protesting to get us out, you donated blood to keep us in?"

"I donated blood because we have classmates, friends and relatives who are over there whether or not they want to be. If they need blood, I want them to have it."

"I've no donated blood," Fiona interjected. "Perhaps I should. Whit is it like?"

"I fainted," Alexander laughed. "The nurse explained that it was not unusual for football players to faint—especially the leaner ones."

Jerry continued, "Songs like 'People Got to be Free' by the Rascals and 'War' by Edwin Starr become even more meaningful if you study the words. I acted on those words. I put my own thoughts into words and poems."

Fiona listened in rapt attention.

"But enough about me," Jerry said. "And I know Alexander. Tell me about yourself, Fiona."

Fiona gave the short version of how she came to be at MU and then added, "I arrived in America, feeling depressed and out of place. I soon became intrigued by the hippie movement. I read everything I could find about hippies and listened carefully to those songs ye mentioned. I watched the news on TV and followed the events related to hippies. Should I become a hippie? I made a tie-dyed blouse and wore a sweatband on my forehead. It was fascinating!"

"You don't look like a hippie!" Jerry laughed.

"Eventually, the drugs, protests, and even some fashions turned me off. The music became psychedelic and heavy metal and was no longer melodic to me."

"Some drugs can be mind-opening," objected Jerry.

They finished their meal in silence.

While walking Fiona to her dorm, Alexander commented, "I did not know of your fascination with hippies."

"I was a troubled teenager seeking solutions and a new way of life. I still wonder about my role in life. Your friend is a distraught young man seeking his own answers. I wish him well."

They continued in silence.

*****

"I'M GOING TO TRY OUT FOR BASEBALL." Alexander put down his coffee cup at their table in the Student Union coffee shop.

"I'm not surprised," Fiona replied. "Ye need to be busy, and ye're missing your sports."

In his youth, Alexander's ambition was to be a professional baseball player. He and his friends played baseball all day and nearly every day. He loved reading about baseball and read every baseball book in the library—especially the youth fiction novels. Watching baseball on television with his father was more than entertainment—it was a learning experience. In those years, Alexander knew baseball would be his sport. Perhaps it could be once more.

"Bonnie. I'll enjoy watching ye. Noo, whit is a baseball?"

"I'll teach you." Alexander laughed. Although not a sports fan, Fiona had been in America for over three years and probably knew a little about baseball.

That afternoon, Alexander handed Fiona his baseball glove. "OK, you throw with your right hand, so put this glove on your left hand. Don't worry about putting a finger into every finger hole in the glove. In fact, put your hand in the glove like this. Now open and close the glove by opening and closing your hand. That's good. I'm going to step away a few feet and then throw you the ball. Open the glove by opening your hand. Catch the ball in the glove by closing it as soon as you feel the ball hit it. Then take the ball out of the glove with your right hand and throw it back to me. This is called 'pitch and catch.'"

After throwing the ball back and forth for several minutes, Alexander handed Fiona a baseball bat. He showed her how to place her hands on the bat and hold the bat over her right shoulder. Alexander stepped a few feet away and threw a slow underhand pitch for Fiona to hit. She swung the bat but released it. The bat flew spinning towards Alexander. He caught it and laughed.

"I think I've played my last game of baseball," Fiona announced. "But I'll be happy to cheer for ye."

*****

ALEXANDER KNOCKED on Coach Parker's office door and was invited in. He introduced himself. Coach Parker smiled. "Certainly, I remember you, Alexander. I wanted you to play baseball for me, and I still do."

"Thank you, sir. In fact, that's why I'm here. I'd like to try out for the baseball team. I don't need a scholarship. Coach Guffy blocked me from playing basketball, but I'm hoping to play baseball since he's no longer here and this is a new semester."

"I need to do some checking, but I think you can join the team." He picked up the telephone, dialed it, and said, "Joey, I'm sending Alexander Gordon to the locker room. Please help him get equipped."

"Thank you, sir. You won't be sorry."

In the locker room, Alexander pounded the baseball into his glove. It was great holding a baseball in a glove again. Now he might play collegiate baseball! He was rusty, but would practice hard. He jogged out onto the field.

*****

AFTER TWO WEEKS OF PRACTICE, an assistant coach noted to Coach Parker, "Alexander hasn't played baseball in a while, but he is rapidly becoming the best player on the team."

"I agree. Now to figure out how best to use him."

Alexander entered Coach Parker's office and found his two top assistants there as well. Coach Parker explained, "Alexander, just as I remembered, you are an outstanding baseball player, and you will improve rapidly as the season goes on. I want you to be on this team, and I plan to use you extensively. One reason you are here today is so we can discuss how to best use you. But first, I have a question about your plans and intentions concerning baseball.

"Thank you, sir, for your compliments. I'm enjoying playing baseball again. Most people assume I'll be a professional athlete, but I won't. The pros are always on the move. The temptations while traveling must be nearly irresistible. Sure, the money is good and the fame tempting, but professional sports are not for me. Instead, I plan to get multiple advanced degrees in engineering and use those skills to develop my own business and company. In a nutshell, that's it."

"Some would disagree and argue with you, but obviously, you've given this much thought. Now, let's discuss where you might fit on this team."

The pitching coach said, "I want you to pitch."

The batting coach said, "You'll soon be the best hitter on the team, so I want you to bat in every game."

Coach Parker interjected, "Since you have no aspirations to play professionally, there's no need to concentrate on any particular position or skill. What are your ideas, Alexander?"

"I want to pitch and bat for myself—that is, without a designated hitter. Also, I'd prefer to not be a designated hitter. I could play defense in the outfield, say right field. I have good stamina, and I'm sure I can do this."

"Alexander, you still have some rusty spots, but I will be gradually working you into the games. Please be patient. I predict you'll soon be a full-time player and starter.

＊＊＊＊＊

AS FIONA WALKED TO BALLET class, a curled, almost crumpled student lay on the steps of the English building, his head on a pillow, apparently sleeping. As she neared him, she recognized Jerry Owens. She called out, "Jerry! Jerry!" but he did not respond. Fiona kneeled and found Jerry taking very shallow breaths. She shook him, "Jerry! Whit is wrong?"

Jerry lifted his head slightly, "Glue," and returned his head to the pillow.

Another student came up and said, "The ambulance is on its way."

The ambulance soon arrived, and a nurse emerged. She glanced at Jerry and grunted, "Him again?"

"Will he be all right?" asked Fiona.

"Most likely. He is a glue sniffer. We've treated him before. Some fluids and bed rest, and he'll recover. Friend of yours?"

"His name is Jerry Owens. He is in my creative writing class."

"Better keep him away from glue."

They loaded Jerry into the ambulance and took him away.

Fiona proceeded to her ballet class. *Jerry had many problems. How could she help him?*

*****

I CAN'T PUT IT OFF ANY LONGER, thought Dr. Richardson, ballet instructor. *I must tell her.* Fiona stretched at the ballet practice rail. "Fiona, could I speak with you for a moment?"

Fiona followed Dr. Richardson to her office. Once in her office, Dr. Richardson motioned Fiona to sit and then sat behind her own desk.

"Fiona, you are an excellent dancer and one of my best students. However, there is a problem with using you in our spring program. I'm sorry, but I must be frank. You are too tall for these young men to manage. In fact, paired with any of our male dancers, the two of you simply do not look right. Therefore, I've made the difficult decision to limit your performance in the spring program. Don't worry. This does not affect your grade in any manner. I'm deeply sorry."

Instead of being upset, Fiona was thoughtful. "If I could find a suitable, tall, strong young man for a partner, would that change anything?"

"Of course, but I cannot imagine finding anyone at this late date. I'm certain no one from the previous semester could manage you either."

"Please, let me try. Will you be in your office this afternoon?"

"Yes, I'll be here."

"I'll be back soon."

*****

FIONA LEFT THE DANCE STUDIO and searched for Alexander. She soon found him and explained her dilemma. She purred, "I ken I'm asking a huge favor, but could ye please try to do this for me?"

"Of course. I'll at least try, but I am not familiar with ballet at all."

Fiona squeezed Alexander's hand. "Let's go talk to Dr. Richardson."

Fiona knocked lightly on Dr. Richardson's door and was invited in. Alexander followed.

"Dr. Richardson, this is Alexander Gordon. He has volunteered to help me by being my ballet partner."

Dr. Richardson studied Alexander carefully. "Let's go into the studio." They followed her.

"Alexander, do you think you can lift Fiona over your head?"

"Yes, ma'am."

Fiona removed her overcoat. She was wearing her practice outfit and an enticing smile for Alexander. Fiona was completely confident Alexander could do anything she asked. She felt warm and excited.

"Try it. Alexander, place your hands around Fiona's waist and just lift straight up. Fiona, give a slight jump to help him." Alexander smiled at the instructions. He placed his large hands around Fiona's slim waist, his thumbs and forefingers touching and his palms on her hips.

Fiona jumped a little, and Alexander effortlessly lifted her over his head.

"Now, Fiona, can you turn horizontally?" She did.

Alexander's arms were extended, but he showed no sign of straining.

"Alexander, can you lower Fiona so her face is just above yours?" He lowered Fiona as she smiled into his face, their lips almost touching.

"Now, Fiona, keep your body straight. Alexander, pivot her body to be vertical at the same time you are returning her feet to the floor." He did.

"Hmm, Fiona, may I speak to you privately?"

*****

THEY RETURNED TO DR. RICHARDSON'S OFFICE. Alexander waited outside. Dr. Richardson did not recall ever having a student who could do what Alexander had done so easily.

Alone with Fiona in her office, Dr. Richardson asked, "How long have you two been dating?"

Fiona blushed and answered, "Since September 22. Is it that obvious?"

"Even if he were not wearing your name on his neck chain, I'd have noticed it immediately. As is said, 'obvious to the most casual observer.'"

"I apologize for being personal. You are not required to answer these questions. How long have you known each other?"

"Since September 22."

"I'll bet there's an interesting story behind your introduction."

"Indeed, there is." Fiona smiled.

"Under normal circumstances, I do not allow dance partners to be dating. There are too many potential problems. In fact, if I had known you were about to bring in your boyfriend, I would not have permitted you to do so. However, this is a unique situation, and I'm glad Alexander will help. Also, my feeling is your relationship will survive the stress of learning to dance together. I may choreograph some parts of your routine to take advantage of Alexander's strength and minimize his inexperience, but I'll take care of that. Please ask him to come in."

Fiona opened the door and smiled at Alexander. He entered the office.

"Alexander, I'm willing to try you if you will try. I must warn you this will take a lot of work and practice."

"Yes, ma'am. I'm sure it will."

"Allow me to explain a few things.

"Partnering in ballet is called 'Pas de Deux.' The lady can jump higher and take positions she could never take on her own with a partner. She can even appear to float about the stage as her partner carries her.

"The man may not be standing in a ballet position or even appear to be dancing because the audience will watch the lady. In a way, the man acts as a third leg for the lady by stabilizing, lifting, and turning her. With Fiona, you will assist with promenades, lifts, turns, and jumps. She can explain these to you in more detail later. Here's a booklet that should help you."

Fiona gushed, "*Moran taing* that much!"

"There is a lot to learn, but it should be interesting."
Alexander grinned. "Also, I'd much rather be her partner than see
her dance with someone else. We may need to practice often."

They walked out of the office hand-in-hand.

*****

FIONA AND ALICE sang in the church choir and had become good
friends. Alice and her husband, Roger, were students at MU. They
lived in an off-campus apartment near other married students.

"Alice, I'd like to ask a favor of ye," requested Fiona shyly as
they were leaving choir practice.

"I'll try to help you any way I can."

"I want to show Alexander I can cook."

Alice stepped back, pointedly sized Fiona up and down,
snickered and exclaimed, "Oh, sweetie, believe me, Alexander is
not the least bit concerned about your cooking skills!"

Fiona turned bright red. "Och, I still want to show him I can
cook."

"What's your idea?"

"Ye ken I'm taking a home economics course. Suppose I plan
a meal and buy all the ingredients. Could I come to your
apartment, use your kitchen, and prepare the meal? Ye and Roger
could join us. It might also be good for Alexander to see a happy
young Christian couple."

"I see. Of course, I'll help you. Sounds like a fun time as
well."

*****

AT LUNCH IN THE MAIN CAFETERIA, Fiona suggested to Alexander
that they have a meal with Alice and Roger.

"I like your idea. It's something different. Plan your meal,
and then let's go grocery shopping."

"Something ye should ken. Alice and Roger have little money. Even though they both are working, their jobs are student jobs. We should be generous in buying groceries. Besides the key ingredients, we should get supplies, spices—things like that."

"Understood. I've got it."

"Nay, I can pay for the groceries. I wanted ye to underston how I might buy a few extra things or large quantities."

"No, I've got it. I eat a lot!" Alexander always paid for everything.

"How won't ye let me share? Ye canna always take care of everything and everyone. I can help."

"You'll be doing the cooking. I'll buy the groceries. We'll get extras of everything, including paper plates and cups."

"Nay to disposable dishes or utensils; I dinna use them."

*****

ALEXANDER CARRIED a large bag of groceries into Alice's apartment while Fiona carried a small bag. Alice welcomed them into her kitchen. Roger was studying in the den. Alexander returned to his truck for another load.

"That was an experience!" said Fiona to Alice. "Alexander doesna shop; he gets."

"Many, probably most, men are like that," Alice observed.

"Alexander doesna dawdle or browse. He doesna check prices or make comparisons. However, we got everything I asked for. There were even some things I wanted for my dorm room, and he just put them in the cart."

"Has Alexander ever said 'No' to any of your requests?"

Fiona turned red. "Nay, he hasna."

"And he probably never will. He will spoil you rotten, girl."

Alexander brought in the last of the groceries—including a bottle of wine and four wine glasses. He laughed, "I discovered how to find a wine Fiona likes: One, it must be made in Scotland and, two, the bottle must use a cork—not a twist-off cap."

"Oh," Alice despaired, "I'm afraid we don't have a corkscrew."

"But I do!" With a grin, Alexander reached into his pants pocket and pulled out his Swiss Army Knife.

"We have salmon to bake," Fiona explained to Alice, "and I wanted chardonnay with it. In Scotland, we have a lot of salmon. Alexander had eaten little salmon until we started dating, but now he really likes it. Today, we'll also have asparagus, roasted potatoes, and sugar snap peas with mixed greens and tomatoes for a salad. I found this interesting garlic buttered bread to go with it. Of course, tea with lemon—hot for me but iced for ye."

"That's a lot of food," noted Alice.

"I ken. Alexander eats a lot."

"Well, let's get busy preparing it."

"Please, let me do most of the work."

Alexander and Roger, an industrial engineering student, were getting acquainted in the den. Roger needed this spring semester plus two more semesters to graduate.

Roger's specialty was manufacturing processes. He hoped to find a job with a major manufacturer of mechanical products. He wanted to remain in the South but was concerned that might be difficult. If Roger could not find a manufacturing job, he planned to go into construction work. He had experience in construction, especially building houses.

The girls worked hard, and dinner was superb. Alexander ate a big meal, but there were many leftovers. Alexander offered to clean up and do dishes.

"You willna ken where to put things," said Fiona. "I will help you."

Alice smiled knowingly.

In the kitchen, both arms wrapped around Fiona, Alexander whispered, "I love doing dishes with you!" Fiona spun a plate on the counter; it rattled.

Alice called out from the den, "Need any help?"

"Nay," Fiona answered, "We have it."

After finishing the dishes, Fiona and Alexander thanked Alice and Roger and prepared to return to their dorms. Alice hugged Fiona and whispered, "In case you were somehow unaware, Alexander absolutely adores you."

Fiona blushed, "I ken."

*****

WITH HIS OWN CLASS CANCELED, Alexander turned toward the English Building to surprise Fiona after her creative writing class. As he neared the building, Fiona and Jerry Owens came out talking and laughing. The twang Alexander had been experiencing lately when Jerry joined them for coffee or a meal struck him like the proverbial arrow. He had to admit Jerry was quite personable and interesting—even exciting and certainly different. Plus, he and Fiona shared a common interest in creative writing. It was natural they had conversation; however, Alexander liked it less each time he witnessed it.

As he approached them, Alexander heard Fiona say, "That was such a braw poem. Ye have braw thoughts."

"Easy when inspired by your beauty."

Fiona blushed, then discovered Alexander, and her blush deepened.

"Hi," said Alexander. "I thought you might want some company, but you're well covered." He skulked away, growing angrier with himself at every step, but continued hurrying away from Fiona and Jerry.

Do not look back. Leave them alone.

Sandlin

*****

ALEXANDER ENTERED HIS ROOM, slammed his books on his desk, and dropped on his bed, his head in his hands.

"My high school football teammate is making a play for Fiona," he blurted to Donnie, "and she is falling for it—and him."

Donnie searched through his stack of records and placed "You Are Always on my Mind" by Johnny Cash on the record player. "You mean the hippie?"

"Yes, Jerry the hippie. Fiona is spending more and more time with him. Of course, they have class together, but still... I wanted to surprise her today, but when I caught them talking and laughing, I just kept going. I felt like the unwelcome third person."

"You've put Fiona on such a high pedestal that even you cannot reach her. Why do you think that no-good hippie can?" Donnie had not liked Jerry from the moment they met.

"Jerry is an intellect and writer. That appeals to Fiona."

"Jerry is not good looking, has already dropped out once and will probably drop out again. He has few prospects. He is even short."

"But still..."

"You're jealous," Donnie laughed. "I've never seen you jealous—not of anything or anyone, much less a guy over a girl. Jealousy is a new experience for you, and you can't handle it."

"I'm afraid Fiona is about to dump me for Jerry, and there's nothing I can do about it. It's over for us."

"Jerry is a dope addict and will come to a bad end."

"Maybe Fiona thinks she can save him; I don't know."

"Sometimes girls get caught up in trying to save a bad guy, but Fiona seems too smart for that. We're studying this in sociology right now. It's called the savior complex."

Donnie glanced at his notes. "The savior person sacrifices their own needs for someone who desperately needs help."

250

"Now you're scaring me. You sound like Mary. There's an idea—I'll talk to Mary tomorrow. Mary will tell me what I should do."

"Here's what you should do: Nothing. You are wrong. Fiona loves you. You're just jealous. Get over it."

The record ended, and Donnie replaced it with Ernest Tubb's "Walkin' the Floor over You." "Now, get some sleep. I need to study some more."

*****

THE NEXT MORNING, almost despite himself, Alexander waited for Fiona outside the coffee shop. He never took their morning coffee break for granted and always invited her, but not yesterday. He doubted she would come after his behavior, but just in case...

Fiona arrived with worry written on her face. "I didna think ye would be here," her voice quivered. "But Mary assured me ye would." She dabbed at her eyes and touched her 'AF' necklace.

Relieved that Fiona wore her 'AF' necklace, Alexander hoped she would not rip it off and throw it at him. "I'm so glad to see you. I was afraid you would not come. I'm sorry about yesterday. Please forgive me. I have no right or reason to object to who you see or talk to. Jerry is a friend, smart, and a talented writer. You are even taking the same class. It is only natural for you to discuss your work with him. I apologize. I was wrong."

"*Mo leannan*, ye dinna have reason to be jealous of Jerry."

"That may be, but he gets a special look in his eyes when you are near."

"And I get a special keek in my eyes when _ye_ are near. I feel sorry for Jerry. He is troubled, and I dinna ken how to help him."

"I don't think anyone can help Jerry. In fact, he doesn't want help."

"That's whit Mary says as well. She reminded me Jerry was her high school classmate and cautioned me against expecting to save him. She said that the hippie is the real Jerry, and the engineer was his attempt to copy ye. Mary said that Jerry always looked up to ye—even idolized ye. She says Jerry is interested in me because I'm your girlfriend—or at least I was. I dinna ken. It's sad. *Tha mi brònach* " She fingered her 'AF' necklace and dabbed at her eyes again.

"Let me start afresh." Alexander stepped back and then stepped forward toward Fiona.

"Good morning, Fiona. You are particularly beautiful this morning. I've missed you. I will be the luckiest man alive if you will be my girlfriend."

She held out her hand, and he took it gently in his own, bent low and kissed her fingers.

"Flatterer!" She smiled, and her green eyes glowed through her tears. "Don't get us in trouble again, *mo leannan*," she laughed.

"Let's go inside for coffee and tea and a different subject," Alexander said. He opened the door for her, and they entered the coffee shop.

*****

A FEW DAYS LATER, during their customary morning coffee time, Alexander hinted, "We are studying portraiture in my photography course. They fully equipped the studio with a large-format camera, studio lights, and various backdrops. Our instructor requires each student to provide their own model. This forces the student to find and ask someone to be a model. The student must also write a modeling contract and get the model to sign it. So, I need a model."

Fiona teased, "Well, let me ask around and see who I can find." Seeing the disbelief on Alexander's face, she giggled.

Alexander understood. "Fiona, would you be my model for a portraiture class?"

"Aye. I'd like that. Whit do I need to do?"

"Come to my photography class to hear the general instructions and get some tips on clothes, posing and makeup. We'll be assigned studio time then."

Two days later, Fiona entered the photography classroom with Alexander. Most of the photographers were boys, but there were some girls as well. All the models were standing near their photographer.

The instructor entered the classroom and called the class to order. "I especially thank the models for volunteering. That is, I assume you volunteered." Everyone chuckled.

"I've already instructed the photographers how to use the equipment. Today, I'll go over some rules and give tips to the models."

"First, there must always be at least three people in the studio, one of whom is a chaperone. The chaperone can be anyone acceptable to both the model and photographer. In most cases, the makeup artist serves as the chaperone."

"Whatever your personal relationship, employ a professional relationship for this class and project."

"No nudity. No exceptions." Everyone groaned.

"No food, drinks or smoking in the studio."

"Now, a few tips for the models.

"Do not expect to dress or change clothes in the studio."

"Use a makeup artist. To you male models, yes, you will use makeup."

"Relax."

"Lean towards the camera but only slightly."

"Turn slightly from the camera."

"Chin slightly down."

"All these instructions and tips are in the handout being passed around now."

"Now reserve a time on the schedule. The photographer should be in the studio at least an hour before the model to set up the camera and lights."

Fiona smiled at Alexander. "Jane will be my makeup artist and chaperone."

*****

AT THEIR SCHEDULED TIME, Fiona and Jane entered the studio. Fiona was wearing an overcoat; Jane was carrying a makeup bag. Alexander had arrived earlier and prepared the camera and lights.

Fiona removed her overcoat, and Alexander gasped out loud. She was wearing a long olive-green form-fitting dress with one shoulder exposed. The "AF" necklace Alexander made for her was high on her neck. The heart-shaped diamond necklace hung below the AF necklace. She sat on the modeling stool as Jane brushed her long, thick auburn hair over the unexposed shoulder. Not only was Fiona gorgeous, but she was also glamorous. Fiona smiled at Alexander and purred, "Mr. Photographer, do ye prefer my hair over this shoulder or the other?"

Alexander had not said a word. Fiona asked sweetly, "Can ye talk?"

"Not intelligently," he murmured.

Fortunately, Fiona had studied the photography tips and practiced with Mary, Anne, and Jane advising her. She knew exactly what to do and how to pose. Alexander composed himself enough to push the shutter button.

Alexander escorted Fiona and Jane to their door. Inside, they giggled all the way to Mary's room.

*****

THURSDAY NIGHT SUPPER with Alice and Roger had become a pleasant routine. "Let's have baked ham this time," Fiona suggested to Alexander. "Baked ham with sweet potatoes. Auntie has cooked those many times. Plus, your mother telt me about using the ham bone afterward to make red beans and rice. I'd like to try cooking red beans and rice as well. Can you go grocery shopping with me?"

"I sure can. Did you know you can buy the ham already cooked and cut spirally? My mother buys precooked and sliced ham. It's not sliced all the way through and still looks like a ham with a ham bone. If the ham were truly raw, it would take hours of baking—like baking a turkey."

"But isn't that cheating? I want to cook."

"You can cook the side dishes and heat the ham. I like to eat—and do dishes," he added. Fiona poked him in the ribs.

After supper, Fiona commented, "Alexander's mother uses the ham bone to make red beans and rice. I'd like to try it."

Alice assured her, "I know how to make red beans and rice. It's simple. You cook the red beans separately from the rice and then combine them in your bowl or plate."

"Mrs. Gordon uses a slow cooker."

"I have a slow cooker. It's a common wedding gift." Alice smiled at Fiona. "That's how I got mine. Come on, I'll show you. Of course, we may dirty a few dishes." Alice giggled.

As Fiona and Alexander were leaving, he thanked Alice and Roger. "I can't tell you how much I've enjoyed meeting you, being with you, and, of course, having meals here. At the risk of imposing, suppose I get a charcoal grill and cook steaks next time?"

Roger replied quickly, "I'd sure like a good charcoal-grilled steak."

*****

"DONNIE, I NEED SOME ADVICE." They were in their dorm room, and the hard rock music next door was deafening. Alexander banged a heavy dictionary against the wall, and the volume diminished slightly.

"OK. Go ahead and propose to Fiona. I don't know why you are putting it off. Get on with it."

"No, that's not the advice I need. I need some guidance in grilling a steak."

Besides growing up on a farm, Donnie had been an apprentice butcher.

Alexander continued, "Although I've watched my dad grill steaks and even helped, the complete process is a bit fuzzy."

"What do you need?"

"Everything. A grill, charcoal, lighter fluid, tongs, the meat."

"OK. Get a classic kettle-style grill, at least twenty-inch diameter. Use a charcoal chimney starter instead of lighter fluid. There should be chimneys for sale near the grills. Use lump oak charcoal. Buy premium ribeye steak; you can afford it. Ask the butcher to help you select steaks for grilling."

"What about a marinade for the steaks?"

"You can make your own—that should impress Fiona. I'll give you a recipe. You'll need soy sauce, Worcestershire sauce, olive oil, lemon juice, and garlic. Let the steaks marinate in the refrigerator for about four hours."

"How long to cook them?"

Donnie continued, "First, make sure all the charcoal is burning well before you put the steaks on the grill. Don't overcook them—something like three to four minutes each side for medium-rare. Oh, while you're at it, cook some hamburgers as well. Maybe even a sausage link or two."

"Got it, thanks."

"The most important thing to remember is to bring me a steak."

*****

Viking Princess

FIONA AND ALEXANDER often planned their day and special activities during their morning coffee break in the Student Union.

"Anne and Jane have invited me to join them and a few other girls flying to Florida for Spring Break. They are so looking forward to being on the beach for a few days. It sounds like fun. I've never been to Florida. They want to work on their tans and hope to meet some nice guys."

Alexander's disappointment must have been apparent in his facial expression. "And are you going with them?"

"Unless I get a better offer," Fiona smiled.

"Oceanport has a nice beach, and my parents want to see you again. We could pass through your aunt and uncle's farm, spend several days with my parents, get in some time on the Oceanport beach, and return to MU via the farm."

"Are ye inviting me to spend Spring Break with ye?"

"Please."

"I'd love to."

*****

"INSTEAD OF FLYING TO FLORIDA, I'll be with Alexander in Oceanport for Spring Break," Fiona informed Anne and Jane.

"As though you ever considered Florida at all!"

"I did. I even bought a bikini. I've never had a bikini. Let me try it on and tell me if you think Alexander will like it." Fiona went to her room and soon returned to Anne's room wearing her swimsuit and windbreaker. She removed the windbreaker.

"Oh my God!" exclaimed Anne. The tiny bikini was pale green with darker green leaves printed.

"Does it fit? Should I wear it?"

"Sweetie, your bikini mostly looks like you. If I could wear something like that, I certainly would. I'm afraid my swimsuit must be more concealing than revealing."

257

Jane contended, "I'm glad you're not going to Florida with us. We'd spend the entire time surrounding you and waving clubs to keep the guys away."

"Will Alexander like my bikini? I dinna want him to keek at the other lassies on the beach."

"Well, Alexander is a guy, but I suspect his eyes will not stray from you while you wear that bikini!"

"I predict he will not only like it, but you will see he likes it." Jane grinned.

*****

AS FIONA WANTED, they made a one-night stopover for a brief visit with the Johnston's before proceeding to Oceanport, where they would stay with the Gordons.

While Robert took Alexander to see timber harvested, Fiona updated Ellen in the kitchen. She told Ellen about Alexander helping her in dance class.

"He is unbelievably strong, Auntie—nimble on his feet and well-coordinated too. I've never had a dance partner who could handle me, but Alexander does it easily."

Ellen smiled. "I'll just bet he does!"

"Auntie!"

Changing the subject, Fiona said, "I helped Alexander with his photography class by posing as his model." She giggled as she described his reaction to her glamour dress and pose. "My photo, that is, the photo taken by Alexander, won first place in the photography classes. They will feature it in the student yearbook."

"Of course, it would win and be featured. You are beautiful!"

"And I'm becoming a good cook. We eat supper with Alice and Roger almost every Thursday night. Alexander and I get groceries together—which has been a learning experience for me. Alexander bought a charcoal grill, and the past couple of weeks has been grilling steak or fish while I make the side dishes and desserts."

"Sounds like everything is going your way."

"My life is wonderful."

* * * * *

AS THEY WERE ABOUT TO LEAVE THE JOHNSTON'S, Ellen whispered in Alexander's ear, "Fiona's birthday is two weeks from today."

"Thank you, Auntie!"

As they drove away, Fiona asked, "Do ye ken that Uncle is beginning to accept ye? He was looking forward to seeing ye again."

"I noticed. What's the difference?"

"He likes ye. Auntie says Uncle likes name-dropping and telling his friends we are dating. He brags on ye."

Fiona continued, "My friends say a big part of the difference is we've been dating for six months now. They say a lassie should not bring her leannan home to meet her parents until they've been dating at least four to six months."

"You girls really discuss subjects like this?"

"Aye, we do. Often."

"So, your inviting me to the farm two weeks after we met must have been scandalous!"

"It was indeed. But that week was scandalous, anyway. Besides, Auntie and Uncle had already met ye."

"So, we've been dating for six months? What do you mark as oor first date?"

"I tell people we met on September 22, and September 22 was also oor first date. They usually assume we met on a blind date."

"Well, in a way, it was."

"Whit do ye consider oor first date?"

Alexander smiled. "I would say our first date was the afternoon we spent together after we met."

"The lassies do not count that as a date."

"I invited you to have supper with me. That was an 'ask and hope she says yes' situation."

"I suppose it could count."

"Well, if it doesn't, then our first date was you inviting me to go to the library. So, you asked me out first."

Fiona blushed. "I was so embarrassed. I could not believe I asked ye. I'm that thankful Mary encouraged me to follow through."

They rode on to Oceanport and its beach.

What in the world could he get Fiona for her birthday?

*****

"WANT TO GO to our new house?" asked Malcolm Gordon. "There have been delays, but it's coming along." They got into Rachel's white Lincoln and drove to the new house.

"Is this a new car?" asked Fiona. "It is nice and roomy."

"Yes, brand new. Got it a month ago."

The new house exhibited the various stages of construction. Some wall frames were not covered, and wiring and plumbing showed through. The wood floor had not been installed, and the textured underlying concrete was visible.

"This is the first time I've paid attention to a house being built," Fiona remarked. "I dinna ken about building a house."

"Alexander knows a little," Malcolm bragged. "He helped me build my workshop, and he even studied architectural drafting and designed a house."

"I took a drafting course in high school," Alexander explained. I thought it would be helpful in my engineering drafting courses, and it was. A section of the high school course was about architecture. We toured and inspected houses under construction. One project was to draw a set of house plans."

"D'ye still have those plans?" Fiona asked. "I'd like to see your house ideas."

"I'll try to find them."

Back at the Gordons, Alexander rummaged around in his bedroom and found his house plans. He and Fiona sat at the dining room table and reviewed them. Alexander said, "I'm no architect, but I concluded most house plans put small boxes inside a big box. I wanted mine to be different."

"Of course ye did." Fiona smiled.

"I liked, and still like, the idea of combining rooms to make the house seem more open. For example, I combined the kitchen, breakfast area and den into a single large room. I minimized hallways. Of course, bathrooms and bedrooms are private. Designing a good floor plan can be a challenge."

I'll remember this, thought Fiona.

*****

"WOULD YOU LIKE TO WORK on your tan?" It was a sunny day in Oceanport, and the beach was inviting.

"Yes, but with my fair skin, I need gallons of sunscreen. Even then, I can only stay a few minutes in the sun. Let me get into my swimsuit."

"I'll get sunscreen on our way to the beach."

Fiona came out wearing a windbreaker over her swimsuit, her long legs reaching all the way to the ground.

The beach was not crowded, and Alexander parked his truck in a relatively isolated area. He removed their beach bags, a small ice chest, and a beach blanket from the truck bed. He spread the extra-long blanket on the sand and placed their bags and ice chest alongside. Alexander removed the large tube of sunscreen from Fiona's bag and turned to hand it to her.

Fiona had already removed her windbreaker and was sitting on the blanket, her legs extended. She leaned over to Alexander and reached for the sunscreen. *"Moran taing!"* Fiona immediately unscrewed the top and rubbed sunscreen on her long legs.

Alexander gulped. He knew he should say something, but what? He had a sense of déjà vu and warmth.

"Do ye like my new swimsuit?" Fiona continued to apply sunscreen.

Alexander gulped again. *Come on, man, think!*

"Fiona," he finally got out, "you are, beyond any doubt, the most beautiful girl I've ever seen. And in your bikini, I..."

Fiona finished applying the sunscreen and turned on her stomach. "Alexander," she cooed "there are places on my back I canna reach. Would ye rub sunscreen there?"

He wrapped his beach towel around his waist. "I'll try."

*****

AS SPRING BREAK drew to a close, Fiona and Alexander loaded into his customized truck and drove to the Johnston's farm, then on to MU.

"Moran taing for a wonderful Spring Break," whispered Fiona as they sneaked a kiss in the dormitory parking lot.

"Believe me, the pleasure was all mine," answered Alexander.

Fiona dropped off her bags in her room and immediately went to Mary's room. Mary's room had long since become the gathering place for the girls, and several were in there reliving their Spring Break.

"How was Florida?" asked Fiona as she entered Mary's room.

"Disappointing, I suppose," replied Anne. "Most of the guys and many of the girls were drunk most of the time. Lots of loud music and dancing. I met a few guys, but no one worth bringing home." She smiled at Fiona.

"How was your Spring Break in Oceanport," asked Jane. "Did Alexander like your bikini?"

One girl interrupted, "Bikini? Fiona wore a bikini on the beach! I bet she was a knockout. But you are not sunburned. With your fair skin, how did you avoid getting sunburned?"

"Alexander liked my bikini that much."

"I'll bet he did!"

"We sunbathed several times, but only for a few minutes each time, so I would not freckle. I used lots of sunscreen. Alexander enjoyed rubbing sunscreen on me." Fiona was bright red.

"I'll bet he did!"

"Weel," Fiona countered, "I had to rub sunscreen on Alexander as well." She mused wistfully. "He is quite muscular, ye ken. There's no fat on him at all."

"We don't know," grinned Jane, "but we're sure you do!"

*****

IN HIS ROOM THAT NIGHT, Alexander picked up his telephone and dialed the Johnston's number. Ellen answered.

"Auntie, it's Alexander."

"I recognize your voice, Alexander. Is everything ok?"

"Yes ma'am. I've been trying to think of a birthday present for Fiona. You know she is called the Viking Princess. She says she doesn't like that name, but I suspect she really does. I'd like to give her a tiara. Can you help me find one?"

"Of course. What do you have in mind?"

"I think the tiara for Fiona should be narrow and dainty, made of silver and fitted with emeralds and diamonds.

"That sounds beautiful. But a tiara like that will be expensive, Alexander."

"I'm not extremely concerned about the cost, Auntie. However, I want Fiona to wear it occasionally and not be forced to lock it away in a safe deposit box."

"I'll talk to my jeweler and see what I can find."

"Thank you, Auntie."

*****

MID-MORNING ON FIONA'S BIRTHDAY, Alexander cranked up his customized truck and pointed it towards Fiona's dormitory. She had requested brunch instead of breakfast on her birthday so she could sleep late. Alexander had made reservations at Fran's Place; a small local restaurant known for brunch. He had already eaten a modest breakfast, knowing that Fran's brunch, although fancy, had dainty portions. Alexander parked his truck in the dorm driveway and entered the dorm.

The receptionist called for Fiona as soon as Alexander entered. She watched expectantly—something was always happening around those two.

The lobby was nearly empty and Alexander had been sitting only a moment when Fiona opened the door to the stairs. Rushing up the stairs to greet her, he remembered falling the first time he did so. Fortunately, he did not stumble this time.

Fiona was breathtakingly beautiful in an emerald green dress that showed off her slim figure, and Alexander marveled at her as always. She wore both her 'AF' necklace and diamond pendant. He touched his 'Fiona' choker gratefully.

"Happy Birthday Beautiful!" Having already ascertained that the House Mother was nowhere around, he gave her a quick, soft peck on her lips. Giggling emerged from the lobby.

Fiona glowed through her blush. *"Moran taing, mon leannan. Madainn mhath. Ciamar a tha thu?"*

They stepped down the stairs and walked to Alexander's truck, hand in hand.

"You have a busy day, my beautiful princess. Just to be sure, let's go over the schedule. First, remember my promise that this is your 'Yes' day. I will do or help you do anything you want. I will not say 'No' to anything. I will be your servant today."

Fiona giggled, then laughed outright. "When I telt the lassies about your 'Yes Day' promise, they laughed until they cried. They said, 'So, this is like a normal day! Has Alexander ever telt you no?'"

Alexander could feel his face flushing. Fiona's friends were correct. "Well, perhaps I pamper you a bit. Doesn't everyone?"

Alexander helped Fiona into his truck and walked around to the driver's side. He stopped at the front of the truck and glanced toward Fiona—a beautiful auburn-haired girl in a beautiful maroon customized hot rod. What a sight! *Why didn't he bring a camera?* He smiled and continued to the driver's side.

Once the truck was rolling, Alexander again said, "Let's go over the schedule for today. I have made reservations at Ruffin's for supper. After supper, we'll go to the special opera performance on campus. The opera is Italian, so I know you'll like it. After the opera, there is a reception at the Alumni Inn with members of the opera cast."

"How braw! I dinna ken how ye got invitations to the reception."

"You can thank Auntie and President Curry for the invitations to the reception. But I don't have plans for between brunch and supper. What would you like to do? Should I stay with you or give you some time by yourself?"

"I have plans for the afternoon. Of course, I want ye to stay with me; dinna be silly. I must get my hair and nails done. Then, we will go to some dress shops. I want something new and special for tonight. I may need to go to the dorm and change clothes a few times."

Good thing I got that book to read, Alexander thought.

After trying many dresses, Fiona finally selected a dark red evening gown. Alexander considered carrying a club when she wore it. He reached for his wallet as they checked out.

"Nay," Fiona insisted. "This is from Auntie. Please take me to my dorm noo so I can get ready for the evening."

*****

ALEXANDER RETURNED FIONA TO HER DORM one last time and then dashed off to his own room to change into his tuxedo.

"Well, you don't look dead," Donnie harassed him. "I thought this was a surprise birthday party. Is it really a wedding?"

"We are going to an opera after the birthday party," Alexander replied. "Not Grand Ole Opera—a real opera. Don't worry, you don't have to go to the opera. In fact, you can't. It's sold out."

"Good. Thanks for getting me out of it. I'm glad to not wear a rented tux."

"After the opera, we're invited to a reception for the opera cast. By the way, I bought this tux. Figured I'd need it again, and it's difficult to find my size."

Donnie laughed until he gasped for breath. "Remember when I told you that the Viking Princess had you wrapped around her little finger after only a few days?"

"Sort of."

"Well, look at you. You've had a fancy breakfast, waited in a beauty salon, shopped for dresses all afternoon, and even bought a tux to go to the opera and reception."

"You're just jealous. Not to mention uncouth."

"Uncouth? I'm wearing a tie to a birthday party!"

"See you there."

Alexander left his dorm, got in his truck, and drove eagerly to Fiona's dorm. *How would she look in her new clothes?*

The receptionist in the girl's dorm notified Fiona when Alexander entered. "Nice tux," she smiled.

Fiona looked truly regal as she stepped onto the landing. Alexander stepped up to her and bowed. She held out her hand to greet him and he kissed it—remembering his faux pas when they first met. Fiona must have remembered as well. She blushed.

"You are so beautiful."

"Moran taing, *cuideigin a nì flatter* Ye're bonnie, yerself, *mo leannan*." She took his hand.

They stepped down the stairs and into Alexander's truck. He drove to Ruffin's Restaurant—the finest restaurant in town.

A valet met them in the driveway at Ruffin's. An attendant helped Fiona out of the truck. At the receptionist desk, Alexander gave his name to the receptionist whose smile suggested, "*Of course you are*."

The head waiter escorted them past the tables. Alexander glanced at Fiona. She appeared confused. The head waiter stopped at a closed door, knocked, hesitated, and opened the door.

"Surprise! Surprise!"

Fiona gasped, "Och! Och!" and put her hands to her face. Everyone gathered around her. "Happy Birthday! Happy Birthday!"

After all had greeted Fiona, Alexander tinged on his water glass and asked them to be seated. "Welcome to Fiona's birthday party. Years from now, you will tell your grandchildren about the time you attended a birthday party for a Viking Princess." Everyone laughed and clapped.

Alexander continued, "I have already ordered starters. The waiters will take your individual orders for the main course. Please order anything you like—anything. Dessert will be birthday cake plus ice cream." He pointed to a beautiful three layered cake with a red haired princess figure on top.

Starters were shrimp cocktails. As they served the starters, Mary spoke out, "Look, Fiona! You don't have to peel them!" Everyone laughed, knowing the story of Fiona at Mary's shrimp boil and Alexander peeling her shrimp.

Alexander ordered stuffed lobster for Fiona and himself. Others ordered lobster, but Donnie, and several guys, ordered steak.

While waiting for their main course, Alexander again tinged his water glass. "This is a good time for Fiona to open her gifts. Otherwise, Mary will try to tell her story of how Fiona and I met."

Most of the gifts were cards. Mary's gift was a package. Fiona opened Mary's gift to reveal a small box marked "String Bikini Kit". She blushed but opened the box to find four pieces of string.

Someone yelled out, "Try it on!"

Mary said, "Just in case you want something more conservative than the bikini you have now!" The group roared in laughter.

Alexander nodded to their attendant. He disappeared and returned with three boxes. Alexander handed Fiona the longest box. She opened it and removed nineteen long stemmed red roses and one white rose.

"Moran tain, mo leannan."

A vase magically appeared and Alexander helped her put the roses in the vase. He then removed the lid from the middle sized box and handed her the corsage from within.

"You should not be the only girl without a corsage at the opera," Alexander explained.

Alexander handed Fiona the small oblong box. "For my Viking Princess," he said.

Fiona opened the box, gasped, and removed the dainty silver tiara trimmed in gold and fitted with emeralds and diamonds.

"Och! Och!" she gasped, her tears flowing, "Put it on me."

As Alexander placed the tiara on her brilliant auburn hair, Fiona threw both arms around him and kissed him passionately.

"Look! Fiona popped her foot again. Good thing Dr. Crawford is not here," said Anne.

The guys gathered around Alexander and were congratulating him until Donnie said, "I hope you realize you've set an impossibly high standard for the rest of us."

"I'm sorry if that's the case," said Alexander. "I just wanted Fiona to have a great birthday."

* * * * *

THE GIRLS GATHERED around Fiona to examine her tiara.

"Fiona," said Jane with an impish grin, "this has been fabulous. Not only the meal, flowers, and tiara, but to have Alexander as your servant all day and never say 'No' to any of your requests. When is Alexander's birthday and what do you plan to give him?"

"His birthday is in August. I dinna ken whit to give him, but I will think of something braw, I hope."

"I just bet you will," said Jane, her grin growing larger.

Fiona turned scarlet. "Jane Cook, ye behave or ye'll have to find another roommate next semester."

Jane laughed. "Fiona, I love you. Living with you has been a fun and educational experience I will treasure all my life. All the same, I predict you will have a new roommate next semester." She stepped to Fiona, gave her a kiss on the cheek, and hugged her.

"Now I must repair my makeup again," said Fiona through her tears.

After the birthday cake dessert, Alexander again addressed their friends. "Fiona and I must leave for the opera. Thank you for coming. Please excuse us. The room is yours."

* * * * *

"DID YOU EVER SEE, OR READ, about such a couple?" Jane sighed. "So in love. Better than any movie—and we've been part of it."

"You're right," admitted Donnie. "Every night since they met, Alexander has raved about Fiona and what they did that day."

"Same with Fiona," said Jane. "She is a different person from the shy girl I met on the first day of school. In fact, I wondered if we would get along. All she wanted to do was stay in our room and study."

"As I got to know Fiona," Mary chimed in. "I realized that she and Alexander were a perfect match. Of course, I had to mislead him about her beauty. I still laugh about Alexander being stunned when he met Fiona. The big ox."

"Remember the night of their library date?" said Anne. "Fiona was embarrassed and excited at the same time."

"Does everyone know Alexander prevented bullies from harassing Fiona when they were in high school? He faced down a group of thugs and told Fiona to run." asked Mary. "After their library date, Fiona told me, 'I have found him again and I will never leave him.'"

"When do you think Alexander will propose?" Jane asked the group.

"Soon and dramatically," Mary asserted.

"Will Fiona say yes?" someone asked.

"She would have said yes a week after they met—maybe sooner," Mary answered.

"Let's make up a betting pool," suggested Donnie.

*****

"OCH, WHIT A BRAW DAY and party!" exclaimed Fiona in Alexander's truck. "Moran taing, mo leannan. Tha gaol agam ort." She leaned into Alexander and gave him a quick kiss on his cheek.

Alexander smiled. He was absorbing some of Fiona's favorite Scottish Gaelic phrases. "And now to the opera!"

"Aye, and my favorite! I canna believe the La Traviata tour has reached MU—and on my birthday! I havena been to an opera since coming to America. Do ye ken La Traviata?"

Alexander admitted he knew nothing of La Traviata. "I was lucky to learn of it and get tickets—much less a box seat."

"La Traviata means 'woman gone astray'. Guiseppe Verdi wrote it in 1853 and it is one of the most popular operas. You may not know the story, but you've probably heard some of the music—at least the melodies. 'Libiamo ne' lieti is a famous duet meaning 'Let us drink from the joyful cups'.

They arrived at the MU theatre and entered to find their box seat. As always, Fiona attracted much attention and admiring gazes. Her form fitting dark maroon evening gown was glamorous but not immodest and accentuated her long auburn hair. In her high heels, she towered over everyone except Alexander. She held her head proudly to show off her tiara as she gave tiny waves to fellow students from her music and dance classes.

In their box seat, Alexander whispered, "Once again, you are the most beautiful girl in the room."

Fiona blushed. "*Moran taing, cuideigin a nì flatter.*"

A photographer approached their box seat, snapped a photograph, and soundlessly said, "Thank you."

The opera began and Fiona watched, enraptured, sometimes mouthing the words. Occasionally, she would whisper a few words of explanation to Alexander. She was in her element.

*****

AFTER THE OPERA ENDED, Fiona and Alexander drove to the Alumni Inn for the reception. As they entered, Alexander could almost hear necks popping as heads snapped around to admire Fiona.

Fiona quickly found a group of her music and dance friends and instructors and led Alexander to them. After a brief round of introductions, Alexander left the group to get drinks.

When he returned, Alexander found Fiona alone with a distinguished looking man, probably in his mid-thirties.

"Mr. Gilbert, may I present Alexander Gordon. Alexander, this is Mr. Raymond Gilbert, the director of tonight's opera and manager of the traveling opera troupe."

Alexander shook Mr. Gilbert's hand. "Pleased to meet you, Mr. Gilbert. I'm not much of an opera fan, but I certainly enjoyed it tonight. Fortunately, Fiona was there to explain it to me."

Alexander felt uncomfortable and wished his tuxedo did not hide his "Fiona" choker. He considered removing his tie and opening his shirt. *Why didn't Fiona introduce him as her boyfriend?*

"Thank you, Alexander. I'm pleased you enjoyed our show. Perhaps you will become an opera fan like Fiona?"

"I don't know, Mr. Gilbert, but Fiona certainly loves opera."

"So I've learned. I also learned that besides being an opera fan and the most beautiful girl in the room, Fiona is a musician who sings and speaks Italian. In fact, I'm trying to convince Fiona to audition for our traveling troupe. What do you think?"

So that's it, Alexander thought. "Fiona is so talented," he said, "I'm sure she would be a welcome addition to your troupe."

"Fiona," said Mr. Gilbert, "would you join me for dinner tomorrow? I can interview you during dinner. Afterward, you could audition in the theatre."

Alexander stiffened.

"Thank ye, Mr. Gilbert. Although my morning and dinner plans are already made, I'd be pleased to discuss opera and your traveling troupe in the mid-afternoon."

"Very well. May I pick you up at, say, three o'clock?"

"Nay, but I will meet ye at the theatre at three."

"Wonderful, I'll see you then." Mr. Gilbert glanced at Alexander before leaving.

He knows, Alexander thought. *He knows exactly what he is doing. This is not his first time to do it, either.*

"Alexander, being in the opera has been a lifelong dream of mine, but I did not expect this. I dinna ken."

"Perhaps you've been discovered. This may be a moment to remember." *I'll certainly always remember it.*

"I ken ye dinna like it, but I must consider this. I hope ye underston."

Abruptly, the magic disappeared.

"Will you at least join me for church and dinner tomorrow, anyway?" Alexander asked.

"Of course, that's how I said those times were already spoken for."

They returned to Fiona's dorm in silence, neither knowing what to say.

*****

IN HER DORM ROOM, Fiona quickly and quietly slipped into bed pleading exhaustion from the long day. She did not want to talk to anyone. Her pillow absorbed her tears. *What to do?* She tossed and turned the night away.

Sunday morning with Alexander was awkward. During worship service, Fiona could not keep her mind on the minister's message. Dinner with Alexander was not much better. They tried to relive the birthday but carefully avoided discussing the reception and opera.

After dinner, Alexander returned Fiona to her dorm in silence. As he was about to leave, Fiona grabbed his arm. "Will ye come with me to the audition?"

"Of course. Thank you for including me. I'll park the truck and wait in the lobby. Take your time."

Fiona rushed to Mary's room and explained the latest developments. "Mary, I've always wanted to be in an opera company. Now I dinna ken. I love the opera, but I love Alexander as well—more, in fact."

Mary thought only a few moments. "Fiona, you are extremely beautiful and talented. Any opera company would be overjoyed to have you. How fortunate that you have choices and are not forced to accept a life you do not want. Let me play the devil's advocate and see if I can help."

"I'm listening."

"This guy, Mr. Gilbert, that you met for a couple of hours last night, is good looking and a smooth talker—an actor, isn't he?"

"Aye, he is that."

"In a few days, he will be in a different town and theatre, right?"

"Aye, I suppose."

"Does he have a girl in every town?"

"I dinna ken, but I get your point."

"Don't you think his traveling troupe is complete? Where would you fit in?"

"I dinna ken."

"Could he be simply trying to hustle you? Seduce you? Is this a couch audition?"

"I dinna ken, but I've asked Alexander to come with me."

"Good. Fiona, do you think Alexander loves you and will propose?"

"Aye, I do."

"So do I."

"On the other hand, the opera opportunity may be entirely legitimate. Suppose you join the troupe. You'll be in a different town every few days, right?"

"Aye, I suppose."

"Would Alexander follow the troupe from town to town, or would you just see each other occasionally? Every month or two?"

"I dinna ken."

"I don't believe he would follow you—certainly not for very long. He would try because he loves you so much, but that's just not Alexander. He could not do it." Mary wiped a tear away. "This is the first time I've acknowledged something Alexander could not do. Oh Fiona, I'm so sorry to tell you this. I know how much you want to be in the opera, but you'll have to choose between the opera and Alexander."

Fiona, tears in her own eyes, hugged Mary.

"If Alexander played professional football, would you travel with him from town to town every week for half the year?"

"He willna play professional football. The day we met, well, the day I found him again, he telt me that even though he loved the game and the competition, traveling would be difficult and the temptations overwhelming. But if he turned professional, aye, I would follow him. I would be miserable without him."

"Just as he would be miserable without you."

"Mary, ye've no given me an answer."

"Interesting, isn't it? Your career situation and Alexander's career situation are strikingly similar, yet I believe you would follow him and he could not follow you for very long. It's not just that he's a man and you are a woman—you are different. I wish both of you the best and pray that you will make the best decision—whatever that may be, I don't know."

"*Moran taing*, Mary. Weel, I'm going to the audition to learn more, and I must change clothes. Alexander is waiting in the lobby."

As Fiona walked onto the landing in her casual clothes, Alexander stepped up to meet her. Fiona noticed he had removed his coat and tie and opened his shirt. His 'Fiona' choker displayed prominently on his neck. She smiled.

"Hello, Beautiful," he said, but his voice sounded flat and troubled.

"Flatterer!" She winked. *He's trying; what should I do?*

They walked in thoughtful silence towards the theatre without holding hands. Alexander's words from months before echoed through Fiona's head. He had made his decision before knowing Fiona. Fiona had also decided before knowing Alexander.

Suddenly, Fiona said, "Let's go this way." She turned off the well-beaten path and Alexander followed. Fiona stopped in a secluded area and turned to face Alexander.

"Alexander, *mo leannan*, I love ye that much. I willna leave ye again." Fiona gently put both arms around Alexander and kissed his lips softly. "I dinna want to be Campused," she explained. "Noo, let's go to the theatre." She took his hand and strode purposefully onward.

To Fiona's surprise, Mr. Gilbert was sitting on the side wall of the theatre steps. He didn't seem surprised at Alexander's presence and stood to greet them. "It's such a pretty day and your campus is so beautiful that I didn't want to go inside," he explained. "Now that you are here, the scene is even more beautiful. I'm so pleased that you came."

"Thank ye. Mr. Gilbert, do ye remember Alexander?"

"Of course, good to see you again, Alexander." Mr. Gilbert extended his hand and Alexander shook it. "Shall we go inside? They have assigned me a temporary office for interviews."

"That willna be necessary," said Fiona. "Mr. Gilbert, I apologize for not properly introducing Alexander at the reception. Alexander is my boyfriend—my that serious boyfriend and I love him that much." She gave Alexander a quick kiss on his lips. "*Mo leannan*, I apologize to ye as well."

"I suspected as much from the way you looked at him," Mr. Gilbert said, "and from the way he looked at me." Mr. Gilbert laughed.

"Mr. Gilbert," Fiona continued. "I am that complimented by the attention ye've shown me, but I willna be joining your opera troupe. I suspect I would not travel well, and I would be especially miserable without Alexander. I will remain at MU with Alexander. There isna need for an interview or audition."

"I'm disappointed," Mr. Gilbert said, "but not surprised. I was warned. However, I'd still like to hear you sing. Can you sing part of the 'Drinking Song' from La Traviata?"

Fiona glanced at Alexander. He smiled and nodded his head. "I'd like to hear that myself."

They entered one of the practice rooms and Mr. Gilbert produced a sheaf of music. He sat at the piano and played "The Drinking Song." Fiona came in and sang the female part.

When Fiona finished singing, Mr. Gilbert said, "That was marvelous. Simply marvelous." He turned to Alexander. "I hope you appreciate Fiona's talent and what she is giving up for you."

Fiona said, "Alexander is a musician and singer as well."

"Oh," Mr. Gilbert interjected, "What do you sing?"

"Could I use the piano, please?" asked Fiona. She sat and played "Perhaps Love." Alexander joined her in their special duet.

Mr. Gilbert reached into his pocket and retrieved a business card case. He handed a card to Fiona. "If you ever change your mind about performing opera—traveling or otherwise, please let me know." He removed a different card and handed it to Fiona as well. "If you are interested, my associate will contact you and Alexander about making demo tapes."

"Aye, thank ye, Mr. Gilbert. Considering oor current circumstances, demo tapes might be an interesting project." She handed both cards to Alexander.

"It was my pleasure to meet you both," said Mr. Gilbert. "Now, if you'll excuse me, I have another appointment."

"Thank you, Fiona," said Alexander. "Shall we take the new route to your dorm?"

*****

277

ONLY A FEW DAYS AFTER THE OPERA, Alexander was uncharacteristically running a few minutes late to meet Fiona for morning coffee and tea. As he approached the coffee shop, he saw Fiona and Jerry in apparent deep discussion at the doorway. Alexander drew in a deep breath and continued toward them, resolving, *stay in control of yourself.*

Fiona noticeably relaxed when Alexander reached them. She smiled and extended her hand to him.

"Good morning, Beautiful. Nice tan." Alexander smiled.

"Cuideigin a nì flatter!" Thank you for coming—and at the perfect time.

Jerry obviously was not happy and did not offer to shake Alexander's hand.

Rebuffed, Alexander offered, "Let's go inside for a cup of coffee."

"No thanks," replied Jerry. "I must go."

Fiona held out her hand to Jerry. "Best wishes, Jerry. Take care." He took her hand gently and held it a moment too long to suit Alexander. Jerry then left. Fiona and Alexander entered the coffee shop and sat at their customary table.

After Alexander returned with coffee and hot water for tea, he said, "I hesitate to ask and probably shouldn't, but what is going on with Jerry?"

"Jerry is leaving MU today and hitchhiking to San Francisco. He plans to write a book of poems."

"I wish him good luck, but I don't see how he can support himself writing poetry books."

"Alexander," Fiona spoke softly. "Jerry asked me to go with him. He wanted me to collaborate with him and convert his poems into music and song."

Alexander was shocked. This was entirely unexpected. He was at a loss for words. He looked at Fiona quizzically.

"I'm not surprised Jerry is leaving MU," Fiona said. "I had a feeling he would leave before the semester ended. His asking me to accompany him was quite a compliment, but, of course, I telt Jerry nay."

Alexander had not realized he was holding his breath until he let it out with an enormous sigh.

"Alexander, I love ye with all my heart and soul. When ye saved me from those bullies three years ago, I ran away and left ye. I will never leave ye again. Please believe me."

Alexander found the words he needed. "I believe you, and I love you, Fiona. Please never leave me."

"I willna."

Sandlin

Chapter 9: Proposal

O, my love is like a red, red rose,
That's newly sprung in June.
O, my love is like the melodie,
That's sweetly play'd in tune.
-- Robert Burns

NORMALLY, ALEXANDER FELL FAST ASLEEP, seemingly the instant his head touched the pillow. His pillow, cot, and dorm room were the same, but tonight was different, and he knew exactly why: It was time, past time in fact, to decide about Fiona—a conscientious, reasoned decision. True to his engineering aptitude, training, and logic, Alexander thought through his options.

Option one was the easiest: status quo. Continue dating Fiona and take a *que sera que sera* approach, but this was unfair to Fiona and becoming a strain on himself.

He did not like Option two but had to consider it: Break up with Fiona in favor of his personal goals and career. Find a new girlfriend. He might even return to football since MU had a new football coach. He laughed at himself. Option two was definitely out.

Option three was more venturesome: Get an apartment and ask Fiona to move in with him. She almost certainly would, even though her conscience would trouble her. His parents and her guardians would not like this arrangement at all. Could their relationship survive this arrangement and its consequences? How would living together affect his personal goals and career?

Option four was obvious: Ask Fiona to marry him. He was confident she would say 'Yes,' but what if she did not? Once engaged, when should they marry? Long or short engagement period? Once married, would his personal goals change? What about his career plans? What about Fiona's plans and dreams? Where would they live? What about Fiona's love for Scotland?

And what about Fiona? Was she agonizing over the same decisions? There were no guarantees. Alexander had to make his own decision and then put his pride aside, act, and adjust his life according to someone else's decision.

Having made his decision, Alexander fell into a peaceful sleep.

*****

DR. TOM SOUTHERN, Professor of Industrial Engineering, smiled as Alexander entered his workshop. He had helped Alexander make the "AF" necklace for Fiona and helped Alexander with some of his engineering projects.

"D-Dr. Southern," stammered Alexander, "I would like for you to make an engagement ring for Fiona."

"I've been expecting this. Thank you for choosing me. It will be my honor to make Fiona's engagement ring. What do you have in mind?"

"Something impressive but not gaudy, I suppose. What do you recommend?"

"Probably a large solitaire diamond, although some people prefer a large center diamond surrounded by smaller diamonds. The average size for the center diamond is about one carat, but my guess is you'll want something larger, say two carats. 'Carat' refers to the weight of the diamond, not the size. Diamonds are judged by the four C's: cut, color, clarity, and carat. Knowing you, I expect you want the best possible of the four C's."

"That's why I've come to you, Dr. Southern."

"I suggest a simple oval shape solitaire in platinum. Let me show you some pictures."

Alexander chose a platinum six-prong solitaire engagement ring. "I don't know Fiona's ring size," he admitted.

"Fiona has beautiful long slim fingers. I can estimate the size, and adjust it later."

* * * * *

"DAD, I HOPE YOU AND MOM can come to the baseball game." From his dorm room, Alexander telephoned his parents. "Coach Parker has scheduled me to pitch. This will be my first time to pitch in a couple of years. Plus, Fiona becomes a naturalized citizen that morning and then sings the National Anthem for the game. The day should be perfect."

"We'll be there. I'll reserve a room at the Alumni Inn. That was a great place to stay. Will the Johnstons be coming?"

"Of course."

"*A really memorable day,*" mused Alexander as he patted the engagement ring in his pocket.

* * * * *

"AUNTIE, I AM SO HAPPY that ye and Uncle Robert can come on Saturday," Fiona spoke excitedly into her telephone. "It will be a wonderful day."

"Honey, we would not miss your Naturalization for anything. And then to sing the National Anthem for the baseball game! What a day this will be."

"And dinna forget, Alexander will pitch the baseball game. His parents will be there too."

Sandlin

"We'll be happy to see the Gordons again. We will be there Saturday morning."

*****

THE NATURALIZATION CEREMONY was held in the Student Union on Saturday morning for the six candidates. Fiona and Alexander arrived early and were soon joined by Malcolm and Rachel Gordon, Robert and Ellen Johnston, Mary, Anne, Jane, and Donnie. Fiona seemed calm but nervously wrapped a strand of hair around her finger.

An official from the U.S. Citizenship and Immigration Services reviewed Fiona's application and appointment letter and confirmed she was eligible for citizenship. She handed him her green card. The official gave Fiona a welcome packet, a small American flag, the Citizen's Almanac, and a pocket-sized pamphlet of the Declaration of Independence and the U.S. Constitution.

The U.S. Citizenship and Immigration Services began the official ceremony with a presentation of videos and music and opening remarks from the Master of Ceremonies, President Curry. He warmly welcomed everyone and gave Fiona a big smile. The next step was to take the Oath of Allegiance.

The citizens to be stood and raised their right hand.

"I hereby declare, on oath, that I absolutely and entirely renounce and abjure all allegiance and fidelity to any foreign prince, potentate, state, or sovereignty, of whom or which I have heretofore been a subject or citizen; that I will support and defend the Constitution and laws of the United States of America against all enemies, foreign and domestic; that I will bear true faith and allegiance to the same; that I will bear arms on behalf of the United States when required by the law; that I will

284

perform noncombatant service in the Armed
Forces of the United States when required by the
law; that I will perform work of national
importance under civilian direction when required
by the law; and that I take this obligation freely,
without any mental reservation or purpose of
evasion; so help me God."

Everyone stood and recited the Pledge of Allegiance.
President Curry distributed the certificates and closed the
ceremony with, "Congratulations! You're now a U.S. citizen,
enjoying the full privileges and responsibilities of citizenship."

Fiona was immediately in Alexander's arms, her eyes misty.
He declared, "I'm so proud of you! I love you so!" Everyone
gathered around Fiona, congratulating her.

*****

ALEXANDER HAD BEEN WARMING UP for the game, but came off
the field for the pre-game interview. He first entered the dugout
and retrieved the box containing Fiona's engagement ring. He
casually dropped the box into his pocket and approached the
television reporter.

"My thanks to you and your girlfriend for agreeing to an
interview," said the reporter. "As soon as she gets here, we'll go
over a few things and then begin filming."

"I have a stipulation to make and a favor to ask. First, no
mention or discussion of football or Coach Guffy. I will not
respond to such questions or statements. I assume you will ask for
my comments towards the end of the interview. Please don't stop
the camera for another minute or two."

"Anything special you'd like to say?"

"Keep the camera rolling. You'll see."

"Here they come." Fiona came to Alexander and gave his hand a slight squeeze. Malcolm and Rachel Gordon, Robert and Ellen Johnston, Mary, Anne, Jane, and Donnie came over to observe the interview in person. They stood back behind the camera, which was pointed towards the baseball field as the backdrop.

The reporter was thinking, "This girl is positively beautiful, plus they are a celebrity couple. This interview could make the national news."

The reporter advised, "This will be simple, short and sweet. I'll begin by congratulating Fiona on becoming a citizen and then add she will sing the National Anthem. At that point, I'll ask Fiona for her comments. Next, I'll point out this is the first game for Alexander to pitch since high school and that he will also bat for himself. Alexander, please talk briefly about playing baseball again. Now put on these lavalier microphones so you'll have more freedom, and our conversation will appear casual. Ready? OK, here we go."

The reporter led Fiona and Alexander in front of the camera. The cameraman mouthed "Three, two, one" and dropped his hand.

"What a great day for baseball! And what a great day for two outstanding MU students. Standing before me are Fiona MacDonald and Alexander Gordon. Fiona has just become a naturalized U. S. citizen. Congratulations, Fiona. Tell us about becoming a citizen."

Fiona was beaming. "First, I'd like to thank my Aunt Ellen and Uncle Robert for not only taking me under their wing but sponsoring me for citizenship. I especially want to thank Alexander Gordon for his support since the day we met— September 22. *Mo leannan*, I love you that much." She stood on her tiptoes and gave Alexander a light buss on his cheek.

The reporter was delighted. Yes, this could go national.

Fiona continued, "I'm noo an American Citizen and also a citizen of Scotland. The citizenship process is no difficult but takes some effort and study. I encourage everyone eligible to follow through and become a citizen."

The reporter added, "And in a few minutes, you will sing the National Anthem."

"Yes, I'm majoring in music, and I love to sing. Noo, the U. S. National Anthem is <u>my</u> national anthem."

The reporter turned to Alexander. "This must also be a proud day for you, Alexander, to have seen Fiona become a citizen."

"It was, indeed, a proud moment. I love Fiona very much." He gave Fiona a light kiss on her cheek.

"Now, let's talk baseball. How does it feel to play baseball again?"

"I've always loved baseball, and I'm excited to play again. I thank Coach Parker for the opportunity to play and being patient as I attempt to shed some rust. My baseball game is coming together, and I'm eager to play today."

"You'll be pitching. This is your first time to pitch since high school. Are you nervous?"

"Yes, I'm nervous, but not so much about pitching."

"Oh, what makes you nervous today?"

Alexander's hand dropped to the ring in his pocket. It seemed to quiver, and he hoped it was not noticeable. He took a deep breath. *Now or never.*

Alexander removed the ring box from his pocket, and in one smooth motion, turned to face Fiona, got on one knee, and opened the ring box.

The reporter had the good sense to step out of the scene.

Alexander extended the ring, still in its opened box, towards Fiona and her bewildered appearance. They had not discussed this during preparations for the interview. Suddenly, Fiona realized the full implications of Alexander's kneeling. She clasped both hands to her mouth. Tears welled in her eyes and began running down her cheeks.

Alexander slowly, carefully, and deliberately proposed.

"Fiona. Flora. MacKenzie. MacDonald.
Meeting you was the most significant event in my life.
You are so beautiful that I was stunned and speechless.

Fiona gasped, "Och! Och! Och!"

Getting to know you has been the most wonderful
adventure of my life.
I love you more than anything.
If you marry me, I will devote myself to you forever and ever.
Fiona, will you marry me?

"Aye! Och Aye! Yes! Yes!

Alexander removed the ring from the box; it came alive in his hand. He let the box drop to the ground, extended the ring, and Fiona held out her hand. Alexander lovingly placed the ring on her finger. It fit perfectly. Alexander kissed the ring. He gazed at Fiona. "I love you, Fiona."

"Tha gràdh agam ort, mo leannan."

Alexander stood and embraced Fiona in a long kiss.

Tears of joy fell like raindrops as the women hugged Fiona and fanned their faces with their hands. "Let me see! Let me see!" they gasped, admiring her engagement ring.

The men gathered around Alexander, shaking his hand and thumping him on his back. Robert hugged Alexander and said, "Welcome to the family, son!"

The batboy ran to Alexander and shouted, "Alexander, Coach says you must come to the dugout now!"

Ellen blurted to Robert, "I told you so, you old fool!"

Robert grinned. "What took him so long?" Ellen burst out laughing.

*****

IN THE DUGOUT, Coach Parker asked Alexander, "Was that what I think it was?"

"Most likely, Coach. I proposed to Fiona, and she accepted."

"Congratulations, young man. I knew this day was rapidly approaching. But can you still concentrate on pitching today?"

"Yes, sir. Please allow me to try."

The loudspeakers crackled, "Everyone, please stand for our National Anthem." Alexander joined his teammates as they lined up across the dugout. He watched Fiona as she sang, "Oh, say can you see…." She was beautiful and sounded beautiful. As the anthem ended, Fiona gave a flourish and waved her left hand high in the air, turning her hand so that all could see her engagement ring.

Alexander stepped to the pitcher's mound and began throwing warmup pitches. After he warmed up, he allowed himself a glance into the stands. Fiona's friends were excitedly gushing congratulations and admiring her engagement ring.

The game broadcaster spoke into his camera. "What a day this has been for Fiona MacDonald! She has become a naturalized U. S. Citizen and sung the National Anthem. Her boyfriend, Alexander Gordon, has proposed marriage, and she accepted. Alexander is the starting pitcher for this game. We'll soon know if he can concentrate enough on his pitching to be effective."

The first batter stepped to the plate. Alexander wound up, reared back, and threw a blazing fastball. The batter made a weak, late swing. The MU assistant pitching coach checked his radar gun in disbelief: 102 miles per hour. Alexander threw again: 103 miles per hour. After seven more pitches, Alexander had struck out the opposing side throwing nothing but fastballs.

The game broadcaster said, "Well folks, that answers my question about whether Alexander Gordon can concentrate on his pitching game. He will be the third batter, so we'll find out if he can hit."

The first batter walked, and the second batter struck out, so Alexander came to the plate with one runner on base. The opposing pitcher threw a strike across the middle of the plate. Alexander swung, connected, and knocked the ball cleanly out of the park.

The game broadcaster said, "Another question answered. I've never seen a ball hit so far in this baseball park."

The rest of the game continued along much in the same vein. Alexander shifted his pitching scheme to include a curveball and changeups. He pitched the entire game and did not allow a run to score. After hitting his third home run, the opposing team refused to pitch to him and walked him every time. It was a fantastic baseball performance.

*****

FIONA MET ALEXANDER outside the baseball locker room. Instantly, she was in his arms and glowing. "*Moran taing* for the most memorable day of my life, *mo leannan*. It was even better than oor introduction! Better than my birthday! When do ye want oor wedding?"

Alexander jested, "Right now would not be too soon for me! But I know you want to be a June bride, so I guess we can wait a little longer. Where do you want the wedding?"

"Chapel on Campus seems appropriate. The reception can be at the Alumni Inn. I'll make the reservations Monday. For noo, everyone is waiting on us for dinner. Come along, *m'fhian*."

That night on the national news, the Human Interest reporter said, "Here is the most touching story of the day. What a day this has been for the Viking Princess, Fiona MacDonald! She has become a naturalized U. S. Citizen, sung the National Anthem and her boyfriend, Alexander Gordon, proposed marriage. For any of you young men out there who are contemplating proposing, here is how it is done."

The replay showed Alexander removing the ring box from his pocket in one smooth motion....

*****

IN THE ALUMNI INN, they had hastily rearranged a conference room to a private dining room. Rachel and Malcolm Gordon, Ellen and Robert Johnston, President Curry and his wife Linda, Mary, Anne, Jane, and Donnie were in the room. Everyone applauded as Fiona and Alexander came in and raised their water glass to toast the newly betrothed.

President Curry naturally acted as Master of Ceremonies. "What a day! What a day! My congratulations to you both. I am pleased to know you and to celebrate with you." He sat down.

From his end of the table, Donnie chanted: "Speech! Speech!" Others joined him.

Knowing they meant a speech by him, Alexander stood with his water glass raised high. "To my Viking Princess, I love you with all my heart and soul."

Mary spoke up. "Tell us about the wedding details."

Alexander answered, "Well, my role is to show up." Everyone laughed. "As to the details, I have not been informed except that instead of getting married tonight..." He grinned at Ellen and Robert. "Apparently, Fiona wants to be a June bride.

Alexander continued, "After the wedding, which we hope can be in the Chapel on Campus, our plan is to honeymoon all summer and forever after. We plan to return to MU for the fall semester and continue our education."

Fiona stood with her water glass held high. "I propose a toast, not only to my beloved *m'fhian, mo leannan,* but to my fabulous friend, *mo charaid*, Mary, who introduced us and helped make my life complete. *Moran taing*, Mary; I'm forever in your debt."

*****

ON MONDAY, FIONA AND JANE strolled to the Chapel on Campus while chatting excitedly about Fiona's upcoming wedding. They discussed colors and color themes, dresses, flowers, songs, photographers, and tuxedos for the men. Jane asked, "What does Alexander say about all this?"

Fiona laughed, "Ye heard Alexander say his role is to show up!"

As they approached the Chapel, Fiona admitted, "I've always wanted to be a June bride like my mum. I ken it's a bit late to expect a day in June will be available, but I'm hoping to get lucky."

Fiona found the manager's office and pointed to the name on the door: Betty Walker. "Mrs. Walker and Auntie were classmates."

Fiona knocked on the door. Betty invited them in with a huge and knowing smile on her face.

"Fiona, I'm happy to see you again. You've been extremely accommodating with your playing and singing for us. Is there something I can help you with?"

Fiona was glowing. "Mrs. Walker, *mo leannan*, Alexander Gordon, has proposed. I am hoping the Chapel is available for a June wedding."

Betty teased, "It's a bit late to schedule a June wedding, but let's check anyway." She opened her planner. "Hmm. How about June 28th?"

Fiona squealed, "I canna believe it! June 28th is perfect! My parents married on June 28th!"

Betty could no longer hold back her laughter. "That's exactly what Ellen said."

"Auntie? How did she get involved?"

"Ellen reserved this date the day after she came to campus to help you with your little Campused problem."

"I remember noo she visited ye that day. But how did she ken?"

"Ellen has a kind of 'second sight' for certain things. She can be amazingly accurate. Let me telephone her for you right now."

Betty picked up the telephone and dialed Ellen. She handed the phone to Fiona.

Fiona, her voice pitched high, squeaked, "*Moran taing! Tapadh leat! Tapadh leat!*" Unable to speak more, she handed the telephone back to Betty.

Betty's eyes were welling with tears, but she managed to say, "Ellen, this is your best prediction ever. I'll see you at the wedding."

*****

LEAVING THE CHAPEL on Campus, Fiona went straight to the coffee shop to meet Alexander. Jane had a class to attend.

Alexander asked, "Any luck?" Fiona wanted a June wedding but he suspected it was too late to schedule a June wedding in the Chapel on Campus.

"How about June 28th?" She knew any day would be more than okay with Alexander.

"Sounds wonderful to me. I can't believe you got it."

"Auntie reserved it. She was a classmate of the Chapel Manager, Betty Walker."

"So, Auntie pulled some strings and called in a few favors, I'm sure."

"*Mo leannan*, Auntie reserved the Chapel on Campus for a June 28th wedding the day after she met ye."

"What? You've got to be kidding me! How did she know?"

"Auntie sometimes has the second sight. She can be remarkable."

Fiona choked, "*M'fhian*, my parents married on June 28th."

Struggling with emotion himself, Alexander acknowledged, "And so will we."

"Will ye walk me to the dorm? I want to tell Mary."

*****

FIONA WENT STRAIGHT TO MARY'S ROOM. As always, her door was open, and Fiona walked in.

"*Mo charaid*, d'ye have any plans for June 28th?"

"No," Mary smiled.

"Would you be my *maighdeann onair*--Maid of Honor? "

"I'd love to. Thank you for asking. Were you able to get the Chapel on Campus?"

"I was. In fact, Auntie made the reservations the day after she met Alexander."

"That is truly remarkable. Unbelievable, except the proof is right there in the reservation. And just think, your aunt came to that conclusion in fewer than 24 hours."

"When did ye ken Alexander and I would marry?"

"Actually, before your aunt. She was not around you and Alexander, and I was. I watched you two quickly falling in love. That first Sunday, when you were autographing 'The Look' pictures, I knew your relationship was serious. I told you Alexander was falling in love with you, but he did not realize it. The big ox."

Mary continued, "The day you were Campused and said, 'I've been serenaded, kissed, Campused and I'm falling in love. It's been a wonderful day.' was the day I became certain you would marry Alexander. So, technically, I beat your aunt; however, I concede to her superior senses."

"Jane, Anne and Alice will be bridesmaids."

"Please don't select ugly gowns for the bridesmaids. You'll be outshining us all, anyway."

*****

IN THEIR DORM ROOM, Donnie glanced up from his books. Ernest Tubb was singing "Yellow Rose of Texas" on the record player. Donnie exclaimed, "Pick it out, Billy Byrd!"

Alexander came back with, "If you don't quit picking that thing, it will never heal."

Donnie laughed. "Just think. Two years ago, you were a big dumb football player trying to get a degree in mechanical engineering, and now you are about to marry a sophisticated...."

"And beautiful," interrupted Alexander.

"beautiful, foreign artist. What happened?"

"Fiona happened. Are you available to be my Best Man on June 28th?"

"I sure am. Congratulations. Where will the wedding be?"

"Chapel on Campus," Alexander told Donnie about Auntie reserving the chapel the day after she met him.

"Amazing. But strictly speaking, I beat her to that conclusion."

"How so?"

"After you met Fiona, that first night you told me she was, by far, the most beautiful and fascinating girl you had ever met. I figured right then it was all over for you. Now I need a new roommate."

"Good luck. I've found my roommate."

*****

PARKED OUTSIDE THE CIRCUIT COURT, Alexander smiled at Fiona and asked, "Ready?"

"I do. I mean, I am." She laughed at herself.

They approached the clerk's desk, and Alexander said, "We've come to apply for a marriage license."

"Well, you're in the right place. Do you have identification with you?"

Alexander had his driver's license, and Fiona used her driver's license plus naturalization certificate. The clerk made a few marks on their application, stamped it, and noted there would be a three-day waiting period until they received the license. The waiting period provided time to check and review the application and gave prospective couples time to reconsider. She added, "That will be ten dollars, please."

As Alexander was reaching for his wallet, Fiona immediately placed a five-dollar bill on the counter. He quipped, "You are determined, aren't you?" Fiona nodded her head. Alexander added another five.

That night, Fiona entered Mary's room and informed her, "I just bought your best friend for five dollars!"

Mary laughed, "And how much did he pay for you?"

"Let's call it a down payment plus lifetime installments." Fiona giggled.

*****

"I'VE BOUGHT THE LAND." It was lunchtime, and they were reviewing their morning in the main cafeteria. Alexander had found a 160-acre farm near the MU campus. The owners, an older couple, were about to sell their farm. They wanted to retire and needed money to move to town. Alexander offered to buy their farm and allow the couple to live there for the rest of their lives. It was a perfect arrangement for everyone.

Fiona and Alexander intended to continue their studies at MU for several years. However, they did not want to rent an apartment; they planned to build a house. Alexander wanted their house to be a log cabin.

Fiona was more than somewhat leery of living in a log cabin, but she was willing to consider it. After all, it would be modern with all the conveniences. They would probably live in it for only three or four years while they attended MU. Alexander was different, and that characteristic had attracted her from their first meeting. Besides, Alexander promised Fiona she could design the next house.

"Let's take a ride toward Jackson and check out log cabins." A company near Jackson built log cabins and had several models on site for touring and examination.

As Alexander was driving his truck towards Jackson, he reminded Fiona, "Even though the house will be made and styled of logs, it can have any rooms and features you want. Any ideas?"

"I'd like perhaps four bedrooms. I expect we'll have visitors, your family, friends, and such. I want a large bathroom and closet for the master bedroom. I'd like to have a music room with a grand piano. I'd like a studio for painting. I remember your idea of a house being open, and I like the idea of the kitchen being open to the den. How about you?"

"I'd like porches all around the cabin. It should have a large common study and library we can use together." He smiled. "I want to be with you and be able to see you. I'd like a large workshop for my tinkering and experiments and a separate barn for outdoor equipment. I'd like to cook and grill outdoors on the back porch. We'll need an enclosed garage for three cars—I intend to keep my customized truck but get a new truck for normal use. We need to get you a nice car; what kind of car would you like?"

"BMW." She was definite about it.

Fiona had been skeptical about living in a log cabin, but she became enthused after touring the model cabins. Her artistic and creative abilities came to the forefront as she selected wood colors and textures. She chose stones for the fireplace and granite for countertops. They discussed room arrangements and locations. Fiona had sound ideas about everything, from lighting to faucets. She was musing about kitchen appliances that were modern but with an antique appearance. Alexander learned his simple log cabin would be, in fact, fancy.

On their way back to MU, Fiona laughed. "No one can believe I'm going to live in a log cabin. But just wait until they see it. It will be beautiful, even elegant.

"And I get a workshop."

*****

WITH HIS NEXT-DOOR NEIGHBORS AWAY, Alexander was strumming his guitar while Donnie was studying.

"Does my strumming bother you?"

"No, I'm OK as long as you don't sing."

The phone rang. Alexander was trying to divine who was calling and whether he should answer. It was his lawyer, Bill Tees.

"All good news, Alexander. Thomas Bennoitt has dropped his lawsuit against you. Completely dropped it. Now, the question is what to do about our countersuit?"

Alexander did not hesitate. "Drop it. I want all this to be over as soon as possible. I want nothing more to do with the Bennoitts."

"I thought that's what you'd say."

"Thanks for all your help."

"Bye."

Donnie asked, "What's up?"

"I'll call Fiona to update her, and you can eavesdrop to learn the good news."

*****

MARY JOINED FIONA AND ALEXANDER in the coffee shop. "What's up?" she asked.

"Mary, sales of my gadget are skyrocketing." Alexander smiled. "I recently received a sizeable payment from General Motors. It is time to organize a company to handle sales, research, manufacturing—the whole works."

"I always knew you could and would succeed and do this. Congratulations!"

"I've reviewed the situation with our accountant and lawyer. Fiona and I agree. We want you to become our first employee."

Mary choked, and a tear fell onto the table.

"But what would I do? I don't understand your inventions. I don't think I could assemble them."

"I'm with ye, Mary," added Fiona. "But Alexander insists that I be part of the company. I have great faith in him."

"Our accountant and lawyer agree we can hire you to help set up our company," Alexander said. "Your first task is to draft employee hiring guides and handbooks. For now, I'll get you a filing cabinet to use and store in your dorm room. Be prepared to stay at MU through the summer. You'll represent the company while Fiona and I are away. We'll honeymoon all summer." He smiled at Fiona. She blushed.

"Of course I accept, you big ox. Oops, guess I better call you boss man. I thought this would be my last semester at MU for a while. Even with my scholarship and part-time job I cannot afford to be here. I was going to find a full-time job and save enough money to return."

"Be sure to include a few business courses in your schedule. We need to figure this out."

Mary noted she must leave for class, and she stood to leave. Alexander stood politely, and Mary impulsively hugged him. "Thank you, Alexander. I don't know what I'd do without you."

"I'm forever in debt to you," Alexander said as he glanced at Fiona.

Fiona eyed Alexander in admiration. "Ye never cease to amaze me, *mo leannan*. I admire ye, but dinna ye ken ye canna take care of everyone?

"Now we need to talk to Alice and Roger."

*****

THURSDAY NIGHT SUPPER with Alice and Roger at their apartment had become almost routine. Thursdays fit everyone's schedule, including Alexander's baseball schedule. Fiona was preparing meatloaf while Alexander and Roger were chatting in the den about their engineering courses.

Around the supper table, everyone was enjoying the meatloaf. Alexander especially liked the sauce on top of the meatloaf. Fiona explained it was a blend of tomato paste, honey, mustard, and brown sugar. She was becoming an excellent cook.

Fiona and Alexander eyed each other without speaking. Fiona gave a slight nod of her head.

"Fiona and I have an announcement." Alice's head snapped over to Fiona. "No," Alexander laughed. "Not that."

Fiona glowed a brilliant red.

"Sorry about that," Alexander said to Fiona. "I need to work on my opening lines."

"Aye."

"Sales of my inventions, especially ultrasonic atomization, are increasing rapidly. I recently sold a license to General Motors. It is time to organize a company to handle sales, research, manufacturing—everything."

"Congratulations! How wonderful."

"We discussed our new company with our accountant and lawyer. Roger, Fiona and I want you come to work for us."

"I don't understand. How would I work for you? What would I do? I really need money; can you pay me?"

"We have a job for you—actually two jobs. Yes, we can pay you."

"What would I do?"

"Your first assignment is to supervise the construction of our log cabin while Fiona and I are on our honeymoon. We plan to be away all summer." Fiona blushed.

Alexander continued, "At the same time and for the longer term, we need a small manufacturing and assembly plant built and outfitted. We need to hire and train employees."

"What is to be manufactured?"

"I enjoy target shooting. I've developed an improved trigger design for small rifles. It can be adapted to fit air rifles, but we'll have to tinker with it a bit. The manufacturing and assembly plant should be flexible so we can make other products in the same plant."

Roger was getting excited, and Alice dabbed at tears in her eyes.

"Roger, I want you to continue your studies and get your degree. You'll be a busy man, but you can do it."

"This is exactly what I want to do. I'm in. When do I start?"

"You are our second employee. I'll introduce you to Mary tomorrow, and she will start the process. Don't be concerned if all this seems new—it is, but we'll figure it out."

*****

AT LUNCH IN THE MAIN CAFETERIA, Donnie appeared concerned and puzzled. "There's something strange going on. A guy was asking me a lot of questions about you today. He claimed to be a magazine reporter, but I don't think he really was. Anyway, I didn't tell him much."

Mary nodded. "I had the same experience yesterday. Plus, a friend who works in the Student Records Department told me there have been many inquiries lately about Alexander."

Fiona said, "No one has interviewed me about ye."

Donnie concluded, "I think you are being investigated for something or other. What have you been up to?"

Alexander said, "You may be right, but I've been on the straight and narrow path for some time. I'm not in any trouble. On the other hand, now that you mention it, I've noticed a new face all too regularly. Thanks for the warning. I'll be watching."

"What about Thomas Bennoitt?"

Alexander grimaced. "I don't know Thomas' status, but the two guys who helped him attack me are dead. They were shot in an attempted armed robbery near Jackson a few weeks ago."

"I'm sorry for them," Fiona said. "But Rab Jansen was well on his way to a life of crime and apparently, so was the other guy, Tim."

"Well, please keep your eyes and ears open," said Alexander. "This is troublesome. I've not applied for any loans. The only things I've applied for are patents and a marriage license." He smiled at Fiona.

Chapter 10: Thomas Bennoitt Again

"The best laid schemes o' Mice an' Men,
Gang aft agley.
An' lea'e us nought but grief an' pain,
For promis'd joy!
--Robert Burns

THOMAS BENNOITT STUDIED HIS FACE in the mirror of his bedroom in Jackson, still not entirely approving of his reflection. Facial scars were only slightly visible, but his straightened nose would not require additional surgery, and dental repairs were complete. His broken but healed arm sometimes ached.

He blamed Alexander Gordon for all this, although Thomas had only a vague memory of that night. He remembered being hit and then becoming conscious in an ambulance before passing out again. In the hospital, he vaguely remembered getting an injection and becoming unconscious.

The police report said the three of them had attacked Alexander Gordon, and Alexander defended himself, but Thomas wondered about that. How could Alexander Gordon have done such damage to him, plus to Rab and Tim? It did not seem possible. And now Rab and Tim were dead—killed in an armed robbery, according to the police report. Thomas blamed Alexander Gordon for their deaths.

Thomas popped two pills in his mouth and put the prescription bottle in his pocket. Today, he would drive to MU on a scouting mission. No longer enrolled at MU, he considered returning in the fall. Out-of-state colleges offered alternatives to avoid Alexander Gordon, but today, Thomas was returning to familiar territory.

He opened the garage door and paused while admiring the dark blue Mustang his father had given him after he wrecked the GTO. It drew lots of attention and was sure to catch the eyes of the girls at MU. Thomas backed out of the garage and drove to a convenience store to purchase a six-pack of beer. It might be a long day.

Nearing MU, Thomas did not believe his eyes. There in front of him was Alexander Gordon's customized and distinctive truck. Fiona rode in the passenger seat with her auburn hair flying in the wind. Thomas took a long drink of beer. This was going to be fun. He jammed the gas pedal to the floor, and the powerful Mustang leaped.

*****

FIONA AND ALEXANDER were enjoying a lazy drive along a winding country road while admiring the greening of trees. It was a beautiful spring day, full of fresh air and sunshine. Wildflowers along the road showed new spring faces. Fiona was bubbling with excitement and telling Alexander about the plans and recommendations from the wedding planner.

Alexander noticed a car approaching them rapidly in the rear-view mirror. He slowed to let the car, a dark blue Mustang, pass. No point in rushing anything today. Instead of speeding past them, the Mustang stayed alongside and then began easing into them. Its windows were dark, and he could not identify its driver. The Mustang bumped into the side of Alexander's truck, then veered away. It swerved into the truck again, attempting to push them off the road. Alexander braked hard, and the Mustang shot ahead.

Alexander stopped and got out to inspect for damage. The side of the truck was slightly dented and scraped. No structural damage, but his truck would need bodywork and painting. He was angry that his beloved truck was damaged. "That seemed intentional to me," he opined to Fiona. She agreed. They continued their tour in silence, a little shaken.

A few miles farther on, the scene of an accident loomed in front of them. A constable and two civilians were present at the scene. A dark blue Mustang had gone off a sharp curve, flipped over the guardrail and was upside down in a gully. Alexander stopped his truck. "Let me see if there's anything I can do."

Alexander walked to the constable and witnesses who were engaged in discussion. Alexander pointed to his truck and then to where the Mustang had attempted to force him off the road. Together they stepped down to the Mustang, and Alexander peered through the bashed-in windshield. He spoke to the constable, who wrote on his pad, and then returned to his truck.

Grimly, Alexander said, "Thomas Bennoitt is dead." Fiona gasped.

The next day, the newspaper noted the accidental death of a former MU student from a combination of drugs, alcohol, and speeding.

Sandlin

Chapter 11: Bridal Shower

It ne'er was wealth, it ne'er was wealth,
That coft contentment, peace, or pleasure;
The bands and bliss o' mutual love,
O that's the chiefest world's treasure.
-- Robert Burns

ELLEN HOSTED THE BRIDAL SHOWER at the Johnston's farm in early May before final exams at MU. Malcolm Gordon drove there with Rachel, Caroline, and Liz. Fiona and Alexander came from MU. Fiona's friends from MU were also there, along with some of her high school friends, church friends and friends of Ellen. After brief introductions, Malcolm and Alexander left with Robert for a tour of the farm.

"Oh, my goodness," gasped one of Fiona's friends from high school. "Please tell me he has a brother—younger, older, doesn't matter."

"No," replied Rachel, "Alexander is my only son."

"How in the world did you meet him?" asked another friend of Fiona.

"It's a long, beautiful, sometimes funny story," answered Ellen. "So, let me get the tea and scones. This is Mary's favorite story."

Mary began, "This past fall semester, I met a freshman girl who had been assigned to my dorm. People called her 'The Viking Princess.'" Mary laughed. "She doesn't like that name, but it fits, don't you agree?" The girls laughed and applauded. "She was brilliantly regal and sophisticated but shy. She was so extraordinarily beautiful that I wanted to introduce her to Alexander just to see his reaction—the big galoot! Fiona declined, saying she was in college to study and not to socialize."

One girl interrupted, "Sounds like something she would say."

Mary continued, "But after being around Fiona for a couple of weeks, I really wanted them to meet. I'm not a matchmaker and rarely do that sort of thing, but they were so suited to each other.

"First, I had to sell Alexander to Fiona. That should have been easy, but it was a tough sell. Fortunately, the other girls helped. Fiona liked that he was a musician and that he was taller than she. She did not like that he was a football player, but she finally agreed to meet him, anyway.

"I telephoned the big ox—he's like a brother to me—and told him I wanted him to meet a new friend of mine. I described Fiona as tall, very smart and with a good personality—leaving out that she was incredibly beautiful. Alexander agreed, but reluctantly. Success! Did I mention how much I enjoy playing tricks on the big guy?

Mary continued her story. "... Alexander turned around and saw Fiona; he was stunned and speechless....

"Now, let me tell you Fiona's reaction. She returned to the dorm after being with Alexander all afternoon—they even had supper together—she came straight to my room and said, 'I can't believe what I've done.' This shy, sophisticated Scot invited a boy she had just met to study with her in the library! To Fiona, this was unacceptably forward. She did not know what to do, but the other girls did. Within a few minutes, we changed her clothes from conservative to glamorous and fixed her hair. We recognized her change in attitude when she wanted to use her mother's best perfume from Scotland.

"When Alexander spotted Fiona on the stairway, he practically ran up the stairs to meet her. He took her books and her hand. One girl said, 'I didn't know Fiona had a boyfriend. How long has this been going on?' They had known each other for four hours!

"Fiona returned from the library with a dreamy look, and everyone wanted to know, 'Did he kiss you?' That's how obviously they were attracted. Fiona said no, but she would not have turned away."

Fiona was blushing. She covered her face with her hands.

"Now let me tell you about 'The Kiss'...."

After Mary had given her latest version of their story, Ellen said, "Now to open the gifts."

Fiona opened her gifts, and everyone oohed and awed as she graciously thanked the givers. She received traditional gifts: bath salts, wine glasses, hand soap, bath towels, slow cooker, scented candles, cloth napkins, wooden cutting board, wooden salt and pepper shakers and a sexy nightgown. Opening one gift, Fiona held up a pair of panties and thanked the giver; then, she noticed they slit the panties up the middle, and her red face turned scarlet. The girls giggled. One of her high school friends carefully handed Fiona her gift, which Fiona opened to find a glass jar full of M&M candies. "Don't worry," her friend said. "I've removed all the green ones—they're an aphrodisiac." Everyone giggled. Another high school friend handed Fiona a similarly wrapped package. On opening it, Fiona discovered a glass jar full of green M&M candies. All the girls howled in laughter.

*****

"PLEASE TELL ME about your Uncle James." Fiona and Alexander were returning to MU after the bridal shower to take final exams and finish the spring semester.

"My grandparents had three children. James is the oldest. My mother, Aileen, was the middle child. Ellen is the youngest.

"Uncle James is a hard-working business executive—the very definition of a workaholic. He has few hobbies and takes little time for recreation. He has always been good to me, and I love him, but, frankly, he can be tiresome. That's one reason I came to America to live with Auntie. She is much more fun.

"Uncle James' wife is Margaret. She is much more social than Uncle James but still almost aloof. They are wealthy and known for entertaining—especially business guests. Uncle James and Aunt Margaret have no children and, I believe, have never wanted children. That's another reason I came to America."

"My dad and James met in college. Dad was also studying business, but not as intently as James." Fiona's eyes were welling. "My dad became a successful businessman, but he was still fun to be around."

"Anyway," Fiona continued, "James introduced my dad to my mother and, as they say, 'That was that.'"

"So, your mom and dad had a short courtship, and your Aunt Ellen and Uncle Robert also had a short courtship?" Alexander teased, "Is this some kind of genetic trait?"

"No, Uncle James and Aunt Margaret dated for two years and then married. My mom and dad dated about five months before he proposed, and they married two months later. Auntie and Uncle Robert eloped three months after they met." Fiona giggled.

"I wonder what they are thinking about us?"

"After ye proposed, Uncle Robert asked, 'Whit took him so long?'"

*****

ELLEN JOHNSTON'S PHONE had been ringing off the hook with questions and plans for Fiona's wedding. She was pleased to take an active part in Fiona's wedding.

It rang again, and she answered. It was Alexander.

"Auntie," began Alexander. "Don't worry. Everything is OK here, but I have a favor to ask."

"You know I'll try to do anything you ask."

"Fiona plans to wear the pearl necklace that belonged to her mother and not the diamond necklace I gave her. She was afraid this would upset me, but I understand."

"Yes, her father gave that necklace to her mother as a wedding gift. It would be appropriate and beautiful for Fiona to wear it at her own wedding."

"I'd like to give Fiona earrings and bracelets to match her mother's pearl necklace as my wedding gift, but I do not know how to go about it. Can you help?"

"Yes, I can. The necklace is in Fiona's room. I'll take it to my jeweler and see what he can do."

"Thank you, Auntie. I was struggling with this."

Ellen had no sooner hung up than her phone rang again.

"Auntie, it's Fiona."

"Of course it is. Getting nervous about your wedding, Honey?"

"A wee bit, but more excited than anything. I've been trying to call ye all day, but your line has been busy."

"Many people have called about your wedding. Even your Uncle James called. James and Margaret will be here a few days before the wedding. James wants to discuss your finances and business interests."

"Good. I want Alexander at my meeting with Uncle James."

"I'm sure James will agree," said Ellen. "Alexander needs to be aware of your situation."

"Auntie, I want to give Great Grandfather MacKenzie's dirk to Alexander for a wedding present. He can wear it during the wedding ceremony. Will it upset ye if I give him this family heirloom?"

"Honey, Alexander is family. Plus, you and Alexander may provide someone to pass it along to."

"Auntie!"

"I'll bring the dirk to the wedding."

*****

THE WEDDING PLANNER conferred with Fiona and Ellen at the Chapel on Campus. "I've planned many weddings here," she informed Fiona. "Time is a little short, but we can do it. Let's go over the checklist."

With the wedding checklist in her hand, Fiona laughed and said, "Yesterday, Alexander telt me that he had not seen any charges for the wedding in our bank account. He said it was okay to spend money on our wedding. He wanted the wedding to be exactly what I had imagined all my life."

"And what did you tell him?" Ellen laughed.

"Ye dinna ken or want to ken how much oor wedding is costing."

Ellen explained to the wedding planner. "I eloped. I want Fiona's wedding to be special. I'll take part vicariously."

"The list seems good to me," said Fiona, "but I have some suggestions and requests. My wedding willna be a full Scottish wedding, but I would like to include some Scottish rituals. I will walk down the aisle to 'Canon in D' played on the bagpipe. Alexander and I wrote oor vows. He will use a slight variation of the traditional vow, and I will vow in Gaelic. After the vows, we will each prick the other forefinger with a tiny sgian-dubh and mix oor blood by touching fingers.

"We'll need a silver Quaich—that's a 'Loving Cup'—to sip from after the wedding. They usually fill the Quaich with whisky, but ours will have water mixed with a dram of MacKenzie Scotch Whisky.

Fiona continued, "At the reception, we'll need a bagpiper to lead us in the traditional grand march before the first dance. The first song will be 'Ebb Tide.'

The wedding planner added, "I'll have to find a bagpiper. A string quartet of MU music students will play before and during the wedding ceremony. Entertainment at the reception will be a dance band composed of MU music majors. Fiona tells me it is the same band that performed when she and Alexander first danced together. Fiona and Alexander both say they do not want to sing at their own wedding. I think this is a wise decision.

"The reception will be in the Alumni Inn. The meal will be buffet-style and delicious with many options. No alcohol will be served.

"For many things on the checklist, I will take care of the details but need your guidance and choices.

"I understand you plan to spend your wedding night at the Alumni Inn. Fiona, I strongly recommend spending your wedding night in an undisclosed hotel somewhat away from this area. I've seen too many instances of harassment on the wedding night and teasing and embarrassment the next morning. There is an excellent hotel about an hour and a half from here, and I recommend you stay there. In fact, you might stay there for two nights."

Fiona took in her aunt, and Ellen winked. Fiona blushed but said, "I need to discuss this with Alexander."

"Very well. Let me know if I can help. Oh, and prepare for a long flight to Hawaii and an even longer flight to Scotland."

After the wedding planner left, Ellen took Fiona aside. "Fiona, about your wedding night..." she began.

"Auntie, I'm well aware of the birds and bees!"

"I'm sure you are. I just wanted to advise you that you will not want to rise early the next morning and travel. In fact, you probably will not leave your room at all the next day." Ellen winked.

"Auntie!"

*****

THEY NEEDED WEDDING RINGS, and Alexander knew where to get them. "Dr. Southern," said Alexander, "allow me to introduce you to my fiancé, Fiona MacDonald."

"Fiona, Dr. Southern helped me make your 'AF' necklace. He advised me on your engagement ring and personally made it."

"Thank you, Dr. Southern. It is a beautiful ring. Everyone admires it. Now I need to choose matching wedding bands."

"Thank you, Fiona. If I may say so, you are beautiful yourself and will be an even more beautiful bride. I'm honored to have made your engagement ring. Let's see what you have in mind for the bands."

Fiona chose simple matching platinum bands with beveled edges and a matte finish.

"Dr. Southern, could you please make for me a tiny sgian-dubh—that's a small Scottish knife. Alexander has made a sketch of my idea. The handle should be nearly full size, with the MacDonald crest on one side and the Gordon crest on the other. The blade will be small. A special feature is that the tip of the blade will be a pin. In fact, we will use the pinprick during oor wedding ceremony."

Tom Southern studied the sketch. "I'll be honored to make this for you."

Alexander cautioned, "The blade doesn't need to be sharp; in fact, it shouldn't be sharp."

On their way out, Fiona slipped Dr. Southern a note. He read, "I will pick these up myself and pay for them. On the inside of Alexander's ring, please inscribe '6-28-70 Le M'Ghaol Uile, Fiona.'"

*****

THE WEEK BEFORE THE WEDDING, ELLEN AND ROBERT picked up Margaret and James Mackenzie at the airport in Jackson and brought them to the Alumni Inn. James had reserved a suite and

314

office since he would be there several days and always had business to accomplish wherever he was. His first and most important piece of business was to resolve Fiona's finances and investments.

After arriving at the Alumni Inn, James and Margaret met Alexander at an introductory supper. James was impressed with Alexander but especially impressed with Fiona's clear love and admiration for him. This was the first time James had seen Fiona since she left Scotland. She was no longer a skinny and shy teenager but a beautiful and happy young woman full of confidence.

The next day, Ellen, Robert, Fiona, and Alexander entered James' office suite. It was unexpectedly large, with a full-sized desk, credenza, filing cabinets, small tables, and extra chairs.

James commented, "This Alumni Inn is unusually accommodating. Not only is my suite spacious and comfortable, but supper last night was excellent."

Robert explained, "Frankly, the local motels are not good. This Alumni Inn was desperately needed. Ellen and I always stay here instead of a motel."

"There are some business matters which require your attention, review and approval, Fiona," James began, "but first, I must make a confession."

James studied Alexander. "Alexander, I apologize, but I thoroughly investigated you. Of course, the agency gave you an admirable—even enviable—report. I want you to know I approve of you and your upcoming marriage to Fiona."

"Eejit!" scolded Ellen. "I could have saved you a lot of money."

James smiled at his impetuous sister. "Now, you tell me!"

Alexander responded, "Thank you, sir."

"With that out of the way, let's get down to business."

Alexander interrupted, "Mr. MacKenzie, before we discuss finances, I need to make a statement. Whatever money or possessions Fiona has is hers alone. I have more than enough money for us to live on and enjoy a comfortable life. I know Fiona has an inheritance coming, but it doesn't matter whether it is a dollar or a million dollars; it is hers. I should not even be in this meeting."

James smiled. "I'm well aware of your net worth, Alexander, and I offer you my congratulations. You are an exceptionally talented and hardworking young man. I'm sure you will continue to do well. However, there are other considerations you should know. Please remain in this meeting."

Fiona interjected, "This is one of the few areas where we disagree. I've pointed out to Alexander that if I were working in a hamburger joint at minimum wage, my earnings would go towards oor family budget. He agrees but disagrees about using my inheritance." Fiona blushed and smiled at Alexander. "First time I've said, 'oor family.'" Alexander returned her smile and visibly relaxed.

James continued, "Alexander, you are technically and legally correct that Fiona's inheritance is hers alone. It is not community property. I understand and respect your wish to provide for Fiona. However, there are unusual circumstances I hope you will consider. Your life is about to change dramatically, and you should adapt your attitude accordingly."

James focused on Fiona. "Fiona, you are quite wealthy. I apologize, but we've misled you into believing you had a million dollars from a settlement with the insurance company. That settlement was closer to five million and is now worth six million. I apologize again, but we did not believe it was in your best interest to be fully aware of your finances.

316

"Besides the insurance settlement, your parents had individual life insurance policies. I've invested that money, and it is now valued at three million dollars. There's more."

"Your dad owned property and all or part of several businesses. In fact, he and I were partners in some of them. Some of those I've sold and invested the proceeds. Those proceeds are worth five million dollars. The other businesses are now in your name, but I manage them. I value them at ten million dollars.

"My father, your grandfather, left his distillery to myself, your mother and Ellen. I own sixty percent; your mom and Ellen have twenty percent each. Of course, you inherited your mom's share. Its value is about thirty million dollars.

"In his will, father attempted to divide his properties equally, but choices had to be made. I inherited more of the distillery. Ellen chose the plantation in Mississippi. Your mom chose the MacKenzie Estate east of Aberdeen. Fiona, you have inherited the MacKenzie Estate." He smiled. "By custom, you are 'Lady Mackenzie.'" James smiled at Alexander, "Even though incorrect, people might call you 'Laird MacKenzie.'"

James returned to Fiona, "To summarize, your current net worth is about fifty-four million dollars. That will generate some four to six million dollars annually for your family budget."

Fiona dabbed at her full eyes. "I dinna ken whit to say." She asked Alexander, "Does this change anything?"

Alexander answered, "You once told me you loved me despite my money and not because of it. Now it is my turn to tell you the same." He leaned towards her and kissed her lightly on her lips.

Alexander said, "Thank you, James, for everything you've done for Fiona and thank you for summarizing her financial situation. Frankly, this is too unexpected and too much to absorb all at once. Fiona and I need some time to discuss this. Can we continue tomorrow?"

All agreed to delay further discussion until the next day.

*****

FIONA AND ALEXANDER sat at a small table in Ellen and Robert's suite, studying James's small stack of papers.

Fiona commented, "Well, one thing I ken for certain is I'll be taking a general business course next semester."

"Me too—let's take it together. It will be our first course together." Alexander smiled.

"No, *mo leannan*, oor first course together was ballet," Fiona laughed.

Alexander laughed as he shook his head. "I still can't believe I took ballet! Suppose we ask James to continue managing your interests and turn them over to you gradually instead of abruptly."

"I like that idea," Fiona agreed. "But I want to deposit enough money in oor joint checking account to cover half the cost of the land and log cabin."

Alexander smiled. "You are determined, aren't you?"

"Aye, I am."

Fiona suggested, "Let's move to the couch; I'd like to discuss a dream I have." Sitting close to Alexander, she held up a picture of her Grandfather MacKenzie's old house and snuggled closer.

Alexander responded, "Why am I getting the feeling that yet another part of my life is about to change?"

"I would like to repair, renovate, and remodel my grandfather's estate. This would probably be awfully expensive, but apparently, I can afford it."

Alexander asked, "But then what would you do with the estate? Rent it out? Bed and breakfast?"

Fiona kissed him and purred, "Live there with ye, *mo leannan*."

"I should have seen this coming! Of course, we could live there. Scotland would be a new and broadening experience for me." He hesitated and then added, "But I'd also like to keep a house in the states. The log cabin being built now would be fine. In fact, I like that idea: an estate in Scotland and a log cabin in the states. We can do it."

Now excited, they made plans. Whether in the states or Scotland, they would continue their education and seek higher degrees. Their courses would not have to be transferable; they were more interested in becoming educated.

*****

THE NEXT DAY, FIONA AND ALEXANDER again met with James while Ellen and Robert gave Margaret a tour of MU.

Alexander renewed their discussion from the previous day. "Mr. MacKenzie, thank you again for managing Fiona's finances. She and I spent time last night attempting to understand and develop a course of action. Frankly, it is fuzzy in our minds. We have questions. First, could you continue to manage Fiona's finances in the short term and gradually transfer the responsibility to her?"

As I expected, James thought. *Alexander will manage Fiona's finances, and he will do it with her full approval and confidence and in her best interests.*

"Of course I can, and I'll be happy to do that. I agree this is the best course of action."

"Uncle James, I have a question about Grandfather MacKenzie's Estate. I loved that auld place. I am considering having it repaired, renovated and remodeled; whit is your opinion?"

James smiled and pulled an envelope from his desk drawer. "I suspected you might want that. I had an architect inspect the house, take pictures, and write a report with recommendations. He included sketches of various ways the old house might be remodeled. It will be expensive, but you'll get a good price,"

James smiled. "You own part of the construction company.". He handed the envelope to Fiona, who placed it on her lap.

"I'm curious," James asked, "What will you do with the remodeled estate?"

"Alexander and I will live there—at least part-time."

"Excellent! I'll be happy to have you closer. Next, let's talk about the distillery."

James addressed Alexander, "Fiona's great grandfather founded a distillery near Inverness to make Scotch whisky.

Alexander interrupted, "Fiona said she worked there as a child."

James smiled and continued, "There is an official governing agency, the Scotch Whisky Regulations. Genuine Scotch Whisky must be produced at a distillery in Scotland from water and malted barley. There are many other regulations. For example, we must age it for a minimum of 3 years inside oak casks in a warehouse in Scotland. Even though our whisky is regulated, there are still many variations. The MacKenzie Scotch Whisky developed by my grandfather is the finest available. It is expensive but not the most expensive Scotch whisky. The MacKenzie Distillery is not the oldest in Scotland; however, it is the oldest owned and operated by its founding family.

"Fiona, as I said yesterday, you own twenty percent of the MacKenzie Distillery. I manage the business and own sixty percent. Business is good, but I'm searching for new ways to promote our products. I've hired a small advertising agency— partially owned by you, Fiona—to develop promotional ideas. They've prepared a report containing their recommendations." James handed a thick report to Fiona, who immediately gave it to Alexander.

Hmm, interesting, thought James.

Ellen, Margaret, and Robert walked in, and all agreed it was time to take a break for supper. Robert said, "I'm about to show

320

you the best barbeque you'll ever have. The place doesn't seem like much, but the food is outstanding."

*****

THE NEXT DAY at their final business meeting with James and Ellen, Alexander ventured, "I studied the advertising recommendations last night. I have a suggestion about promoting MacKenzie Scotch Whisky. Since you three are the owners, I can make my suggestion directly to you."

James urged, "Let's hear your idea."

"One of the promotional ideas from the advertising agency is to build on the historical development and the family ownership. I like that idea. My suggestion is to make television commercials using a family member to narrate the history, guide the viewer on tour through the distillery, and show how the whisky is made. Fiona that would be you."

James was enthused. "Of course. What a great idea!"

Ellen agreed. "I like it!"

Fiona objected, "But I dinna ken those details."

James pointed out, "The advertising agency will research and write the scripts. This is a wonderful idea. I'll get them to work on the details."

Alexander observed, "When Fiona appears on television, every man's eye will turn to her."

"*Cuideigin a nì flatter.* But I'll need you with me, Alexander. I dinna want to seem like a giant. Besides, women buy whisky too."

"I'll be in the background shaking a big heavy club!"

"And no 'Viking Princess' either. This is Scotland."

"Can I be paid for doing this?" Fiona blushed. "I've no had a paying job in my life."

James laughed. "Of course!. In fact, you must be paid, and you must join the actors' guild."

James reached into his coat pocket. "This reminds me. Here is your wedding gift from Margaret and me. Round trip, first-class tickets to Scotland via Hawaii.

"We are looking forward to seeing you in Scotland."

*****

FIONA SAT ON THE COUCH close to Alexander in the Johnston's suite. She showed him photographs and sketches for the proposed MacKenzie Estate modifications. "What are your ideas?" he asked.

"I like the architect's advice and would combine some of his recommendations. He says the old house should be partially demolished so that piping and wiring can be properly replaced. I hope that three outer stone walls can be repaired and kept—this would preserve the original appearance of Grandfather's house. Floor space can be increased by adding towards the rear. It was already a large house, so not much expansion is needed. The stone fence needs extensive repairs. The long driveway needs to be covered in gravel.

"I want at least four bedrooms. I expect we'll have visitors, your family, friends from MU and such. I want a big bathroom and combined closets for the master bedroom. I'd like a music room with a grand piano and a studio for painting that faces the landscape."

"I want the MacKenzie Estate to fit your vision, Fiona. But I have a few requests. My requests are like the log cabin. I'd like a large common study and library for us to use together." He smiled. "I'd like a large workshop for my tinkering and experiments and a separate barn for outdoor equipment. I want a place for outdoor cooking at the rear of the house. I assume we'd need an enclosed garage for at least two cars."

Fiona commented, "The architect has estimated construction would take at least eight months and probably more depending on whit I wanted."

"Good thing we're having our log cabin built! We can go to school at MU for the fall and spring semesters and live in the log cabin. We can move to Scotland the next year when the MacKenzie Estate is ready. I'd better find out about getting a visa and enrolling in a Scottish university."

*****

THE NEXT DAY, Alexander walked over to his old dormitory to visit Donnie. With baseball tournaments, wedding plans, and visits, he hadn't seen Donnie in several weeks. Donnie had examined his schedule and saved an entire semester by attending summer school. He glanced up from his desk as Alexander came in.

"So, how's the old married man?"

"Not quite," grinned Alexander. "Not quite."

Donnie waved his arms around the dorm room. "Just think about what you are giving up. Not to mention having me to help you get through school."

"Donnie, do you know anything about distilling whisky?"

"One of my uncles is a moonshiner, and I've studied the theory of distillation in chemical engineering class. Why do you ask?"

"We've been meeting with Fiona's Uncle James from Scotland. We just learned that Fiona has inherited twenty percent of the MacKenzie Whisky Distillery in Scotland."

"Wow, that must be worth a lot of money!"

"There's more. Fiona inherited property, cash and investments besides the distillery."

"So, all the time you were concerned about Fiona learning about your money. She was filthy rich?"

"Fiona did not fully know about her inheritance. She knew she had a little money but did not want to think about it because it reminded her of the death of her parents. Yes, she is wealthy."

"So, is she calling off the wedding? Are you calling off the wedding?"

"Absolutely not. But I should learn about distilling whisky. Do you have anything simple?"

Donnie fumbled a moment among his stack of books. "Try this. But I'm sure you'll need to go to the library."

"Thanks, oh and Donnie, please don't mention this to anyone."

"When are you moving to Scotland?" Donnie smiled.

"As a matter of fact, Fiona also inherited her grandfather's estate in Scotland. She wants to restore and modernize it so we can live in it part time."

"See, you should have known. How do you feel about that?"

"Happy and kind of excited. It will be an entirely new experience for me. And, of course, I'll be with Fiona."

"What will you do in Scotland? Run Fiona's businesses? I don't see her being involved in the business."

"In the short term, we both plan to attend the nearby university. We may even take a different course of study in Scotland than in the U.S."

"Don't forget your old roomie—especially if you need an expert in distillation."

"Oh, and Donnie," Alexander added, "about the Bachelor Party, I really don't want to go on a wild all-night drinking party with strippers and such."

"What? I was planning on three- or four days partying in Las Vegas!"

"Right."

"What do you have in mind?"

"How about if you and I, plus a few friends, go to our favorite barbeque joint, drink a beer, eat some barbeque, and reminisce? You can even harass me about giving up my bachelor life."

"Sounds right. I'll cancel those strippers I've booked."

"Thanks."

*****

SINCE SHE NOW HAD A FULL-TIME JOB with Alexander's new company, Mary remained on campus for the summer and took a business course. Fiona entered her dorm room.

"*Mo charaid*, I need to tell you something—don't worry, it is good news."

"We've been meeting with my Uncle James from Scotland. To be blunt and to the point, I've inherited a lot of money and property in Scotland."

"How wonderful! You were unaware of this?"

"Almost entirely unaware. I kent an inheritance, but I associated it with the death of my parents and didna want to deal with it."

"Does this affect your wedding plans?"

"Nay, of course not." Fiona shook her head. "It may affect oor lives but not my love for Alexander."

"Among other properties and investments, I inherited twenty percent of the MacKenzie Whisky Distillery in Scotland and my grandfather's estate. I want to restore and modernize the estate so we can live in it part-time."

"How does Alexander feel about this?"

"A little peculiar, I suspect. He fully expected to provide oor sole support. And ye ken how independent he can be. But he is excited about living in Scotland for a while."

"When are you moving to Scotland?"

"It will be at least a year until the estate can be restored. After we get there, we plan to attend the university. Mary, please dinna tell this to anyone."

"I won't, but let me ask you something." Mary had a twinkle in her eye, "In Scotland, is it customary to have a Bachelorette Party before the wedding?"

"Aye, it's called a Hen Party. These can be simple tea parties or wild shenanigans with lots of alcohol and male strippers." Fiona paused, "Och, nay, Mary, dinna tell me ye are planning a wild Hen Party for me!"

"Why not? You'll have time to recover."

"But I dinna want a wild party with male strippers."

"Why not? It might be your last chance. Besides, what about the rest of us?"

"Please, just a simple tea party."

"OK, but don't complain that I didn't allow you to see male strippers."

*****

MALCOLM AND RACHEL GORDON had driven to MU for the rehearsal and wedding and were staying at the Alumni Inn with Alexander. They listened incredulously as Alexander informed them of Fiona's newly discovered wealth.

"Fiona is a very sweet and humble girl," Rachel acknowledged. "I love her, but I knew she was accustomed to being around money. At least, now she has some."

"Mom, I have plenty enough money to support Fiona, as they say, 'in the manner to which she is accustomed.'"

"Does this mean you'll move to Scotland?"

"Yes. In about a year. Until then, we'll live in the log cabin being built near MU. I think we will be back and forth between here and Scotland often. I hope you will visit us in Scotland."

"I'm sure we will," said Malcolm. "Maybe even do a little genealogy research."

Alexander added, "Please say nothing about this."

*****

ALONE WITH ELLEN IN HER SUITE at the Alumni Inn, Fiona said, "Auntie, I dinna want to pry into your personal business, but my situation might be like yers, and I would appreciate your advice. Am I to understand that most of your income comes from the MacKenzie Distillery holdings?"

"Don't worry, Fiona. I'm probably delinquent in revealing certain things. Most of our income comes from the gas wells on this farm—plantation, your Uncle James calls it. Calling it a 'Plantation' amuses him. The plantation belongs to me, not to Robert; it is not communal property—not that it would matter. Your inheritance is not communal property either—it is all yours, just as Alexander wanted. Anyway, getting back to my income, as the gas wells become depleted, the distillery profits will become our primary income. On the other hand, new gas production methods are being discovered, and gas production might even increase in the future.

"Robert was a poor farm boy. He had no idea of my potential financial worth—these things were not mine twenty years ago—and neither did I. Robert studied hard and worked even harder. We were struggling, but managing when I inherited more money than anyone has a right to. I did nothing to earn my inheritance except to choose the right parents. In fact, I was so rebellious, I probably should have been disinherited. I thank God and my parents I was not.

"So, Alexander is, in a way, in the same situation as Robert was, except that, frankly, Alexander is already more successful through his own efforts. Robert works hard and manages the farm well, but we would struggle if the farm proceeds were our only income. I suspect that, if your inheritance were to vanish, you would still live well based solely on Alexander's talents."

"*Taing* for telling me this, Auntie."

"Fiona, you must learn how to manage your husband and his feelings. Somehow, you must make him feel he is truly your main support, even if he isn't your primary financial support. One way you could do this is to reinvest all earnings from your inheritance."

"But I want to contribute to oor needs."

"You could establish a budget and make regular, but modest, contributions to your bank account and reinvest all other earnings."

"I like that idea."

"Fiona, there is no need to tell your uncle about this discussion."

"I underston."

Chapter 12: Wedding

And by thy e'en, sae bonie blue
I swear I'm thine for ever
And on thy lips I seal my vow
And break it shall I never
--Robert Burns

* * * * *

WHILE WAITING FOR THE WEDDING rehearsal to begin, Alexander had been anxiously and formally introducing people. Fiona and Mary were standing beside him in the Chapel when David approached. "David," said Alexander nervously, "allow me to introduce you to Mary. It was Mary who introduced me to Fiona. I'm forever in her debt." *There, another introduction done.*

David smiled and extended his hand. "Pleased to meet you, Mary. Are you the same Mary who was a classmate of Alexander's and mine all our lives?" Mary was guffawing in disbelief.

"Why, yes, I am. How very pleasant to meet you."

Alexander turned bright red.

Fiona had to turn away to hide her laughter.

* * * * *

THE REHEARSAL DINNER was held at the Alumni Inn. Following customary welcomes and introductions, Mary unexpectedly took the microphone from Alexander. "Let me tell you a story."

Alexander, knowing what was coming, was bright red but sat down. Fiona blushed and took his hand. Mary grinned at Alexander. "Don't worry, I'll give the short version."

"I grew up living next door to this big galoot. We played together, swam together, fished together, learned to ride bikes together. For pickup games in sports, Alexander always chose me even though I was terrible." Mary grinned at Fiona. "I've not told you this, but I even kissed him once. It was like kissing my brother. That's what Alexander became to me: my brother and best friend."

"Even though I love him, I must confess that one of my great pleasures is to play tricks on Alexander. Everyone thinks he is so smart—and he is—but he can be gullible.

"I met Fiona the first day of the fall semester and was extremely impressed by her. Besides being exotically beautiful, she was different, a foreigner. I immediately wanted to introduce Alexander to her—just to show her off, I suppose—but she was not interested. She was a profoundly serious student and kept to herself most of the time. As I became better acquainted with Fiona, I was more and more convinced that she should meet Alexander. Still, I had to build him up quite a bit before she agreed to meet him. That may have been my best sales pitch ever.

"I telephoned Alexander and told him I wanted to introduce him to my new friend. I described her as a music major—tall and slim with a good personality." Mary laughed out loud. "He reluctantly agreed to meet her in the Student Union snack room the next day. He didn't even ask her name.

"The next day, I had to drag Alexander across the snack room. Everyone wanted to talk to him, and he did not see Fiona until we got to her table. He finally turned to see her. Everyone thinks Alexander is always in control. Well, I can tell you that when he saw the 'Viking Princess,' he was so stunned he could not speak. He just stood there, not so much staring as stunned, with a blank expression.

330

"This was my best prank ever! I ordered Alexander to get us some coffee. He still had not spoken, and even I was feeling embarrassed for him. He came back to our table not only with coffee but with every other drink available. Fiona felt sorry for him. She tried to help by holding out her hand and saying, 'Hello, I'm Fiona' but instead of shaking her hand, Alexander bowed and kissed it! I was in hysterics!

Mary's audience was laughing out loud. Alexander was beet red but laughing while shaking his head.

"Fiona invited Alexander to join us, and he did. When he finally regained his speech, the first words out of his mouth were something like 'You are the most beautiful girl I've ever seen.' At that, I sensed he was recovering, so I excused myself and left them alone. They stayed together for the rest of the day and through supper.

"After supper, I was in my room studying when Fiona returned. She was quite upset with herself. She had invited Alexander to study with her in the library! He was waiting in our lobby. To this shy and reserved Scot, she had been overly forward. She didn't know what to do, but the rest of us did. We quickly got her out of her conservative clothes and dolled up. She was a knockout! When she chose to use her mother's best perfume from Scotland, we discovered just how special her library 'date' had become!

"Fiona went down the stairs, and Alexander practically ran up the stairs to help her. She probably used those stairs five or six times every day. I guess he worried she could not negotiate them that night because he took her books and purse in one hand and her hand in the other. They walked out hand-in-hand. One girl remarked, 'Well, you can remove him from the available list.' Another added, 'and remove her from the list of competitors.' Everyone agreed.

"When Fiona returned from the library, everyone was waiting to hear the rest of the story. What they really wanted to know was, 'Did he kiss you?'" At the head table, Fiona was rosy.

"Fiona said Alexander did not kiss her, but she would not have turned away."

Alexander whispered to Fiona, "I didn't realize that."

Fiona whispered in return, "A kiss would not have been appropriate."

Mary continued, "They spent all their spare time together, and we watched them fall in love. One time, Fiona invited Alexander to a 'Meet and Greet' social at our dorm, but she wouldn't introduce him to the other girls! Watching those two was like watching a fantastic romance movie. The ending was obvious, but you wanted to enjoy the process.

"Fiona and Alexander became celebrities with their picture on the front page of the newspaper." Mary held up 'The Look' photo. "I got their autographs."

"We watched them dance, holding each other so closely that a sheet of tissue paper would not have fit between them— and they continued dancing after the music stopped.

"Perhaps the most notable episode of their romance is famously called 'The Kiss.' I was not a witness, but hundreds of people claim to have been there. Alexander had carefully planned to serenade Fiona from the steps of the library."

Mary shot Alexander a look, "Don't deny it; you know you did."

"Fiona knew the song and joined him in a duet. When their duet ended, they kissed. Unfortunately, the Dean of Women passed by and witnessed their kiss. This led to their being Campused.

"That night, I asked Fiona about her day. She said she had been serenaded, kissed, Campused and was falling in love. At that point, I knew this day was coming soon.

"There is more. Much, much, more, but I'm going to stop my little story at this point and allow others to tell their version."

Ellen stepped to the microphone. "Fiona telephoned me only a few days after meeting Alexander to tell me she had met someone, and I knew right away he had to be extraordinary. I finally met Alexander the Monday after they were Campused." Ellen turned to Fiona and Alexander and smiled.

"Alexander apologized over and over to us for getting Fiona in trouble. He claimed all responsibility and said he would accept all punishment for the PDA. However, Fiona objected and said she was a most willing participant in the PDA." Ellen laughed.

"I was extremely impressed by Alexander—especially the way he and Fiona acted towards each other. The next day, I visited my friend Betty at the Campus Chapel. I reserved June 28th—her mother's wedding anniversary—for their wedding even though I doubted they would delay that long."

Betty was nodding her head in agreement.

Donnie came to the microphone holding a small scrap of paper. "That night, after they met, I asked Alexander, 'How was the nerdette?'" He cast a glance at Fiona, "Sorry about that."

He read from his notes, "Her name is Fiona. She is, by far, the most beautiful and fascinating girl I have ever met. I spent the rest of the day with her."

"I could tell, right then, this day was coming. In fact, we could have saved a lot of time and money if they'd just got married that night." Donnie smiled, "Of course, then we'd have missed playing our part in their story."

Fiona stood from her place at the head of the table, her eyes misty. Donnie gave her the microphone. "I loved ye, Alexander Malcolm Gordon, from the day I met ye. Although I didna ken for a few days, apparently everyone else did. That will always be my most memorable introduction. Ye were so sweet, standing there speechless. *Moran taing*, Mary." She picked up a long, wrapped package and handed it to Alexander, who carefully unwrapped it. It was an old Scottish dirk about eighteen inches long with a twelve-inch blade in an oak and leather scabbard. The pommel featured the MacKenzie Crest at the top of the black oak handle. "This was my Great Grandfather MacKenzie's dirk. I give it to you, *mo leannan*, with all my love. Please wear it at oor wedding."

Alexander stood and embraced Fiona, saying, "I will be honored to wear it." He took the microphone from Fiona and picked up a small package. Alexander said emotionally, "I thought I was doing Mary a favor meeting her friend who had 'a good personality.' Instead, that introduction was the defining moment in my life. I was stunned and still am. Learning about you, Fiona, has been the most wonderful adventure of my life. Thank you, Mary, for introducing me to the love of my life." He handed Fiona the package.

Fiona opened her gift, discovered the pearl earrings and bracelets, and understood immediately. She choked, then gasped and covered her mouth as her tears flowed, and she embraced Alexander all at once.

*****

ALEXANDER, DONNIE, AND DAVID were standing near the back of the chapel, waiting for the wedding ceremony to begin. "Alexander, it's not too late to back out," David teased.

"It was too late many months ago," Donnie laughed.

Alexander smiled. "I'd best move to the front."

With the guests seated by the ushers, the wedding planner motioned for the orchestra to play.

An usher escorted Ellen to her seat. Alexander came through a side entrance and stood alone near the front of the chapel, wearing the MacKenzie dirk at his side. Donnie and Mary walked down the aisle, followed by the bridesmaids and groomsmen. The wedding party assembled at the front of the chapel.

The wedding planner whispered to the little Flower Girl, "OK, sweetie, now sprinkle those flowers just like you practiced." She floated slowly down the aisle, tossing petals left and right.

The young Ring Bearer solemnly walked down the aisle, carefully holding a cushion with Alexander's grandmother's wedding band sewn onto it and Alexander and Fiona's rings in a ring box. He placed the rings on a table near the podium.

Fiona stepped into the aisle, and, after a moment's hesitation, her Uncle Robert joined her. Bagpipes played "Canon in D." Fiona and Robert started down the aisle to the front of the chapel. They turned around to face the congregation, and Alexander joined them. Robert gave Fiona a kiss and placed her hand in Alexander's.

The minister came out and welcomed everyone. He commented theirs was one of the most beautiful love stories he had ever heard. "How wonderful it was to watch them falling in love," he recounted. "Now they are about to be married. I'd like to say a few words about marriage and this ceremony you are about to witness."

Next, Caroline stepped to the podium and read 1 Corinthians 13:4-13 "Love is patient and kind..."

Fiona and Alice's choir director led in singing the hymn, "Morning has Broken."

Liz stepped to the podium and read 1 John 4:16-19: "So we have come to know and to believe the love that God has for us ...."

The choir director led the congregation in "Amazing Grace."

"Fiona and Alexander, since it is your intention to marry, join your right hands, and with your promises, bind yourselves to each other as husband and wife."

Alexander nervously repeated after the minister,

"Today, in this special place
I, Alexander, take you, Fiona, to be my wife.
To have and to hold from this day forward:
for better, for worse,
for richer, for poorer,
in sickness and in health,
To love and to cherish forever.
And this is my solemn vow."

Fiona recited the wedding vow in Gaelic,

"An-diugh, san àite sònraichte seo
Mise, Fiona, glac leat, a Alexander, le bheith i mo bhean chéile.
A bhith agad agus a chumail bhon latha seo air adhart
nas fheàrr, airson nas miosa
nas beairtiche, airson bochda
ann an tinneas agus slàinte
A ghràdhachadh agus a mhealtainn, gu bràth.
Agus seo mo bhòid shòlaimte."

The minister picked up the rings. "By your blessing, O God, may these rings be to Fiona and Alexander symbols of unending love and faithfulness, reminding them of the covenant they are making this day, through Jesus Christ our Lord. Amen."

Alexander placed Fiona's ring on her finger and whispered, "Fiona, I give you this ring as a sign of my love."

Fiona placed Alexander's ring on his finger. She spoke softly, *"Bheir mi an fhàinne seo dhut mar chomharra air mo ghaol."*

Alexander reached to his side and removed the small sgian-dubh from its scabbard. He hesitated but pricked Fiona's finger and said,

"I give you my body, that we two might be one.
You are blood of my blood, and bone of my bone.
I give you my spirit until our life shall be done."

Fiona took the sgian-dubh from Alexander, pricked his finger and said,

"Is leatsa mo bhodhaig, chum gum bi sinn 'n ar n-aon.
Is tu fuil 'o mo chuislean, is tu cnaimh de mo chnaimh.
Is leatsa m'anam gus an criochnaich ar saoghal."

They placed their fingers together, a tiny drop of blood on each. The minister quickly wrapped their fingers in a white silk ribbon and tied a knot.

"Before God and in the presence of this congregation, Fiona and Alexander have made their solemn vows to each other. They have confirmed their promises by joining hands, giving and receiving rings, and sharing their blood. Therefore, I now pronounce you husband and wife. You may kiss without fear of being Campused." The minister smiled.

As Fiona was about to put her arms around Alexander, but their hands were tied together. She put her hand on her hip with his tied to hers. They then put their free arms around each other and kissed. Their lips separated, and Fiona giggled.

In closing the ceremony, the minister blessed them:

"May God be with you and bless you,
May you see your children's children,
May you be poor in misfortune,
Rich in blessings.
May you know nothing but happiness
From this day forward."

Fiona and Alexander turned and strolled up the aisle, now husband and wife.

Donnie observed to David, "It only takes a few minutes, doesn't it?"

After everyone had exited the chapel, the wedding party re-entered for formal photographs.

Some guests left the chapel for the reception at the Alumni Inn. Others stood in a small receiving line to congratulate the newlyweds.

Outside the chapel, Malcolm Gordon waited in his white Lincoln to chauffeur them to the Alumni Inn for the reception.

*****

DONNIE STOOD AT THE HEAD TABLE and tinged his water glass to get everyone's attention. "Could I have your attention, please? My name's Donnie. I've had to take care of Alexander for the past two years, and I'm more than happy to pass that responsibility on to Fiona. Before we get started, I have a few announcements and suggestions to pass along to you. ..."

Next, Donnie announced, "Please welcome Mr. and Mrs. Alexander Gordon." The audience applauded and moved around for a better view. Fiona and Alexander entered the room and walked to the head table.

Alexander spoke. "Thank you for attending our wedding and for coming to this reception. Fiona and I especially thank you for your support during the past two semesters."

Donnie then announced the first dance. Alexander and Fiona moved to the dance floor and began dancing to "Ebb Tide"––the first song they had ever danced to together.

Donnie again took the microphone. "Just in case any of you have not heard the story of how Fiona and Alexander met, here is Mary to tell you."

Mary said, "Let me tell you a story," and began her well-rehearsed story of how Fiona and Alexander met.

"I grew up living next door to this big galoot for years...

The reception audience was applauding and laughing, with some sniffing in tears.

Next, Donnie announced the buffet dinner was ready. The head table would be served first, followed by the other tables in a clockwise pattern. He waved his arm to make the serving order clear.

Seeing most people had finished their meal, the wedding planner got Donnie's attention and pointed to her watch. Donnie glanced at his schedule and tinkled his water glass. "The newlyweds will cut their wedding cake." The photographers and videographers were already waiting near the cake.

After the cake cutting ceremony, Donnie announced, "Fiona will now toss her bouquet; anyone hoping to catch it, please move near Fiona. Fiona moved to one side of the cake, turned her back to the crowd of girls and tossed her bouquet high in the air. Jane caught it and gleefully waved the bouquet in triumph.

Fiona sat in a nearby chair and raised her gown to her knee. Alexander, crimson, reached his hands under the gown and emerged with her garter. He turned his back to the unmarried men and tossed the garter high in the air. It fell to the floor, untouched. Laughing, Alexander picked up the garter, walked to Donnie, and handed it to him.

While others were serving and eating cake, Fiona and Alexander slipped away to change into casual traveling clothes. Ellen and Mary were already in Ellen's room, prepared to help Fiona. Fiona's suitcase was on the bed. Ellen unzipped it and, with a smile at Mary, slipped in a bottle of champagne and a Mason jar.

Back at the reception, Donnie announced, "Now for the dance." He approached Jane and handed her the garter. "May I have this dance?"

Fiona and Alexander got into Malcolm's Lincoln, and he drove them a short distance to where Alexander had parked their rental car. Alexander helped Fiona into the car and gave her a small kiss. He stepped around to the driver's side and got in. They drove away smiling as husband and wife.

*****

"What a beautiful and touching wedding," ventured Alexander to Fiona. "All the same, I'm glad it's over, and we're alone."

"I agree," responded Fiona. "Now we have the rest of oor lives to spend together."

"I just thought of something. What will you call yourself now that we are married?"

Fiona did not hesitate. "I am Fiona Flora MacKenzie MacDonald Gordon. Ye may call me Fiona." She giggled. "This will be confusing for a while. I suppose some will call me Mrs. Gordon, but to me, that is your mother. I like the sound of Fiona Gordon, but, professionally, I'll use Fiona MacDonald."

"What about our joint checking account? Should we leave your name as Fiona MacDonald on the checks?"

"No. I want oor checks to read 'Alexander M. or Fiona M. Gordon.'" Fiona smiled.

Fiona teased, "And now that we are married, whit will you call yourself?"

"Your Uncle James says that you will be 'Lady MacKenzie' and I will be 'Laird MacKenzie' in Scotland. Both have a pleasant sound."

"Fiona, one thing I must correct you on, though," Alexander said. "You often say Mary is my best friend. Fiona, you are my best friend; I've just known Mary longer." Fiona gave a little sniff and reached over the console to put her hand on Alexander's leg.

They drove on, reminiscing about meeting and falling in love and planning their future.

Nearing the hotel, recommended by the wedding planner, Alexander's stomach growled, and Fiona laughed, remembering their first supper together. He said, "I'm starving. We were so busy at the reception that I hardly ate." He pivoted the car into a fast-food restaurant and to the drive-through window. He ordered a dozen beef sliders and a dozen chicken sliders and

340

handed the bags to Fiona. "They only serve sliders," he explained to Fiona. "Sliders are good, but they're small."

Fiona removed a slider from the bag, unwrapped it, and handed it to Alexander. "Better eat one now. I want ye at full strength." She giggled, "I canna believe I said that!"

"Better give me another one then."

A few minutes later, they drove into the entranceway of the hotel. Alexander said, "Swank!" and then realized it was probably typical for Fiona. A bellman came to get their luggage. Alexander turned the keys to the rental car over to the valet. Fiona and Alexander stepped inside to the registration desk. Alexander gave his name and a credit card to the clerk and turned away a moment to check on their luggage. The bellman had their luggage and was waiting for them. Alexander turned back to the registration desk. Fiona was signing them in. Curious, he examined the registration. Fiona had written: "Mr. & Mrs. A. M. Gordon." She smiled, "My first time to write oor names."

The bellman said, "Follow me, please," and led them to their suite. Ellen had teased and convinced Alexander to reserve a "Honeymoon Suite," for two nights, saying, "My guess is you'll spend nearly all your time in your room, so be sure to reserve a good one."

Alexander gave the bellman a large tip and pointedly hung the "Do Not Disturb" sign on the door. Fiona was opening her suitcase to get into something more comfortable. "Oh, look," she exclaimed and removed the bottle of champagne. "Thanks, Auntie!" Beside the champagne was a Mason jar with a lid and a note inside. Fiona opened the jar and read, *"During your first year of marriage, every time you make love, put a penny into this jar. After the first year, remove a penny every time you make love. Most couples never get them all out, but you just might."*

"Auntie!" Fiona exclaimed. She put the jar and note back into her suitcase.

Fiona held up the champagne bottle as Alexander strode from the door to her. He gave Fiona a passionate kiss and said, "How about a glass of champagne and a slider for supper?" Fiona found champagne glasses. Alexander popped the top off the champagne, and it flew away like a bullet. He filled the glasses. Fiona removed two sliders from the bag and placed them on the table. They touched their glasses to make a tinkling sound and then linked arms with the champagne glasses. Alexander whispered, "I love you with all my heart and soul."

Fiona whispered in return, "Is leatsa mo bhodhaig, chum gum bi sinn 'n ar n-aon."

THE END

About Sandlin

SANDLIN IS THE PEN NAME for Gordon Sandlin Buck, Jr., a retired mechanical engineer with various technical publications over the years. He also has self-published genealogy and photography books. Gordon lives in southern Louisiana, where his hobbies include photography, genealogy, and woodworking. This is his second proper novel, and he hopes to continue professional writing in the future.

Other novels by Sandlin:

Timepath: Nature Abhors a Paradox, ISBN: 9798450600147, 2021.

Sandlin

Made in the USA
Columbia, SC
15 March 2022